The Vendetta of Felipe Espinosa

THE VENDETTA OF FELIPE ESPINOSA

ADAM JAMES JONES

FIVE STAR

A part of Gale, Cengage Learning

GALE
CENGAGE Learning·

Farmington Hills, Mich • San Francisco • New York • Waterville, Maine
Meriden, Conn • Mason, Ohio • Chicago

LIBRARY OF CONGRESS CATALOGING-IN-PUBLICATION DATA

Jones, Adam James.
　　The Vendetta of Felipe Espinosa / by Adam James Jones. — First edition.
　　　pages cm
　　ISBN 978-1-4328-2991-9 (hardcover) — ISBN 1-4328-2991-2 (hardcover)
　　ISBN 978-1-4328-2984-1 (ebook) — ISBN 1-4328-2984-x (ebook)
　　1. Espinosa, Felipe Nerio, –1863—Fiction. 2. Serial murderers—History—
19th century—Fiction. 3. Frontier and pioneer life—West (U.S.)—Fiction.
4. West (U.S.)—History—Civil War, 1861–1865—Fiction. 5. Biographical fiction 6. Historical fiction. I. Title.
　　PS3610.O568V46 2014
　　813'.6—dc23　　　　　　　　　　　　　　　　　　2014025062

First Edition. First Printing: November 2014
The Author is represented by MacGregor Literary, Inc. Of Manzanita, Oregon
Find us on Facebook– https://www.facebook.com/FiveStarCengage
Visit our website– http://www.gale.cengage.com/fivestar/
Contact Five Star™ Publishing at FiveStar@cengage.com

Printed in the United States of America
1 2 3 4 5 6 7 18 17 16 15 14

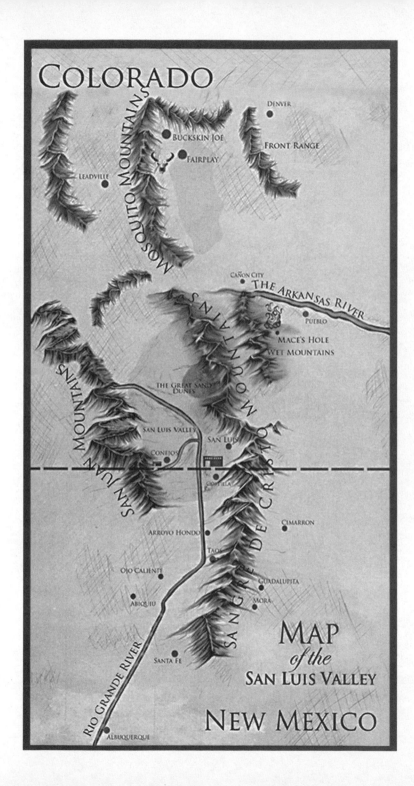

For Catharine

In the evening of life, we will be judged on love alone.

—St. John of the Cross

PROLOGUE

An excerpt from the autobiography of Tom Tobin:

Even as an old man now, far removed from the turmoil in the East and blissfully occupied with the operations of my ranch, I think of things like the depravities committed by Espinosa and I worry it is impossible to trust any man entirely. He is too susceptible to change and too prone to desperation: an able lawman who becomes a crippled thief; a wronged priest turned a vindictive blasphemer. I knew of men hurting children because their own fathers hurt them, and I worry over bad and good and whether there is such a thing as a choice.

I remember a man I met once at Bent's Fort, a fellow Missourian traveling alone into the West. We all shared our suppers that evening and I recall the man keeping especially quiet until William pulled out a few bits of pig fat and began rendering some lard. Suddenly the man gets real excited when he sees it and he points at it and declares, "You get that lard good and boiled and it'll burn a face clear down to the skull!" At this each one of us gets quiet. We were baffled. He had said it so innocently, so boyishly, as if in the same manner one might point out his knowledge of a star constellation. As if it were something everyone should know. So then I ask him, "What do you mean? How do you know this?" And the man proceeds to tell us this story about how as a boy in Saint Louis his stepfather once got fined ten dollars for publicly beating his mother. He said the

11

three of them had been walking down the street and leading a packhorse when the argument started and the stepfather had simply unhooked the horse's lead rope, told the young man to hold the animal by the halter, and commenced thrashing the poor woman with the folded-up rope. A few nights later, the stepfather began taking after her again, this time though in the privacy of their home. The man says when it started he had merely ducked out of the room, into the kitchen, grabbed a big pot and a couple pounds of pig fat, and slipped outside. Then, while inside his stepfather raged and his mother yelped, the young man made himself a little campfire in the front yard. He cooked up that pig fat, boiling it down to a fine oil, and when finally the house had quieted, he took up his pot and carried the boiling grease inside. There he found his mother unconscious on the floor and his stepfather snoring on the couch, and the young man, so little at the time with this big pot between his hands, tiptoed over his limp mother to the couch and poured the scorching grease over his stepfather's sleeping face.

I didn't know what to make of that story when I first heard it, and I still don't. I think of how Espinosa and that young partner of his shot decent fellows they didn't even know, then jabbed crucifixes into the bullet holes. I think of these things, and it occurs to me that the question is not whether a choice exists between bad and good, kindness and cruelty, but whether certain men are even aware of the difference.

At what point, I wonder, does it stop being revenge?

★ ★ ★ ★ ★

PART ONE:
THE TRIALS OF
IGNASIO ESPINOSA
1848–1851

★ ★ ★ ★ ★

CHAPTER 1

Outside he was killing the birds, those little mourning doves that had only just hatched. She could hear it through the wall, their tiny little shrieks. The nest hid within the overhang of the roof and she had seen the boy do the very thing with its previous hatchlings. She had watched him sit, as she envisioned him sitting now, with the chicks between his legs, plucking one up at a time, pinching the little belly between his thumb and forefinger, throwing it like a dart. And when they did not fly he would rise and collect them, their hay-needle bones broken, then sit and try again until the birds chirped no more and the boy left sulking either at his own failure or that of nature.

María rolled onto her side and covered her head with a pillow. She was almost asleep when the door shouldered open.

"Mamá there are men on horses."

She didn't move. "Indians?"

"I don't think so. They wear hats."

"Indians can wear hats."

She sat up, slid into her shoes, wrapped the quilt around her dress, and let the boy lead her out the door.

To the south, the land was flat and unbroken except for two distant sentinel cottonwoods. Two riders, their horses colored gunmetal against the snow with breath fuming from their snouts, approached from behind the trees.

María saw why the boy had fixed upon the hats. They were blue forage caps with golden insignias glinting above the bills.

15

"Army men," she said. "Gringos."

She turned back into the house, the boy trailing, the quilt falling to the floor. She slid the rifle out from beneath her bed and was almost to the door when she stopped. Eyeing the boy, María unsnapped the ramrod from the gun's underside and inserted it into the barrel. It glided until, half an inch from being swallowed completely, striking lead.

"I have not touched it," he said.

But he had before.

María pieced the rifle back together, grabbed the door handle, closed her eyes, and prayed a Hail Mary. She pulled open the door and together they stepped into the cold.

A few large snowflakes fell sleepily around. The men were close now and María saw them to be young, little more than boys. One wore glasses, brown stubble, and was of medium build. The other had blond hair hanging to his jaw. He was gangly, long-necked, and small-headed like an ostrich.

Both wore long, smoky greatcoats that hung below the waists of blue trousers with white stripes along the seams. Rifles bounced in scabbards against the horses' haunches and sheathed on the hip of the blond was a saber. Its handle was black pearl and etched crudely below the hilt was a cross.

The boy began to step forward but María snatched him by the collar, pulling him into her and barring him in with the gun.

The one with glasses smiled and waved.

"They want our food and our beds," she told the boy. "We must give them both."

"We want no such things, *señora*," he said, drawing up his horse. He had said it in Spanish, startling María, sharpening her senses. She did not like the surprise commonality with the man or his apparent friendliness. She wanted barriers, would rather he be hateful.

"No need for the gun," he said, nodding at the muzzleloader.

"I'm Curtis Lee, and that one's Jesse Talford. How do you do?"

María didn't answer.

He looked past her. "You *live* here?"

She remained silent.

The blond soldier, the one called Jesse, studied her thoughtfully. He leaned forward in his saddle, ran one side of his hair behind an ear, and slowly, as if to a child, asked if she spoke English.

María snorted.

He looked to his companion who only coughed into his fist and blushed.

She turned her attention back to Curtis.

"I wonder *señora*, where is s*eñor*?"

"Gone," she said.

"Oh. I'm sorry."

"He is not dead. Just gone."

Below her the boy squirmed. She squeezed him tighter.

"Will he return?"

"Possible."

"May I ask, *señora*, where he went?"

The boy struggled, pushing at the rifle and wriggling downward, and before it caught his neck, María released him. He dropped into the snow and quickly rose. She grabbed for his collar but he ducked and hopped from her reach. She lunged after him and again he dodged. María felt her face growing hot under the eyes of the soldiers.

"*Señora—*"

"He is fighting," she said, whirling back on the soldier. "All of them are gone fighting you."

She saw it register in his face; his nostrils flaring and his lips parting slightly. He turned to Jesse and translated. Jesse nodded but watched the boy who was timidly approaching with one hand outstretched as if to pet the horse.

17

"Felipe!"

Jesse raised a palm. "Is good, *señora*. Is good." He reined the horse so its nose faced the boy, but at this the boy paused, dropping his hand.

"*Señora*," Curtis said, "it is no wonder living here that you have not heard. The fighting is no more. They signed a treaty."

He smiled and looked pleased. But María had anticipated this announcement, had prayed for it, dreamed of it, although not like this. In her prayers as in her dreams the news had only one harbinger, and because this soldier was not him, María could not be pleased.

"What do you want here?"

"Nothing, *señora*, except maybe a point to Costilla. We are only passing and sharing the good news as we go."

"You have no good news. Not for me."

"An end to war is always good news."

"When did it end?"

"February, but—"

"Then my husband and my sons are dead. So it is bad news."

The boy circled back to the side of the horse. Once more he reached out, and María realized it was not the man's horse he wished to touch, but the sword hanging from the rider's hip.

"Oh," Jesse said, snapping open the scabbard and drawing the sword. It was a cavalry saber, its blade long, delicately bowed and golden. The soldier held it up for the boy to see and smiled proudly. The boy gaped open-mouthed.

Curtis eyed the scene with some impatience, then turned back to María. "It's important you know that from now on everything west and south along the big river, including this spot, belongs to the United States."

She scoffed. "Your army has been here two years, the *Tejanos* even longer. We never know where we are living. Mexico, America, Texas—"

"The treaty is official and undisputed."

María looked beyond the soldier into the falling snow. Everything was so very white—the ground, the sky, even, with more snow falling, what was between. The picture added to her isolation. She thought of the center of the moon. Her lungs sucked in and María, if she would allow it, could cry.

Jesse was handing the boy the saber. María made for him but the man held up a hand. "No, no, *señora*. Is good. Is good."

María slowed before him as the boy lifted the blade in both hands. It wobbled and she saw its shine reflected in his wide, unblinking eyes. The other soldier said something reproachful to Jesse but Jesse only waved him off, saying in English what sounded like the same assurance he had just given María. He continued watching the boy, amused.

"We have to leave then?" María asked.

"Not at all, *señora*. See that is more good news. Under the treaty what property was yours will stay as such. You will never have to leave."

"And then whose citizens are we?"

"If you choose to keep this as your home—but I can't see why you—" He stopped and started over. "If you stay here, you can become an American citizen in due time. Or, if you wish, you can remain a Mexican citizen. Your land is still yours either way."

Jesse had started to giggle. The boy had the sword above his head and was trying desperately to keep it there, his arms trembling under the weight. Jesse turned to his companion and tried to speak through his laughter.

María screamed. She had seen it coming but was too late. By the time she dove for him the sword was already on its way down, the boy merely guiding the hilt as gravity pulled the blade. It struck the soldier's knee, slicing the trousers, and cutting a gash that spit blood. The man shrieked and the boy jumped back, dropping the sword.

María caught him by the scruff of his coat and tugged. Jesse howled and clutched the wound with one hand while the other yanked the reins of his horse. The animal reared and spun, sending the soldier's cap flying and whipping his hair about his face before finally coming to a stop, its flanks swelling out and in. The man sat still a moment, hunched over and huffing. Then, lifting his head, he peered at the boy.

"Jesse . . . ," Curtis said.

María had dropped the muzzleloader. Dragging the boy with her, she bolted back for it just as Jesse swung off the horse, yelped and crumpled in the snow. He scrambled up onto his good knee and tore open his coat, sending buttons flying while one hand fished wildly inside for the pistol stuck against his side.

"Stop."

The man looked up and into the barrel of the muzzleloader. María held it atop the boy's shoulder, her left arm looped around his neck and balancing the barrel. She tapped her finger against the trigger, showing it was set. The soldier froze, half-risen on one knee, the pistol still clutched in one hand. The boy was still, quiet.

"Set it down," Curtis said.

In the corner of her eye María saw his own pistol gripped and hanging by his side.

No one moved.

"I said set down your gun, *señora*." He kicked his horse and moved close enough that María felt the heat of the animal's underbelly. The cold end of the pistol pressed down on top of her head. He let it rest there a moment. "I said—"

"You said the war is ended," she said. "That we may stay if we like."

It was quiet. The snowflakes built upon the barrel of the rifle and caught in the hair of the man before it. The boy was still.

María felt the pistol drop from her head and heard Curtis command something of Jesse. For the first time Jesse took his eyes off the barrel. He began to protest and Curtis repeated his order until, for a moment, the two were arguing fast and loud.

María whispered into the boy's ear.

Jesse threw up a hand in exasperation and reholstered the pistol. He climbed to both feet, wincing, and limped back to his horse.

Not until both figures were gray shadows in the distance did María lower the rifle. She released the boy.

He turned to her. "How are you sure?"

"Because they are only boys," she said. "Boys that have killed nothing in their lives. And because, maybe, your father is not dead."

CHAPTER 2

When he was little, Ignasio Espinosa made a game of way-marking life by the places he went and then returned to, noting changes in both his self and the world since last he was in that spot. He told those interested—often his parents, more often himself—observations like how the last he had visited the mountains he still had baby teeth, that last week in church the baby was not yet born, how last they were in the plaza there stood over it the Spanish flag.

He continued it as a teen, although only to himself and as less a musing at time and more a compulsive appraisal of his maleness. He noted rivers he once walked but now rode, woods in which he was now the hunter, fiestas where before he stood in corners and danced with no one.

Years passed, and the more that did the faster they would. Ignasio became a man, a husband, a father. Eventually he ceased his habit of marking time, all but forgetting it.

Now, along his lone walk from Old Mexico, he remembered, and the function of his retrospection changed yet again. He no longer marked his passage into manhood but his digression from it. Suddenly, it was nothing like a game. It was a torment for he who had no one to speak to and nothing to mind except the bleak trail he had walked twice before. The first and second times he had been a husband, a father, and, unquestionably, a man. Now he was not so sure, for he decided that—a man—was lesser if not a husband and father.

He spotted a bluff, abrupt and green with brush and billowing in the heat, far ahead beyond the two great cottonwoods. It appeared a single molar, steep and square and with slight knolls at each overlooking corner, and if it was a molar Ignasio knew it to be cavitied, for from its sunken top there honeycombed a network of channels that bore into the bluff and out its sides. Days after a rain Ignasio had witnessed those channels still seeping as if the bluff was letting itself of blood.

A ball rolled upward from Ignasio's stomach into his throat and he swallowed the last drop in his canteen to wash it down. He unslung his pack, his damp back instantly chilling, and removed the last bit of food—half a biscuit, pulpy with sweat. The last time he was this close to the bluff his belly was full with eggs, beans, bacon, tortilla, and coffee. He scratched the scar on his head.

As he walked, the bluff grew larger and the home came into view. The ball rolled and swelled. Ignasio stopped and squinted but still could not make out more than the form, a tiny brown dot all but swallowed by the green, looming tooth behind it. His pace quickened.

Two figures moved outside the house. They were on their knees and seemed to be digging. Ignasio knew what dress the woman wore. It was blue, and once she had wanted to wrap and bury it somewhere in Old Mexico lest the savages of the north, seeing such a bright and beautiful thing, steal it to hang in strips from the manes of their ponies. The boy was long-haired and shirtless, appearing half savage himself.

Ignasio's mouth quivered. He put a thumb and finger between his lips and whistled, the shrilling echo sweeping across the valley into the mountains. Both heads went up. The boy stood and began to run, bounding over the sage and the few snowmelt puddles. Ignasio waited, savoring the sight, loving what it was and not what he had feared. The boy landed in a patch of clay that sucked his boot off the foot. Ignasio laughed and the boy hopped on one foot back to the clay patch and stuck the other into the protruding boot.

He resumed his run but shortly before reaching Ignasio, he stopped, suddenly unsure.

Ignasio looked down at himself, the black toes showing from the boots with cut tops, the frayed trousers snipped away below the knee, a shirt stained with dirt and blood. He felt his beard, course and dusty, then his left temple and the burn scar running to the back of his head with just a few stray, stubbly hairs.

He eyed the boy and wriggled the toes in his opened boot. "At least I have boots that fit."

Now the boy smiled—an animal grin, huge and toothy—and finished the sprint into his father's arms.

They walked home together, toward the woman standing with hands on hips in the distance. The boy held Ignasio's hand. He had never been known to hold his father's hand, but in this moment Ignasio allowed it.

"Where are Hector and Jacinto?" the boy asked.

"They are dead."

"And your horse?"

"Dead also."

The boy nodded as if he had long known these things to be. "Our horses died, too. No. One died, the other we killed. Both we ate."

"What else did you eat?"

"The first summer we grew many beans and much grain, some tomatoes, onions, and peppers. The next summer there was a snow very late and we grew only a few beans. Mostly we ate beef and elk. We were sometimes very hungry, Papá, and very cold."

The boy slowed the closer they got, pulling back on his

father's hand.

"Elk?" Ignasio asked. "So you are hunting?"

"No. Chief Blanco gives us the elk. He gave one last night. Mamá is cleaning it. Once he gave us a buffalo but the meat was so much that some spoiled."

Ignasio observed what the two had been digging into was indeed the carcass of an elk. He saw too that the woman's once beautiful blue dress was now sullied with blood.

"I worried the Indians had driven away you and your mother. But you tell me they are feeding you."

"Papá, Blanco said that you were alive. He said it all the time. How did he know, Papá? Did you see him?"

"No. And where did you get beef?"

"*Tío* Lino."

"Lino! He came to you? Why?"

"To give us beef. But Mamá would never let him stay. I felt sad for him but Mamá always said not to."

"That is good. Do not be sad for your *tío.*"

Ahead, the woman looked at her bloody hands and disappeared into the house.

"You have taken care of your mother?"

"Yes."

"Tell me, *hijo,* how do you think she is?"

The boy squinted at the house. Ignasio looked at him and knew his son considered not his reply but whether to voice it.

"Can you pray too much, Papá?"

Ignasio squeezed the boy's hand then released it. "No."

She stepped outside, closed the door, and stood before it, her hands once again propped on her hips like a guard.

"She will be very sad about my brothers," the boy said.

They stopped before her. Her hands were still wet and Ignasio saw moisture in her hair like she had combed it back with her fingers. The hair was streaked with silver, her cheeks sunken, her neck frail. She had aged far more than two years. Still, she was beautiful. She trembled as she looked at him.

He took her face in his hands. "*Mi amor. Mi* María. I tried so hard."

CHAPTER 3

When they had eaten, the three walked to the river carrying buckets and pots that they filled, carried home, and poured into the tin washbasin. Once the boy ran up behind his father and jumped on his back and María cried out. Ignasio, holding the boy by the legs, looked at her puzzled. He appeared to her so frail, not entirely weak but nonetheless diminished, especially in the face and in the shoulders. Embarrassed, she said only to never mind and together they continued the walk, Ignasio carrying his son all the way.

She boiled two large kettles atop the stove and told the boy to disappear until she called him. He protested and just as he was on the verge of a tantrum Ignasio lowered his voice so that she felt it in her feet and started a countdown from three. He was out the door by two. María had missed that.

She stirred lavender into the water and he undressed. Dust floated upward in a fine cloud as his clothes hit the floor. Standing naked, María saw the true toll on his body. Grime, scratches, and scars were everywhere. His knees were swollen freakishly like twin aspen burls. His abdomen caved in under his rib cage and a bruise the color of egg yolk covered almost the entire side around the liver. His left shoulder below the collarbone was encased in a bandage, black and hard with crusted blood. María stood and peeled off the wrapping, revealing a puss-filled stab wound in which crawled several butter-colored maggots.

"I put them there," he said.

She helped him into the basin, noting him wince as inch by inch he submerged. He sat finally, his knees huddled against his chest in the small tub, the water already turning to silt. She knelt and began to wash him, wiping the maggots from his wound into her hand and tossing them in the stove.

"Our home needs repair," he said. "It smells of rot and rodents."

She followed his gaze around the home; a one-room jacal built of aspen poles twined together and chinked over with mud and hay. Pieces of wall had crumbled and María had patched the holes with dead brush which allowed for poor insulation and an ever-increasing population of mouse squatters. The floor was tamped clay and covering most of it were two beds made of hay-stuffed grain sacks. Toward the end of winter, when the contents of the sacks grew moldy, María felt little lumps roll down her back and legs—the mice tunneling about her mattress.

Next to the door was a single window, a tiny square opening covered taut with lambskin glowing orange with the setting sun. Against the walls of the room was the small potbellied stove they had hauled from Taos, a few pots and pans hanging from hooks above it, a pine sideboard containing lanterns and lantern oil on one level, sheets and clothing on the other, and finally, in the corner, a homemade altar on which there perched a portrait of the Virgin, a cross, and, hanging each from a nail, two rosaries. Three more nails protruded empty.

Outside the house against its western wall was a woodpile, while attached to its eastern side a corral and a chicken coop. Both the corral and the coop had been empty for almost a year.

"Yes, I think I shall build a second room. This house is too small," he said.

"You did not think it too small when there were five of us."

His eyes stopped wandering, flicked past María's, and turned downward to focus on the water.

"Do you grudge me?"

"No. But I should like to hear how they were killed."

"They were killed on the battlefield."

"On the battlefield."

"Yes. Very quick. Both were shot once. By the time I found them they were already dead. *Murieron rápidamente.*"

"That is it?"

"That is it."

"Mm, I see." She leaned close so that her lips brushed his mane. "Or maybe you spare me the truth because it is too much for me, and perhaps too much for you."

The muscles along his shoulders relaxed. Tenderly she ran a hand down them.

"Yes. It is both."

"Then you keep the truth and forget it. I shall never ask again."

"They are buried. Hector received his rites, but Jacinto—"

"*Bueno,* Ignasio. I think I would like very much that other room. And possibly a new roof. This one is like a sponge that drips on your head while you are sleeping."

"As I walked, I thought of irrigating from the river."

"That too," she said, filling her cupped hands with water and letting it run over his head. "You are here to stay then?"

"Of course. What a question."

"What if there is more fighting?"

"There will be no more fighting. The Americanos got all they wanted."

"But if there was?"

"Then I would refuse it."

"You could have refused it before, *marido*. You were never forced to go."

"If I had known, María . . . oh if I had known . . ."

She could not tell if it were memories he gathered, or the courage.

"We marched to Santa Fe but we did not fight for it. For days we dug trenches, felled trees, set cannons. But when the Americanos approached, the governor balked and instead of attacking we loaded all his clothing, paintings, and gold trinkets into wagons and left the city for the Americanos to take.

"We entered again El Jornada del Muerto where the men pissed in their canteens and cut strips from their dead horses. There were the men whose skin baked like turnips and walked with nothingness in their eyes until finally they simply sat and stayed sitting with that same nothingness as the other men relieved them of their weapons and then continued the march, leaving them to die. And oh, María, the ice in the nights. Jacinto woke one morning, his toes so gray I had to cut them. They . . ."

He stopped himself. María soothed the cloth against him. "Yes. I remember the cold."

"We rode through it to Paso del Norte, which had become a nationless city, for every day a new man would claim it. On Christmas, the current of the Brazos carried empty bottles of brandy, and tracing it we discovered the Americanos, camped out and drunk on the holiday. We charged them. I was a lancer and among the first but before my tip could strike they fired and my horse toppled. I landed hard, and when I rose it was to a great thundering like seams ripping open in the sky. The Americanos were firing their howitzers. It ended in our retreat, and I don't think a single Americano fell.

"We wandered south into Old Mexico. Along the way we were attacked by Apaches that crept up on us in the night and as we slept covered our mouths and cut our throats with blades, antlers, and sharpened stones. They had painted themselves black and were so quiet we did not alert until many were dead and our few horses gone."

"It is a Godless land," she said.

"Yes. We would talk of how He was never felt. No one felt Him until Chihuahua."

"Chihuahua? You went home?"

"No María. It was not our home. You wouldn't have known it. There, too, was a battle, only greater, the Americanos even bigger in number and with more howitzers, rifles, and grapeshot cannons, and when it was over they moved into our city like termites, blighting everything and honoring nothing. I saw men bathing in the fountains. They turned our homes to stables, leading horses through our doorways and shutting them in. Women were raped and men beaten. One day all dogs within the city were herded then let loose in the hills to be hunted for sport."

"Dios."

"No. It became that He was not there. At first they kept us jailed or chained in long rows along the sidewalks, and in that imprisonment we knew that He had left—in sadness or in expulsion. Only when our keepers saw that our faith was gone, they released us. We wandered the city in our decaying uniforms like haunts, the Americanos knowing us leaderless and beaten, allowing our presence like one might allow barn cats. We waited for news of Mexico's surrender, and when it came, the war was over, except that to me it had been that way long before. I tell you, I would not have gone."

Suddenly his hand burst from the water and clutched her wrist. "Oh but María, do not repeat that. Please tell no one I said it."

She shook her wrist free. *"Idioto.* Why would I tell? Who do I even have to speak to but a priest that rarely comes and an old Indian chief? And he is mostly crazy."

"Don't tell Felipe."

31

"Don't tell Felipe? Aye. He makes a lion of you for the wrong reasons. If they are mistakes to you then they should seem as such to him. A son should know the mistakes of his father, lest he make them for himself."

"Please."

"If you demand it, then fine. Let him too bang his head with rocks to prove that it is thick."

"Or Lino."

"Lino? When do I talk to him? I would not tell Lino the time."

"Felipe says that he comes to you."

"He gives us cows and chickens, but I do not speak to him. I send him on his way and he goes with his tail down. *Cabron*, what a suspicion! Turn your face so that I may shave your beard, and maybe cut you by accident."

"I like my beard."

"I hate it. Look to me."

She cupped his chin with one hand and worked the knife with the other. It reminded her of skinning the elk earlier that morning, rasping the blade in little motions as great tufts of fur fell away. Except that with each patch of black gristle that fell away from Ignasio there revealed something underneath she found beautiful. It was his face how she remembered it. It was him coming all the way back.

Their eyes met for a moment and her cheeks turned hot. He traced little wet shapes with his finger along the front of her dress.

"We will stay here then?" she asked.

"This is our house. You were hoping to leave it?"

"Here is our house, but not our home."

"I tell you again it is not home as you remember it. Pray that you shall never see it as I have."

"But here is not even Mexico. You cannot even call your home

32

your country. Why would we stay?"

"Because here there are no *castas*. No one cares who is *Mestizo* and who is *Criollo*, or what you can prove about your mother. What matters here about a person is land, and land we have."

"Do we?"

At this he stiffened and she observed his fists slightly clench. "We have a claim."

"They will care we are Mexican."

"The war is done."

"That, Ignasio, we will see."

María finished shaving him in silence. She ran a hand over his face and throat, flicking the thick mane of hair to indicate that that, too, would soon have to go.

The lambskin over the window was now faint with color, the sun now set.

"I wonder where Felipe is," Ignasio said.

"Either sitting with his ear against the door. Or, more likely, he is in the willows looking for frogs to lance."

"Aye. The Ute boys have made him violent. And his teeth—".

"Leave him alone about his teeth. He is sensitive of them. It is being here with his mother while elsewhere he knows his father and brothers are at war that has made him violent."

The heaviness Ignasio had brought back with him once more pressed down upon his shoulders. "I'm sorry."

"So you have said. And I know you are, for if you were not I think I should hate you."

"I'm sorry I left you."

She rose, picked up one of his hands, and kissed it. "I am too."

And slipping off her shoes but not bothering with the dress, María climbed into the tub.

CHAPTER 4

They walked east, the sun hanging in morning behind them. It burned over the San Juans and onto the pink burn scar along Ignasio's head. He held one hand above him to shade it. He would wish for a hat if only that too was not so painful, and he would wish for clouds if only they would not rain. He wished then for nothing.

A breeze swept over the valley, baked and dry, carrying grasshoppers that leapt crackling into Ignasio's chest. Ahead, hazy in the heat, were the Sangre de Cristos, their peaks furrowed with snow and rising sharp in an otherwise gentle pasture. He journeyed to the feet of those mountains; to a village that had sprung up during Ignasio's absence. It lay forty miles away and was the nearest village to their home. The boy led the way. He had walked without stopping and mostly backward in order to face his father. At the moment, he held up a knife that was ancient looking and dark with rust, and, judging by its brass handle, likely a precious instrument in its time.

"It was on Ba'ga Ka'ni," the boy said, "just behind our home. Me, Appah, and Ojos y Nariz."

"You mean the big bluff?"

"Yes, we—"

"Who says it is called Ba'ga Ka'ni?"

"The Utes because it looks like a headless cow and there are little stomachs inside."

"It doesn't look like a cow; it looks like a molar. What the

Utes say about something doesn't make it so."

"Oh," the boy said, slowing as he considered the statement and almost bumping into his father. He was thin and lithe as he swept around the brush, his straight black hair whipping about his shoulders. His teeth were sharp, crooked, and oversized; the jaw so under-bitten his face appeared L-shaped. He spat as he talked and every other word seemed to start or end with a *tthh*. A half inch separated one tooth from the next, hinting that many were missing or simply overgrown by the others that thrust out so obscenely the whole mouth could not always fit over them. When he closed his mouth, his lip would often snag on the left lower canine that reached halfway to the nostril.

He continued the story: "We crawled on our bellies inside a very narrow, very long tunnel inside the bluff. Appah in front and me in the middle. There was no light, Papá, and we crawled until in front of me came the clashing of something metal and Appah said, 'Aye, what is this?' and I heard more clashing and more metal. We didn't know what Appah touched because we were stuck behind him like worms in a line. We guessed from the sounds and from the excitement that he had discovered something rare. Appah, not even knowing what he handled, said 'Brothers, it is treasure!'

"He began to pass us the findings. I tell you, Papá, it was so dark we could never know the things we passed. The first was a great cut of smoothed, curved metal, as large as half of me and very heavy. The next was also something steel, not a plate but a ball with what seemed little rocks that clattered inside it. Then there came something smaller and jagged and feeling like a rock. And then came something that made us all whoop. Anyone who held the thing, even in dark, would know it. It was this . . ."

He held the knife close to Ignasio's face. Ignasio nodded and wondered if María knew about the weapon. He wondered why she allowed his hair to grow so long and why she permitted him to play with those savage children.

"Then something very bad happened, Papá, something frightening. We lay there in the dark and in a line on our bellies feeling our treasure when before us Appah began to scream. It was a scream anyone would understand, one a screamer makes when he thinks he is about to die. At first we were very confused but still very frightened because, Papá, you would know that scream. And then I hear it. It is a rattle. Appah is yelling for us to back up, for you see on our bellies behind one another Appah is stuck until I back, and I cannot back until Ojos y Nariz backs. Appah is kicking me in the face and I am kicking Ojos y Nariz in the face until finally we are all scuttling backwards like blind gophers.

"Appah was still yelling but I could no longer hear the rattling when I saw the first splash of light on the walls. Then we were free, sitting on a ledge with our hands over our eyes because the sunlight was blinding. We were careful not to step because somewhere before us was a long dive to the bottom. As our eyes adjusted to the sun, I saw Appah crying, rocking in a ball, and sucking on the side of his finger—

"Oh but, Papá, do not tell I said he was crying."

Ignasio nodded.

"Anyone who had heard that rattling and watched Appah suck at those two little red dots on his finger would have known what happened. But, without even thinking we had carried out the treasure. And if the bite had been a curse, then the knife we had found—this one here—was a blessing.

"I held up the knife. Appah looked at it, cried a little, and nodded. He laid his hand out flat on a rock and said to do it quickly. I said I would try. I set the rusted, dull blade at the base of the finger, above the joint, and with one hand held the handle while the other palmed downward on the back of the blade, here, Papá, where it is not sharp.

"Then, without warning him so he could not jerk away, I pressed. The skin broke, blood sprayed, and the knife sunk. But only halfway because, Papá, you can see that this blade is very dull and rusted even after I have cleaned and sharpened it. Appah shrieked so that my ears buzzed and he yanked his hand back with the knife still stuck in the bone.

"I grabbed his hand and forced it back down and told him to close his eyes. Then I called Ojos y Nariz. Again I held the ends of the blade far apart, and now I told Ojos y Nariz to stomp on it. He did. It sounded like a carrot snapping and like that the finger was off."

The boy held the knife close to his face and ran a finger along its side. He looked up at his father and grinned. The grin was anarchy.

"It worked too, Papá. The women had to cut off his whole hand but my cutting the finger gave him time to get to the women. He is alive because of me. Because of this."

Ignasio pushed the knife away from his face. He was tired of looking at it.

"Do you know what else was in the treasure? The big, smooth, metal piece was a breast plate—part of a suit of armor. The metal ball was a helmet and it had a faceplate that was closed and when we opened it there were bone shards inside. The jagged thing was just a rock. We each took one of the items, but I got the best."

Brown and black shapes appeared in the valley ahead and for a moment Ignasio thought he was looking at a boulder field. Then the shapes took form. Little square hovels, their roofs all caved so that the homes sat like opened boxes next to each other in an almost perfect rectangle with a pasture in the middle. Some of the walls were crumbled and Ignasio saw heaps of rain-packed ash and metal scraps turned sepia from flame and rust. It was a village, dead and burnt.

"So there it is," Ignasio said.

They approached it in silence and entered as if through cemetery gates; even the boy grew solemn.

Ignasio walked between two adobes, the smell of charcoal filling his nose. "Did you know I helped build some of this? I had a say in its design."

"I helped too, Papá. Don't you remember? I carried mud from the river. We all did. Do you really not remember?"

But Ignasio was lost in memories. They weaved through the outer buildings until reaching the center to what was once the plaza. They halted. Long mounds of earth blanketed with weeds and brush filled the old plaza from one end to the other. There had to be more than thirty, each one staked at the head with two sticks wrapped crudely together with twine; unmarked crosses that leaned in all directions as if in mass celebration of the very confusion of the place.

"Who did this?" Ignasio asked.

"Me and Mamá, and also Padre Montoya but he did not help much with the digging, mainly just said the prayers and went back to Abiquiú. Mamá said it was because he is old, but he is not that old, Papá, just fat."

"You and your mother did this? All of it?"

"And Padre Montoya but, Papá, he mostly sat during the digging."

Ignasio strained to picture the boy and his mother dragging and shoving thirty-some corpses into graves.

The boy sensed his father's confusion. "We smelled the smoke before we saw it all the way from home. When we stepped outside we saw it pluming in one single string into the sky. Mamá knew what it was right away but she would not let us come until fetching the padre. We brought the muzzleloader with us but everyone alive was already gone and everyone here was already dead, except for one man. When Mamá and I had his grave dug we went to drag him but when we picked up his feet he opened his eyes and kicked at us. The man was bleeding in his chest and his scalp was cut so we had thought for sure that he was dead. Mamá had to shoot him. It took us four days to dig and cover all the holes. I did not mind except that we slept here during the nights to keep a fire going to ward off the coyotes. And, Papá, how it stunk. I hated sleeping with so many dead."

"Come," Ignasio said, putting a hand on his son's shoulder, turning him around. "This is not getting us closer." He walked behind the boy through the narrow alleys until they reemerged in the openness of the valley.

"Blanco left us alone though, Papá. The Utes would do nothing to us."

"No, they would not."

"Because I am their friend."

"Because that was our deal."

"What deal?"

"The deal I made with Blanco. I gave him almost all the money we had. You didn't know this?"

The boy stopped.

Ignasio looked over his shoulder. "Keep up with me. Why do you look hurt? Did you never wonder why they killed every other Mexican, even the women and the babies, why they burnt and scalped the entire town but never bothered you and your mother?"

"Because we are friends." It was almost a whisper.

"*En absoluto.* Friends bought and paid."

"Even the food? All the meat they left at our door? All the things they gave us, Papá?"

Ignasio whirled on the boy, hooked a palm behind his neck,

knelt, and pulled his face close. "Look at me, Felipe. You are done with those savage boys, with Blanco and his Utes. Do you understand?"

Ignasio saw acceptance slowly forcing its way in painfully. He felt the neck relax, shoulders slump. The boy nodded.

The rest of the way they said very little. Around noon they forded the Río Grande. Beyond that the land remained flat, dry, and unforested. Shortly after sunset they came upon a great sprawl of tiny firelights in the shadow of the Sangre de Cristos. A mile out of the village, they ate a cold dinner, smoothed out places in the brush with their boots, and laid out their blankets.

Ignasio lay a long time with his eyes open. The meat had never been part of the deal.

He awoke to the sound of roosters and the smell of cooked meat. When he opened his eyes the sky was gray with dawn. The boy sat quietly beside him, his knees against his chest, peering out at the morning. Ignasio blinked and the boy looked down at him and smiled. Ignasio turned his head, embarrassed, and rose.

The village was Costilla. Ignasio counted more than twenty homes, their packed-earth exteriors still dark with moisture. Like the dead village of the day before, Costilla had been arranged rectangularly around a communal plaza. Horses swished at flies in tiny pens beside some homes, while staked goats paced and bleated beside others. Chickens wandered between alleys.

Oxcarts had begun to cut a rutted roadway into the village. It entered the plaza and extended southerly where it branched eastward into the mountains or south toward Taos. Between this junction and Costilla, Ignasio observed what he thought to be a smaller, satellite village. Upon studying it, he realized it was a single, sprawling hacienda.

The main building was U-shaped with real glass windows.

Next to this was a stable, and behind that what Ignasio guessed to be servants' quarters. Fenced at the very rear of the estate and backing against the first inclines of the mountains were what had to be more than two hundred cattle; half a dozen side pens milled with horses and sheep.

"Is that him?" Ignasio asked.

"Yes, that is his house."

"Look how he has set it before the town, like he is some great gatekeeper."

The boy did not reply.

Ignasio turned on him. "I said does it not seem he thinks himself a gatekeeper? A king?"

The boy looked toward town and nodded.

But Ignasio saw the obedience in it, that he nodded not in agreement but in pity of his father's cluelessness, of his having mocked a truth. Ignasio felt his grief swell inside him like it was something breathed in.

"Papá?"

Ignasio closed and massaged his eyes.

"Papá?"

"Hmm."

"Does *Tío* Lino love Mamá?"

The words invoked a bodily response akin to falling, for inside him Ignasio's heart leapt and tingles of energy surged through his limbs as if in preparation of a hard impact on a rough surface. He opened his eyes, shielded them with one hand, and looked at his son. The boy, however, did not look back, merely peered down at his boot which kicked distractedly in the dirt.

"He tried to," Ignasio said.

"But you would not let him?"

"No. And neither did she."

They entered the plaza. Two dirt-faced children collided with Ignasio as they chased each other and continued past him.

Smoke, sweet with baked bread, billowed from a few squat *hornos,* looking like four-legged beehives. The smell of meat wafted from the center of the plaza wherein blazed a great fire surrounded by a large gathering of people. They were packed tight and holding out pans, twine-wrapped to sticks, or long skewers of sizzling meat. What hands were empty they held before their faces in protection from the heat.

Ignasio tapped the shoulder of a man a little shorter than himself.

The man did not turn but swatted behind him. "*Vaya* beggar. I have little enough for myself."

"I am not a beggar. I am a buyer."

"You want to *buy* my breakfast?"

"Not breakfast, a horse."

"For that you must see Hermano Mayor."

"Who is he?"

The man tossed his head in the direction of the hacienda. "Lino Espinosa."

The gathering around the fire had quieted. Glancing about them, Ignasio saw that one of the faces was white. Surrounded by Chicanos the face seemed to glow. Ignasio was startled that he had not noticed the man sooner. Their eyes met and his heart jumped and the scar on his head pulsed.

He leaned closer to the man in front of him and lowered his voice. "Who else do you know that would sell a man a horse?"

"Here, no one. But in Taos, or Santa Fe—"

"*Amigo!* I have a horse to sell!" A stout man with a helmet of dark, tightly curled hair limped his way through the crowd with a skillet in one hand and fried eggs in the other. He wore a soiled, white shirt that was open to display a bulging gut with tight curls sprouting sporadically from it. He stopped before Ignasio, sucked the handful of egg into his mouth, and wiped the hand on his trousers. "You want a horse, *amigo*? I will sell you one right now. Call me Cesar, and follow me to my home."

"Your limp," Ignasio said as they walked, "from the war?"

"No, I knew better than to go to that. I limp because there is glass in my shoe."

"Glass? Why don't you shake it out?"

"Because I put it there."

"Why?"

"To remind me of the suffering and sacrifice of our Lord and to keep me close to Him."

The man led them to a tiny adobe on the northern end of town. The door was open and walking past, Ignasio observed a mat of muddy blankets on the floor, some cookware, and a humid billow of body odor. At the rear of the home and attached to its back wall was a small wooden pen in which circled a single burro.

"Her name is Solymar," Cesar said. "Back when I still had my looks I asked a girl to marry me but the girl's mother refused it. The mother's name was Solymar. I named this animal for her because they looked alike and so that I would not feel bad spurring it."

"You said you had a horse."

"Yes, but look at her. She is only two years old and thus strong and with yet much room left in her head for whatever commands you wish to insert."

"But you told me you had a horse."

"*Amigo,* Solymar is much better than any horse. You do not want a horse in such a land where one month there are blizzards and the very next painful weeks of drought and heat. A horse is like a handsome woman and will complain and throw its head at you because it thinks it deserves better. Burros are like ugly women; they do not complain or throw their heads at you because they know you will not hesitate to give them a kick. Also they will eat anything, and this is important here where fine hay is rare as seafood. *Símon,* to live here a man needs only a strong burro and an ugly woman."

Ignasio looked to his son. The boy shrugged, pursed his lips as if to say, *makes sense,* climbed atop the pen, and rubbed the animal between its ears. The burro blinked sleepily.

Ignasio turned to Cesar. "How much do you want for it?"

"Not much."

Ignasio took another look at the burro rubbing its head in rhythm against the boy's hand. Ignasio nodded. "*Bien.* But I am curious why you would sell it if you say it is so important to have?"

"Because if I sell it I will have enough for a horse."

They settled on two of Ignasio's gold pieces for the animal plus its saddle.

"What else?" Cesar asked.

"Chickens."

"I have no chickens but can show you who does. First though, what more here? I have many pans and bed stuff, a shovel, somewhere a timepiece left by my mother—"

"Who was the gringo in the plaza?"

Cesar scratched at his belly and cocked his head. "Lynchburgh? Is that who you mean?"

"If he was the gringo in the plaza."

"Yes, you are talking of Lynchburgh. He is from somewhere east but not all the way east, more like Tensi or Tenseesee, however they call it. His wife will make you blush she is so pretty, as is true of the daughter. For those reasons the Lynchburghs will not do well here. It is like I said."

"Why are they here?"

Cesar shrugged. "It is the same reason for me and everyone: Don Carlos gave them a plot."

"Who is Don Carlos?"

"*Amigo,* where is it you are from?"

"Chihuahua."

"Chihuahua! What of the battle there? People said it was very big and most terrible. Is that why you have the wound on your head?"

"Who is Don Carlos?"

"Don Carlos is Charles Beaubien. But do not call him that unless you are ready to hang. Although he will act as if to have forgotten it, in truth he is *Canadiense*. He came to Taos and married a *señorita* and thus became a Mexican. That is when he began calling himself Carlos, then Don Carlos once he received his land. The first grant was in his name, but when he wanted another he put it in his son's, and when the son was killed in the Taos Revolt, Don Carlos inherited it. As far as you can see in every direction is Don Carlos's land. And if you were to climb to the top of the mountains and see all there is on that side, that too, belongs to him. Oh, and he is the appointed judge for all of northern New Mexico. *That* is Don Carlos."

Ignasio snorted. "He is *barón feudal.*"

"He is *El Jefe Supremo.*"

"Then what is Lino Espinosa?"

"Lino? Lino is *El Jefe Miniatura.*" Cesar guffawed but not before glancing warily around him.

They left for home around noontime, both atop the burro. Tied to the pommel of the saddle were too clucking sacks of hens and one rooster. When they were more than a mile out of the town, Ignasio finally spoke. "They too will be scalped and burned. Watch. It is only time."

CHAPTER 5

It was an autumn evening, the wind biting at her ears and smelling of dead flowers, that María heard a dim bellowing choir floating north from Santa Fe. Then she saw them, a dark herd frothing dust as it approached. A lone horseman rode ahead holding the lead rope from a single cow trotting at his side. Behind him the other vaqueros chided and paced the rims of the herd. She imagined she could feel the earth below her thudding with the steps. Not that of the herd. His.

Ignasio and the boy joined her at her side.

"Is that him?" Ignasio asked.

They answered in unison: "Yes."

The vaqueros halted the herd around the two cottonwoods and waited while the outrider and his cow moved closer. María noticed he had shaved. He slowed, and although he was not close enough for her to see his expression María knew it was confusion slowing him, and then realization that stopped him.

"He thinks you dead," María said.

Ignasio said nothing.

The rider waved.

María looked at her husband who only laced his hands over the end of a shovel and rested his chin on it. "We could use the beef," she said.

"I can get beef."

"But this one is right here, and it is free. I did not say you cannot provide."

"Then do not suggest it."

The rider glanced over his shoulder at his herd. He faced them once more, offered a wave of dismissal, turned his horse, and retreated back to the herd, the cow in tow.

María shook her head. "You think too much, Ignasio. You think too much than what is good for you, and what is good for us."

Lino never returned. The Utes disappeared. And although María hardly spoke to these visitors when they had come, their withdrawal saddened and isolated her. Another nonpresence.

Three years after Ignasio's return, the Espinosas had constructed a new roof for the home and added a second bedroom. It had an exceptionally large window which, when uncovered by its lambskin curtain, revealed the giant bluff looming over the home. They planted, harvested, and traveled for their provisions. They were sick and healthy, sorrowful and cheerful, hateful and loving, shunning then embracing one another, wiser and prejudiced.

The family developed and so did the land, the country around them. Many of the United States' Mexican War veterans took the one hundred sixty acres of land warrants in the new Territory of New Mexico. Nonveterans went to Don Carlos who, urgent to establish his sprawling grants, doled out plots indiscriminately. The Espinosas and their fellow Mexican landholders watched the migrant homes spread like pockmarks: watched them stretch like an encroaching blight.

It troubled Ignasio most of all. María saw the insult constantly smoldering inside him, turning him inward. She suggested again they return south but once more he refused, this time not for what had become of Old Mexico but to spite what had followed them—him—here.

While her husband crumbled under the weight of his

acrimony, María concentrated on her son. At fourteen, the boy was nearly as tall as his father. His shoulders and jaw broadened. He remained lanky and his mouth worsened with the squaring of the jaw. And in replacement of his once naiveté, María observed a solemn conscientiousness of himself and his family.

For a long time, both parents worried over how the boy felt about the death of his brothers. Never were their deaths, or rarely even their existences, mentioned. But María knew they all thought about them. She saw it catch in her husband, saw his eyes flinch with the shame she knew it carried, saw him dig his nails into his thighs, saw their bruises later. In those moments María would usually excuse herself to go outside and weep in private, knowing that everyone knew and thus that no one would follow.

When the memories struck the boy however—when they seemed to drift about a room more like a smell than a thought—he turned to stone. At first his taciturnity suggested to María he did not understand it, that perhaps he thought his brothers would return, or that perhaps death was not so dichotomous to life but rather an aspect of it, like birthdays and getting sick, instead of its terminus. But in his developing maturity María soon realized something different. It first occurred to her while observing his fidgeting in those difficult moments, then confirmed itself when he, too, began leaving the room; not to cry like his mother, but to play.

Ignasio declared the boy insensitive and that he must never have cared for his brothers. María, however, recognized it for what it was. He was distracting himself, choosing not to feel the sadness of his mother or the regret of his father. He was removing himself from the emotions. It was a self-created acceptance, a self-crafted understanding, a regimen or filter of sorts, and in many ways it was healthier and more sensible than his parents' languishing.

His disposition and youth kept him the only bright light among them. María lamented his upbringing, simultaneously cherishing and worriedly monitoring his spirit like it was a clear sun surrounded by dark, drifting clouds. For him she did what she knew best: she taught him the religion. Together they prayed for hours, and although no one in the family could read, María regularly opened their bible and recited passages by heart. And in the end it was her greatest solace: the indefatigable, unquestioning faith of her son.

Ignasio tried increasingly less with him. The two worked beside each other only because Ignasio needed the help. He took his son few places and shared with him few stories. He took to riding to town alone, and the boy would stand and watch his father trail off into the sage. María watched, too, wanting desperately to embrace her son but restraining herself because to do so would be to acknowledge her husband's mistreatment.

She asked Ignasio why he did not take his son hunting and he replied that he was too young, which María knew was a lie; the truth being something to do with whatever fulminated behind her husband's eyes.

Distanced from his father, isolated from others, and forbidden from the only other playmates he'd ever had in this country, the boy wandered alone and began to talk to himself, continuing nonetheless to venerate his father, and seeing this became the most powerful source of pain in María's life.

She was alone in the house. Outside Ignasio called her name.

She found them side by side near the burro pen and henhouse, shielding their eyes with their hands as they stared off toward the river. "What is it?"

Ignasio spun, his eyes wild. "Come here. Look."

She followed their gaze beyond the river. About half a mile

away, María spotted a man in a white hat walking with his head down along the creek's east bed. Three horses waited behind him, one saddled, the other two appearing twice their bulk with packs.

"You should go over. Best to prod him along now," she said. Ignasio did not answer.

"I will go with you," she offered. "All of us will go."

"Yes, I will go too," the boy said.

Ignasio simply remained squinting, his lips pressed and thin, and in his silence María knew that none of them would be going, that he had called her out only to confirm his fear.

Beyond the creek, the man stood with his hands on his hips looking their direction for a long time. Then he turned his back to them, walked to his horse, and began to unsaddle.

CHAPTER 6

All day and all night the overcast hovered, unmoving, and in that darkness shone no skylight to mute the flicker of the men's fire coming in through the window and dancing on the ceiling, nor wind to thwart the carrying of their voices.

Ignasio slid out of bed and away from his sleeping María, crept lightly through the main room past his son in his blankets, and out into the night. There came no greeting from the henhouse as he neared it but in the little corral Solymar, who always slept flat on her side, brayed and rose. Ignasio paused at the fence and stroked her nose. He whispered to her to go back to sleep, and when he felt she was calmed resumed his walk toward the river.

He stopped about fifty yards from the water. On the other side five men in dark silhouettes sat in a loose circle around a high fire. Every so often the fire flickered just right and Ignasio glimpsed their faces. If they had been speaking Spanish, Ignasio suspected he could have picked up most of their words. Even so, he remained listening, watching, and after a while he sat.

Beyond these men more fires twinkled, the closest seeming less than two miles away, and concealed in the darkness between these night fires scattered yet more camps and shelters—new homes whose lights had earlier this night been extinguished.

He felt the world plummet around him, gaining momentum like a heavy boulder down a steep mountain, and Ignasio, sitting secret and cold in the night sage, could do nothing to stop it. He thought back to how this land looked when first he saw it and his heart sunk—not simply for the change in the land but also for that within himself. He remembered the first time he laid eyes on this land, and how his sons had been beside him.

When the Espinosas left Chihuahua City for the land to the north, Hector, their eldest, left behind a fiancée, and upon returning to the city less than two years later as a soldier, he went searching for her. It happened on a night after the failed battle of Sacramento, that long period when Mexican soldiers wandered their occupied city aimlessly.

Hector found the girl, as well as her new husband. A fight erupted. An American officer intervened and somewhere in his confusion, or in his rage, Hector swung on the officer with a table leg and shattered the man's cheekbone. He fled and was eventually discovered hiding in a dress shop, disguised in one of the dresses. He was arrested, led into the back alley, and shot in the chest by three riflemen.

At dawn, Ignasio and Jacinto were awakened by an American soldier who, having obtained their identities and location from Hector moments before his death, related the story including where they could find his body. They found him still in his dress and slumped against the wall, a shovel waiting beside him.

With news of Mexico City's capture and the end of the war Ignasio and Jacinto set out on the long journey north, back to María and Felipe. They joined up with a Santa Fe trader who provided them with horses as well as the group's single source of protection—a .31 dragoon.

They embarked along El Camino Real northward through Chihuahua, skirting wide the mountains west of El Paso. On the afternoon of the fourth day the craggy hills finally tapered into flat, passable desert, and swaying in the heat, half-asleep in the rhythm of the saddle, Ignasio suddenly felt a hard *thock* somewhere short of his thigh, followed by the boom of rifle fire.

The horse whinnied and dropped and Ignasio rolled backward onto the ground, crawling behind the flailing animal. The shots came from the mountain slope, little puffs of smoke floating from behind a boulder spill.

Weaponless, Ignasio lay flat with his head tucked while more bullets ripped into his horse. A bubbly wailing rose somewhere behind him and Ignasio turned to see the trader on his back, clutching his stomach and bemoaning the sky beside his own dead horse.

Ignasio looked for his son and spotted him galloping away in the direction they had just come. Once more the rifle fired and Ignasio saw it strike home in the boy's back. He heard a short yelp as Jacinto suddenly started bouncing limply inside the saddle before finally dropping and rolling to a stop on the desert floor.

Ignasio was alone. After surviving two battles—two years of war—Ignasio would die not in battle but in some random ambush. He felt a sudden relief in the knowledge, a thankfulness that he would not live long enough to know the grief of surviving so long only to lose so much.

But, slowly, it occurred to him that the shooting had stopped. Ignasio lifted his head to see three men approaching, their uniforms filthy and tattered.

American soldiers.

They raised their guns as he stood. They yelled at him in English and one kicked him behind the knees to the ground. They were patting him down when the call came, a wet and desperate cry that caused all three soldiers to jump. The trader's left hand rested on his opened stomach while the other stretched upward, clutching a folded piece of blood-smudged paper.

Cautiously, one of the soldiers took the note; the other two keeping their rifles on Ignasio. He unfolded it and read. Ignasio watched his lips whisper over the lines, his face growing pale.

"This is real?" he asked the trader in Spanish. The other soldiers, watching with obvious concern, let their rifles droop. One of them asked something but their comrade stared only at the trader.

The trader opened his mouth to speak but all that came out was gurgling followed by blood. The soldier turned from him to Ignasio. He held the note before Ignasio's face; gingerly, as if, Ignasio thought, scared by it.

"This—" he started, flipping the paper to read again, "this treaty, it is real?"

Ignasio nodded.

The other two soldiers were speaking quickly at the same time. The third stared at Ignasio, the document hanging limp at his side, his face thinned out and grimy. He was yet a kid, surely not even twenty. He had an empty holster on one hip, a canteen on the other. Besides these few things the soldiers appeared utterly provisionless.

The kid broke his gaze with Ignasio and relayed the information to his comrades. When he finished, the group stood silent for a long time. Ignasio, still on his knees, followed their gazes to the carnage: the horses, bullet-ridden, tongues purple and dangling; the trader, hand still on his stomach but unmoving; the lifeless form of Jacinto.

"Forgive us," the kid said.

He buried his son and the trader that evening at the foot of those mountains, shallow graves dug through rocky soil and cairned with stones. Dissecting the events of that day Ignasio would later pinpoint this moment, the desert growing black and icy, he on his knees with only a flat rock to rhythmically bore the graves, when the possession happened. For truly it was possession in every way Ignasio understood the word. He lost all sense of reason, conscience, morality, cruelty, and excess. Replacing these was a fierce and unintelligent emotion: a sudden hatred for everything. *Every thing.* He thought of nothing but his veins surged hot with purpose. He dug: driverless yet driven, empty yet brimming.

He dug.

And he hated.

Ignasio left the graves of his son and the trader, neglecting their rites but not the trader's dragoon. He snapped it open and counted its bullets before setting off on foot into the mountains: a lone shadow on moon-bleached desert.

He slunk through boulder fields and shimmied down ledges, feeling nothing each time he banged a knee or scraped his back or shivered against the piercing bite of the cold night's wind. The obstacles were somewhere in his unconscious alongside the smell and sting of lye from the time he had held his hands in a bucket of it as a young boy just to see how long he could, the feeling of a dozen little paws scratching frantically at the sides of the burlap sack that he once had to press below a river's current, and every other painful and vicious and invigoratingly real thing that he had ever known.

He found them asleep in the murky haze of dawn, each one shivering in a ball with his arms tight about his chest around the smoky remnants of a campfire. He crept until he stood directly over them. Then, before his presence—a presence that seemed to him as large and fiery as the rising sun—could be felt, Ignasio aimed the dragoon and fired. The sound exploded across the mountains and over the desert below. He saw the man's face blast apart at the bridge of his nose and for a flashing moment Ignasio had the strange image of a squeezable coin purse opening.

Already Ignasio was aimed on the other two, one of which,

the kid, had made it to a sitting position while the other remained on his side. The kid felt around for a weapon, and when he caught eyes with Ignasio, Ignasio shook his head and the barrel of the gun. The kid froze. His eyes widened in recognition.

In Spanish, Ignasio told him to be still and to tell his friend the same. The kid relayed this and the man remained on his side, peering up at Ignasio.

"Where is your gun?" Ignasio asked the kid.

The kid felt around perplexed. Then he looked over his shoulder. Ignasio followed his eyes to a rifle leaning on a rock about ten feet away. The kid's shoulders slumped.

"Good. And that of your friend?"

The kid looked over at the other soldier. He pointed at the man's hip and Ignasio saw the loaded holster. Ignasio caught eyes with the man and nodded.

"Please, we got separated. We got lost," the kid said. "We went into the city for the night except that when we woke up our company had left. We tried to catch them but couldn't and since then have just been wandering these mountains. We're lost and starving and we never heard. Please, we never heard . . ."

His head dropped and he began to sob. They were long wails, soft little howls.

"El Paso isn't far," Ignasio said. "And I'm ready to let one of you go, but only one."

The kid looked hopefully up at Ignasio.

"You took two of us and so I want two of you. I'm giving you the choice of who is dead by the time I leave and who is allowed to go to El Paso. Since you speak Spanish, *niño,* you appear to have the advantage in this decision."

The kid kept his eyes firmly on Ignasio.

"This may be obvious, *niño,* but is it your choice that you be the one I let go. Is it your choice that *el companero* dies?"

The kid stole a look at the other soldier, then back at Ignasio. He nodded. His face was striped where the tears cut through the grime.

"You will cooperate in this decision?" Ignasio asked.

"Yes."

"*Bueno.* Take that rock at your right foot there, and bash in his skull."

The rock was sharp, about the size of a grapefruit. The kid peered at it as the other soldier finally spoke, saying to the kid what sounded like a question. The kid did not acknowledge him.

"Why can't you do it?" the kid asked.

"I want you to. Was that not our decision, that you cooperate with me and I let you go on to El Paso? If it's not, I'll offer the same deal to *el companero.* Enough signaling and I believe he will understand."

"No, I'll cooperate. But maybe I could shoot him instead?"

"No guns."

"A knife then? I'll stab him."

"The rock."

The boy exhaled. He stared at the rock and began to sway, his breathing heavy as he considered the prospects. Again the other soldier spoke, this time more urgently.

Ignasio sighed and squatted on his knees in front of the soldier. *"Companero—"*

In a flash the kid lurched forward and snatched the rock, brought it up, and slammed it down on the soldier. It landed high on his cheek near the ear and Ignasio heard what sounded like an egg cracking. The officer pushed himself to his knees, his cheek concave, but already the kid was upon him. He swung the rock again and caught the man in the back of the head. The man collapsed and the kid knelt on his chest and drove the rock up and down until all that was left was a splattering of skull, hair, and brain.

When he was done the kid rolled back to his seat and pressed his face into his hands.

"Bueno," Ignasio said, bending down and removing the pistol from the dead man's hip. Then, with the trader's dragoon still tight in his grip, Ignasio pressed it against the kid's forehead. The kid dropped his hands and looked up teary-eyed at Ignasio. Ignasio pulled the trigger and the hammer clacked against the empty chamber.

Ignasio motioned his head to the eastern horizon. "There's El Paso."

A twig snapped somewhere in the sage. Ignasio jumped and scanned the darkness but saw nothing. He looked down at himself, seated on the valley floor and surrounded by a leafless autumn sage. A thin coating of frost had spread atop his pants and he brushed it away. Beyond the creek, the fire had dwindled, the voices disappeared. Only the one man remained. He lay on his side, his elbow propped, smoking a cigarette, and staring into the fading embers.

Ignasio didn't know what his thoughts had been while turning his back on the weeping kid or how long he had walked. What he remembered was noticing the setting sun, and it occurring to him that he had walked all day in no specific direction. He also realized he was carrying something in each hand. He lifted them and saw the two pistols gripped so tightly his knuckles had turned blue. Reality, memory, swirled up from his stomach and Ignasio dropped to his knees and wretched. All that came was water and bile, yet all Ignasio could do was heave until the sensation became yet another association—like the smell of blood and the feel of a pistol—of the madness lairep inside him.

And now, watching the man beyond the creek lay by his fire

and smoke his cigarette, Ignasio felt the tingles of that madness like a coming electrical storm. He had sensed it the day he first saw the white face in the Costilla, had sensed it every day thereafter. It hovered over him, a fear that he could not trust himself. A fear that his family, most of all his one remaining son, should ever be witness.

CHAPTER 7

Alone in the bedroom, María squeezed and rolled the wooden beads of the rosary between her fingers, a late-winter sun beaming through the tiny window, the crackle and occasional cough through the closed door where Ignasio fed the stove. The front door banged—five solid thuds that sounded like a boot kicking. María's eyes shot open.

She remained on her knees and held her breath. The thuds came again: harder so that they rattled the door. After a moment, the grate of the stove creaked shut and Ignasio's feet padded across the floor and to the door.

The knocker's greeting was muffled, unfriendly, but María thought it to be in Spanish, broken and accented. It demanded something about a cow.

She crept to the bedroom door, pressed her palm flat to stifle the reverberation and inched it open. She saw Ignasio with the front door open just wide enough to peer through it. His back was to her and over it bobbed a head, bald save what little hair tufted wildly from the sides. She glanced around for Felipe but he was nowhere to be seen, and María realized he'd been absent since morning. A glimpse of the bald man's face revealed him to be sunken and thickly bearded.

"What cow?" Ignasio asked.

"No cow," the man said, "*es toro*. Bull. He is Sidney's best bull."

"You're asking if I killed a bull?"

"I did not ask if you killed the bull; I ask why you killed the bull."

"I know nothing about any bull. I was inside all day and have enough meat anyway."

"You killed the bull yesterday. Sidney found it today thawing from night freeze. I see it myself now and when I stick my finger in the bullet hole it is ice inside. And its meat is not cut so you did not kill the bull for meat. So tell why."

"I didn't kill your bull."

The man turned his head to the right and began speaking English. María realized there was a second man, hidden behind the door. He replied something barely above a whisper.

"Sidney wants recompense and you can have the meat," the bald man said. "He wants twenty dollars."

Ignasio began to close the door but the man's palm smacked it back open. The force jarred Ignasio's grip and the door swung wide. There stood Sydney, his hand flat on the door. A broad white plainsman hat squatted over a round, pasty face with two tiny eyes, cold like rusted nail heads.

He said something to the bald man who then asked, "Was it your boy done it?"

Ignasio knocked Sydney's hand away. "My land is not your pasture. You got your stock ranging so that every day I got to step in their shit and drive them off."

"So it was the boy?"

"No. Let me close my door."

Sydney banged the door and sent it buzzing. The bald man took a step forward, leaned his head in, sniffed, and wrinkled his face.

"You know, me and Sydney was in Mexico. For me it wasn't the hot I hated because Texas is hot. It wasn't the water either because Texas got bad water, too. I could stand the hot and the water and even the disease in the women since women you can avoid, unlike hot and water. It was the stink I hated. It is like shit, earth, and beans all in a mixture that floats up from the people into buzzing clouds of flies. Stink, stink, buzz, buzz all the time. I hate to come from Texas to see this land we won square, and find the very same stink. And it just won't leave."

For a minute there was only the sound of the pops in the expanding stove despite the cold that had long since overtaken the house.

"Sydney," the bald man said, rocking back on his feet and nodding to his companion, "he was with Doniphan. He and Colonel shoot many, many Mexicans."

María watched her husband leaning slowly to his left, his arm creeping toward the muzzleloader leaning against the wall behind the door, he apparently having poised it there between the two sets of knocks. She saw one of Sydney's hands go to his waist.

She wobbled forward and the bedroom door screeched at its hinges. Sydney and the bald man looked at her.

"Oh," the bald man said, appearing surprised and amused. He and Sydney shared a quick volley of words. Ignasio stood frozen in place, his arm still half-stretched for the rifle.

"Fine, Mexican, Sydney will give you time to choose to pay for the bull or else choose not to pay. You know where his house is. He hopes you will pay." The two men turned and Ignasio shut the door.

Ignasio spun and marched toward María. He shoved open the bedroom door, brushing wordlessly past her and dropped to his knees in front of the dresser. He opened its bottom drawer, shifted through a stack of clothes, pulled out the pistol. She watched as he clicked open the cylinder and cycled through. When he was done counting he exhaled and shook his head.

"Where is he? Where did you see him go?" he asked.

"I haven't seen him since morning."

"Where did you see him go?"

"To the butte. This morning. Only please—"

But already he was past her and out of the house.

"Do not be harsh . . ."

The sun had barely risen the next morning when the boy tapped his mother's sleeping head. She opened her eyes and he put one finger to her lips and another to his. He looked scared. Beside her Ignasio snored. The boy tugged her arm and motioned for her to follow. María slid from under the quilt, grabbed her shawl and boots, and tiptoed out.

A cloud of black and white magpies burst from the pen as the boy led María to the corral. There lay Solymar, a windblown drift of snow crested against her back. Below her head, blood pooled black and frozen in the icy mire. A single bold magpie hopped in the mess as it pecked and tugged at the burro's opened throat.

"I didn't mean to kill that cow. I only shot at it to scare it or to . . . I . . . I don't know, but not to kill it," he pleaded, looking about to cry.

"I know Felipe. I know." She cupped a hand around his head and brought it into her bosom. His fists squeezed and wrung the back of her shawl. He was shaking.

"Maybe he doesn't have to know this," he said. "He doesn't have to see it. If you keep him inside for just a moment I'll hide her. I'll break the fence and he will think she escaped. That a lion or coyotes—"

The front door swung open and the magpie lifted away as the boy released his mother and wiped at his eyes.

Ignasio trudged toward them. "What is it?"

María stepped aside. Ignasio stopped and took in the carcass, neither surprised nor angry. He said nothing and for a second María and the boy looked at each other while Ignasio strolled up to the pen. He set a foot on its bottom rung, hooked his thumbs in his pockets, and spat.

"I wondered if this would happen. I should have been out here. I should have been waiting for him." He chewed on the inside of his cheeks and gazed off toward Sydney's.

"What are you going to do?" María asked.

"About the burro?" Ignasio shrugged. "Seems fair."

"What are you going to do about everything?"

"Right now, nothing." He thought a moment. "But come spring I think an *acequia*. And maybe a big damned fence."

Spring came, and with one final chop of the shovel the ditch met the river. Water rushed into the fresh rivulet and down. All three of them turned to watch with the shovels at their sides as the water rolled its virgin course down the trench, picking up clumps of dirt and dissolving them. In the midday sun the water shimmered like a streaming line of mercury.

The digging had begun more than a month before with a small pond near the corral and then trenched upward to the river. The channel split the river, Y-ing down in a straight line to the Espinosa homestead where it filled the pond before cycling back toward the crops via a spout-like cut in the opposite bank of the pond. They had worked feverishly since the thaw, Ignasio bent on irrigating before the Texan.

María peered beyond the river to the figure watching, his plainsman hat pulled low and gleaming. He had watched most of the spring, his tiny eyes hot on their backs from half a mile away. He turned, strode to a waiting horse, untied it, and spurred off.

"He's going somewhere," María said.

Ignasio scowled. "What of it? All you do is worry and scare, worry and scare. You have become *un quejica,* a nag."

"And you have become something unrecognizable."

He dismissed her with a wave. "Come on, Felipe. Help me with the posts."

"The posts?" María asked. "You're going to start the fence now?"

The boy trotted off beside Ignasio, beaming from his father's recent attention. María, suddenly alone and with the shovel clasped in her aching hands, wanted to cry. Instead, she followed.

The posts they had accumulated over the winter, an impressive cutting of shaved aspens and pines stacked to size next to the rickety cart that had moved them from Chihuahua. They loaded the cart and hand-pulled the posts over to the river where they drove them into the western bank. It was slow work, the posts slushing in all angles until finally pounded deep enough into dry earth. Water rushed over María's legs, numbing them; the lift and pound of the posts burning the muscles in her arms. She had no idea how big Ignasio planned the fence, only that there would be no rest until it suited him.

Two riders approached from the opposite side of the river. María recognized Sydney and the bald man.

"Ignasio—"

"I see them."

The riders pulled up short of the river and watched for a moment while Ignasio pounded a post, ignoring them.

"Mexican," the bald man finally said, "if peacefully we asked you to stop this fence and fill this trench, would you?"

Ignasio rubbed his brow with his shirtfront, and drove at the post.

The bald man looked at María. It was an appeal.

"Ignasio," she whispered.

He finished the post and slushed out of the water for another one. "Not his side," he said under his breath, and hoisted the next post.

The bald man looked to Sydney whose eyes burned down on Ignasio. Without a word the two men turned their horses and left.

Ignasio drove at the post. "Do not say anything, woman. I'm ready for him."

CHAPTER 8

On that first Christmas of the war Ignasio and more than a thousand Mexican soldiers had stalked up the Brazos River north of El Paso following debris and rumor until cresting a ridge overlooking a great blue-and-white sprawl of drunken enemy.

As a lancer, Ignasio waited in the forefront atop a soot-colored gelding. Below, a single Mexican captain trotted up the river valley to the Americans with the terms while at the same time obliterating the Mexicans' surprise advantage. Ignasio had watched with the pound of the gelding's heart through his legs, his lance suddenly a hundred pounds in his hand, all the while praying for surrender as the enemy camp swarmed into readiness like ants over a boot-mashed anthill.

Now, more than six years later, Ignasio stood on the one wooden step below his front door and peered through the evening at Sydney's cabin, reliving his anticipation and fear in those moments before the Battle of El Brazito. At least then, he thought, he had been able to see the enemy and what they were doing. A hailstorm of lead balls had sent the body of the lone captain whirling, and before they were fifty yards out another had opened the chest of Ignasio's soot-colored gelding.

María stepped out followed by the boy. "Is it your plan to patrol with that gun all night, every night?"

"Go back to your rosaries," he said.

"Maybe I could take up the rifle?" the boy asked. "I'll watch with you."

Ignasio shook his head.

"Perhaps you should be the one saying the rosaries," María said. "It's obvious you're the one with all the say. Go see if the Virgin will listen to your demands."

Ignasio ignored her and after a moment she clasped the back of her son's shirt and pulled him inside, shutting the door behind them.

Ignasio watched the June sun peel away from the valley and up the mountains. He clung to that departing light, unprepared and anxious for whatever might happen tonight. There had been no anxiety or fear when hunting the three American soldiers, only pure, trancelike resolution. He wanted that resolution now, that nonemotion; had, in fact, counted on it. Instead, now that he summoned it, that demon possession eluded him like tiredness at bedtime. Courage at wartime.

He stayed outside until the last light left the valley and the stars poked through their sockets. When he returned to the house, María's door was closed and the boy sat keenly at the edge of his bed. Ignasio told him to go to sleep and—the lie rising out of his throat like bunched cotton—that everything was fine.

He sat at the table. What if nothing happened tonight? Would he go out in the morning and continue working on the fence? Yes, he had to. He had done too much not to. And in the evening he would return home where he would spend the night pacing with the handle of the dragoon sweaty in his palm until either Sydney or exhaustion finally killed him.

Why were his hands shaking? Ignasio went back outside, loaded an armful of wood, and built a fire. The squat iron stove warmed to life and Ignasio sat on the floor next to it facing the door. He leaned his head back against the wall and absently spun the cylinder of the dragoon, every so often snapping it back into place then out again. The air in the room grew warm and thick.

He awoke, unsure if the whispers he heard came from his dreams or outside. In the low burn of the fading lantern Ignasio saw the boy asleep on his bed.

He rose, set the hammer on the pistol, walked to the door, and put his ear to it.

It exploded open. Little pieces of plaster burst apart where the still-latched bolt smashed through the frame, and the thick pinewood slammed into Ignasio's face and threw him backward. His pistol fired into the ceiling, showering down pieces of clay.

They were upon him. One took two long strides and kicked Ignasio in the mouth. He glimpsed blood speckle the sole before once again he was launched onto his back. A tornado of stomping boots surrounded him and suddenly two men had him pinned to the floor by his arms.

One of the men grappled with the boy, a bicep hooked under his neck. A few feet away, another man stood grinning with his back pressed against the bedroom door while on the other side María screamed and pounded.

Ignasio lifted his head to see Sydney, his hat low over his eyes and standing at Ignasio's feet, a shotgun in one hand. He said something to the two men kneeling on Ignasio's arms and both, counting down from three, leapt away.

Ignasio shot up but was too late. Holding the shotgun like a javelin, Sydney jammed the stock into the bridge of Ignasio's nose. His head whipped back and he hit the floor. With one quick step Sydney straddled him and Ignasio's eyes cleared just in time to see the Texan raise the shotgun straight and high, stock first. It came down, driven vertically like all those posts into the muddy flesh of the creek, hard into Ignasio's face. Sydney lifted the rifle and rammed it down again, again, repeatedly until all that remained of Ignasio's vision were a few specs of lantern light as if viewed through a tattered curtain. Far off in the distance the boy cursed and María wailed.

Sydney paused, looked around, took a step back, and twirled the rifle until he gripped the barrel like an ax. He sucked in a breath then swung the rifle down on Ignasio's forehead, shattering the stock into a dozen pieces.

Ignasio had always pictured his father being the first person to greet him in the afterlife. After a few words between the two of them, his mother, sons, and everyone else he once knew would then appear. Instead, after Sydney's assault removed him from the living world, Ignasio found himself atop a horse and greeted by the Ute chieftain Blanco.

The old chief sat bareback atop a tall ashen pinto. The animal's ribs protruded and war paint flaked in fading streaks from its fur. The two were alone in a brown autumn valley surrounded by an unbroken mountain ring. The sky was a charcoal overcast, the valley floor a shadow. Wind ripped at Ignasio's body and howled against his ears. It was the harshest wind he had ever known and it blew the chief's white cobweb hair straight back as he hunkered low to the pinto's mane. Even his one eyeless socket seemed to squint. The two horses rubbed noses.

"Where are you going, Espinosa?" Blanco yelled over the wind, the words gummy from his toothless mouth.

"Heaven," Ignasio said.

"Heaven? Why there?"

"Then Hell I suppose."

"Hell?" The chief laughed. "That might make more sense. But I did not mean you must be going one way or the other." The chief smiled, his lips sucking in over his gums. "Wherever you are going, Espinosa, do you even know how to get there?"

"Over those mountains."

"Are you sure?"

"I think."

Blanco glanced around. "Those look like very hard mountains to cross. Do you really want to climb them if it is Hell on the other side?"

"Is it?"

"I do not know, never crossed them. I only come here to ride my horse."

Ignasio looked down to see the chief's pinto rubbing its head against the front of Ignasio's mount, and it struck him that the horse he sat upon was the soot-colored gelding, shot through now many years ago. The pinto raised its head, a fresh crimson streak running along its nose. Ignasio leaned over. From a hole in the gelding's breast little droplets of blood dripped and flew in the wind.

Blanco rubbed the neck of the pinto affectionately. "Like I said, I have never crossed those mountains. You can though, if you want."

Ignasio looked at them. They were menacing, serrated ridges crescendoing spear-like into sharp peaks. The only possible passageway that he could see switchbacked up and over the ridge between two peaks strewn with tumbled boulders—remnants perhaps of some crumbled summit. The chief turned the pinto and kicked it into a trot, yelling something to Ignasio as he sped away.

Wait.

Ignasio jammed his heels into the gelding and chased him.

What did you say?

He wasn't sure whether he thought it, or screamed it.

The chief looked back over his shoulder and pulled on the pinto's mane.

"What did you just say?" Ignasio asked.

"I said control your horse or you will fly."

"Oh," Ignasio said, and the chief galloped away.

But that was not what Ignasio had first heard.

What he had heard was, *"Control yourself or you will die."*

Ignasio took one last look at the mountains and decided against them. And, when he opened his eyes, he saw María.

CHAPTER 9

The office was compact, stuffy, and poorly lit. With its separate entrance it clung like an afterthought to the side of an otherwise massive two-story residence looming two blocks west of the Taos plaza. Framed along the walls there poised flamenco dancers mid-twirl and bullfighters post-parry, whilst in between, portraits of Santa Anna, Governor Armijo, and George Washington glared as if in contempt at the exuberance of their fellow decor.

A squat, ring-stained oak bookshelf held half-drunk wineglasses, stacked collections of law, history, and fiction in languages ranging from Spanish to English to French. Opposite this stood a large rosewood desk on top of which sprawled a pencil-drawn and meticulously detailed map of northern New Mexico Territory. A mess of pencils, rulers, razors, and drawing compasses spilled haphazardly atop the map. A pistachio chair, its leather bulging and plush, had been turned to face opposite the desk. Slumped with one suited leg over the other and wineglass in hand sat Don Carlos.

"Where is it you say this was?" he asked.

"In our home," María said.

"I mean where is your home? From whom did you acquire your property?"

"On Río de Conejos. We are of the grant."

"The Conejos Grant? I don't think so. That savage Blanco massacred every one of those settlers five years ago. You must

73

have your location or perhaps your date of arrival confused."

Don Carlos sipped uninterested from his glass. He was a large man, paunchy but not fat and a little over six feet tall. His hair was brown, curly, and receding, his chest puffed and his nose sharp and bird-like. He wore polished dress shoes, creased suit pants, and a shirt that was white and ruffled at the collar and stained below both armpits. A small Mexican flag pin glimmered over his left breast.

"I'm not confused. I remember when Conejos burned. So does my son," María said, gesturing beside her to the boy.

"My god!" Don Carlos set his glass on the table and leaned forward. "Lino told me of you. You are the cousins! I have thought you a tale of his, a legend. A mother and a child living way out there like survivors of a dead race. Two helpless people stranded as if on a sheath of floating ice. My God, it is turning me poetic! I shall have to write of it, the inspiring fortitude of the Mexican people. Tell me, how is it you were spared?"

María glanced at Ignasio who had so far said nothing. He stared hunched at the floor, his head a disfigurement of purple swells and blood-crusted bandage.

"We had a . . . we made peace with Blanco," María said.

"Inspiring! *Los Diplimaticos.* Yes I will write of this, the inspiring fortitude!"

"You will help us then?"

It took him a moment to respond as he followed out the fantasy in his head. "Oh, yes, the *Tejano.*" His face became sour as he gestured to Ignasio, outlining the mashed face with one circling finger. "He did all that?"

"Yes. He attacked us."

"Even the big scar on the side of the head? That looks old."

"That is from the war. A musket jammed and exploded beside his head."

"The war, yes, seems like only a day ago. Such terrors, such persecution. I, too, sacrificed much for Mexico. More than most, in fact. You see, I lost two sons to the war, one being a son-in-law. My real son was only thirteen. They dragged him out from under a water trough and gouged him to death. Granted, he was not a soldier and the mob that killed him consisted of Mexicans. But if it were not for the Americans and their invasions, their manifest destinies, those Mexicans and Indians would not have been beguiled into rioting over Taos, and neither would they have mistaken my son for one of them. Unfortunately, my gringo skin often betrays my Chicano heart."

"Will you help us with the Texan?"

Don Carlos slouched back in his chair, his finger running along the rim of his wineglass and his eyes deep in memory. "*Los Tejanos, sí* . . . So it was a trespass and assault with absolutely no previous provocation?"

"We irrigated a creek and had begun a fence, but all on the land granted to us."

"Mm, then yes, Espinosa, I will help you. Even though you're not tenants of my own grants, where such squabbles are nonexistent, you're lucky I'm district judge. Obviously this man is in encroachment of land deeded by a pre-treaty Mexican grant and, since it has been continually occupied, said deed must be recognized by the US court."

"Thank you, Don Carlos."

"Of course, *señora*. Just bring me the deed."

"Deed? We have no deed."

María looked to Ignasio who continued staring at the floor and was no doubt, she thought, secretly gloating.

"God, yet another error of Lino and Armijo. I'm afraid we can't proceed further until you obtain the deed."

"How can I get one?"

"For the Conejos Grant? Go to where it was originally issued. There will be a record."

"Where was that?"

"Mexico City."

He said it as if it lay at the end of the street and again María appealed to her husband. Between his torn and bruised cheeks she sensed the hint of a smile. She was, as she had been in almost everything for many years now, entirely alone in this.

"What else can be done?"

Don Carlos brightened. "I would be pleased to give you a lot in Costilla."

Ignasio's face dropped.

"You would finally be close to an actual village, to civilization, not to mention your cousin," Don Carlos said. "Although I can understand how that might be difficult considering your, what should I say, *failed* relationship with Lino. He told me about it a long time ago."

"What did he tell you?" María asked.

"There is no need to repeat it now, in front of your son. Besides, what we do in the past is—"

"What did he tell you?"

Don Carlos blushed. His eyes darted briefly toward Ignasio who, for the first time since stepping into the office, appeared interested in the conversation. "Lino said that you once tried to, ahem, force yourself upon him."

For a moment it was silent. Don Carlos picked underneath one of his fingernails, concentrating on the task as if it a pressing matter. Then María began to laugh. "I forced myself on *him*?"

Suddenly the door barged open, flooding the room with light and the wide silhouette of a woman. She was dark, short, and heavyset with gold loop earrings framing a steely face. Noticing María and the two beside her, the woman appeared surprised, then quickly annoyed.

"My love!" Don Carlos exclaimed. "Where have you been?

What took you so long? I have been eyeing that door for hours."

"Let's go," the woman said.

"Don Carlos," María said, her face once again grave. She clutched the shirt around his shoulder as he stood, ignoring his wife's scorn. "Will you buy our property?"

Don Carlos shook free. "Next to that brutal Texan? I would be crazy."

They departed Taos unnoticed and without saying a word to one another. The sun set behind their backs and stretched their shadows long in front before they dissolved into the all-encompassing shadow of the evening. They dipped through arroyos and stumbled through rabbitbrush and María's mind went out of her body and above it. It looked down on her, on them, unattached yet still committed to her memories, wants, and emotions.

From above, María took in their situation: three Mexicans on a sixty-mile journey home, a family of three bound to a black future. One of them was crippled, the other two on each of his sides lest he fall. They were hungry and with little food, cold and with few garments. They were a family severed; bereft of two members and in their devotions to those left. María's mind fed all this cordlessly from above her head down to her heart and her heart wept not for the future but because it had never foreseen this present.

The lights of Taos flickered behind them. "I do hope you're still happy we tried," Ignasio said. "For all our sake, I really do."

"Quiet Ignasio. Please."

"A deed in Mexico City, a 'Chicano heart,' bah. That man's heart is as pallid as his skin."

"I said shut up, Ignasio."

"Then what, if you lead this family, *madre querida,* would you have us do?"

"You know what I would do. You've known this whole time."

"Leave, María? Abandon the home we built, the one you spent two lonely years keeping with 'inspiring fortitude'? Shall we wave a white flag at Sydney as our farewell?"

"Those two years were lonely. But can't you see that they're still lonely? This land has been a poison. So tell us then, like you always do. Shall we die here?"

"No."

"What does that mean?"

"It means no. We will leave this place and you will have your way. Congratulations, you have won."

María slowed, instinctive of a trap. "Really?"

"It's not my decision María; it's yours."

But underneath his cynicism, María knew he was ready to leave. She knew he pinned the decision on her because to do so was to pin all future hardships and misfortunes on her. Very likely he even hoped for such things, just like he had hoped the appeal to Don Carlos would end in embarrassment. It was a victory on all fronts for him, and she didn't care. If this was what it took for them to leave the cursed jacal and the Texan across the river, María would bear forever her husband's disappointments.

"Where will we go?" she asked.

"You tell us, Don María."

"Chihuahua. Home."

"Is that your choice, that we again travel the Jornada del Muerto? Through the desert and mountains and Apache canyons? You realize I've made this trip already twice more than you. But if that is your choice—"

"It is."

"Then fine."

From behind them came a small voice. "It is not my choice." Both of them turned to see the boy.

"Don't tell it to me," Ignasio said. "Tell it to your mother. It's her decision."

"Please don't do that Ignasio," María said.

"I will look at you, Papá."

Ignasio scowled. "All right Felipe, what is your choice?"

"We stay. We get rid of the *Tejano.*"

Ignasio scoffed and looked at María but María offered him nothing.

"If that's what you want I won't stop you," Ignasio said. "I even encourage it. Stay here. You may have my house while your mother and I are gone. Build that fence, get a woman, start a family. Do what you like."

"Yesterday I'm too young to do anything. Now you say I can have the house and do anything I want."

"Jacinto was younger than you and he fought in a war."

"And he and Hector would be ashamed to see their father now," the boy said.

Ignasio chuckled and shook his head.

In his growing redness María saw it coming. She cried out as Ignasio swung. The boy dodged and the swing grazed his ear. The boy crouched, leapt, tackled his father. The two went down and rolled and suddenly the boy had his father pinned and was fighting against Ignasio's flailing hands, pummeling his father's battered face.

María hurried to grab her son and an elbow—or a fist, she would never know—smashed into her eye. She saw a flurry of colors, stumbled backward, fell. Everyone froze.

"María?"

"Mamá?"

María sat hunched in the sage, rocking, her eye buried in her palms.

"I cannot do this," she said, sobbing into her hands. "Not anymore."

CHAPTER 10

When they reached home Ignasio ate with his family and made plans. In the morning they would begin packing and by the end of the week the Espinosas would vacate the land to arrive in Chihuahua by mid-autumn.

After the meal Ignasio joined his wife and son in prayers. It was not so much to feel closer to God, but to feel closer to them.

Preparing for bed, Ignasio paused with his hand on the lantern, and as the boy sat on his bed pulling off his shoes Ignasio said his name, then told him good night. The boy replied the same and Ignasio snubbed the light.

He maneuvered through the darkness using the vision of the room preserved temporarily in his mind, except in the vision standing out more than any obstacle in his path was the boy's face. It was his reaction to the bid of good night, the tilt of the head and the flashing confusion as if the words seemed unusual despite them being said countless nights. Then again, Ignasio realized, they had also been unsaid on countless more. By the look on his son's face he had not expected them to be remembered this night. But Ignasio had said them pointedly, and for that reason along with everything else that had happened and all the things that yet still might happen, *good night* had come out an unintended, indicative riddle.

He found the bedroom door handle near the foot of the boy's bed, pushed it open, and closed it behind him. In the moonlight of the open window María waited for him sitting upright in their bed, the sheets in her lap.

"He will forgive you," she said to him.

"I did not ask him to."

"No, but he will."

Ignasio undressed and sat in bed next to his wife. She took his head, leaned him into her lap and stroked his hair. He didn't fight it. He fell asleep, wanting to fight nothing.

When he awoke it was dark and the air was thick with the smell of lantern oil. Ignasio wrenched out of bed and into the main room. The boy was gone.

The smell in here was stronger, the vapors hanging trapped like a sweet-smelling cloud. From the dim white glow of the window Ignasio spotted the lantern standing upright in its place where he had left it on the table. He picked it up. It was light and its base greasy. On the table little droplets reflected the moon.

He went to the cupboard on the opposite end of the room, opened it, and felt along the bottom shelf. Where two one-gallon jugs of lantern oil usually sat, his hands felt only empty space.

María shuffled out of the bedroom behind him, the blanket around her shoulders. "What are you doing? What is that smell?"

He tore past her into the bedroom and yanked open the dresser drawer. His hand fumbled through the clothes until grasping the pistol. From the other room María called the boy's name.

"He's gone," Ignasio said, pulling on a pair of pants and making for the door. "Stay in here. Don't leave the house." He clicked open the chamber of the pistol and held it to the light of the window, checking that it was full.

"Ignasio!"

"What?" He whirled around to see her pointing toward the

door frame. He hadn't noticed it before, hadn't even thought to check. The muzzleloader was gone. Ignasio slipped out the door behind and began to run.

The night air was still and frigid. A gloss of ground frost stretched shimmering under a crescent moon. It crunched under Ignasio's bare feet as he ran, calling out his son's name in loud whispers that brought with them plumes of breath.

Scoping the ground he spotted a boot print in the frost. Relaxing his eyes and taking in the whole spectral valley before him, Ignasio saw a line of tracks running through the frost and fading in the direction of the river.

He veered into the tracks, his feet burning, the handle of the pistol already slick with sweat. Every time he called out he slowed and listened, and every time there answered only silence. Between his panting came the trickle of the river. He paused at the bank and noticed the prints continuing past the opposite side except now with splatters of water around each step. Less than a hundred yards beyond, Ignasio made out the outlines of Sydney's cabin, the moon glinting on its windows and casting black shadows along its sides.

He sloshed through the river, the water shallow and icy, climbed up the bank, and listened. He held his breath, his heart pounding through his chest and into his temples.

He saw movement around the cabin. At first it appeared only a shadow within a shadow, some dark shape creeping through and dissolving into larger, darker shapes before the movement came to the front of the cabin. In the skylight Ignasio realized the silhouette was that of a person.

Ignasio ran. He called out again and this time the figure paused. Ignasio waved his arms and the figure disappeared into another shadowy corner of the cabin.

"Felipe!"

Somewhere close a cow bellowed.

"Felipe!"

Ignasio froze. Before him a sudden flash of deep blue flared at the cabin's side. The blue flickered to orange and spread around the cabin, traveling slowly at first as it circled like a fiery halo working to connect one end to the other. Ignasio watched as the fire ring stretched along its predetermined trail until the whole lower perimeter of the cabin was alight in flames. The blaze hugged tight against the log walls in flames that licked to the roof. He squinted and shielded his face from the suddenly searing heat. At the side of the cabin someone was running. And in the firelight Ignasio saw the dark hair and wild eyes of his son, the muzzleloader swinging in one hand at his side.

Run, Ignasio thought. *Run as fast as you can.*

Ignasio took off to intersect him but as he did the boy abruptly stopped, spun back to the flaming cabin, crouched, and raised the rifle.

"Felipe!"

From the cabin there came a thick bang as the front door kicked apart. A perfect dark rectangle opened amid the orange flames and from it Ignasio had time to see a spark of light before something heavy slammed into his chest. The blast spun him sideways and he toppled. The earth tilted on its axis and stars dazzled before him. Lying on his back he forced his lungs to breathe and the hole in his chest sucked and spat. There came a second gunshot, this one bigger, louder.

Ignasio lifted his head and saw Sydney in long white pajamas come stumbling through the fire like some pale demon out of an inferno. He dropped his pistol and both hands clutched at his side. After a moment the Texan teetered and fell, the spreading flames nipping at his form.

Ignasio heard a woman's voice. She cried his name and that of the boy's but Ignasio did not answer. His concentration was elsewhere, for somewhere someone was trying to tell him something, something very important. His chest sucked and the stars blurred and Ignasio stopped his breath and closed his eyes in order to shut out all distractions.

This time he heard the words and realized it was he who was trying to speak, he who had something important to tell. Earlier in life it would have shamed him to say such words, especially if they were his last. But now they felt right and good like only the truth does, and understanding this Ignasio wished he had said them more often in life, that he had obeyed them instead of others. What he wanted to say but in the end could not was:

Run. Run as fast as you can.

★ ★ ★ ★ ★

Part Two:
The Resentment of
Lino Espinosa
1851–1862

★ ★ ★ ★ ★

CHAPTER 11

Ernesto De La Vara was eighty-eight years old when he died. He was one of Costilla's first citizens, and its oldest.

His death came as a surprise, the surprise being that time had not killed Ernesto but rather his single companion in old age: his pet goat Chaco. The two had migrated together and the goat seemed as ancient and immortal as its master. But unlike the old man who had always been short-tempered, Chaco was imperturbable. The animal often stood coated in horseflies with its tail still or asleep in a hot afternoon sun while shade offered itself just a few easy steps away.

Despite the docility of the goat and its lifelong relationship with its master, one evening as Ernesto bent over and set down the animal's food bowl, Chaco—for reasons uncharacteristic and decidedly unknown—reared up and slammed his two knobby horns deep inside his master's soft head. They found Ernesto the next morning facedown in the pen's muck with Chaco standing over him, sleepy and bored, the food bowl empty.

Since the discovery, Secundina had not left the dead man's side.

She was there dutifully as the men peeled the body from the frozen mire, and she followed them to the morada where they left her to strip the soiled clothes from the carcass and wipe it with soapy rags. She worked quietly with the doors shut and a mystical glow radiating from the candles above the body, her breath fuming in the cold interior. When he was clean she dressed Ernesto in a brown *habito* before finally seating herself on a pew in utter darkness.

The morada was the first building in Costilla. A wall separated the structure into two rooms, a common room at the front and a chapel in the rear. Wooden perches jutted from the interior's stone wall above Secundina's head to display wood-carved santos in enactment of the Passion. The chapel held twelve rows of pews, each one a smoothly-halved pine tree with legs.

When Secundina shifted, the whole row wobbled, and hooking her fingers at the edge of her seat she felt the roundness of the underside, the rough bark of the tree from which it was cut. The rows split into two sections of six facing the other. Ernesto lay on the rostrum at the head of the room. The walls were windowless and this, coupled with the mausoleum-like cold emanating from the stones, gave Secundina the sensation of walking into night every time she entered the morada, as if it beyond such things as temperature and time. She tightened the shawl around her neck and wondered what things took place here when women were not allowed. She snaked a hand up her dress and adjusted the cicilo, the bracelet of cactus around her thigh.

When finally the first of the mourners entered she lowered her head and removed from her pocket her kerchief—a green folding of silk with the figure of a rabbit embroidered in one corner. Her father had given it to her. He had told her it came from Europe.

As the mourners passed impervious to her in the dark, Secundina bunched and twisted the kerchief distractedly in one hand while the other, the dead one, curled lifelessly in her lap. The entire arm hung withered, its pale skin sagging from a lack of blood and muscle. It was a congenital deformity: a curse, just like her pole-like physique, her towering height, her stretched and horsey face, her table-flat chest.

Hours passed and her head began to ache from dehydration. Nonetheless, she felt thankful to have no water. Better to fight an aching head than an aching bladder. Her stomach had stopped growling hours ago as if in acceptance of its neglect. Whenever sleep tempted her, which was often in the chapel's quiet darkness, Secundina tightened the string of cactus. By now she figured to have seen every family in the village walk by to say their rosaries over Ernesto. She began checking off names in her memory, flying down the streets of Costilla and its outlying pastures to deduce who might be left.

The door moaned open and Secundina turned to see her mother silhouetted in the candlelight.

"*Vayamos hija.*"

A tingling pain flared in her leg when she rose, and walking through the pews Secundina feared it would fold. It didn't, and with her hands cradled before her she let her mother place a sympathetic hand on her back and lead her through the common room to the exit.

Night had fallen and the air smelled of smoke as bonfires raged along the trail east of town leading up to the hilltop cemetery. Outside the morada's entrance the Brothers formed a gauntlet that Secundina and her mother now walked through. Secundina kept her head down and said nothing and she felt their eyes like fingers brushing her cheeks. The men at the back of the formation were shirtless and wearing white trousers that shimmered against the fires.

When she was past them, Secundina watched the men file into the morada and close the door. She followed her mother to the *auxiliadora,* the women's morada, where the sights and smells of a recent feast greeted her. Wooden platters lay empty and smeared. Bits of corn, beans, and rice littered the room's clay floor. Secundina absorbed the scene for a moment, inhaling deeply, then took a broom from behind the door.

Her mother caught her hand and removed the broom. She led Secundina to a cabinet and from one of its drawers pulled out a plate of food.

"Sorry it's cold."

A lump rose in Secundina's throat. "Thank you."

She ate standing up while her mother cleaned. Soon the other women began to arrive and Secundina stuffed away a few more bites before forfeiting the plate lest she be the only one not cleaning. When they were done, the women took seats in a large rectangle around the room and talked mildly.

"Did you feel the spirit of Ernesto today?" one of the old women asked Secundina.

"Yes."

"Did he say anything to you?"

"Not that I could hear."

"Mm, I am surprised. I thought he would have told you to go shoot that old goat. Heee!"

The laugh came out a wheeze and the smell of it reminded Secundina of musty clothes. She smiled at the woman who, once the moment was over, looked to the ceiling and crossed herself. When finally the woman keeping watch outside the door announced it was time, pensiveness floated about the room. Silently the women funneled out.

The bell atop the morada clanged and echoed while below it the procession formed. At the head and dressed in white robes were the Hermanos de Luz. Behind them, adorned in gray and hoisting the shrouded body of Ernesto, were the Hermanos Salidos a Luz. And in their white trousers at the back waited the Hermanos de Sangres, the flagellants. The women took their place behind the Brothers at a respective following distance.

Everyone was still, the wind and the flutter of torches the only sounds. From the front of the procession a voice began to sing:

"Adios acompanamientio, pues ya todo esta cumplidoooo; Poner a hombres en las tumbas. En la tierra del olvidooooo . . ."

The procession started down the street toward the first of the bonfires. In the intermittent beats between each verse, whip cracks filled the air, an anxious burst of leather snapping skin.

Secundina walked at the back of the line with her hands once again cradled over the rosary. When the procession reached the base of the cemetery hill it stopped. Wedged into the earth was a large cross, the first of the bonfires flaring behind it. The hymn paused and the mourners bowed their heads. The Hermano Mayor walked from the front of the formation to its middle and gave Ernesto the first of his blessings. He said amen and a salvo of whips hissed in reply.

The procession recommenced its slow, snaking march up the hill, but Secundina remained where she was. She stared through the fire. Behind it something had moved. It had been slight, merely a shadow, yet unmistakable. Someone, something, was back there. Secundina peered toward the procession and realized they had reached the next station. Suddenly she was alone. Or was she? She felt her thigh bite and tingle.

She started to run, one hand holding up her dress and the other clutching the rosary. She peered over her shoulder just as two figures emerged in the middle of the path. The flames blazed at their sides and Secundina observed one to be a man and the other a woman. She glanced back up at the formation, hesitated, turned around, and approached the two shadowy figures.

The woman was hooded with wavy gray hair falling out of her shawl and over her front. Her face was grimy, her clothing filthy. She shivered. The other Secundina realized was not so much a man but a boy, his mustache thin and glinting silvery in the firelight. Dried sweat caked his brow.

"Who are you?" Secundina asked.

"Please," the woman said, "help us."

"What are you doing here?"

The woman snatched Secundina's hand. "We need Lino. Please. We are family."

CHAPTER 12

Vivian sat snug between his mother and sister on the parlor room sofa. Lino paced in short, pivoting steps before the fire. The newcomers had just finished eating and were telling their story. Vivian listened, spellbound.

María told it through heavy sobs that heaved her chest and arched her back from the chair. So far the boy had said nothing, just kept his hands in his lap, his eyes on the floor, and Vivian wondered if he could even talk through that muddle of crooked teeth.

The dad was dead, killed by a gringo. Vivian understood that much. He felt sorry for the boy who was like a statue as his mother cried. Both were so dirty Vivian thought it incredible his mother had allowed them in the house. They had been led in quickly, Secundina immediately fixing them dinner. Vivian couldn't remember Lino ever treating guests so special, and this confused him since no one appeared particularly happy to have them here.

María finished the story and the room fell quiet. Lino stopped pacing and stood with his back closed to them. Vivian's eyes wandered over the other parts of the room: the brass crucifix near the fireplace standing taller than he, the shelves lined with his mother's books, the mounted heads of the steer, elk, bear, and mountain goat—glassy eyes that had all at some time or another played parts in Vivian's nightmares. On one side of the parlor room connected the hallway, leading to four bedrooms and an office, while on the other the home hooked into a dining room and kitchen. It was, as Lino called it, Hacienda de Espinosa.

Finally, Lino turned. He looked to the three of them seated on the couch and Vivian's mother gave her husband a slight nod. The boy looked at them too. Only not them, Vivian realized. Secundina.

"So now you are here," Lino said, spinning so that he peered down upon the mother and her son. "Now you are here because you know they will look for you. You know they're going to look at your papá, little Felipe, as well as this *Tejano* of yours, and they're going to wiggle their fingers inside those bullet holes and wonder if maybe there's more to the story."

"Lino . . . ," María said, but didn't finish.

"Now you are here." Lino looked at her, tapping the front of his teeth with one fingernail. After a moment, he sighed and put a hand on her shoulder. "Today we buried one of our townspeople. He had no kin and thus no one to grieve him. But if this man had, say, a wife and a son, it would be customary for them to grieve their husband and father for one year. It would be their obligation."

Now Lino put a hand on the heads of María and the boy, bowing them down in penance. "In respect of your loss, I think it best you follow custom."

For the first two months of their mourning, Vivian saw very little of his cousins. Their door remained closed and the few times he snuck behind his mother as she took them food the scene he glimpsed inside was always the same: María lying on her bed with a small crucifix resting on her chest and the boy sitting on the floor, his back to the other bed, staring at nothing. When the door closed, the air whooshed out hot and stale. On Christmas the two accompanied the family to the morada, and while most in the chapel wore festive colors, María and her son wore black and stood isolated in a corner with their heads lowered uninvitingly.

In the new year, the two began taking their meals at the table, María always helping Vivian's mother and sister with the dishes until gradually she joined in all household chores, including caring for little José. She seemed to Vivian a kind woman like his mother except always tired, always sad. When she smiled at him her eyes were wet and she would hold the smile even after turning away as if to release it would be to allow in whatever crept behind her eyes.

The boy's despondency took a stranger, more distant shape. His consciousness seemed to exist in other places. He talked to himself in short bursts that immediately trailed off like whatever thing muting the conversations in his mind had merely slipped and recovered. They might be feeding the horses when suddenly he would blurt out some word or noise and both Vivian and Lino would jump and look at him. But each time the boy only kept working, unaware even as his lips went on mouthing some secret monologue.

He did, however, prove an expert in the pastures. He was fearless atop a horse. Whenever one bucked or tossed its head, the boy gripped the loose ends of the reins and quirted them across the animal's face. Vivian had never seen anything so bold.

Branding day came on a soggy morning in early spring. The boy worked with the men while Vivian toyed outside the fence with a puppy. As they played, the puppy bit at Vivian's glove, tugged it off, and scurried away with it into the release pen. Vivian ducked under the fence and went after the dog just as the men let loose one of Don Carlos's freshly branded bulls. The bull, singed and wild, charged. Vivian turned, saw the bull, and froze.

But suddenly Felipe was inside the fence, whooping and waving at the animal. When the bull cut for him, Vivian seized the distraction and squeezed back through the fence just before Felipe jumped and rolled under the fence behind him.

The bull snorted and followed them along the fence for a moment before darting off into the pastures. The boy brushed Vivian off and grinned. "Be careful brother, or next time you'll be cowpie."

He stepped aside as Lino and the rest of the men rushed around, and in the commotion Vivian could think only of how the boy had called him his brother.

Vivian's mother, Cecilia, taught lessons in Costilla's one-room adobe schoolhouse. When she proposed that it was time the boy begin lessons, Lino agreed but only if done inside the home. At first, Vivian and Secundina sat in on these private lessons, and secretly Vivian was pleased to find that where his cousin excelled in horsemanship he fell short in reading and writing.

Nevertheless, he proved a fast, eager student. He did not stare off and talk to himself around Vivian's mother. His eyes followed her finger as she ran it along a sentence in a book and his mouth read aloud, and eventually Vivian accepted that with his pace and with his appetite Felipe would soon surpass him in school, too. Stuck in his room so long, the boy even read by himself and once he saw that Vivian knew it wasn't even worth trying to compete.

During Holy Week, the boy and his mother were finally allowed to attend a public event outside the morada. Still wearing black, they stood with Vivian and his mother and sister watching the Good Friday *parada* stream by in the plaza. Hermano Mayor Lino Espinosa in his flowing white robe led the procession. Two men with red rags over their faces pulling an oxcart loaded with rocks and a perched skeleton labored behind. The skeleton was made of wood except for the head, which was a polished human skull. Dressed in a black cloak it held a bow and arrow.

"What is that?" the boy asked.

"That is Death in his cart."

"Don't you think it's odd that Death should have to be escorted."

"Do not make fun. When I was a baby, a man mocked this processional. He began to laugh and the arrow slipped and struck the man in the heart."

The *parada* weaved to the morada where it stopped and reorganized. The mood became solemn as the Cristo emerged wearing white and a crown of yucca. Two Brothers appeared dragging a cross and hoisted it atop the Cristo's shoulders. The Cristo heaved forward. Behind him the flagellants cracked their whips. The march began.

They followed him for more than an hour, waiting patiently each time he fell or dropped the cross. They ascended to a hill overlooking the village and topped with a small stack of stones. The whips stopped and the crowd quieted. At the foot of the stones, the Cristo laid the cross flat and stretched himself across. The Brothers surrounded him and together they hammered the stakes through the Cristo's hands and feet; the Cristo looking deep into the sky and uttering no sound.

The Brothers lifted the cross and notched it into the mound. The Cristo peered benevolently down at his audience, rivulets of blood etching down the yellow and green of the freshly carved cross. A line formed and the first of the townspeople approached to offer their prayers. When it was Vivian's turn, the Cristo looked down at him and smiled, his eyes blood burst and compassionate. Vivian stepped aside and watched the boy do the same except that after the prayer he bent and kissed the dying man's bloodied feet.

★ ★ ★ ★ ★

On Vivian's birthday the women cooked a feast and nearly every boy in Costilla came to Hacienda de Espinosa. After the meal they remained at the table and one by one presented Vivian with gifts. He felt like a king. When the last of the gifts had been opened, the boy, who had so far sat silently and unnoticed at the edge of the table, suddenly rose and told everyone to wait. When he returned from his room he held in one hand what Vivian thought was at first a walking stick. Looking closer, however, he saw the juniper had been shaved flat and carved elliptically with the ends tapering down to two notched points that bounced lively from the leather-wound middle where the boy held it.

"We'll have to string it of course," he said. "And then make arrows. But that will be the fun part."

He handed it to Vivian and stood back. Vivian gripped and felt its flexible, snapping power. He had no idea how Felipe had made it or how he had concealed it from everyone, only that it was the best gift he had ever received.

After Vivian's friends left and the boy and his mother were once again shut away within their room, Lino confiscated the bow; Vivian threw a tantrum that shook the walls.

The next day Vivian sought out the boy. "Why does Lino hate you?"

"Because my father hated him."

"He took my bow."

"He's your father and can do what he wants."

"But he's not my father," Vivian said. "My real father fought in Taos and was killed for it. He would not have taken the bow."

"You call Lino Father."

This surprised Vivian, hurt him even that the boy could not do so much as pretend to understand. "It is not how I think of him."

★ ★ ★ ★ ★

Secundina's birthday was a month later. She had no party, no friends to join her, only a dinner. Again, however, the boy surprised them by presenting her a bouquet of flowers. The family said nothing as Secundina accepted her lone present, thanking him in open spite of Lino.

The next morning Vivian discovered the bouquet discarded in a heap outside his sister's window. Hurriedly he scooped the flowers and stuffed them under a rock.

Summer passed and the air began to cool. More families moved into Costilla. One night Vivian was awakened by a bright, silvery white light that filled his room. Sitting up he saw the pastures frosted over in a pristine, unbroken frost radiating a crescent moon.

The following morning was Sunday and on the way to the morada Vivian was pleased to find that the boy and María no longer wore black.

CHAPTER 13

Lino Espinosa, wearing a lambskin coat and a sombrero pulled low over his eyes, waited in the middle of the roadway leading to the hacienda. Approaching him were the three Mexican raiders and, tied single file to the rear man's horse, their string of captives. Grime crusted their faces, and their clothing was a stained variegation of sweat, soil, and ash.

A distant cheering rose from the town. Lino glanced that way, rolled a cigarette, and stuck it in his mouth. He fumbled in his pocket but found no matches.

"Here," the first of the raiders said, swinging suddenly off his horse and trotting up to Lino. He held up a book of matches, struck one, and held the flame to the cigarette as Lino puffed it to life.

"There they are?"

"Yes," the raider said, pointing to the prisoners. "Take a look."

"I am looking. Not much to choose from."

"Possible. But this time we made the mission one of quality, not quantity. Come see."

"What are they?"

"All Navajo except for the boys. Caught them on our way back straying a little too far from the nest. Got lucky."

"What are the boys?"

"Ute."

"Then that rules them out," Lino said, coming to a stop before the captives. There were seven in all, four of them female.

Two of the males were no older than ten, Lino suspected, while the third had to be at least fifty. The women were split equally in age, two of them old and two little girls. Their hands were tied behind their backs while another rope coiled around their waists and attached to the prisoner in front to create one long leash. They all appeared well-beaten with purple bruises and days-old blood caking their faces and matting their hair. The males were shirtless with buckskin pants while the women wore dresses faint with dust. On the dress fronts of the two girls Lino observed matching stains of blood. "And it looks like you decided to rule out the girls, too."

"Why?" the raider said, pretending to look confused.

Lino pointed to the stains. "I have a policy against anything traumatized, whether it be a horse or a servant."

The raider glowered. "The rest then, you take them? Nothing wrong with the Ute boys."

"Except they're Ute. We have a delicate agreement with Blanco, and I'm not going to be the owner of these two objects of incitement."

The man looked back at his companions. Lino finished his cigarette and flicked it at the man's shin to get back his attention.

"Of the other three, the two old ladies and the man, any of them speak Spanish?"

"That woman there does. Aye!" The man strode up to the woman in question and clutched her chin. "You speak Spanish?"

The woman winced and nodded.

"*Bueno,*" Lino said. "Give me her and then take those Utes anywhere but here."

Lino paid the men, letting them murmur over the small sale, and led the woman to the skinny adobe behind the stables that was the slave quarters. She was their first woman servant; his surprise for Cecilia.

Another chorus of cheers floated from town. Lino considered saddling a horse but, finding brittle autumn air invigorating, decided to walk. He felt cheery with the recent purchase and he wanted to savor the feeling alone. He walked slowly down the small foot trail between the stable and the house. Over the past few years he had developed along this walk a habit of admiring everything around him: the sprawling acres of pastureland to his rear and its floating brown and black islands of cattle, the half dozen corrals of horses, the sheep pen, the stable and tack room, the servants' quarters—all situated in a sort of spreading fan reaching from the rear of the ranch's massive five-bedroom home. This was Hacienda de Espinosa, and knowing it Lino's heart swelled.

But simply admiring wasn't enough, for what man, Lino figured, would not regularly admire such a property? And so Lino did not simply admire. He intensified his appreciation for what was around him by contrasting: by reminding himself that it was not so long ago that he had tried to kill himself.

It was seven years earlier in a Taos *prostíbulo*. Lino had left home in Chihuahua four years before that and so far his venture as a *ranchero* was failing. He was homeless and spending almost every night in a saloon. A few months before, he had ridden away in the night in order to escape recruitment for the war. Of course, it didn't help that what few livestock he did own he was steadily, guiltily, donating to María, while the small ranch home he had built up on the Conejos Grant had, along with the entire Conejos town site, been destroyed by Blanco and his Utes. Ironically, his running away upon news of the approaching recruiters had removed him from the Ute attack just days before it happened, saving his life. But when he awoke that morning cripplingly sick from Taos Lightning in the stale room of a whore, in one final irony Lino found himself wishing for death.

It had not been the pure Taos Lightning but the much cheaper Indian version diluted with chewing tobacco and the muddy river water running through the pueblo. When Lino opened his eyes that morning his world rippled as if the bedroom was a sunbaked desert. His memories of the night before were nightmares of a great spinning battle in which Lino fought alone against a horde of personal demons, his only weapon the venomous Lightning. He sat up, noticed the sleeping body next to him—the swath of sticky black hair, felt the soured liquor swish in his stomach, and realized he had lost the battle. He leaned his head over the side of the bed and vomited.

His vision upside down, his uncut hair dangling into his mess, Lino looked for something familiar and spotted his saddle stuffed into a chair in the corner of the room. He eyed the lasso tied to its horn.

Lino slid out of the bed naked and crawled to the saddle. He untied the lasso, stretched it out, and looked up at the ceiling. Almost straight above him, one of the room's ceiling beams buckled, revealing a slight gap between it and the adobe mud above.

He stood, swaying as blood soared to his head, took the saddle out of the chair, slid the chair forward, stood on it, and snaked one end of the rope through the gap. He worked it down until the honda was at his chest and tied off the other end at the beam. He didn't bother making a noose, instead simply looped the lasso over his head and snugged it around his throat.

Knowing what he was about to do a sin, Lino made no prayers and asked no forgiveness. He merely looked down, decided the drop was too short, climbed higher onto the arms of the chair and, his knees trembling, he leaped.

The rope twanged taut, the loop clenched. Lino choked and for a moment saw a shock of colors burst before his eyes. But at the same time he remained aware of a loud noise screaming above him, the sound of twined rope burning across wood. Lino opened his eyes to find himself lowering to the ground. He landed neatly on his seat, the rope drawn tight under his chin.

The woman sat up in the sheets, her face cocked and confused. She looked at Lino, nude, with his feet out in front of him, struggling at the coil around his throat, and erupted in laughter. Lino's head went hot from a lack of blood and humiliation. As the woman roared he stood, unhooked the loop, tugged the rest of the poorly knotted lasso down from the ceiling, and recoiled it.

"Lino Espinosa," she said between laughs, "goes to bed with a limp dick, wakes up with a limp noose."

He held up a weak backhand that he knew he was incapable of delivering, lowered it and began to dress. The woman shook her head, rolled over to her bedside table, and took a swig of tequila. She found a cigarette, lit it, and sat back against the headboard watching Lino struggle into his pants.

"*Hombre,* you are going to wish you'd hung after I tell the girls about this one."

Lino ignored her, concentrating instead on his imminent second attempt.

"If you wanted to die a little more, what should I say, *heroically,* you should just wait around another morning."

"What happens tomorrow morning?"

"Why, everything," the woman said, exhaling a billowing cloud of smoke over the bed. "Uproar is happening. *Caos total.*"

"I don't know what you're talking about."

"Then I would say that makes you the most oblivious Mexican in Taos, and for that I pity you more."

"Tell me."

She snorted. "Tomorrow is the revolt, the rebellion. Do you live in a hole? That Montoya is getting everyone stirred up, even the Indians. They're going to kill every gringo in sight. *Los*

Americanos exterminarán." She laughed. "That is what I'm saying. Instead of hanging yourself with a lariat in my bedroom
how about you run into a gringo's blade or something? That
way you can die a hero, maybe even a martyr."

Lino considered her, his mind whirling, scheming. Already a
plan was forming, one with the potential to make all his failings
of the past few years, all the reasons he had to kill himself,
insignificant. He might have been the last one to learn this
secret but suddenly Lino Espinosa felt like the most powerful
Mexican in the whole besieged country.

When he left the saloon into the white January sun, instead
of seeking a proper rope to make a noose or a secluded place to
shoot himself, Lino veered west to a tall adobe residence outside
the plaza with a squat little office attached to its side. Lino had
met Charles Beaubien, or Don Carlos, three years earlier when
Lino sat down with then-Governor Manuel Armijo to discuss
the prospect of a new land grant to the north. Don Carlos, who
had recently lobbied Armijo and been granted a million-acre
spread, as well as a second of the same size in the name of Narciso, his twelve-year-old son, sat in on the meeting with an
unconcealed interest in this latest idea of populating the so-far
inhospitable Indian country to the north. At the time, in
company with perhaps the two most formidable men in New
Mexico, Lino could not help feeling on the verge of becoming
the third.

Of course, the grant had failed, and when General Kearny
and the Americans marched into Santa Fe, Governor Armijo
fled to Old Mexico (and, as Lino found out later, with a
company of Mexican Volunteers containing Ignasio and two of
his sons). With Armijo gone, so too was Lino's ally. Don Carlos
was still there and amazingly with even more power after Kearny
appointed him district judge. Yet without Armijo, Lino had no

excuse to reach out to the Canadian-turned-Mexican Don Carlos.

Until now. Going straight from the brothel to his residence, Lino rapped on Don Carlos's office door.

The door inched open. "Yes?" Don Carlos peeked through the door frame. It was total darkness behind him and bluish pouches sagged under his eyes.

"Don Carlos, do you remember me?"

Don Carlos scrutinized him. "No."

"We met three years ago with Governor Armijo, we were talking about—" Lino saw that none of this was registering and suddenly became self-conscious. "No matter. My name is Lino Espinosa and I have important, urgent information for you. It concerns your safety, possibly even your life."

In the dim light of the stuffy office, Lino told Don Carlos everything. Much of it he exaggerated considering he knew next to nothing of the plan after having first heard it moments before from a tequila-slugging whore. Still, Lino pretended to be in the know, influential even in the execution of it all. He told the Don that while he knew better than to mistake Don Carlos for anything other than a Mexican patriot, the others, the Indians especially, might not.

"I have feared this very thing," Don Carlos said. "Feared it for months. The air has become thick with premonition. Do these people not know I am their brother? That I am a son of Mexico? An adopted son, yes, but of her bosom no less than Santa Anna himself. It is this *gringo* skin Lino, it betrays my *Chicano* heart."

"You must go Don Carlos. Ride away in secret with your family and inform no authority lest the people decide you're a traitor."

Don Carlos jumped to his feet and threw on his coat. He began to rummage through his shelf and then his desk, collecting things. When his eyes passed over Lino, his eyes widened as if he had just remembered him and he gestured Lino up out of the chair. "Of course I must thank you. How can I? Here—" Don Carlos dumped his armload of books and papers and trinkets onto the desk and reached into the pocket of his coat.

Lino caught Don Carlos's arm. "No. There is no need. I came here because I know where your heart truly lies; for that reason you had to be warned." He wrapped Don Carlos's hand in both of his, shaking it a little. "If you feel you must do anything for me, promise me only that you will return, and that when you do you will remember me as your friend."

That night Lino camped in the mountains overlooking Taos. He made a fire and slept well despite the January cold, and when he awoke it was to the sound of distant screaming. Lino sat up, rekindled the fire, boiled coffee, and enjoyed the morning view of the massacre below. He thought of how he had saved Don Carlos's life, and how no man could ever forget a thing like that.

Thanks to Lino's warning, Don Carlos slipped unseen out of town. But, as Lino found out days later in the aftermath of the revolt, his warning had provided the Don an opportunity he had not foreseen; one that prior to knowing the man he could never have even fathomed.

Don Carlos had followed Lino's suggestion and rode discreetly out of town, except that in fleeing he left behind him not only the storm-hovered village of Taos but also his family. Being women, his wife and daughter were safe. Narciso, however, had been doomed. The insurgents discovered him cowering under a water trough, dragged him out, and speared him to death. Don Carlos became the surviving father and sole inheritor of his son's million-acre land grant, bringing his total landholdings to two million acres.

Following the war, Don Carlos retained title to his land as

per the Treaty of Guadalupe Hidalgo. But similar to Mexican conditions for ownership, grant owners now faced pressure by the United States to develop their properties, to populate and civilize the otherwise untamed Indian country or face forfeiture.

Lino meanwhile spent his time after the war holed in an abandoned jacal east of town watching over his few cattle and conspiring pretexts for visiting Don Carlos. After a while though, convinced the baron had forgotten him or at least held no intention of rewarding him, thoughts of the noose once again crept into Lino's mind like smoke under a closed door.

Then one day, a messenger for Don Carlos came to him carrying a letter detailing big ideas to civilize the frontier, and at the center of each one of these ideas Lino saw his own name sketched in ink. The Don had not forgotten him. The smoke sucked back under.

The Utes had agreed to a peace treaty and Don Carlos needed settlers ready to forget the attacks, trust the agreement, and go north once again. He reasoned that for any future settlement to be successful in such isolated conditions it must be self-governed and tightly communal. The people would require not only faith in the Indians' promise of peace but faith in each other as well as, most importantly, in God. With past settlements extending more than fifty miles from the nearest priest, the last item proved difficult to exact. But recently Don Carlos had happened upon a discovery that could solve these problems, and he needed someone willing, someone with nothing, to embark upon a grueling mission of severe faith.

Lino had been aware of the Penitente Brotherhood since migrating to New Mexico. In his first year while riding in the hills above Santa Fe in search of a stray cow, he had come across a man trudging through the snow barefoot and hauling a wooden cross the size of two men over his shoulder. When Lino asked what he was doing, the crossbearer said only that he was becoming closer to the Lord and moved on. Back in town, Lino learned not only what he had seen but, in this ancient, remote land, how remarkably common it was.

Los Hermanos Penitentes came to the New World with Coronado and his company of Franciscan priests. They were laymen, dropped into the territory and adapting over the centuries to its harsh landscape. Distanced from the church and without ordained priests to deliver mass, the Penitentes sought their own pious and progressively more extreme devotions. They enacted passion plays, whipping themselves and, in some chapters, even going so far as to crucify their brethren in belief that to die on the cross guaranteed a place in heaven. They wore hidden crudities of constant torment—a sharp rock in a shoe, a loop of barbed wire around the stomach—as everyday reminders of Christ's suffering.

But if their sodalities were radical they were at the same time exceptionally communalist. Each chapter of the Brotherhood had its morada, a meeting place acting as both a center of faith for its village and also its administration. Small taxes were collected from each household, the revenues distributed toward such things as funeral services, the caring of the sick, spiritual observances, and dispute resolution.

The members of the moradas were organized into three ranks. The Hermanos de Sangre, the brothers of blood, were at the bottom. These were the novices, the newly initiated and still burdened with sin. They were the purgers. Above these were the Hermanos Salidos a Luz; the brothers approaching the light. Then there was the council, the Hermanos de Luz. These were the elder men of the morada, the elected leaders of the Brotherhood.

Women were not permitted membership and although they had their auxiliaries, or *auxiliadoras,* the women, like virtually every Mexican in the village, followed the governance of the council. They followed the leadership of one man most of all, the head of the council and, in effect, the village. This was the Hermano Mayor.

Lino learned all this the night after meeting the crossbearer, and ever since he had yet to ride through a New Mexican town without noticing its morada.

It seemed then only common sense for Don Carlos to imagine transplanting a pious, self-sustaining, tax-collecting colony of people into his land grants. Lino couldn't deny that it was a brilliant idea and in every one of their meetings leading up to its deployment he was mindful to tell his soon-to-be benefactor that very thing regularly.

The Don sent him to Abiquiú where Lino spent half a year studying the Brotherhood, learning from its members until finally becoming one himself. The initiation was the most harrowing experience of his life, one from which he would forever carry the scars, but when it was over he found that never before had he known such peace of mind. The morning in the whorehouse, like most things in his past, was ancient memory. Now all Lino had was the future. A whole wealth of it.

With Don Carlos proffering the land Lino recruited from Santa Fe northward, and within a year what began as eight families clustered in leaky huts along the Costilla River became fifty-four men, women, and children, each one of them a devout subscriber of the morada. Under Lino's guide, the Brotherhood assembled.

A council formed, and Lino, without opponent or question, was named Hermano Mayor of New Mexico's newest and northernmost settlement. Don Carlos provided Lino not only a hacienda and a herd of one hundred cattle but—and this being perhaps the most momentous addition to his life—a family. This last part, Lino knew, was less a gift than a stipulation. The Don reasoned a settlement engineered on faith and family would suspect a leader who exhibited only half those things. Lino agreed.

Still, long after the wedding ceremony, and especially during its consummation, Lino felt only the forcedness of the marriage, its hollowness. He admired his bride. As a schoolteacher, Cecilia was learned. Slender with a Pueblo Indian physique while at the same time comfortingly warm in the face with her Mexican features, she expressed a *Chollo* exoticism, dark but not forbidding. But she was also sad, and Lino couldn't help reminding himself that he was part of that sadness. Her first husband had died fighting the Americans. He had been everything Lino was not.

Then there were the children, *her* children. Secundina had been cold to him from the beginning, her resistance never explicit, never vocal, but at the same time unmistakable in every disdainful look and snubbing silence. But for every degree of disregard the girl offered him Lino matched it and more. To him, Secundina was a dark cloud ever present. Her deformed arm embarrassed him and Lino sought to hound the girl with overwork and implied contempt until she moved out of his home willingly because as long as Cecilia was around he would never be able to force her out.

Vivian was younger and so not as closed to him, but Lino could still tell the boy had his doubts. He reminded Lino of a skittish horse, easily spooked and easily tricked. Like his sister Vivian hesitated in calling Lino his father and so instead called him nothing at all. But Lino paid no attention. As long as they obeyed him, he couldn't care less whether they chose to love him.

Who he did care about was José. Unlike the other two, José was his. Cecilia had given him the child after their first year in Costilla and ever since Lino had doted on his son and dedicated himself to his prosperity as much as he did to that of the village. After all, some day Costilla and all of Hacienda de Espinosa would be his to look over. The idea thrilled Lino. If Secundina and Vivian could sometimes hurt his pride, José, even as a baby, bolstered it.

Then there were his newest, most unexpected charges: María and her son. Costilla and Lino's new life in the town were five years old the night his cousins appeared with the news of Ignasio's death. Lino had thought himself rid of them, with that part of his life. The last he had seen Ignasio had been during his last visit to the remote jacal with his offering of beef; his last failed attempt at forgiveness for a drunken night many years ago shortly after his cousins' arrival in the north. The night he had come knocking on María's door even though he knew her husband was not home. The night he had knocked *because* her husband was not home.

So it was that the night María and her only living son fled to him with their frantic story of Ignasio's death, Lino felt a sudden and unexpected wash of relief. When Ignasio died, so too did the man's grudge, his hate. And if María still loathed and feared him—as she no doubt did—that fear and resentment were more deeply buried with each plea she made for help, buried and covered with hard-packed humility. Lino could think back to all those times she had taken his cows and offered nothing in return except reproach. He savored that humility. It enriched his life, his contentment, and he would hold it gleefully over María's head until the day she died.

But while María's entrance into Lino's hacienda created a newfound source of satisfaction, of twisted redemption, the boy presented an unexpected, underestimated source of opposition. The boy made no pretensions at gratitude, and this disturbed Lino not simply because it challenged him in a way similar to Vivian and Secundina, but because at first he could not understand it. Lino barely knew the boy, had in fact never even spoken to him before he and his mother moved into the hacienda. What did the boy have to hold against him?

The answer was obvious. The boy was his parents' son, raised with their grudges. It took Lino nearly a year of living with him to see this, and when he did he realized what it was about the boy that shook him deep in his gut. The boy was like his father. It was as if Ignasio had never died. As if all the dead man's memories had come back.

Lino finished the quarter-mile walk from the hacienda to the skirting adobes of the village. Up ahead in the plaza there came another burst of cheers, and approaching it now Lino saw the very form of his burden. He was grinning, and so, too, were what seemed every resident of a flourishing Costilla. The town Lino, with some distant help, had built.

A young man he knew as Otilio moved out of Lino's path, stopped, and nodded. A bow, Lino thought. He looked at the crowd in the plaza again, at the boy, and thought to himself no matter how troubling he or any of his bastards might be, they would never be so troubling as to make a man wish himself dead.

He joined the crowd, and silently thanked God the knot had slipped.

CHAPTER 14

The plaza swirled with dust. Secundina felt it in her eyes, her throat. She reached into her pocket in search of her kerchief before remembering it was gone. She crossed the hand concealingly back over her left arm. As far as she could see through the haze almost every woman, old man, and child in the town lined the plaza in a large rectangle. They stood watching and cheering the men atop their horses and burros in a condensed, hoof-stomping cluster at one end of the plaza as they waited their turn at the half-buried rooster in the middle.

The game was Carerra del Gallo. A live rooster was buried up to its neck in the center of the plaza, the soil around it tamped hard. The bird twitched and flung its head wildly about as one by one the men swooped by on their running mounts, leaning low to one side of the saddle in an attempt to catch and pluck the rooster from its hole. When a man succeeded, every other rider whipped into a frenzied chase after him in the confines of the plaza, leaping off their mounts and tackling him to the ground, piling on top of him, and fighting to rip the rooster from his clutch until nothing was left of the animal and the point was awarded and a new round begun.

So far the morning's game had gone through two birds, the first going to Sergio, an old veteran of the sport, while the second victory belonged to a newcomer, Felipe Espinosa.

Secundina and Vivian watched at the end of the rectangle opposite the bunched riders. About fifteen yards before them the rooster flailed its tiny, screaming head as one of the men rushed over it, his outstretched hand missing by a foot. The crowd groaned then clapped respectfully. The man turned his horse, kicking up a new cloud of dust, and returned to the end.

Vivian checked over his shoulders and whispered to Secundina, "Look at that Sergio, the *cabron*. See how mad he is, how determined? Like a little hornet."

"Mm."

"He can't stand that Felipe is tied with him. Look how the other men slap Felipe's back. See how Sergio hates it?"

A small side group of men clustered around the boy, excited by his surprise triumph. Secundina had to admit she was glad Sergio lost. The boy smiled but spoke little. Even from a distance, Secundina could sense his attention fixed on her.

"That little hornet, if he loses again, *dios mio,* can you imagine? I hope he does just so we can all see it. That way Sergio will have lost to a single man instead of tying with a few. I bet everyone is hoping the same thing. They're tired, too, of Sergio and his strutting."

"Felipe is a boy," Secundina said.

"Even better. He will hate it worse, angry little hornet."

Another man galloped by and missed. The rooster called and flailed.

"Still, he is a very good horseman, no?" Vivian said. "Felipe I mean, not Sergio."

"Possible."

Away in his cluster, the boy darted a glance at her.

Vivian smiled and shook his head. "I think he is sweet for you."

"And I think he is hideous," Secundina said, and immediately grew hot with self-awareness. Out of the corner of her eye she checked to see if her brother scrutinized her, whether he frowned at where her wrinkled arm folded below the other but

Vivian was looking at his cousin with the same mixed expression of amusement and admiration.

"The others all like him," he said.

"That is because they don't know how strange he is, that he is *un pervertido.*"

"Why do you say that?"

"Because yesterday I caught him spying on me in my bedroom. I was trying to nap, and I became aware of someone watching. I felt his staring, *his* staring. You know what I am talking about. When I lifted my head I saw my door had been cracked open and an eye was looking through it. Later, I caught him following me to the river to do the wash. Of course, he tried to deny all of it, and for that he is even worse."

Vivian only laughed. "Like I said, he is sweet for you. *Él está muy en amor.*"

"He also stole my kerchief."

"He did?"

"I think so."

Another rider galloped and missed. In the crowd behind her Secundina heard a series of greetings followed by a parting of feet that informed her Lino approached. She peeked over her shoulder and saw him, a cigarette in one corner of his mouth, his hands stuffed into the pockets of his lambskin coat.

"Children," he said, putting a hand on each of their shoulders and making a place for himself between them. They greeted him in turn but said no more, Secundina pretending to focus on the game.

"Where is your mother?" Lino asked.

"She was here but left when José started crying," Vivian said.

"She's not at the house. I have a surprise for her."

"She's probably at the schoolhouse. What's the surprise?"

"If I told you it wouldn't stay a surprise." Lino sucked on the cigarette and exhaled through his nostrils onto Secundina's neck. He studied the action in the plaza. "What happened? What was all the cheering?"

"Two birds were nabbed, this is the third," Vivian said.

"Sergio?"

"He got one, the other—"

"Felipe got the other," Secundina finished.

The group around him had broken and now he stood his horse in line just a few turns away. He waited—purposefully, Secundina felt sure of it—directly behind Sergio. He winked at her.

"Why did he just wink at me?" Lino said.

"It was not you he winked at," Secundina said.

"Yes it was."

"No, it wasn't," Vivian said. "It's Secundina. Felipe is sweet for her. He is in love."

Secundina fought back a smile. Next to her she felt Lino fuming, despising the two of them for teaming up. She felt him wrestling with the very notion of the boy.

"That boy does not love you," Lino said. "He's only looking to be loved, and knowing how ugly he is it makes sense for him to start with you. You are the only girl in Costilla who can offer him no challengers. That's not love. That's desperation."

Another rider rushed in, this time actually swatting the rooster's head but failing to clutch it. He clenched his fist and winced toward the sky, spurring the horse away from the crowd at the last second.

Looking around, Secundina realized that since Lino had joined them the other people had drifted away and the three of them now stood in a small island within the great ring of the plaza. Secundina glanced across Lino to her brother. He stared directly ahead, his lower lip quivering.

"Well, I think he is handsome," Secundina said, "and a gentleman too. Just yesterday he surprised me in my room with flow-

117

ers. He is always bringing me flowers. I thanked him and we talked for a long time. Then he insisted on walking me to the river and assisting me with the wash. I told him he was a *caballero* of the highest form and a role model to the other boys of this family."

Sergio was up. He stood in his stirrups, shifting his weight from one foot to the other in an exaggerated display of checking his cinch. A few members of the crowd applauded. Sergio whooped and spurred the horse. He hunkered low to its heaving mane and leaned over one side toward the ground, his opposite foot out of the stirrup hooking below the saddle horn. The horse raced toward the target and with his palm out and his fingers stretched Sergio made for the waving rooster head. There came a high shriek as the beaked head lurched and, Sergio's pinky catching its side, batted to the ground. Sergio gripped into a plume of dust. He cried out. The dust floated, cleared, and the rooster remained in the ground looking dazed.

The crowd roared. Vivian yelled and Secundina clapped her good hand against the back of the other. Sergio yanked back on his horse and glared at the crowd, his teeth clenched. Trotting back to the waiting riders he narrowed his gaze on the boy.

"Here comes Felipe," Vivian said, sticking two fingers in his mouth and trying to whistle. All that came out was a *phhhh*.

The crowd quieted as the boy wrapped the reins around one hand and stuck it on the horn, the other clenching and unclenching at his side. He took a final glance at Secundina. She nodded at him.

He charged. He stood spectacularly high in the stirrups, his hair blowing behind him, the horse thundering below him. The bird shrieked and writhed. He braced himself as the flailing head drew under him, and in a sudden leg-lifting arch he swept his body downward. There came a burst of debris as if the earth below had just exploded open, and finishing his sweep upward he raised his hand to display the hanging rooster.

The crowd erupted and the other riders broke into a wild dash after the boy who began to wave the thrashing rooster above his head and race along the perimeter of spectators. He ducked and pivoted on the horse, dodging his pursuers and turning them into one stringing line. One of the riders broke and raced to cut him off at one of the corners. The man stood on his saddle and leapt, tackling the boy to the ground. With that, every man was suddenly on foot and racing for the pile.

The crowd howled as the men ripped and tore to get to the now completely covered boy. They wrestled until one by one they rolled off laughing and stepped back to see the results. Five of them remained grappling, including Felipe. When finally they broke apart, each rose holding up some piece of the rooster—a wing, a leg, a glob of torso. The crowd cheered in approval.

The boy was the last to stand and when he did the noise surged loudest. He hoisted the rooster's head, its neck chords dangling wet underneath. He held it there, beaming at Secundina.

"That is two for Felipe," Vivian said.

Lino flicked his cigarette into the dirt, turned, and left.

CHAPTER 15

They led the ox through the main street of Costilla, Vivian on one side and the boy the other. The wooden wheels of the *carreta* rumbled over the rutted path and at the bottom of the bouncing cart the saw twanged. The animal kept a slow, lumbering pace as the two tapped their *romals* against its flanks.

At the edge of town, they followed other cart tracks through the sage to the forests of the western mountains. Tree stumps appeared along the path, some of their tops gray while others yellow and still smelling of sap. Once deep into the forest at the base of the mountains the incline became so steep that the ox wheezed and fought at its whips. Vivian and his cousin cut off the path, veering deep into a swallowing of pine and juniper.

They worked quickly, saying little while volleying the saw back and forth through the trunks. The buzz of the saw was the only sound in the woods. No birds chirped, no pine needles brushed against each other in a breeze. When the *carreta* was loaded to the point that its undercarriage sagged below the axles, the boy stepped back and declared the work done. He found the shirt he had taken off and put it back on. He picked up his sombrero and then the pistol that had been under it. Vivian pulled four .31 cartridges from his pocket.

"That is all?" the boy asked.

"Any more and he would notice."

He slid the bullets into the chamber and snapped it closed. Beside them the ox sighed and shrugged its shoulders, shifting the straps laced around them, and shut its eyes.

"How about I follow you this time, brother?" the boy asked, hoisting Vivian's hand and slipping the dragoon inside it.

They stalked upward through the trees, the loaded pistol pulsing something dangerous and prophetic in Vivian's hand. It was a cold, mature energy. Grasping it, Vivian fought away any creeping feelings of callowness. The boy had taught him the basics of shooting. The rest he said would have to be revealed by the gun itself. At first Vivian had not known what to make of this. He wondered if it might even be a tactic of his cousin's to maintain an upper hand. But the boy had spoken the truth, for gradually Vivian realized that whatever he wished to know about the gun, the gun told him.

It told him it shot best when held tight in both hands but that when one hand was the only option a pinky placed along the underside of the handle helped steady the aim. It informed him that one of its six chambers had a tendency to slip upon revolving into action, a tendency Vivian figured very good to know. He learned the damage the pistol was capable of at close range as well as at distance. He observed how the pistol left jackrabbits and coyotes still recognizable after penetrating their fur, whereas all that remained of crows and prairie dogs were spatterings of falling black feathers or sand-clotted gore.

Once, while Vivian and his cousin crept through a spot not far from where they patrolled now, a lone deer had spooked a few dozen yards ahead of them. To Vivian, it had been just a flash of brown through the trees, and before his mind had the chance to process the movement the boy drew the pistol and fired. It didn't even seem like he had aimed, just flung up the barrel and pulled. An impossible shot—in distance and response time—yet Vivian could not help but be impressed by the speed of his cousin's draw, even if he had wasted a bullet.

But as Vivian scanned the trees for the bolting shape of the deer, the boy surprised him by saying calmly, "Got it."

They found the deer exactly where Vivian had glimpsed its fleeting form, a limp, scrawny doe. Its eyes stared wild and forever confused. The bullet had landed two inches and a little in front of the right ear. There was no exit wound meaning the bullet lodged somewhere in the middle.

"I never shot a deer before," the boy said.

"What have you shot?"

"I got a bull once."

"A bull? Why shoot a bull?"

He just shrugged and fingered the seeping hole in the deer's head.

"What else have you shot?"

He looked up at Vivian, squinting slightly so that suddenly Vivian knew he was being sized up. He was disappointed then, for his cousin only turned back to the fallen deer and said the bull had been it.

After every outing, they cleaned the gun meticulously and wrapped it in a damp, oil-sweet shirt. The boy said when it was not cleaned and put away properly he felt bad. Then he would send Vivian away while he returned the pistol to its hiding place. Vivian didn't mind. It wasn't his pistol after all. What mattered to Vivian was that the secret remained theirs.

As they continued their walk up the mountainside, Vivian noticed their footsteps seemed louder than normal. The ground was a carpet of pinecones and tiny twigs that crunched under his boots no matter how lightly he stepped. The air felt thinner even though Vivian knew they were still low on the mountain and far from timberline. When he looked up, he saw patches of clear blue backdropping the treetops, the sun straight above fighting to break through. It seemed to him the whole forest should be chattering with squirrels and birds. He slowed down and did his best to step even lighter.

Behind him the boy whispered.

"What?" Vivian asked, turning and immediately realizing his error. The boy stopped and looked at him quizzically. Most of the time Vivian didn't think his cousin knew he was talking to himself, as if it were something as unconscious as grinding one's teeth. Vivian never asked him about it, partly not wanting to embarrass him but mostly because something told him the boy would be unwilling—perhaps unable—to explain. With his cousin still looking at him curiously, Vivian said, "Never mind."

After walking in silence a few more minutes Vivian said, "There is not a damn thing out today."

The boy put his hands on his hips and clucked his tongue. "We might as well shoot something." He looked around and pointed. "That knot."

Vivian saw the knot, a deformity bulging from the center of a limbless pine. "It's going to be loud," he said.

"It's always loud, no matter what you shoot."

Vivian felt his face redden. He turned around to square the target, setting his stance. The boy moved behind Vivian's shoulder and Vivian felt his breath on the back of his neck. He brought the gun up and squeezed one eye shut. He gripped the handle tight in both hands, peered down the barrel. The hammer clicked back. He held his breath.

It happened fast. Vivian's world seemed to tense and pause before suddenly erupting in violence. In the corner of his open eye he caught a blurred glimpse of his attacker hunkered low like an animal and pouncing from behind a juniper. He was on him and batting the pistol skyward before Vivian had time to even turn his head. The gun fired and flew into the air and Vivian fell to the ground. The man went down with him, wrestling Vivian flat with a taught, ropy strength and pinning the boy's neck with one dark forearm. Stuck to the ground Vivian became aware of men pouring out from behind the trees. Somewhere nearby his cousin grunted and cursed. Vivian stared at the man above him, the fiery eyes within the painted red-and-white face, and let go his bladder.

A single calm voice in a strange language rose over the assault, and the man holding Vivian eased his grip. He turned his streaked face to the speaker and pressed a hand over Vivian's mouth. The palm tasted of sweat and earth. Abruptly the man climbed off and lifted Vivian to his feet by his armpits, slipped behind him and placed a firm, reminiful hand on the back of his neck.

Despite having been taught to fear Indians his whole life, Vivian had never fully believed the warnings. The only Indians he had ever seen were those skinny and starved vagrants standing in lines outside the Taos ration office, or else the few resigned-looking Navajos Lino kept as slaves. At the time he had wondered how people who looked so broken could be capable of the atrocities attributed to them. Vivian had thought that the stories of raids, kidnappings, and tortures were tales meant simply to keep him from wandering too deep into the woods. Now however, finding himself strayed perhaps a little too deep and surrounded suddenly by men looking nothing like those outside the ration offices, Vivian believed the stories.

More were coming into sight every moment, stepping into the scattered crowd holding rifles, lances, clubs, and bows. A few led horses, their flanks and noses matted with the same colored streaks as their masters. He looked to where the boy struggled on the ground beside him, his attacker suddenly jerking a knife up to his throat and stilling him. A dribble of blood trickled down his nose. The warriors fell silent, each one appearing to hover around one man in particular.

He was old. Very old. Thin wisps of cloudy white hair hung to his shoulder and looked as if a hard breeze might blow him bald. His lips sucked inward into a gray and toothless mouth. A leathery scar marked an empty eye socket. Scattered across his face and torso were innumerable dried and flaking pockmarks.

From somewhere in the crowd came a shout, followed by a rumble of what sounded like agreement. The chief raised one hand and silenced them. He appeared transfixed by Felipe, approaching him and stopping just a few inches before his face to study him, ducking his head and looking upward as if to observe from a different angle. He brought his hands to the boy's mouth, hooked his thumbs into the boy's cheeks, stretched the lips apart, and grinned.

"Espinosa!" he declared, spreading the cheeks even wider. He looked over his shoulder and said in Spanish, "Look, Appah, it is Coyote Mouth!"

One of the braves smiled back and nodded. The brave stood out from the others, for situated awkwardly over his undersized chest was a rusted and ancient-looking breastplate. One hand held a lance while the other arm hung in a nub above the elbow.

"I did not recognize you at first with your new hair," the chief said. "You Mexicans grow mustaches like the white women grow their fingernails. Who is your *amigo*?"

The boy shook himself free and wiped the blood from his face with a sleeve. "That is my cousin."

The chief eyed Vivian. "You are Espinosa, too? Then you are one of Lino's. What is your name?"

"Vivian."

"Vivian, I do not like your papá as I used to," the chief said. "I can like Mexicans but not Mexicans that try to be Americans. Tell him that. Tell Lino Blanco says it."

Whatever sense of hope Vivian had begun to feel at the apparent familiarity between Felipe and the chief vanished upon hearing the name that had long been a source of paranoia throughout the valley. Vivian's father had warned of him in numerous addresses in the morada, especially following the massacre at nearby Fort Pueblo.

It had happened last Christmas Eve. As the story went, Blanco and a few of his Utes had been invited into the fort to celebrate the holiday with drinks and a feast. The atmosphere was friendly until, for no apparent reason, Blanco gave the sign and the Utes turned suddenly on their hosts, slaughtering every resident of the fort save for two children and one of the men's wives. Later, the woman was found dead and scalped; killed, according to her captors, because she had cried too much. The children were never seen again.

"Felipe," Blanco said, "what about your father? Is what I heard about his dying true?"

"He is dead."

"I know he is dead. I asked you if what I heard about his death is true."

The boy did not reply.

Blanco studied him for a moment. "Now Ignasio, *he* was a good Mexican. He I always liked."

"What happened to your skin Blanco?" the boy asked.

"You mean where did all my beauty go?" The chief flashed a smile. "I was given the smallpox. Given them by Carson. He had us sign a treaty and then tricked us by presenting coats cursed by some *bruja*. Many of us were killed. So now I am to kill Carson."

The boy looked toward the other braves, their weapons held ready. There had to be close to thirty of them. Blanco followed the boy's gaze.

"We are not all going to Carson. I will do that alone. No, now we are just riding. We have no food, no place to rest without catching sick or being attacked. There are Appah's two sons taken one day while playing in the woods, just like you and Vivian today." The chief shook a finger at Vivian but did not look at him. "So all we have left to do is ride. And today we ride through Costilla."

The boy's face grew panicked. "The large hacienda south of town . . ."

"Yes?" The chief cocked his head.

"My mother is there, and so is a girl with a bad arm. Everything else though . . ."

The chief closed his eye and nodded to show he understood. "We will not ride hard."

Behind him one of the horses scratched at the earth with its hoof. Some of the warriors shifted from one leg to the other.

"We are going now," the chief said. "Good-bye, Coyote Mouth. I am glad I saw you today." He turned.

"Wait," the boy said.

The chief stopped but did not look back.

"There are four gringo homes," the boy said. "Two are next to each other and you will see them as you approach. They are adobe. The other two are in town and made all of wood."

"Is that all?"

The boy was quiet a moment. Then: "The red-painted jacal behind the morada with the black mare in its pen. A man lives there named Sergio. Him."

"*Bueno*," the chief said and started back to his warriors. Again though he stopped short, noticing the brave in front of Vivian who had picked up the fallen dragoon. Blanco held out his palm and the brave, visibly disappointed, handed it over. Blanco raised the weapon above his head and examined it. He opened its cylinder and stuck his eye through an empty chamber and for a moment Vivian saw through the tiny hole the eye aimed directly on him. The chief flipped the chamber shut and held the gun out to Vivian.

"Do not shoot me in the back, eh Espinosa?"

Vivian and his cousin raced through the trees higher up the

mountain. They ran until coming to an outcropping of rock that jutted high over the forest in a tight cluster of round towers. They scrambled up the rocks, the boy stopping every so often to offer Vivian a hand until finally reaching the summit. They looked down on the valley, the San Juans hazy far off to the west, the shimmering string of the Río Grande and, directly below them, the little village of Costilla.

In silence they watched the wave of screaming warriors spill out from the forest and onto the plain.

CHAPTER 16

The two adobes on Costilla's eastern edge were flattened rubble. A few scorched posts reached out from the debris like gross appendages. The air smelled of smoke and blood, and the dead sprawled scattered in the street before the ash heaps. In one corner, a man lay facedown in the dirt with arrows stuck in his back. Around him were the children—three boys and two girls—their throats cut and feeding congealing dark puddles. Broad scrapes of hardened blood and glimpses of skull showed where the children, like their father, had all been scalped.

"I know it might sound terrible," Don Carlos said, distractedly lifting an arm of the dead man with his boot, "but I wish his wife was here. No telling what further horrors await her. It is a blessing they killed the children."

Some of the survivors had already begun collecting the corpses, wrapping them in sheets and hoisting them into waiting oxcarts.

"I should help," Lino said.

"No, no," Don Carlos said, stopping Lino with a hand to the chest. "They can see you are talking with me."

Lino thought how that was probably worse. He pointed a short distance up the street. "There is one of them."

Alone in the middle of the street one of the Utes lay on his back, his war club still laced around his wrist and a painted white horse lying dead beside him. One whole side of the Ute's head was missing and a flapping cluster of crows ducked their heads in and out of the breach with strings of brain dangling from their beaks.

"Ha, a musket ball. Great shot!" Don Carlos said. "I know we Mexicans don't always like gringos living among us, but you must admit they are good to have around when a great shot is needed. Too bad there weren't more of them."

"If there were more of them the whole town would be burned."

"Or none of it," Don Carlos said. "But all that is only speculation, and anyway, you are probably right. If it were my choice we would have no gringos here at all."

"It *is* your choice," Lino said, immediately regretting it.

Don Carlos hesitated. After a moment he put a hand on Lino's shoulder. "Keep walking with me, Espinosa. Show me what else."

Together they navigated Costilla's smoldering plaza. To either side of them men carried bundles of broken wood and charred artifacts. Cows, sheep, pigs, and the occasional horse milled about as if hesitant of their sudden freedom. In one corner Lino noticed Miguel Flores fighting one of the pigs as it tried to nip at the carcass of Miguel's son. Wails of women pierced through alleys and doorsteps until they seemed to coalesce above the plaza into one bodiless salvo of catcalls. At one point a woman ran up to Don Carlos, dropped to her knees, and buried her face in his long overcoat. Don Carlos patted her hair, soothing her with his eloquent, sympathetic Spanish before sending her away with a coin.

Passing one particular cow, Lino stopped and examined it. "This is one of mine," he said. "One of yours I mean."

"How many did they run off in total?"

"I don't know yet but at least half. Most of the sheep, too. I've sent Vivian and Felipe to look for any strays."

"They will be lucky to bring back any," Don Carlos said. "I'd bet those Utes had the cows skinned and filleted before they hit the ground. My men say the trees in the forest are losing their coats, that the Utes are so hungry they're stripping the bark off the aspens. How do you eat aspen bark I asked. They said they did not know but the Indians find a way. They find ways for lots of things it seems to me, just none of them peaceful."

They came to the two smoking heaps on the northwestern side of the plaza and passing by Lino felt the heat still emanating inside them. One of their doors, ripped from its hinges, lay twenty feet away in the street along with seven scalped and charred bodies.

"How is it that no one was ready for this?" Don Carlos asked. "Could you not hear their whoops from the hills?"

"We heard them but by then they were too close. My son was in the mountains where they came from but even he heard nothing."

"He was lucky. You all were."

"Like I say, Blanco was so absorbed with the cattle it was as if he forgot about us in the hacienda."

"Still, you should have been better prepared."

Lino gestured behind him, back toward the crow-picked Ute. "We got some."

"Not enough. But what more can be expected from . . ."

Don Carlos let his thought trail off, making Lino angry and nervous all at once. He had known Don Carlos long enough to convince himself the man's dealings with Mexicans like Lino were not the only deals he made. He understood that just as he understood the admiration Don Carlos poured on Mexicans like Lino undoubtedly contradicted the complaints he made behind closed doors. Sometimes he wondered if Don Carlos continued his accent when there were no Mexicans around. Nonetheless, the man had made Lino, as Cecilia described it, the only Mexican in Costilla with glass windows, and so Lino rarely questioned Don Carlos's opinions, no matter how auspicious they often seemed.

"What about Fort Massachusetts? Where were they to protect us?" Lino asked.

"Do you really have to ask? They were fifty miles away!"

Fort Massachusetts had been erected three years previous along a trail of military forts following the Río Grande from Texas. Upon its completion many claimed it the first sure sign of peace in the feral Indian country of the San Luis Valley. It was to be a lighthouse for those traveling either edge of the compass. So far, however, it had been anything but, especially for villages like Costilla. For one, the fort was a long day's ride away. It was also hidden deep against the mountainsides of the Sangre de Cristos, allowing easy passageway for Indian parties that didn't mind a wider swing through the valley. As far as Lino and the people of Costilla saw it, Fort Massachusetts had only brought further sign of impending Americanization. Already talk circulated of building a second, better-positioned fort.

"When they came looking to lease that land I told them to pick a spot somewhere lower, somewhere on the valley floor. But they did not listen. What American does?"

Lino nodded. He stared at the caved remains of the two homes. Somewhere a child wailed.

"Listen to me *amigo*," Don Carlos said, "because the discussion began let me attempt to finish it. I permit Americans here because I have no choice. They file their applications with me just as orderly as our Mexicans. If it were possible I would refuse them and see only Mexicans inhabiting this place. But I am forced to permit the applications because it is inevitable.

"You see, Lino," Don Carlos continued, guiding him with his hand on the back of Lino's shoulders, "the Mexican way of living is the very best. We live honorably and peacefully and under

God. But to the Americans, these things matter very little since they cannot be put on balance sheets, maps, or draft registries. Their concern is with civilization, and to them ours is not American or modern enough. Your—*our*— habit is to step out our doors and wonder about our family back inside it. Sometimes we might even glance at our neighbor and wonder about him, and we may ask ourselves if he wonders about us in return.

"The Americans, however, wonder about the whole world. They feel as if every eye on every continent is on them, and this obsession has led them into a perpetual habit of always upgrading and making a show of themselves. They are never content. With Mexico they saw a poor nation made poorer by internal problems, and so for the Americans the prize was not only the coast but also the opportunity to crush another nation for all the world to see. An easy victory.

"With Britain they saw an equal power and past enemy threaten to rise up again, and in this case, wanting to prove to the world they could be assertive as well as diplomatic, they gained Oregon via a compromise. And now even their own Southern states are flaring their feathers. As for this conflict, I doubt either conquer or compromise shall be a solution, but what I am sure of is that once again we Mexican people will find ourselves in the middle despite our being so very far apart."

Ahead of them children circled the body of a fallen Ute. They stabbed the body with sticks and yelled curses, and when they noticed Lino and Don Carlos they paused. After a moment, seeing they were in no danger of reprimand, they resumed their assault.

"Why then do you help place us in the middle?" Lino asked. "Why do you assist in their proliferation?"

"Because if I chose to fight back that would be me," Don Carlos pointed to the Ute, "lying dead in a street getting poked with sticks. Blanco and his warriors have chosen fighting, and they consider themselves brave for it. Dios, they *are* brave, who am I to say they are not? But just as inevitable as American expansion is the extermination of the Indian rebel. Soon enough they will be stopped by the American howitzer, or because they have run out of bark to eat. As for those Indians who have relinquished, those that have been tricked into peace by the Indian agents, well they died the moment they lined up outside the agency to collect a watery bowl of soup. Their hearts might still beat, but they are dead."

"So what will you have us do?"

"When one finds himself stuck in the middle of something, it is best to walk the middle ground. The Mexicans of this land are like trees that have, in their isolation, magically escaped the change of seasons. But an autumn forest is encroaching all around us now, Lino, whether we like it or not. Would it be so bad then to yellow our leaves just a little?

"Railroads are coming. So are miners, militaries, and someday even cities. All these things are going to bring better security, more food, bigger houses, and more money. And ultimately is that not what we all want, gringo or Chicano?"

Upon circling the morada the two stopped shortly before the doorstep of the house behind it. A stake had been driven into the ground by the door, the bloody, sharpened end pointing toward the sky from the opened mouth of Costilla's best horseman, Sergio. He was naked, the stake running from his anus and up through his throat. His genitals hung on a nail tacked directly above the door.

"I said they might be brave," Don Carlos said, "but I said nothing about being honorable. If there is a difference between the two words, there it is."

"It's going to be difficult returning the town to order," Lino said. "Many will flee."

"No, they won't. Not this time."

"Are you going to impose fines? No one will have the money."

"That is both why I am not going to impose fines and why I will not have to. The people have been here too long to leave now. It's going to take more than an attack like this to persuade them otherwise. The Conejos attack was different. Those people had only been there a few months and so had little invested. It was easy for them to leave and never return. Here, though, the people have lived six years and their stake in this land is all they have."

Lino pulled a couple cigarettes from his jacket pocket and offered one to Don Carlos. The Don stuck the cigarette into his lips and leaned forward for Lino to light it.

"No, they will not leave," Don Carlos said, a puff of smoke coming out with the words, "but they will need some reviving. Some morale."

"Can you give them something?"

"I cannot. But you can."

"What?"

Don Carlos breathed out one more cloud of smoke before flicking the cigarette away. "You will revive the town through the same institute that built it."

Lino looked at him blankly and Don Carlos motioned with his chin to the morada. "You must hold something special. A ceremony or something."

"There are no ceremonies planned until Holy Week."

"Is anyone engaged?"

"No."

Don Carlos thought for a moment. "Initiate someone."

"But there is no one close to being ready. Every boy old enough has already gone through. The only one who—"

He realized himself mid-sentence.

Don Carlos scraped what appeared a burnt piece of skin

from his boot. "It's about time that nephew of yours contributed something," he said, a little distracted.

CHAPTER 17

María lay on the bed, one pillow under her head and another propped against the headboard so it covered her eyes but not her nose. It was an old trick that not only shut out the light but forced her head to remain still, which in effect helped her mind become calm. It was a trick that more and more no longer worked.

The house was quiet, the only sounds the buzz of hummingbirds as they considered María's window. It was a welcome silence after the constant racket of construction and repair floating from town in the weeks following the Indian attack. Lino and Vivian had gone to Santa Fe with a herd and María didn't know where the others were. In the past she yearned for and seized opportunities like this, these lapses in the day when nothing was needed of her and she could just rest.

Lately though, María found she no longer enjoyed these moments like she used to. At first she wondered if the first year in Costilla had worn out all novelty of relaxation, those long twelve months of mourning when all there was to do was lie on her bed with a pillow over her eyes. But looking back, she decided that that was only part of it.

The truth was that ever since moving into Lino's home María had lost the ability to ease her mind. Now every time she attempted to shut out the light—to expel the world around her—she found herself alone with her thoughts, enclosed with her memories. It was in silence and solitude that she best felt her depression, in relaxation that she felt unforgivable and longed for Cecilia to hand her some chore or even for Lino to say something disdainful if only to make her feel faraway.

She moved the pillow from her face and opened her eyes. The bed next to her was neatly made. Every morning during their sixteen months in the room María had made her son's bed, a chore she appreciated as another preoccupation. But that morning he had surprised her by doing it himself, carefully stretching flat the sheet, folding the top end neatly over his pillow and all the while never acting like anything he did was unusual.

Lino had kept the two together in the same room despite the boy being close to eighteen now. María wished her son would move into a room with Vivian, except Lino would never allow it. She knew he meant their physical detachment from his family to be congruent with their emotional.

María heard the outside door open. She listened, curious, as someone shuffled in. Footsteps clacked on the wood floor through the main room. They moved into the hallway and down it and as they passed the door to María's bedroom they paused, hesitating. María lifted her head. The footsteps turned around and there came a soft knock.

"Come in."

Secundina leaned through the door, a great heap of clothing, jewelry, a pair of shoes, a blanket, and a few plates and cups from the kitchen cradled in her arms. The girl balanced the pile with her chin.

"Did I wake you?"

"No," María said, sitting up. "What are you doing with all that stuff? Where are you taking it?"

"I am taking it back to where it belongs. I think you should know something."

"What?"

"Felipe just asked me to marry him." On the word *marry* she rolled her eyes, suggesting she expected María to find it as ridiculous as she apparently did.

María remained expressionless. "What does that have to do with you carrying around all your things?"

"I am carrying them *back*. Felipe took all of it from my room and had it stuffed on a packhorse. He thought I was going to say *yes.*"

"He wanted you to go away with him?"

"He had horses ready and everything. Still does. That is what I thought you should know because now I am not sure what he is going to do."

"Where is he?"

"The stables."

María weaved her way through the hallway and living room and out the door. Panic struck and clutching her dress with both hands she began to run. A thought suddenly possessed her, an image that would not go away—the idea of finding her son gone.

She swung around the house to the stables. A few horses milled about the mud of the adjoining corrals and scanning them María saw three tied alongside each other outside the pen. Two wore saddles while the other shifted under a pair of bulging panniers. A short distance from them in the shade of a juniper sat her son. María stopped, placed her hand over her chest, and breathed. He wore a crisp black dress shirt with ivory buttons and a collar hanging loosely halfway down his chest. The black pants were similarly baggy and the polished boots appeared clownishly large. A wide sombrero dipped low atop his head. The clothes belonged to Lino.

He glanced up at her and back down as she approached. He sat hunched over on the ground with his chin in one hand and the muzzle of the dragoon held lightly in the other, the gun's handle drawing distracted little shapes in the dirt. A once-bouquet of flowers lay strewn to the side.

"Is that empty?" María asked, stopping over him.

He pulled the gun's trigger. *Click.* María scraped her foot to smooth a spot on the ground and sat. She folded her knees against her chest. "Were you going to tell me good-bye?"

He paused his tracings but did not answer.

"It seems to me, considering all that has happened, the distrust between us is wrongly sided."

"I trust you."

"Then why were you not going to tell me good-bye?"

He was silent.

"Where would you have gone?"

"Back home."

"Back home? To Mexico?"

"No, to the Conejos."

"You think of the Conejos River as home?"

He shrugged. "It is where we built our house."

The thought touched María, this memory of the small and lonely jacal that had housed the two of them during the long two years of the war. She remembered how hard they had all worked to build it; she, Felipe, Ignasio, Hector, and Jacinto. The family when it was whole.

"And then what?" she asked.

"What do you mean?"

"What would you have done once on the Conejos? How would you support your wife?"

His head came up and María realized he had yet to consider this. "Maybe I'd be a vaquero."

"You would do well as a vaquero."

The boy looked up at her, his eyes suddenly bright with the compliment. He pushed his hands into the ground and spun himself to face her. "Then *we* can go."

"You and me?"

"Yes."

"I cannot. We cannot."

"Why?"

"Because we have nothing there."

He dropped the gun in the dirt. "We have nothing here! Mamá no one wants us here. Lino hates us and someday he will drive us out. Why wait to be made to crawl away when we can leave on horses? Why not leave now and say good-bye to no one?"

María took hold of her son's hand. "I'm an old woman with no husband. I'm unwanted no matter where I go, but at least here we are cared for. You're not ready to care for me, but neither can you leave me for to do so would be to leave me to die." It was an unfair tactic she knew, but one so true; her heart was still recovering from the panic moments ago when she had feared the scenario real.

"Besides," she said, "if you left, your cousin would be upset."

"No she wouldn't."

"I mean Vivian. He thinks of you as his big brother. You should be proud of that."

He shrugged. Only one person in the world was capable of making sense to him right now, and María knew it was not her.

"Did you know I used to consider attempting a trip back to Chihuahua, just the two of us? I thought about it all the time, back when we were alone and so far away from everything. I would look out our door and see nothing at all, and I would think how lonely and sad it was. I would think how your father and your brothers must all be dead, how I wanted to just call you, pack up, and begin walking south. But then I wondered, even if we made it to Mexico, what if they were not dead? How would they ever find us?

"The war would be over and I would never know if your

father and your brothers lived or died. So we stayed with me never sharing these thoughts nor asking for yours, and we endured all that time without questioning it until the day your father finally returned.

"The orators, authors, and generals all preach how you must seize what you want, that if you desire it you must act quick to get it. But sometimes this is wrong. Sometimes going after a thing only distances it from you, like me taking us from that house would have distanced us forever from your father and we would have spent the rest of our lives wondering."

María touched the back of her fingers against her son's face. "I know it hurts right now. I know that *she* hurts. But sometimes, Felipe, there is such a thing as waiting for what you want."

Chapter 18

Lino leaned against the wall in the kitchen, his arms crossed. The rest of the family was seated and the Navajo woman weaved in and out among them, setting a steaming chili pot in the middle of the table followed by a plate of roasted vegetables and a dish of warmed tortillas. Secundina had her eyes on her lap and beside her María wore her tightlipped smile. Cecilia sat opposite Lino's place at the head with José, Vivian, and the boy perched quietly between. It was a late meal and Lino knew the family was hungry.

When finally the table was set Lino said, "All of you find your coats and go outside except for Felipe. We must all wait for him to tell me something."

In silence Cecilia, María, Secundina, Vivian, and José went to the parlor, put on their coats, and filed out the door into the lingering cold of early spring.

Lino had planned tonight's discussion for days, devising ways to pressure his subject and make him self-conscious, and in the end this, to infer blame for withholding dinner from everyone else, was the best he could do.

He rolled his fingers along the back of his chair at the head of the table, alone now with the boy who stared straight ahead. An evening light fell in from the dining room's small window, catching the vapors swirling upward from the food.

"I am considering your induction into the Brotherhood," Lino said. "Is this something you want?"

After a moment the boy nodded.

"Do you know what is required of you?"

"Yes."

"How? How do you know?"

"I am told things."

"Are you aware you will need a sponsor, that you must have a Brother attest to your worthiness? Your induction is not the decision of just one Brother but that of the whole morada."

"I know."

"The testament of the Hermano Mayor should carry much weight." It was not a question, but to Lino's chagrin the boy nodded all the same.

"You understand, too, that your induction is also dependent upon a *promisa*? Something you can offer the morada."

"Yes."

"I want you to tell me then, before you tell anyone else, what you are capable of promising? What do you have that anyone would want?"

"I'll promise whatever the morada asks of me."

Lino shook his head. "That's not good enough. You may think it will be for them, but it's not for me."

The boy frowned and looked away. He had suspended his insolence while Lino dangled the prospect of initiation before his face. Now the defiance returned and Lino felt rage and even a little fear, his confidence wavering.

"I want to tell you a story," Lino said. "It's from when I was a boy. It's about a *tío* of mine, a man you never knew because he died long before your birth. When I was very young, my father became sick with pneumonia. He didn't die but in the weeks my mother cared for him she sent me to stay with this *tío*. In the neighborhood where he lived the people knew him well. They called him a hero for his part in the war, his fighting for Mexico's independence. He raised his family lovingly and because of this his family loved him back. Thus, my parents trusted my *tío* in keeping me, and I trusted him, too.

"He was a carpenter, and during my stay he was called to do work on a home outside the city, one set alone far off behind the Cerro Grande. My *tío* brought me along, his own son being little more than an infant at the time. A widow lived alone in this home. It had to have been a lonely life and to this day I wonder why she stayed. Still, she was cheerful, and as we began our work she sat next to us talking.

"Very soon however, I noticed the woman spoke mainly to me, and that perhaps because of this my *tío* started acting peculiar. It was a manner that even as a young boy I knew to be hinting of evil. He would say something innocent to her and then end his sentences with words like *'preciosa'* or *'hermosa.'* Once, he said to her *'mi amor'* and the woman replied very quickly 'do not call me *tu amor.'* My *tío* grinned as if it was only a joke but even I could tell she was serious. After that the woman stood up and went somewhere else in the house.

"My *tío* told me to leave, that he did not need me anymore and that I should go home. I pled with him, saying I was afraid to walk alone all the way back to the city even though I was not. I had to stay, you see, because my presence was everything keeping the devil away. I even began to cry. I remember how he tried to soothe me then, how he patted my hair and told me it was all right while at the same time his eyes floated about other parts of the house.

"With his hands on my back he ushered me out and closed the door. I didn't return home however, but snuck around the back of the house and huddled against the wall. I think I did this because I was more afraid of leaving and for the rest of my life wondering than staying and actually knowing. I heard a bedroom door force open. I heard the woman, her surprise at first, and then her protests. There came the sounds of her struggle and then, like sound that is suddenly muted by the shutting of a thick door, silence. I waited like this, hearing nothing for a long, long time.

"When I saw my *tío* exit I waited until he was far down the trail before entering the house. I called out for the woman but there came no answer. I went to her bedroom and when I opened the door I saw her. She lay on the bed, her pants still tangled around her ankles. Then I saw the marks around her neck. Not cuts, Felipe, hand marks. I remember how her whole face was the color of a finger whose base has been laced tight with string. I remember how I could still smell the struggle that had happened in that room, how it was copperish and hot with breath and how fast that hotness was growing cold.

"I ran back to the city, crying all the way. I wondered where to go, yet because I was only a boy I had no choice but to return to my *tío*'s. I wiped my face outside the door and even made up a story about where I had been. But when I stepped through the door my *tío* didn't even notice, and the first thing I saw was him bouncing his son on his knee, laughing. And when my *tía* stooped over to retrieve the boy from his lap I watched him grasp her hand and pull her close to his face and kiss her. I watched it, and I knew right then that I would not be able to tell anyone what I saw. You, Felipe, are the first to hear this story."

The boy trembled, his eyes firm and glossy.

"You know who the man in my story was Felipe, who he was to you?"

The boy stared ahead. He chewed on the inside of his cheeks.

"There is a dark vein that runs down your side of the family Felipe. I don't know where it originated but I saw it that day in your grandfather. And I see it in you."

The boy shook his head. "It's my father you were afraid of. He is who you hate."

Lino winced. "I don't hate Ignasio. There was a time when I hated myself *because* of your father but before then I had great respect for him, despite his feelings toward me. That is not to say I don't have plenty reasons to hate him."

The boy wrung the tablecloth in his lap. "You didn't know my father like me."

"And he didn't know his like I did! When you can believe Ignasio knew nothing of what his father did to that widow, then you can believe your father was also capable of things you never suspected."

The boy was quiet. He moved his eyes to the twisting tablecloth and for a moment Lino thought he might cry. To his disappointment, he did not.

"What do you want from me?"

"I want you to understand why I distrust you," Lino said. "And now that you do, maybe you will understand the promise I want you to make."

"What promise?"

"It is not the same promise you will give the Brothers, but one separate from them. Separate even from God. This promise will be for me only."

"Tell it."

"I want you to give up Secundina. No, not give up. I want you to hate her."

The defiance fell out of the boy and suddenly he was the vulnerable, breakable boy Lino had always wanted him to be. For the first time since moving into Hacienda de Espinosa he became something Lino understood and felt comfortable with. He was begging. His eyes were no longer dark. His eyes were soft.

Invigorated by it, Lino expounded: "You must do more than ignore her. When she calls Vivian to her, you must call him instead. If a new relationship in the village is announced you must ask why no one wants her. When the children in town laugh at her and tease her about her arm, or every time she drops something because of it, you must laugh and tease too. And when she asks the reason for all your loathing, all your disgust, you must answer because it is how everyone else feels."

A tear fell down his cheek. "What if I can't?"

"Then your admission to the morada is denied, and you and your mother shall leave and find your home anyplace but here."

The boy looked to the front door, toward where everyone still waited in the cold. The food on the table had ceased to steam. Despair floated in his eyes.

"Is that a promise?" Lino asked.

A late freeze struck Costilla. On the first day the aspen buds hardened and fell in blasts of wind that seemed to stiffen and shake the entire valley. Overnight a pale overcast rolled in from the south, covering the sky until the sun grew pallid. Snow began early the morning of the second day, blanketing the streets and contrasting starkly the recently charred homes. The animals stood transfixed as snowflakes stuck in their fur and ice oozed in their nostrils. The wind-driven snow drifted against buildings. Tracks of boot prints marked routes between doors and woodpiles.

As night fell on the third day, snow still piling and wind howling, the town gradually came to life. Lanterns hung glowing above doorways and women and children stepped into the cold with blankets wrapped about their bodies. They watched, crossing themselves, as the men trudged to the morada.

Lino sat in the living room next to the fireplace with the boy across from him. When the knock came both stood. Lino did not invite the visitor in, merely announced that it was time.

Lino and the boy marched unspeaking through the snow, the messenger trailing slightly behind. As they entered town and neared the morada the snow became packed and easier to traverse. Lino slowed in front of the door and allowed the boy to step ahead of him.

The boy raised his hand and knocked three times.

From inside a voice answered faint and muffled: *"Quien en esta casa de la luz?"*

"Jesús," the boy replied.

"Quien la llena de alegria?"

"María."

"Quien la conserva en la fe?"

"José."

A long silence, then: "Who knocketh on the doors of this morada?"

"They are not the doors of the morada, only the doors of your conscience."

Very quietly, being careful not to so much as lean forward lest even the messenger notice, Lino whispered to the boy, "Good."

Shuffling sounded from inside and with a great release of the bolt the door opened. Felipe entered, followed by Lino and the messenger. Lino made his way through the first room and into the chapel. The air around them was numbing, scarcely warmer than that outside. The air smelled sweetly of tea leaves and wax from what seemed a hundred candles flickering along the wall. Ahead of them the Brothers formed a gauntlet leading to the rostrum; the Hermanos de Luz at the innermost edge while clustered behind them swayed the descending ranks. Lino held up a hand and gestured Felipe to stop, then made his way through the men and took his place at the front of the room. The boy stood facing him at the back while two Brothers stripped him naked and handed him a pair of white trousers.

The Sangrador, the bloodletter, emerged from the throng carrying a cup of alcohol in one hand and a sharpened piece of flint in the other. He stepped behind the boy and looked at Lino who nodded and ordered the boy to begin.

"With what most profound respect which divine Faith inspires, O my God and Savior Jesus Christ, true God and true man . . ."

The Sangrador dipped the flint into the cup, its tip shining silvery in the candlelight, and began the first cut down the back.

". . . in reparation of all the irreverences, profanations, and sacrileges that I, to my shame, may have until now committed, as also for all those that have been committed against Thee, or that may ever be committed for the time to come . . ."

The boy did not wince nor stumble his words. The Sangrador dipped the flint in the cup again and returned to the initiate's back. The second cut paralleled the first, the wounds trailing deep along each side of the spine—allowing a free flow of blood as well as a permanent, visible seal of obligation.

". . . but also so supply the defect, and for the conversion of all heretics . . ."

As the boy finished the prayer Lino observed blood running like veins down the inside of the white trousers before trickling into a pool around his feet. The Sangrador let the flint drop inside the cup and retreated inside the ranks. Felipe swayed and for a moment a confused look curtained his face. Lino watched him, waiting for him to collapse, but the boy squeezed his eyes shut and opened them, and like that the confusion disappeared. He looked to Lino, and the Brothers did the same.

"What led you here this night?" Lino asked.

"God," the boy said.

"How do you seek admission?"

"A promise."

"What promise?"

"I promise to live by, listen to, and execute God's will."

"As I am both sponsor of this candidate and head of *el frater-*

nidad," Lino said, "I accept the pledge of the candidate pending the cleansing of his soul." He peered hard at the boy. "And what of the sins on your soul?"

"For these I ask forgiveness, now and until they are gone."

Lino eyed the dark stains still flowing down the sides of the pants, the knees wobbling. He waited to reply, waited in vain for the initiate to fall, before announcing finally, "You may begin asking."

The boy dropped to his knees, his arms dangling and the tips of his fingers dipping into the pools of blood beside him. Immediately there came a swishing of liquid as Brothers soaked their whips in buckets of silver sage tea and brought the tightly knit wool lashes dripping to the front of the ranks, and handed them to the elders. They formed a circle around the initiate, Felipe all the while gaping open-mouthed up at the ceiling.

Then, as if whatever string held his face upward had suddenly been cut, the boy's chin dropped and he crawled to the man in front. "Hermano Losada, *por el amor de Dios, por favor, perdóname.*"

The hand of Brother Losada rose into the air and struck down. The balled end of the lash cracked on the boy's back, tearing open a red gash. He collapsed to his stomach. He lay there quivering as the circle looked on in silence. Then, slowly, he rose and crawling once more he approached the next man along the circle.

"Brother Higuera, for the love of God, please forgive me."

Fwick! The whip snapped down and once more Felipe fell to his stomach. Then, again he rose, shaking, and crawled to the next brother.

This time, when the boy asked for his penance, the brother holding the whip did not raise it. Instead he smiled at him and offered a prayer: "Many are the woes of the wicked but the Lord's unfailing love surrounds the man who trusts in Him."

"Amen," the boy said, and resumed his crawl around the circle.

Lino watched each Brother give his whip or his prayer before falling back as the next man assumed his whip and spot in the circle; the cord ends cleansed and soaked in the buckets of sage tea at the end of every cycle. Soon the individual gashes along the initiate's back were no longer discernible, the skin around the spine and shoulders gnashed apart into one great wound of tattered, bloody skin.

Lino saw the boy's tendons strain, powering the shoulders as he crawled. A smeared track of blood formed within the circle where the boy's knees dragged continually around, and eventually Lino no longer smelled the candles or the tea, only blood. But despite his blood loss, the boy had ceased to collapse after each lashing, and Lino recalled that it had been the same for him, how after a time the pain is no longer even felt as if once a certain amount had been achieved there could be no more. It was true his words had begun to slur, but after a while it appeared the strokes of the whips no longer even registered. His track around the circle had become unwavering, systematic, and observing this Lino decided all previous doubts regarding the boy's endurance tonight would prove invalid.

The circle dispersed until only one Brother stood before the initiate. He answered the boy in prayer, turned, and looked at Lino. Everyone looked at Lino.

Leaving his place at the front and accepting a whip he approached the bloody, crouched figure in the middle of the room. Lino looked down. He waited. The boy lifted his head. His pupils were all but hidden by the blood that filled his eyes, yet Lino could not mistake the unnerving consciousness in them.

"Brother Espinosa, for the love of God, please forgive me."

Eyes locked, Lino brought the cord up and cracked it down

with all his might. Then, aware even in the moment that the others would talk of it later, Lino whipped the cord down once more.

It was late now and only three remained in the morada. The interior had cooled although the smell of blood lingered, the evidence of the night's violence hung in the air.

Felipe lay on his stomach on a cloth-draped table. Next to him the *enfermero* sponged his wounds with a cloth that he dipped in a cup of silver sage that had long ago turned a dark, hazy red. Lino stood by Felipe's head watching. The only sounds were from the cloth dunking and squeezing into the cup.

Lino put his hands on the back of Felipe's head. "You are no longer a boy. Now you are with *us*. Now, you shall be peaceful."

CHAPTER 19

Secundina was giving up on ever having hips, a waist, thighs, calves, cheeks, and, especially, breasts.

Her mother told her that she had a niece that was thin and homely into her twenties when suddenly she bloomed like a cactus and found a husband immediately.

"Am I as homely as she was?" Secundina asked.

Cecilia blushed and waved her hand. "Oh no, no, I don't mean *you* are homely, only that you may bloom late."

"Do you think I need to marry?"

"I think that *someday* you should. No woman wants to live her life a *soltera,* an old maid."

When she turned twenty, shortly after Felipe's induction into the Penitentes and his abrupt turn against her, Secundina set up an experiment based on her mother's suggestion. Standing naked beside the corner wall of her room, she pressed the length of her body against the cool adobe. She stood the way she normally carried herself, and with a pencil traced her silhouette on the wall. She stepped back to take it in and was surprised to find a few things she liked. The chin arched out gracefully from a straight neck and a torso that, while perhaps a little feature-less, impressed elegance. The figure was undeniably, delicately feminine.

Keeping her eyes on the sketch, Secundina backed in front of her bureau mirror. Just as before, she stood straight but relaxed. When she moved her eyes to the mirror the first thing she noticed was her left arm hanging alongside her, so withered and pale against the light brown of her abdomen that it seemed to belong to another being, a thing dead and trapped in ice. She observed the pronounced cords like an old woman's in her neck, how small her chin, how oval her eyes. As for the bumps on her chest, Secundina could laugh and cry at the same time.

She wanted to become the figure on the wall, to melt into that womanly base shape and redesign herself from there. She dressed, slipping on the long black glove she wore over the dead arm before anything else. She hung a quilt over the tracing on the wall.

In the years that followed Secundina removed the quilt one evening a week, stripped, pressed herself into the silhouette, and looked for change. Four times a month became fifty-two times a year. She did this as gold was discovered in the mountain ranges to the north and as a network of stage roads and settlements blazed throughout the valley. She did it as the Territory of New Mexico fractioned, the entire southern half under the banner of Confederate Arizona while to the northeast and just a hair over Costilla's head there cut the invisible border of the new Colorado Territory. Never once did Secundina's real figure extend beyond the one etched in pencil, and in the end all the experiment taught her was to feel as preordained and lifeless as a marking on the wall.

She finally erased the tracing and decided against rehanging the quilt. She considered this blank space on her wall, the sudden reconfiguration of her room, and thought how everything could change but her.

Omar Chapa lived near the center of town in a tiny one-room jacal that, like its occupant, reeked of fungus. Secundina smelled it walking past the home just like she smelled it walking past

Omar, and every time she wondered which one was the proponent.

He was a Penitente of course, a Hermano de Luz. He held no profession and subsisted off a few chickens, one meager vegetable patch, and every so often the charity of the morada. Considering how slow he moved and the hunch in his back, Secundina guessed him to be sixty-something. His hair was gray yet youthfully curly, as if all his vigor went to the hundreds of tight little coils.

He used to have a wife back when the town was first raised. Secundina remembered little about her except that she always appeared somewhat colorless and sleepy-eyed. The people had found her a few years ago frozen to death less than a hundred yards from their home. It had been a peculiar case; no one knew why she had ventured outside, where she had been going. Omar explained only that it had been some demon inside her. He exhibited no remorse and, according to rumor, she had not been the first wife to die on Omar.

Secundina never gave him much thought until one afternoon she discovered him sitting at their dining-room table next to Lino and her mother. She entered the room and everyone rose except Omar, his eyes peering out at her below that helmet of bouncing gray curls, the air thick with his smell.

"Secundina," Lino began after he told her to sit, "I think what I desire for you is the same that you desire for yourself. Do you agree?"

"It's possible."

"No young woman should want to live as a burden in her parents' house, just like no parents should want their daughter appearing useless and forever dependent, no? At a certain age, unwanted women become unwanted daughters."

Secundina glanced at her mother who only winced.

"Brother Omar, you know him?" Lino continued. "Yes. Well,

he understands this. He is also considerate of the predicaments of others and willing to help us. Willing to help you."

Omar nodded.

Lino continued to speak but Secundina's attention turned elsewhere. Behind her she heard the front door unlatch and squeak slowly open. She felt a not-unpleasant chill sweep along her neck as someone tiptoed through the parlor and stopped a few feet from her behind the half wall separating the parlor and dining room. No one else at the table appeared to notice and Secundina made no sign of alerting them. Instead she kept her eyes trained on Lino, comforted in her secret knowledge of the man behind the wall. She felt defended.

"Omar and I have spoken for a long time now about it, about *you*. And, providing you are capable of making yourself a good one Secundina, he has agreed to take you in as his wife."

It was plain he expected her to be surprised, except Secundina had understood since the moment she spotted Omar sitting at the dining-room table. She knew the only one shocked was the man eavesdropping behind the wall.

"Thank you, *Señor* Chapa," she said.

Omar tipped his head.

Boots shuffled behind the wall.

"*Bueno,*" Lino said, standing. "It will be next week then." He extended his hand to Omar who shook it limply. Omar put on his sombrero and moved along the table.

Secundina turned to him thinking he might take her hand and kiss it, but he neither made notice of her or, as he passed through the parlor, of anyone lurking behind the wall.

She lay in bed that night fully dressed, a lantern burning dimly beside her. Staring at the glow on the ceiling she thought of marriage, sex, and motherhood.

She had listened to the women of the *auxiliadora* tittle over

these three pillars of womanhood, gossiping and waving away
their personal details and all the while underlining the voids in
Secundina's life. She started to yearn for them, not as supple-
ments to life but as fillers of voids. She didn't crave the love of
marriage, the ecstasy of sex or the responsibility of motherhood.
To her, women that described such things did so to appear
normal, and ultimately that was all Secundina wanted. It was
the same reason she wished for a healthy left arm: not because
it would make day-to-day life easier or more enjoyable but
simply because it was normal.

As if to advocate against her intuition, Secundina closed her
eyes and envisioned happiness with Omar. She pictured herself
a newlywed, being led by Omar into his small dilapidated home.
She imagined how dark the house had to be, how unkempt and
leaky it surely was in order to permeate such a constant
pungency. She coaxed the sound of his door shutting tight
behind her and bolting, and she felt the permanence of marriage reinforcing the bolt and enveloping the whole tiny, stink-
ing house with her in it.

In her vision, a bed, nothing more than wheat sacks stuffed
with molded hay, flopped unmade in the corner of the room.
She let Omar guide her to it until unceremoniously the two
stepped apart and began to undress. Omar kept his eyes on her
as he unbuttoned his own shirt and trousers, and Secundina
kept her eyes elsewhere. He looked at her for a moment or two
and then grasped her in the hope she might feel less disappointing than she appeared. He was let down.

When Secundina finally lifted her eyes and gazed upon a
naked man for the first time she saw only the bones lumping
within the hump on his back and thought how thin and leathery
his skin was, how old this man really was. Then, because she
could not fathom kissing him or offering any soft words of affection, she imagined him simply laying down and, perhaps

massaging himself first, telling her to get on. She would, and for minutes that felt like hours she thought how ugly their two bodies looked connected as they were, how profane their act.

And then their baby would be born. During the birth Secundina saw herself screaming and wishing more than ever to be dead. Later, Omar would want little to do with the baby and this would please her. She would care for it and she would fret. She might even love it. But never would she feel grateful. Even when the child was grown and Secundina was so old that her life seems only a dream cast from a lantern-lit bed, still she would feel only disdain for Omar, Lino, and God. She would congratulate herself that her life was not spent an old maid, and she would be thankful it was almost over.

Secundina opened her eyes and wiped them. Through the wall next to her she heard the late-night murmurs of Lino and her mother. She thought how it would be good not to hear them anymore, not to wonder so painfully if the conversations concerned her. The hacienda had grown increasingly lonely over the years despite more people residing inside than ever. Her mother, at one time Secundina's closest ally, succumbed more and more to Lino. Her brothers kept loyal, especially little José, now almost twelve, but as each one grew older Secundina observed them growing less concerned with their sister's stagnant life and more with their own.

Secundina turned on her side and slid an arm below the pillow. Her hand brushed over something. Lifting her head, she tipped up the pillow and swept her hand until finding a folded piece of paper. The paper was lightly brown like the pages of her mother's sketchbooks. Turning up the wick on the lantern, Secundina unfolded the note.

She recognized the handwriting instantly, curvy and almost femininely elegant. The handwriting could have been that of a burgeoning calligraphist. The person who had written this enjoyed writing, enjoyed it more than talking. More than once Secundina had heard him admit this to Cecilia. He said writing gave him time to better plan his words, and also that a personally written message was more affecting. You could hold it in your hand, keep it in a safe place unlike a verbal message that dilutes and eventually seeps out of the memory. When he said it, Secundina had cut in by asking why, if he loved writing so much, was his spelling so horrendous?

Now, years later, she continued to sense that this comment alone explained why he remained the oldest pupil still taking lessons from her mother. His idea that written messages were more effective, despite how damning they could be when found in the hands of the wrong person—a fear this particular messenger must consider—surely explained why he had stuffed this note under her pillow.

The note was simple: *Si quieres casarte con prudenca, casarse con su igual.*

If you want to marry wisely, marry your equal.

It was a proverb Secundina had read before, had actually even considered while flipping through her mother's books—no doubt the same book that had inspired this message.

She clipped the note between the metal base of the lantern and the glass. The dark inscription of the writing emboldened within the glowing brown of the paper and created a blurry reverse shadow against the wall. It felt good to receive Felipe's message, just like it had pleased her to have him hiding behind the wall earlier that day. It was now six years ago that he had proposed. On that day Secundina had laughed at him and rolled her eyes while relaying the story to María. But underneath all that, even while she laughed and rolled her eyes, Secundina had secretly been flattered. It was a new feeling, and for days after she felt a new sense of optimism and confidence as she floated on the lie that she might be desirable after all.

But as time ushered in so too did reality, and eventually Secundina saw the lie for what it was which, synonymously, was also seeing Felipe for who he was: the only man who wanted her.

Then, as young men in Costilla tend to do, Felipe became a Penitente. After that, although Secundina did not exactly see less of Felipe, she did suddenly seem to become invisible to him. His affection (she was reluctant to call it love) for her had disappeared, and failing to understand why but missing it all the same, Secundina went looking for it. She would tease him in the hallway, which would only make him pause and slide silently past her. Or she would spot him brushing one of the horses and go out to join him, only for him to blatantly move somewhere else.

Once, while seated around the dinner table as Lino made yet another of his unsubtle hints about how Secundina had worn out her welcome in his house, Secundina had replied that he better be careful or one day he might wake up and not only would she be gone but José, Vivian, and Felipe as well. Looking to bolster her attack with a display of coalition, Secundina had turned to the one person she had once considered Lino's most reliable opponent and said, "Right Felipe?" Every eye had switched to her cousin.

It was an excruciatingly long moment before finally, quietly, his eyes cast on his lap, Felipe said, "When I leave, it will not be with you."

If the avoidances in the hallway and the stables perplexed Secundina, this denouncement crushed her. After dinner she had taken a walk deep into the night sage, and falling to her knees, alone and hidden amongst the brush, violently she had cried.

And so now, rereading Felipe's note, Secundina felt rejuvenated. He had not given up on her after all. By the looks of it, he was still trying to win her.

Even so, while knowing Felipe still yearned for her restored some of Secundina's self-worth, she nonetheless entertained no ideas of encouraging him, although the idea of him proposing a second time excited her and, guiltily, so too did the idea of laughing at him once more.

Secundina would always see Felipe as the boy with the monstrous mouth who talks to himself and does stupid things like plant messages that could all too easily become evidence. She had felt that way even as a girl, and because she had not wanted him when he was a boy she felt incapable of wanting him as a man. To give him a chance now seemed somehow un-virtuous, against principle. He was in his twenties now, and to be a man still living under Lino's roof Secundina had lost even more respect for him, despite sensing perfectly well the flatter-ing reason for why he stayed. To Secundina, Felipe had become a vagrant who sooner or later must find a new home either by himself or with people who did not mind his odd mutterings and the disquieting things floating about his past.

Secundina picked up the note and ran her fingers over the elegant letters. At the very least, she should say something to him about the fine handwriting in the note but she knew she wouldn't. In the morning, when he looked at her expectantly, Secundina would make no unusual notice of him. In fact, she would get married and never give Felipe any acknowledgment of his secret message to her.

She would tell nobody anything, least of all the truth. Know-ing Felipe still wanted her made Secundina feel better about marrying Omar. She hoped Felipe would yearn for her his whole life. Perhaps then maybe her picture of marriage, sex, and motherhood would not be all that bad. She could never say it out loud, but there was reassurance in knowing a man's heart hurt because of her.

She pitied Felipe. She pitied him because deep down some

ugly part of her did want him to know these things. She pitied him for being so ignorant to her ugliness.

Smiling, the light dancing in her pupils, Secundina lifted the glass from around the lantern and held the tip of the paper to the wick. She carried the flaming piece of paper to her window and dropped it. Sticking her head out she watched the note burn into a cindering dark crisp that floated and scattered.

A few mornings later, Secundina saw Omar through her bedroom window shuffling down the snow-drifted lane leading to the Espinosa estate. She heard his knock followed by her mother calling her name only to immediately tell her to never mind and to stay in her room.

Then Cecilia called for Lino, and when she was sure the three were seated at the dining-room table Secundina snuck down the hallway and stopped at the entryway into the parlor. She sat down on the floor cross-legged, and with the side of her head against the wall and her eyes shut, she listened.

Omar's speech came through the walls like an old man rambling in his sleep, parched and emotive. He said that he *did* want their daughter but that he wanted another woman more and that she had agreed to have him. He explained how it had come to him in a dream, a dream sent by God, in which Secundina and this other woman knelt before Omar and took turns pleading their cases for who should be his wife, and that in the end even Secundina had agreed the other to be the wiser choice. Thus, Omar concluded, he could no longer marry Lino's daughter and that surely Lino could not disagree with such divine instruction.

Silence followed Omar's story. There came a stomping of footsteps outside the front door. It started to open.

"Shut that door! Out!" Lino barked, and the door slammed shut.

He began softly then, calmly even. He asked Omar questions about his dream, questions to which Omar remembered only some of the answers. He asked him why the other woman had won out and Omar said it was because she showed more compassion. When Lino asked why he favored the other woman, Omar said she was of more esteem. Lino asked if it was because of his daughter's arm and Omar said only partly. He asked Omar if it were because he could not bed with Secundina. Omar admitted this was so.

Lino's chair grated back against the floorboards and Secundina peeked around the wall and watched him pace and chastise Omar, declaring him a slave of the flesh and self. Omar merely hung his head, the gray coils hanging over his eyes like half-hooked bedsprings. Cecilia sat locked in a stare, her face a cold statement of scorn and sorrow.

Lino ordered Omar out and Secundina retreated back into the hallway. She lingered at the hall's back, watching with the detached interest one might offer a bratty child being publicly scolded as Omar trotted through the parlor to the door with Lino still raging at his tail. He stepped out the door after the man, stopping on the stoop to yell one final judgment before jumping in surprise at the three waiting figures he had apparently forgotten about.

"Well, come in then," he said, returning to the house with Vivian, José, and Felipe following him. José had the telltale runny nose and blotchy eyes of a boy who had been crying. If Secundina had to guess, she would say Vivian had just finished another unattractive attempt at belittling José in front of Felipe in his ongoing efforts to buffer his younger brother out of the duo-come-trio.

"Now what?" Lino asked him, noticing José's trembling lip. Vivian had his head down, bracing for the tattle. But Felipe had forgotten them. He stared past the parlor, down the living room, and through its shadows to where Secundina saw his eyes catch her own.

The engagement had lasted three days, and each night Felipe had left Secundina a message, each one written on a carefully torn piece of brown paper and tucked under her pillow. While they were not original thoughts—each being a proverb from one of Cecilia's books—each was nonetheless deliberately chosen and rewritten in Felipe's delicate hand. She had come to look forward to them, even going so far as to stay away from her room in the evenings to allow him the opportunity to sneak in.

After encouraging her to marry an equal, two more messages followed. The first said: *Dejar pasar el primer impulso, esperar a la segunda.*

Let the first impulse pass, wait for the second.

The next: *En el atardecer de la vida, seremos juzgados sobre el amor solo.*

In the evening of life, we will be judged on love alone.

On the night after Omar's last visit, the day the engagement ended, Secundina had not expected a note. If she thought of Felipe at all in the hours to follow she figured him to be reveling. Wishing to see and think of no one, Secundina had gone outside and buried herself in chores, finding them where they barely existed, like in unnoticed bridle knots or the unpatched tears in forgotten saddle blankets. When she finally went back in the house, the bottom of her dress crusted with ice and her nose running, the family had already eaten supper. The only person still up was Lino who, smoking a cigarette in his rocker next to the fire, only frowned at her as if just now reminded of *that* whole predicament.

She walked past him straight to her room and dropped onto her bed. She hoped her mother might at least try to come in and console her, but after a while Secundina gave up on Cecilia and fell into a light, dreamless sleep.

When she awoke it was still dark out and the foot of her bed was wet with the melt of her dress. Feeling around in the dark, Secundina found the lantern and lit it. She sat at the edge of her bed, feeling, wanting. It was a barren feeling she knew well yet rarely so intense, the feeling of emptiness after a strong taste of fulfillment.

Perhaps simply out of habit, she lifted the pillow. There was a note. She unfolded it and read: *I wept when I was born and every day explains why.*

Secundina stared at the note for a long time. The line of black ink blurred in her eyes like words held behind a glass of water. The room grew dim. Secundina turned up the wick on the lantern, swung her feet off the bed, walked to the other side of the room, and found a pencil in her dresser. Returning to the bed she placed the note on top the end table, flipped it over, and began to write.

She went to her closet, changed out of the wet dress, put on her coat, and slipped out the bedroom door. Darkness filled the hallway and she let her eyes adjust before tiptoeing past her brothers' room to the door leading into Felipe and María's. She put her ear to it and heard the quiet, steady breathing of sleep. She tapped a finger against the door. When no sound of movement came, she rapped once more. This time she heard shuffling, the sound of bedcovers being pulled, and quickly, stepping lightly on the balls of her feet, Secundina fled to the parlor. Unlatching the bolt as quietly as she could she opened the front door and stepped into the night.

The cold shocked her, as did the revealing white light of the moon and a million stars. The surface of the snow was a crust that she broke through, a subterranean level of powdery snow filling her shoes. No lights burned in town and the thought that

Secundina was the only one out right now, that she defied the village and looked upon it as it slept, felt empowering.

Reaching the stable, she unlatched its great door and pulled it wailing on its hinges just enough to slip in. A few surprised nickers and snorts greeted her from the darkness of the pens. The air was a warm potpourri of hay, saddle oil, fur, and manure. Secundina sensed the horses around her but could see nothing except the sliver of cold, white light breaching the cracked door. Stepping carefully, one hand feeling about in front of her, she came to the first of the pens. She held her hand over the top panel, smiling as it was met by a soft, sniffing nose. She turned and waited with her back to the wooden paneling and her face to the door.

She heard the crunching of his footsteps. They approached slowly. A shadow passed over the light of the cracked door and filled it. It creaked once more as he nudged it open, stepped inside, and closed it entirely. Complete darkness.

She wasn't sure how he knew where she stood, but he did. He walked straight up to her, whispering nothing, and when he stopped before her Secundina pulled upright from the paneling and stood against him. She felt his breath where her neck met her chest and goose bumps spread across her chest and arms and down her thighs. He put his hands on her waist and slipped them into her jacket around the curve in her back. She let him pull her closer. She put her lips to his ear.

"You be so, so quiet."

★ ★ ★ ★ ★

Part Three:
The Love of
Secundina Espinosa
Winter 1862

★ ★ ★ ★ ★

Chapter 20

The camp consisted of a dozen tepees connected by footpaths of frozen mud set on a sunken meadow within the forested hills outside Guadalupita, New Mexico. It was night and a large fire illuminated the center of the camp. Two bands of men formed two crescents around the fire separated only by a few feet of empty space where the last man of one band met the first of the other like the opposing ends of two horseshoe magnets. On one side were the Jicarilla Apaches, the men adorned in ratty pelts of coyote, bear, and elk, while behind them a huddle of women used chipped stones to shave clinging flecks of meat from the upturned ribcage of a deer. On the other side were the rogue soldiers, dressed not in uniform but soggy boots, knee-holed trousers, duster overcoats, bandannas, soiled cavalry hats rimmed with snakeskin. One man from each party stood, he of the soldiers being the storyteller and he of the Apaches his translator.

The men quieted, the women stopped their work, and Garret Kelly—twenty-four, tall, trim, toothy, golden-haired, green-eyed, Confederate, polyglot, and self-proclaimed swordsmith, professional gambler, whiskey distiller, riverboat engineer, author, and one-time paramour to the First Lady of Kentucky—began his story:

"There was a man who lived not far from here and not long ago. He had a home in a village that he shared with no wife and no children. Instead, the man lived with a profound collection of pets. They were not regular pets like cats and dogs but rather creatures of typically abhorrent species. Tarantulas, centipedes, scorpions, snakes, toads, lizards, mice, and rats crawled about sawdusted and soggy cages made of chicken wire or glass that cluttered and stunk the man's home. Of this collection the man was boastful, proud the way such men are, as if their peculiarity was rather courage to live as others dared not to. Like boys who flip their eyelids and laugh at their friends' repulsion.

"But there was one pet among them the man was especially fond of. Obscenely so. It was a snake, one whose breed was not known but could only be speculated upon mythologically. It measured thirteen feet. The midsection was muscly and thick as a man's thigh, its eyes large black beads—round and unslitted. The man claimed to have acquired the animal when it was young from a traveling Mexican out of the Yucatan.

"The snake did not live like the other man's pets, cooped in one of his many stacked cages. It was of course too big for that. Instead, the man allowed the creature free roam of his house. And so attached did he become to his prized animal that he openly admitted to sharing his bed with it, inviting the snake nightly to coil under the warmth of his sheets, to glean the heat off his own body. Behind the home the man raised rabbits and chickens, and from these pens both man and snake sufficed dietarily until, as inevitably the animal's appetite paced its physical growth, the man was forced to begin raising goats. Of this stock the snake was fed one pre-killed goat every two weeks, each time unhinging its jaws to swallow and then slide the bulge deep into its length. Like this the two lived, contentedly sharing home, bed, and diet, for more than two years.

"But then the man grew worried, for suddenly the snake stopped eating. When he set the biweekly goat before his pet's nose, the snake simply darted its tongue and then turned its head, uninterested. A month passed and the man decided the snake had grown tired of goats, so he tried a freshly shot fawn, still to no success. And when two whole months passed with the snake not eating a single thing, the man's concern turned to panic; anguish even at the fear of his most beloved companion being sick and dying. More than this, the animal's sleeping behavior had changed. No longer did it rest peacefully tight in its coil by the man's legs. Instead the man would wake in the night to find it stretched out stiff and lengthwise against his body, its head near his own and its tail draping off the bed and into the doorway.

"Desperate now, the man sought out a farmer clever in the biologies of exotic things. The story of the snake, along with its symptoms, were related in great detail to the farmer, and as he spoke the man observed the face of the farmer become so disturbed by the time he finished he had already concluded the worst for his cherished pet. He asked if his snake was dying and was surprised when the farmer said no, the animal was not dying.

"The snake, the farmer solemnly informed him, was not dying and neither was it sick. It was instead, as members of their species do, hollowing its stomach and building up its appetite as it prepared for a very large meal. And the reason it lay outstretched in bed close against the man's side was to confirm the meal would fit."

When he finished, Garret surveyed the men around the fire. For a long moment no one spoke or moved. Then, finally, his face grave and understanding, the Apache chief nodded at Garret Kelly.

Later that night while making up his bedroll, Garret was interrupted by the runt of the group, Connor Rutledge. Of all the men in their party Connor was the youngest, the smallest, and also, in Garret's estimation, the dimmest, which was all vexing as Garret had never understood what it was that had qualified Connor for this mission except that he, like Garret, spoke Spanish. Otherwise the young man was clumsy and unconfident and, consequently, dangerous. Adding to all this, Garret had somehow found himself after two nights of poker forty dollars in Connor's debt.

Connor took a seat next to Garret's bedroll. "Is that a true story?"

"Hell yes it's a true story," Garret said. "Happened in the town of Pine Bluff. Feller's name was J.B. Wooten. He had that thing where one eye is a different color than the other. I forget what it's called."

"I never know when you're lying."

"I ain't asking you to." Garret lay down on his roll with his hands folded under his head, allowing Connor in the silence of the stalled conversation to feel like a prick.

"So you weren't just yarn-spinning?"

"You think we wasted an afternoon of riding and gave away half our food just so I could spin a yarn?"

Connor was quiet.

"You watch, when this thing heats up Indians are going to end up our best and perhaps only ally. Because way out here who else is going to take our side? Not the Mexicans, that's for sure. Sibley and them are all Texan for God's sake, and anymore Texans fighting Mexicans is almost a virtue. The Indians on the other hand, they hate the bluecoats. Granted, they hate us too, along with anyone else who's ever shot a rabbit or drank from one of their creeks, but at least their hate is negotiable, gullible even. We're not trying to get them to stop hating us, just to keep hating the other side more. Them burning wagons and attacking forts is the reason so many federals are being kept here instead of going east."

"I already know all that," Connor said. "I'm asking about the story."

"You're too stuck on the drama of the tale and not my reason for telling it. See, Indians like to have their arguments made allegorically. Legends and yarns and such. They'll tell you a dozen stories about some god slaying another just to explain why the sun sets red. Tonight's story wasn't really about a man and a snake. It was about a people that allowed an inherently evil being into their home, an entity that over time grew so large it required not just the space of the home but also its food. And it continued to grow until even that which had come to trust it eventually and inevitably became yet another thing for it to swallow."

"You were instigating."

"And how."

"The snake was the Union."

"Really I could have made it stand for just about anyone, Mexicans too I'd bet." Garret could almost hear Connor's mind whirring as it replayed the story, little mechanical arms picking up and connecting metaphors.

"Why did the chief call you aside afterward?" Connor asked. "What were you two talking about?"

"He wanted to know the end of the story."

"That wasn't the end?"

"He wanted to know what became of the snake."

"What did?"

"Well, there are two versions."

"You said the story was true!"

"It is, save for one of the endings."

"So what are they?"

"In one version the man returned to his home after meeting with the farmer, picked up an ax, and hacked the snake to pieces. But in the other, the man, so trusting of his pet and unbelieving of the farmer, did nothing until one night as he slept the snake wound its coils about his body and squeezed the life out of him. And when the man was dead it devoured him just like one of its goats."

"Lord. So what version did you tell the chief?"

Still resting on his hands, Garret tilted his head backwards to look at where the young man sat behind him. "Since my mission was to instigate the chief, it doesn't matter which version I told, does it?"

The band went north—fourteen cloak-and-dagger rebels under the guise of cattle buyers from Albuquerque—hugging the bottom tail of the Sangre de Cristos, keeping their distance from Fort Union to the southeast. They crossed Raton Pass into Colorado and, thirty miles short of Pueblo, cut abruptly west into the maze of canyons in the Wet Mountains.

Deep within belly-high snow and lifting their stirrups so as not to drag, the party soon came upon boot tracks trailing deeper into the snowy pockets of the surrounding peaks. They followed the trail as gradually more tracks joined from other directions like converging streams until soon the once-lonesome trail expanded into something of an inner-mountain highway.

Wood smoke and the steady hum of voices wafted in the breeze. A large boulder-strewn hill rose before them. Here the men dismounted and led their horses and paused on the summit. Below them, inside an extinct lake surrounded by mountains on all sides, lay a city of tents, lean-tos, cabins, weapon racks, clotheslines, washbasins, and campfires. At the center, strung high on a stripped aspen and presiding over everything rippled the stars and bars. This was Mace's Hole.

The moniker extended from the Hole's previous occupant, a Mexican bandit named Juan Mace who used the natural mountain fortress as a hideout and storage place for his plunder. After Mace was killed, the hideout went unused for some years until Southern prospectors from Pueblo discovered it and began using the location for secessionist rallies. By the time war was declared, Mace's Hole had attracted so many sympathizers living in the territory it found itself headquarters of the Confederate army rapidly manifesting in Colorado, a home base for the territory's displaced, censored, and mostly destitute Southerners.

They were the sons of Green Russell, the Georgian who had set off the Pike's Peak Gold Rush three years prior and ushered in a flood of fellow Dixie prospectors. It was an organization that had recently gained leadership, not to mention legitimacy, in the arrival of the new camp commander, Colonel John Heffinger. Via subversive campaigns to rouse dissension and muster recruits, in the five months since his arrival the colonel tripled the population of Mace's Hole to a booming six hundred plus.

Now, to spreading waves of welcome-home cheers, the colonel led the most recent of these campaigns down into the mountain bowl. Behind him, Garret waved his hat.

The camp featured a spectacular circulation of whiskey, and Garret didn't dally in getting stupendously drunk. He remembered singing in a great circle, his arms around a pair of gray-bearded men, reveling in the chorus of bouncy Georgian drawls. But that was about all he remembered.

He awoke the next morning to the sole of Colonel Heffinger's boot tapping him on the forehead.

"Time to go," Heffinger said.

It was after dawn and a few handfuls of men stirred about the camp while hundreds remained asleep in their tents or else shivering alongside small fires. Before the main path climbing out of the camp, seven men, all of whom had likewise been part of the previous day's mission, waited atop their horses. One of them held the reins to Garret's horse and seeing that someone else had saddled his horse for him Garret knew it had not been done out of friendliness or for time's sake.

Climbing into the saddle—the horn jabbing into his sour stomach—Garret hated himself for ever having boasted to the colonel that he knew Spanish. Or that he had once taken a university course in diplomacy, or that he was an expert survivalist, or that war or Indians or strange lands did not scare him, or whatever other thing that might've hopped from his mouth and cemented his place in what seemed now to be every one of Heffinger's outings when all Garret really wanted to do was mill about in the Hole and slug whiskey with the Georgians.

The party wound over San Francisco Pass and down into the San Luis Valley. It was a welcomely warm February day and as the sun rose higher over the flat plains the road grew slushy. They were headed east with, to Garret's knowledge, no main destination when in the distance ahead there sprouted the bouncing, boxy figure of a wagon. The colonel said nothing, merely peered over his shoulder at the others as if to check they were ready, although ready for what Garret could hardly guess.

The wagon rumbled toward them and the colonel waved. A single driver rode atop the wagon's buckboard: an older man with a gray ponytail, his jacket unbuttoned in the day's warmth to reveal a boney and sunken torso. He waved back and Garret watched him shift the reins of the two horses into one hand and then reach behind into the main compartment of the wagon with the other. He brought it back clutching a shotgun, which he rested in his lap. He slowed the animals to a stop.

"Howdy," the colonel said, scanning the empty land around them.

"Howdy," the driver said.

"Mail huh?"

"Mail, yes sir. Nothing more and nothing less." The driver scratched a fingernail against the shotgun.

"Mail from the fort, I take it."

"Why? Who's asking?"

"Just a few very tired fellers that've ridden all the way from Albuquerque and are looking for a respite of sleep and hot food. Relax friend."

The driver eyed the colonel, unsure.

"I said relax," Heffinger said. "We're just asking you to point us in a direction."

The driver looked past the colonel and examined the others behind him; looking, Garret thought, for sincerity. After a moment, he nodded. "All right, stay on this road. 'Bout fifteen miles you'll see—"

It was like a gust of wind had swooped in and struck the colonel, the front flaps of his coat bursting open. The driver raised the shotgun but never had a chance as Heffinger fired the pistol twice into the man's stomach. The blasts swept down the valley and the driver doubled over and went head first to the ground. Garret's horse reared and sent him toppling.

He landed hard on his back, the air socked from his chest. Dazed, he pushed to his seat and saw a flurry of stomping hooves and between them his own horse bolting far off into the sage, its reins dragging. He remained seated, only dizzily aware of his apparent helplessness, while the others dismounted and rushed the wagon and its two horses kicking wildly within the harnesses. One of them, a paunch-bellied Texan by the name of Orton, clutched a Bowie knife and now lifted the moaning driver's head up by his ponytail. Orton jammed the knife into the driver's throat and Garret darted his eyes, back to where his own horse shrunk away in the distance.

"Kelly!" Heffinger yelled. "What the hell happened?"

Garret fought for his breath, his composure. "My horse took off."

"I'll say," the colonel said, climbing up the wagon's buckboard. Behind him some of the men tore through the contents while the others soothed the horses.

"Well forget about it for now. Get up and help."

Garret rose and approached the wagon, his head swimming. "What do you want me to do?"

Orton stood up from where he had been searching the pockets of the driver. In one hand he gripped a mash of folded papers and a billfold. "Here," he said, handing Garret the knife. "Scalp him."

Garret only looked at the colonel.

"That's right. Use that knife to cut the top of the head off. Do it close to the skull so you get it all in one piece."

Garret looked down at the crumpled form at his feet, the two bullet wounds and the opened throat. "But . . . ," he said, little white sparks twinkling in his vision. "But why?"

"Because that's what Indians do. Hurry it."

Now, whether due to a stomach entirely empty except for some undigested whiskey, the gunshots still ringing in his ears, the impact of being thrown straight onto his back, the sudden prospect of sawing off the top of a man's head, the fact he had never seen a man killed, or the memory that only a short moment ago he had been sitting comfortably atop his horse under a warm sun suspecting nothing, Garret found himself sick and wobbling.

"Colonel, I—" he started before a swell of bile surged from his stomach and out his mouth and splattered around the driver's corpse. Garret dropped backward, landing once again on his seat, his legs out in front of him and his palms flat on the dirt. He heard a chorus of laughter and curses soaring from someplace far away. Above him the twinkling white sparks polka-dotted a clear blue sky.

During the following week Garret lost himself in the boisterous, drunkenly oblivious or drunkenly forgetful throngs of Mace's

Hole rebels. Colonel Heffinger, no doubt circumspect himself following the wagon attack, led no further missions out of the Hole.

On the eighth day, Heffinger summoned Garret to his tent. He found the colonel reclined in a camp chair, a table scattered with papers before him.

"I figure you knew we'd be talking," he said.

Garret took a seat across from him. "Yes sir."

"You don't got to do that. Not here."

"What sir?"

"Talk to me in those two-syllable sentences with your head down like you're a dog and me a man with a rolled newspaper."

Garret lifted his face. "All right. I mean, all right *then,* since that makes three syllables."

"You neglected to tell me you didn't have a stomach."

"I got a stomach. Just not for certain things."

"Like for shooting people?"

"Like for scalping them."

The colonel pursed his lips and nodded. "Fair enough. Few people have such a stomach. Fortunately for you, what you lack in stomach you make up for in mouth. You, Kelly, got what they call the power of persuasion. Means you're a good talker, although sometimes I think your talk contains a tad much bullshit."

"That's because when you're planting something you always begin with shit, whether it's a rosebush or an idea."

The colonel laughed. "I don't know if that supports your point or mine. Either way I need your help. There's a special place in war for men with big mouths and weak stomachs, and it's not in the front lines."

"Where then?"

"In politics," the colonel said, shimmying his shoulders as if the word were a pompous coat he had just donned. "Politicians don't do the fighting. They talk other men into doing it. That or they talk them out of it. It's pretty much everything we've been doing so far on these excursions. It's what you did the other night with those Apaches, and what Smith, Carey, and all the other slick tongues I bring along do in the villages. They politick."

"I can do that."

"I know you can. That's why I'm considering you for a job that just opened up." Heffinger picked up one of the scattered papers. His eyes running abstractly over its lines, he explained to Garret, "General Sibley has been in touch with a man in Taos. Not just a man, an emperor by the sound of it. This guy must own half of Colorado and part of New Mexico. This emperor ain't dumb either.

"Are you aware Sibley's marching our way as we speak? Four days ago he took Valverde and soon he'll have Albuquerque and Santa Fe. This emperor knows which way the tide is turning and has apparently worked out a deal with Sibley to keep his land holdings. The part of the deal that concerns us is this Charles Beaubien—that's the emperor—has set a few stages for people like you in the villages along his land grants. He's got a place for you to stay and apparently even an audience waiting to listen."

"What am I going to be saying?"

"Same thing we've been saying. Tell the white folk to come our way. Tell the Mexicans to do nothing. More and more the beaners are hitching up with the federals. Talk them out of it. Here, and take these." Heffinger set down the letter and handed Garret a stack of neatly cut, twine-wrapped sheets of paper.

"What are these?"

"Proclamations from Sibley to the people of New Mexico. They read, 'An army under my command enters New Mexico to take possession of it in the name, and for the benefit of, the

Confederate States. By geographical position, by similarity of institutions, by commercial interests, and by future destinies, New Mexico pertains to the Confederacy.' Duh da duh da da . . ." The colonel made U shapes in the air with one finger like it were a baton and he a composer of some halfhearted symphony. "The rest is all about coming as friends, the evilness of the Union, liberation. You get the picture."

Garret looked over the papers, wondering if the colonel really had the whole proclamation memorized. "You want me to hand these out?"

"That's right."

"But, sir, what if they don't want them? Wouldn't you think, Sibley being Texan and all, that these Mexicans are leaning Union?"

Heffinger snorted. "Mexicans don't lean. They might hate another side more but that don't mean they *like* the other one. We could be Confederates, Chinese, or green bug-eyed Martians. It's all the same to them. This is the stuff you've got to learn, Kelly.

"With Mexicans in this country it doesn't matter who rules the land they live on because they know it's never again going to be them. In reality a large portion of them ain't even Mexican. Last they knew they were Spaniards, whole generations of them scattered here since the time of Coronado. They've lived under the flags of Spain, Mexico, the Union, and some have probably never even known it. All that matters to them is whoever governs their land allows them their little crops and to worship Jesus as they see fit. That is all we're promising now that their flag's about to change yet again."

"What are we promising?"

The colonel leaned forward and tapped the stack of papers in Garret's hand. "Not to *change* anything."

"Where am I going exactly?"

"Ummm." The colonel snatched back the first letter and scanned it. "Here," he said, handing the letter over to Garret with his finger tapping a spot in the middle. "Costilla."

Garret read the letter. "I'm staying with Mexicans?"

"Is that a problem?"

Garret raised his eyebrows. "Not at all."

The next day he returned over San Francisco Pass into the valley. He diverted a few miles into the sagebrush near where the previous week's ambush had taken place and rode the entire day, the sun sucking into the mountains behind him as he approached the village of Costilla. A few dogs roamed the streets. One of them ran up and began yapping underneath his horse's nose and Garret took one end of the rein, leaned over his saddle, and whipped the animal's snout. The dog yipped and darted. Swinging back up Garret noticed a leathery old man standing on his porch, stone-faced and watching him.

Garret pulled up his horse in front of the man. *"Buenos noches,"* he said. *"Sabe dónde puedo encontrar la hacienda de Espinosa?"*

CHAPTER 21

When the knock came (days earlier than he had been told) and Lino opened the door, a young man—handsome and self-assured even in plain clothes—stepped in and introduced himself as Garret Kelly. He whistled as he looked around the parlor and said, "God, you got a nice place for a—" and stopped himself.

Lino beckoned José to take care of the soldier's horse and Garret tipped the boy a coin. Realizing everyone had assembled behind him to watch in alternating faces of confusion and worry, Lino introduced them one by one.

Garret kissed the hands of the women, taking Secundina's black glove in his palm and playfully pronouncing her name "Secundeeeena." Felipe refused to shake hands and set the example for Vivian. It was Cecilia who finally asked the question that was on everyone's mind: "What are you doing here?"

Garret laughed. "How about we call it missionary work."

"Where are you staying?" Cecilia asked.

Everyone, Garret included, turned to Lino.

"Hungry?" Lino asked.

They sat around the soldier at the table and served him a reheated plate of lamb and steamed pintos. They listened spellbound, politely or seethingly, depending on which face Lino surveyed, as Garret spoke mainly of things like the oppression of the Union, the virtue of the Confederacy, Sibley's forthcoming emancipation, and finally a strange story about a

man-eating snake. Unlike Lino, who stole glances inconspicuously, Garret went purposefully from face to face while he talked
as if tightening the spokes around a wagon wheel. The lanterns
burned low.

The rebels appeared unstoppable in the east and now here,
too, as a force of more than three thousand of them led by
General Sibley marched northward through New Mexico. They
had triumphed at Valverde and already the federals were clearing out and deserting Albuquerque just like the Mexicans had
Santa Fe sixteen years prior. But even before Valverde, Don
Carlos had been busy securing his assets against yet another
shift in territorial power.

"How are you sure?" Lino had asked him a few weeks earlier.

"I am *not* sure," Don Carlos said. "But for fear of later finding myself out in the cold I am best sticking my foot in a few
doors now."

"But what if the Texans fail? What if the whole rebellion is
stopped? The federals will see your actions as treason and you
will lose everything."

"*Verdad* but the federals will not see that. All they will see and
remember, should this feud end in their favor, are my many
generous patriotisms and support."

"You are helping them, too?"

"Long before the Texans. I give them land for their forts,
resources, money, and even my people. All for the Union."

"What do you mean give them people?"

Don Carlos had laughed and wrung his hands. "No, not like
that. What I mean is I have presented the federals opportunities
by which to garner the services of our people."

"How?"

"I am giving the federals the same fair chance I give the
rebels. The bluecoats were recruiting in my villages before the
war was even declared. In some, they have built recruiting sta-

tions, stations on *my* properties. Should they win the war, things like that are what the Union will remember of me. Not that I did the same for the Texans. Mind you, Lino, I am not asking you to raise their flag over the town, just to share your house with one of them. That is, share *my* house."

Lino had known about the recruiters visiting the other villages along Don Carlos's grants, promising food and pay in exchange for enlistment. Despite this, Lino strived to remain unmoved and untouched by the conflict that was inevitably stirring emotions in his own town. He knew it was ignorant to do so, yet still he hoped that somehow, miraculously, the war would miss Costilla. But now Don Carlos was not just bringing the war, or at least a representative of it, into Costilla, but also turning Lino's home into a base of operations, a center of propagations as meanwhile, unbeknownst to each other, a Union counterpart to this solicitor would likely be doing the same thing one village over.

Back at the dinner table, a lantern fluttered and died. Cecilia, looking thankful for the excuse, rose to relight it. The light's extinguishing was like a snapping of fingers; everyone at the table seemed to suddenly shift back in their chairs as if just awakening from Garret's spell.

"Well there I went again," Garret said. "Talking my head off. I have been told my mouth is so big there is never space in a room for someone else to open his." He chuckled and gazed about the table, looking to see which one of them would accept the invite. When no one did he said, "*Señor* Espinosa, you have anything to drink? Maybe some tequila or beer for us men, you and me. Oh, and Felipe."

Cecilia began to rise again but Lino told her to sit down. He went to the kitchen and poured two glasses of whiskey and returned to the table, handing one of the glasses to Garret and keeping the other for himself. Garret took a sip and followed it with an exaggerated *"ahhhh,"* causing Secundina to giggle and the soldier to smile at her and wink.

Lino watched, swirling his glass before setting it down. "On Saturday I will arrange an audience in the morada to hear you, *Señor* Kelly. And of course you are welcome in my home. However, it is best you know most people will likely be unsympathetic to your assignment."

Garret waved a hand. "Fine, fine. Just as long as they don't get sympathetic to the other side. Actually, as far as real recruiting goes, I'll mainly be talking to your Anglos. You have some of us here I take it?"

Lino had not been aware of this part of the soldier's strategy, and learning it now brought some relief. "There are a few Anglos here, yes."

"Why not take some browns?" Felipe asked. "Is it our smell?"

Garret blushed. He looked at Lino in appeal but Lino offered no help. Garret shifted in his seat as if squirming back into some composure. "Believe me, Felipe, if smelling good was a prerequisite for joining the Army, the world would be a very peaceful place. No, all I'm saying is we are not trying to fool ourselves. For half these men currently marching upward through New Mexico, this will be their second war. The opponents have changed but the territory remains the same. The hosts remain the same. I'm an Arkansas boy but even I know there's a wound that hasn't healed over this part of the country. Most Mexes are still sore over the Mex War and most Americans are too nonchalant or forgetting of it, which makes the Mexes even sorer. The Texans are the worst, boasting of the Alamo, a battle they didn't even win.

"Try and convince Mexes and Americans to come together now, let alone Mexes and Texans? Not me. If the Mexes want to harp on things over and done with rather than accept the Texans as their liberators, well let them harp. I, of course, exclude you,

Felipe, as well as your father there and—"

"That is my uncle," Felipe said. "My own father got killed by a Texan."

"I'm just saying I got no prejudices is all. The only conflict here is between rebels and federals. Why, I was half raised by our Mex servant, what with my mother dying early and my father being so busy in the Congress. That's how I learned Spanish. I even had myself a real cute *señorita* girlfriend once. Not a day goes by when I don't wonder if my choosing Yale over her was the right choice."

"Yale is a school?" Secundina asked. It was the first Lino had heard her speak since her engagement to Omar Chapa was called off two days ago.

"A university," Kelly said. "Best in the country. It was my father's fault for knowing practically everyone in Connecticut law and politics that I got in there."

"You said you were an Arkansas boy," Felipe said.

"When? I don't think I did."

"Less than a minute ago, when you said that even though you were an Arkansas boy you could still see Mexes were sore over the Mex War."

"I meant that Arkansas was the last place I came from before here. I've lived a few places but when it comes down to it Connecticut is my home."

Lino's eyes went to Felipe. He had immediately disliked Garret for putting him in such an uncomfortable position within his own home and village. Seeing him in this oddly fought battle where Felipe cut at his legitimacy and he in turn, whether he was conscious of it or not, shrunk Felipe toward the point of inconsequence with braggadocio was like watching two personal enemies going at it. Whoever lost, Lino won.

"What is someone from Connecticut doing in the Confederate army?" Felipe said.

"Good question. It's the very reason I left Connecticut and why my father and I aren't exactly pen pals. It's pretty simple. I don't care much about keeping slaves or not keeping slaves, and I don't think any better of a man who has them or doesn't. *Señor* Espinosa has slaves, slaves of another breed but slaves nonetheless, and I think nothing less of him. If states want to go off and be on their own, well then let them I say."

"You are not really willing to die for that," Felipe said. "You are doing it to spite your father."

"I'm not spiting him. I very much respect him, just not his politics. Thing is, last we spoke he was in a rage about me going off west. And so what do I say to him? I say, 'What are you going to do, wage a war against me for leaving Connecticut? Are you going to come after me with a gun just because I want to be independent?' Well of course he says no and to that I say, 'Right, because that would be wrong. Can't you see that is exactly what we're doing to the South?' "

"But by that very reasoning you demerit your whole assignment here," Felipe said. "The Confederates are invading New Mexico. You are in a campaign to conquer a territory whose majority population is a nonaligned third party. Where is the justness in that?"

Garret looked surprised, as well as a little trounced. Further down the table Vivian and José were struggling not to let their gleeful admiration of their cousin betray their cold squints at the soldier. Seeing this, Lino regretted ever wanting to side against Garret and became suddenly desperate the man not give up. Near the end of the table Cecilia and María looked uncomfortable while Secundina glared at Felipe with hate in her eyes. Of this, Lino wasn't sure what to feel. Hope?

"You have me there," Garret said. "At least, I can see how you see. But I will tell you something, let you on to a secret, the real reason behind this campaign and the reason why I myself cannot help but believe in it. Like you Felipe, it at first seemed to me counterintuitive invading a territory of bean farmers and wild Indians when all the real excitement was happening in Sumter and Manassas. It was like Sibley and his Texans were out to settle a score, claiming a territory they had already tried to claim but been denied. So I had it explained to me and they say it's not just New Mexico we're after, it's Colorado all the way to California. New Mexico is just a gateway, an easy first domino to topple into these territories where gold is snatched from streams like handfuls of gravel. This is what they say to me, and I have to agree it makes sense. For wealth like that not only makes men rich; it wins nations their wars.

"Thing is, Felipe, it is much more than about the resources of these territories, it's their essence—their cities and histories and passageways and people—their very existence, that we are after. And even though I bet none of them say it out loud, every one of those men marching up here right now is feeling the same thing.

"Manifest Destiny is not a newspaper invention and neither is it a fancy of a few men like Polk or Jefferson. It's an urge inside the blood of all Americans, even young nobodies like me. The desire for expansion, of spreading your own nation, your own people and decree, from one ocean to the other, runs in our loins like the compulsion to procreate. It can't be helped. It's just there and you crave it. And if Manifest Destiny is an American birthright, then it is in the veins of her secessionists. Is that wrong? Is a poor man that sires hungry sons wrong? Maybe. Or maybe not."

"You thought that was a secret?" Felipe asked. "Any Mexican old enough to remember knows Americans have to take land where they see it. And yes it is wrong. Childbirth is a will of God. War is not."

"Isn't it? What is the Spanish war cry, *'Santiago'*?"

Felipe opened his mouth, but nothing came. For a second, only a second, Lino and everyone at the table could see him trip, stuck with his mouth open until it became too late to attempt a retort. The hesitation had pushed him into free fall.

Seizing it Garret cut him off. "Who burnt Sodom and Gomorrah, drowned the Egyptian army, plagued the Israelites? In whose name was Jerusalem invaded? Be it by His name or His will no one has more to do with war than God. All those cravings that we feel—for another man's land, a woman, revenge, for violence—who is to say that is not God within us? If it were not, why then, when in the throes of those yearnings, do we call out and pray to Him? You are an intelligent man, Felipe, clearly well read for a . . . what I am saying is there's a big difference between being a smart man and being just a thinker."

Felipe was no longer falling. He had hit bottom. He had given up trying to speak. He cast his unblinking eyes on his hands as if perplexed by their very sight.

"Don't you look stupid now," Secundina said, sending everyone around the table slightly back like whatever heat in the middle had suddenly flared too hot. It had been obvious Felipe was beaten and done, but Secundina, before the moment could be extinguished, had taken this vicious stab at Felipe while also, Lino suspected, declaring her last-minute allegiance to the gringo.

Felipe's eyes were suddenly watery and now even Garret appeared speechless.

Lino threw back his glass of whiskey, rose from the table, and announced the evening to be over. He escorted the soldier to the bed they had made for him in Lino's study and as he closed the door behind him he heard sobbing coming from Felipe and María's room.

Lino paused outside the door and listened. He heard María's mechanized little condolences, her *shh shh shh,* and underneath that Felipe repeating—muffled, as if into a shoulder—"That's all I want. That's all I want . . ."

CHAPTER 22

Two nights into his stay, Garret slouched into Lino's rocker with one leg over the other, a glass of tequila in one hand, a fire crackling at his side. When Lino and Felipe, returning from their impromptu meeting of the Penitentes, came through the door, Felipe scowled blackly at him. Lino made no effort to acknowledge Garret.

Garret heard Lino turn into one of the bedrooms and tell Secundina to go clean the morada. A few moments later she appeared and Garret told her not to have too much fun and, as she usually did with him, Secundina flared with color before walking into the cold night without a coat.

He remained in the chair, enjoying the warmth of the fire and the tequila until whispers began to float from the kitchen. Garret rose and slipped into his jacket, sauntered over to the kitchen entryway, and peeked inside to see Lino motioning vehemently with his hands and hissing at Cecilia who leaned against the counter, arms folded. When he appeared, both froze and looked at him. He informed them that Ben Whitely, one of the Anglos living outside of town, had invited him over for a drink and that he didn't know when he would be back.

He stepped into the shocking cold, stuck his hands in his jacket pockets, and turtled his chin into his collar. He felt paranoid walking alone along the lightless road from the hacienda into town, worried that someone might recognize him. His address to the Penitentes earlier that day had not gone well.

Entering their chapel, their morada, finding what appeared to be the entire population of Costilla, minus its few Anglos, crammed in the pews had heartened him at first. It was a relief that he would not have to repeat his message from house to house but knock it out in one big address. It was also encouraging to think, by the looks of it, people might actually be interested in what he had to say.

He had started out reading Sibley's proclamation, highlighting the cruelties of the Union and its oppression of freedom. He warned against those sympathetic to the federals and warned against joining them. He urged them to continue in their peaceful vocations. He promised them amnesty and liberty.

As he spoke, however, Garret grew increasingly aware that no one seemed to be listening. Almost from the start a droning murmur underlay his speech, virtually the entire audience whispering among themselves and viewing him out of the sides of their eyes. By the time he began his story of the snake, the grumblings had increased so much Garret strained to hear himself and turned to Lino sitting off to his side. Lino, his face panicked, stood and raised his arms over the congregation as if about to part a sea. This gesture, this plea for silence, was all the audience needed to open its revolt.

The murmurs surged to an all-out roar. Men jumped up and pointed at Garret, spewing condemnations Garret suspected never before uttered in the room. One of the men, bald and stout, actually began to push his way through the aisle toward him, the others holding him back by his waistcoat as finally the council—that row of hoary men in white robes seated at the front—rose to shepherd the entire audience out the back door, leaving Garret and Lino staring at one another in silence.

For the remainder of the day Garret had sat nursing tequila by the fireplace, brooding. He ate dinner with the women and the two boys while Lino and Felipe attended their emergency meeting. Dinner was painfully quiet and afterward, before everyone scattered, Garret felt pretty sure he had overheard Cecilia telling the children not to talk to him.

The day's events had frazzled him, hurt him. Never in his life had so many people been against him, especially so passionately and in such a confined setting. Looking back, he realized there were a few moments when he had felt actually afraid, none more so than when the muscly bald man had made for him. He wondered what the man would have done had he reached him, to what extent this Catholic layman would have carried out the fury Garret saw in his face.

The whole incident left him not only anxious but lonesome. To be so wholly rejected in a place so isolated and so far from home was to feel rejected by the whole world. Worse, Garret still did not understand why the people of Costilla had so prematurely made up their minds about him. He had suspicions, but nothing certain.

Later however, after brooding on the matter late into the evening, something had occurred to Garret; something that immediately soothed his rancor and replaced it with a cool sanguinity.

Fuck them.

It took a depressingly long time to realize it but what did he care how these people felt toward him? What did he care about these people at all? Garret had never heard of Costilla until a few days earlier, and in a few more he would likely never hear of it again. Its residents were cultish, their way of living founded on superstition and religious rites stupefyingly archaic. They lived in houses made of mud and straw that recalled the fairy tale huts of the three pigs. The kids were dirt-faced, the women undignified by labor and ragged dresses, and the men all filthily uniformed in stained overalls and oily sombreros. They were all suspicious, humorless, irrational, and—with only a few exceptions—astonishingly poor and uneducated. And finally, as Felipe had suggested, most of them *did* smell.

Most of all though, what alternately riled and relieved Garret was the fact that no matter what the Union, the Confederates, or they themselves might think, the Mexican people counted for nothing in this war. Garret had heard other men speculate on this, especially after news of the Valverde battle and the rumored performance by the New Mexico Volunteers. Word had it these regiments of Mexican farmers had fought with such disorganization and halfheartedness the federals were already discussing relieving them of duty. If what was said of how the Mexicans defended their own country was true, Garret could only wonder how they would fight for someone else's.

Thinking of these things as he entered town and walked down the rows of mud huts, lights burning from under the doorways and the moon dazzling on the snow, Garret chided himself for taking the events of that day so personally. Whether his stay in this town was a failure or a success would not only be indeterminable (unless the federals themselves came in and recruited, the Mexican people in Costilla would remain out of the ranks of any army) but in the entire scheme of things, irrelevant.

Even if the people of the town wished to conspire against him, Garret happened to be in the care of their mayor, their Hermano Mayor. While he didn't know much about Lino Espinosa or his benefactor Don Carlos, Garret knew a man following orders when he saw one. And because he could also see Lino valued living in the only home secure against being blown over by a wolf, chances were orders would stay followed.

He veered toward the plaza. Through the padding of his pocket, Garret felt the steely bulk of the pistol hidden against his waist. He stepped as lightly as possible—the snow groaning under his boots—and tried to appear casual. The process left him frustrated. Despite his resolutions on the people of Costilla, Garret still felt vulnerable walking their streets.

The door of the morada was ajar, its dead bolt resting against the frame, and faint yellow candlelights flickered from within. Garret stopped, took one last look behind him, then slipped inside.

She had her back to him and stood at the opposite end of the room near the dark entryway leading into the chapel. She bent over a wooden table and scraped at a dried puddle of wax with a knife.

Garret leaned a shoulder against the wall and crossed one foot over the other, waiting for her to notice him. She wore an old, unflattering dress; its frayed bottom swept back and forth along the cold, packed earth of the floor with each thrust of the knife. Not that it had much to flatter, Garret thought, making out only the faint contours of hip and buttocks. Her shoulders were slumped and somewhat sinewy, the result of too much labor and not enough self-worth. Still, with the exception of the one arm (he hoped never to see it ungloved) she was not entirely unappealing. Garret felt blood rush to his groin.

The knife stopped and Secundina turned her head. She jumped and dropped the knife clattering to the floor.

"Hola," Garret said.

"Oh. Hello. Sorry."

Garret strode to where she stood, picked up the knife, and set it on the table. "It's cold in here," he said, looking absently about the room as if the temperature might be the color of the wall.

"It's always cold in here, even in the summer."

Garret observed Secundina fold her hands in front of her, noting how she concealed the gloved hand inside the other, how she lowered her head. She looked like a child being disciplined. In the past, he had found most Mexican girls to give this appearance, this crippling shyness which appealed to him over those girls unafraid to speak whatever they thought. He had attributed this Chicana reserve to an awareness of ethnic and societal inferiority. In Secundina's case, however, he suspected her self-consciousness around him was something more, and whatever it was enticed him more.

"I was on my way somewhere. Thought you might need help."

"Thank you. I am almost finished."

He glanced down at the puddle of wax and picked at it. "You happen to know what this meeting was about?"

"I never know what the meetings are about. Women are mostly only allowed in the morada to clean it. But I can guess."

"Me?"

Secundina nodded.

"You know, most places I go I'm a popular fellow. At least I think so. I always try to be respectful. I'm an honest man."

"I believe you."

Garret smiled. She was loosening up. This, too, was unlike the other Mexican girls he had known. With Secundina, from the very beginning he had witnessed a woman dying to be free of her self-perception and her father. It was obvious the girl cared nothing for Lino and, given the chance, would relish keeping a secret from him.

From inside his jacket Garret pulled a flask of whiskey. He unscrewed its top, took a swig, and handed it to Secundina.

"Today was a bad day for me," he said. "Very bad."

"Sorry."

"And I have a feeling that its being bad was someone's fault besides my own. Do you know what I'm talking about?"

Secundina took a drink from the flask and winced. She nodded. "I know exactly."

"Who?"

"Felipe."

"What did he do?"

"He went around telling people things."

"Like what?"

"Things that were the opposite of what you tried to preach today."

She held out the flask and Garret took it. He held it, lost for a moment staring at a candle flame.

"Does your father know?"

"He is not my father," she said, a little vehemently. "And I think he does by now. Not that there is much he can do about it. The people have long distrusted Americans, and now our own Hermano Mayor has brought one among us."

"You seem pleased."

"I am pleased you are ruining Lino's credibility." She reached out and gently took the flask.

"Why would Felipe do that to me?"

Secundina had the flask up to her mouth. Again she winced. This time however, something suggested it was not the burn of the whiskey.

"For many reasons," she said, looking past him now as if debating which of those reasons to divulge. "But mainly because he is in love with me."

"In love with you? You're his cousin."

"No, I am not. The two of us share not a drop of blood."

"All right, but what does Felipe's being in love with you have to do with me?"

Secundina blushed and seemed suddenly to revert back to the shy Mexican girl with the downturned eyes. "I would think for the same reason you followed me here."

Garret smiled at the retort and its attestation. He put a hand out and touched her waist. Secundina moved closer to him and put her hand on his, moving it to her breast. He bowed over her and they kissed.

She pulled away, told him to wait, glided to the door, and latched the bolt. She returned to him and took his hand, leading him into the darkness that was the chapel section of the morada. The air inside was somehow cooler, as if preserved in the sheer blackness through which she so assuredly navigated. She slowed and Garret's toe kicked a step and immediately he realized it to be the very rostrum on which he had stood and spoke only hours earlier. The sudden memory of that disaster sent an adrenaline through him that coupled with that which was sexual and already coursing. He felt her hike her dress and sit on the stage's edge, her legs hugging his waist. Garret threw off his coat as she worked at his belt, until, with one hand, he found the back of her neck and cupped it so that her face was up to his and once more he lowered himself to her lips. They kissed a second time, much longer than the first.

When they were satiated, they lay next to each other, their feet hanging off the end of the platform, the sweat of their backs soaking into its wooden planks. Both knew they couldn't linger long, yet neither would rise. In the darkness, with this girl, Garret felt insulated and oddly closer to home. Yet still he could not keep his mind from reeling the events of the day and the reality awaiting him tomorrow. His mind kept reverting to Felipe; how the Mexican had sabotaged him and for what reason.

Garret turned to Secundina and kissed her head. "We will have to do this again."

CHAPTER 23

Vivian rushed around the side of the house toward the door, a blood-red snowball pressed against the swelling cut below his eye. A minute ago he had been shoveling snow in the pastures when the horse he was riding stepped in a prairie dog hole hidden beneath the snow and whipping its head back in an effort to recover, smacked into Vivian's face. Felipe and José had seen the whole thing.

Had he not been reeling in embarrassment and fury as he raced to the house to quickly bandage the cut, he would have paused before dashing through the door, for even from outside he could hear the girlish moans that even at fourteen Vivian recognized to be sex carrying through the walls. But in the few seconds between trotting up the front steps and reaching for the handle, all Vivian thought about was what José might be saying to Felipe.

Vivian burst inside. The sounds stopped and so did Vivian. The air in the house was thick, and as he inhaled it Vivian swept into the present. From a bedroom down the hallway there came panicked whispers followed by a ruffling of sheets. Vivian shut the door softly behind him and crouched behind the sofa.

He heard a thud as two feet dropped to the floor. Vivian still had the snowball pressed against his face and could feel his pulse throbbing against the ice which was beginning to melt and run down his cheek into his mouth. He heard the bedroom door creak open and the feet—too heavy to be his sister's—

creep toward him. They stopped where the hallway met the parlor. Vivian felt the hairs on his neck bristle as if suddenly passed over in a shadow.

"Hello?" the person in the hallway asked.

Vivian held his breath.

"Hello?" The floorboards creaked as the caller shifted his weight. The ice melt trickling down Vivian's face felt warm and Vivian realized it was blood. He remained still until after one more unanswered hello the caller turned and retreated down the hallway. Vivian exhaled, listening first to the relieved report of false alarm, a little bit of laughing, then, gradually, the resumption of cries and moans. Vivian got up, tiptoed to the door, and escaped outside. He spurred his horse into a gallop across the snowy expanse, racing as if the secret might escape him were he not fast enough.

It was only when Lino came into view, whipping angrily amid a churning mass of cattle, that Vivian slowed. Further down the pastures Felipe and José worked on their feet, digging out a long snowdrift piled against a length of the fence creating a potential escape ramp for the stock. Vivian seethed seeing the two working so closely together. It seemed his brother had to be everywhere Felipe was, always bragging and trying to impress Felipe even though he had nothing worth bragging about. He was only eleven after all. What made it worse was that when Vivian told Felipe how annoying José was, what a tagalong he could be, Felipe became impatient. Once he had even declared Vivian to be the annoying one for always complaining about his brother. Secretly it had broken Vivian's heart.

Now Vivian's heart pounded with anticipation. He had a secret capable of devastating Felipe, one that would crush for good his obsession with Secundina and quite possibly drive him to do something wild. It was information Felipe needed to be free, and whatever he did or became with that information, Vivian would be remembered as his liberator.

Avoiding Lino, Vivian trotted up to Felipe and José deep in snow. José's head peeked above the rim. "Why were you running? Hey, you're still bleeding!"

Vivian touched the back of his hand to his face and brought back a thick smear of blood. By now the bite of the air had half frozen the wound. Gripping the reins and the saddle horn in one hand, Vivian leaned over his horse and scooped a handful of snow and scrubbed it over his face.

This got José laughing. "Oh please, let me help!"

Vivian ignored him. Through the mess of white and red in his peripherals he saw even Felipe appeared amused. It had been a long time since Vivian had seen his cousin happy.

He prepared to change that. "Felipe, I have to tell you something."

Felipe jabbed his shovel back into the drift. "So tell me."

"It is something only you and I should know."

"Pendejo!" José cried. "You can't do that, say you have a secret and leave me out of it!"

"Shut up! You are too young to understand it."

"I'm three years younger than you and I'm smarter."

"How are *you* smarter? You can't walk across town without someone holding your hand."

He was referring to an incident six months earlier. José had been playing in the woods east of town with a few other boys when the others deserted him. Despite being only at the edge of those trees with the town visible on the other side, José decided he was lost and panicked. He wandered every direction but the right one, bawling like a motherless bear cub until finally a nearby shepherd had heard the cries and, thinking them to from a dying animal, followed the sounds into the woods with a pistol to end the animal's misery. Since then José had been afraid to even walk through town alone. Vivian probed at this relentlessly, and every time he did the impact on José showed immediately.

"Tell us your secret Vivian," Felipe said, "but get off your horse and come help as you do."

"Come walk with me just a second," Vivian said.

"No, we are the three Espinosa brothers and among us there are no secrets."

"It's about Secundina and the soldier."

Felipe stopped shoveling and looked toward the house. His eyes widened with understanding.

"Right now?" Felipe asked.

Vivian nodded.

"What?" José said.

Felipe stood silent, peering in the direction of the house with the shovel in his hand. Over the years, Vivian had become both jealous and thankful for Felipe's love of his sister. The love inhibited Felipe in ways Vivian wished it wouldn't (Vivian hated that Felipe submitted to Lino) but he sensed it also kept him from leaving, for what else was there for Felipe in Costilla? He was grown up now and still living under the auspices of a man who disdained him. Surely even María could not blame her son for deciding to leave.

Felipe had grown intensely loyal to the Penitentes, even becoming somewhat popular among them ever since warning them of Garret Kelly's design. But the Penitentes were everywhere and Vivian knew Felipe would have no difficulty finding another morada to join. In his heart Vivian liked to believe that it was he, and maybe even the combination of his brother, who kept Felipe from venturing out and making his own life instead of having it made for him, but deep down Vivian knew this to be merely wishful thinking. He knew it by the sad yet determined look in Felipe's eyes when looking at Secundina, by the green kerchief he secretly kept inside his breast pocket, by the partly burned though still-legible note Vivian had found one morning beneath his sister's window. Felipe loved Secundina profoundly, and the love bound him in turn.

Felipe looked like a man who had just stood up too fast, and suddenly it occurred to Vivian that telling Felipe about Secundina and Garret might have been terribly underthought. Felipe glanced at him, turned back to the snowdrift, and resumed shoveling.

"What is right now?" José asked.

"Be quiet," Vivian said.

"Secundina is in love with *Señor* Kelly," Felipe said.

"The soldier?" José asked. "Why do you think that?"

Vivian ignored him. "You already knew, Felipe?"

Felipe kept shoveling.

"How though? Did you see them—"

"I was told it."

"Told it? By who? Secundina?"

"No."

"María?

"You know."

"The Virgin?"

"Yes."

Vivian caught eyes with his brother and for a moment the two shared a rare moment of empathy. The metallic *srink* of Felipe's shovel jamming into the snow's crust sent a shiver down Vivian's back. He remembered the cut on his face and realized he was still atop his horse. Until now Vivian had been poised for action, although what type he wasn't sure. Riding across the pasture, his feelings had been something close to a man running with a torch in hand, looking to scare up a mob. Now he wondered just how far those feelings had been from his actual intentions.

"What are you going to do?" he asked finally, no longer liking the idea of *we*.

"There is nothing that needs to be done," Felipe said. "Kelly leaves tomorrow and none of us will ever see him again. In a week he will likely die in a battle, and Secundina will never know it and it won't matter. She might love him, but he does not love her. He would never come back for her anyway, although he is probably promising that very thing right now. Her heart will be broken but it will recover."

He said it as if it were in the past and already manifested. Feeling sorry now, though he didn't know why or for whom, Vivian dismounted, tied his horse to the fence post, and joined the shoveling.

CHAPTER 24

On the afternoon before he was to leave, with everyone out of the house except for them, Secundina hooked her calves over Garret's thighs, hugged both arms around his naked back, and squeezed with all her strength as he finished on top of her. She felt the muscles up and down his body tense, tremble, and gradually go weak, yet still she held on, afraid to let go and vexed at her failure to savor the moment for her inability to forgo the knowledge it would pass. She let go only when he said, "Aye *chica,* what else do you want out of me?" And even though in certain nonliteral ways it was the kind of question she had wanted him to ask, Secundina said nothing and released him.

He rolled over and lay panting for a moment. Sensing it to be polite Secundina panted, too. Garret sat up, swung his legs off the bed, and reached for his pants. It saddened her how hurried he became each time they were through, although she knew he had to. She hated that he had to.

She rolled to her side, his back to her as he wiped himself with a corner of the bedspread. "Don't leave tomorrow," she said.

"I have to."

"Why?"

"Because I got orders."

Standing up and putting on his trousers, Garret ruffled through the mess of clothing and sheets at the foot of the bed until locating her dress. He snatched it up in a ball and dropped it on her.

"You said there are lots of orders you don't follow. And that you hate the Army."

"Well this is a big order. Just because I hate the Army doesn't mean I'm still not in it."

"Is it all that important you go back tomorrow? Will they even notice?"

"Yes. Put on your dress."

Secundina sat up but did not get dressed. Instead she rested her bad arm in her lap and, as inconspicuously as she could, as if it had just fallen that way, covered her lap with the wrinkled dress. Someone would be walking back into the house at any moment, yet she felt no urgency. Secundina had no fear of being caught. Often she actually hoped for it, imagined it legitimizing their relationship. The very thing had happened only a few years ago in what had been something of a town scandal when a young man, only seventeen at the time, was discovered secreting the bed of a widow. The Penitentes, with Lino at their head, forced the two to marry or be shunned.

Of course, what would Garret, who had been shunned since he arrived and who was leaving tomorrow, care about a threat like that? Besides, that was not how Secundina wanted Garret—scandalized and forced to stay. If she hoped them to be caught it was because she imagined Garret defending himself which, in effect, would mean defending her, too. Surely then it would not be so easy for him to leave without her.

But as things stood, it was easy for him. He had reasons for why he must go, and even though she could hardly argue against them, she was about to nonetheless. She had been preparing for it since their first night together in the morada, if not before. For all she knew, she had decided to do it the moment he walked in their door. She had no hope beyond him, and she didn't know whether to dread him knowing that or to want it. She abhorred the thought of Garret pitying her, yet at the same time could not let him go without knowing how few options he left her.

"Come on now, get dressed," he said but when their eyes met Secundina knew he had read the question she was about to ask. Suddenly his face took on a shade of preconceived exasperation, and in that moment Secundina saw that he too had prepared for this moment and her heart fissured like ice dropped in hot water.

"What if we left together?" she asked.

Garret sighed and took a seat on the bed next to her. "And go where?"

"California."

He shook his head. "Too many federals in California, as of now anyway. Be best to go once General Sibley gets there, which is kind of the reason I got to be going."

"Mexico then. They would never find us. Mexico has no federals or rebels."

"Yes, but it has Mexicans, and an American like me is not too popular with them. Besides, the French rule Mexico now, and I've never been one for them."

"Then you tell me. I don't care where it is or what we do there, only that we leave here together. Won't that make you happy? Can you not be happy with me?" She knew she was guilting him and sensed how unattractive it must be. But if guilt stymied the defensiveness she felt rising in him, then so be it.

He looked at her dolefully and put an unconvincing hand on her thigh. "I *would* be happy with you. I have been this entire time. Actually you are probably the only reason I didn't leave days ago. Those orders I could have slipped and gotten away with, but not these. You got to understand that." He patted her leg and stood up.

She clutched at his pant leg. "Please—"

He slapped her hand away, an ungentle thwack that caused Secundina to suddenly see herself through his eyes—a naked girl, unattractive, bleary-eyed, pitifully attempting to hide a withered arm.

"Quit it," he said, "just quit it! I gave you a good time, so why not leave it at that? I didn't come here to rescue you and I am not the only person in the world who can, so stop being so goddamn helpless."

She felt her lip quiver. She started to cry.

"Jesus."

She couldn't help it. She sobbed uncontrollably. She pulled the dress over her head, wanting desperately to no longer be naked, but her head got stuck somewhere in the cloth and so did her arm. She could still see herself; not from within the damp material against her face but out of it, a heaving half-creature of woman and cotton, agonizing as it fought to become one or the other.

"Jesus," she heard him say again.

He helped her into the dress and with her head finally free Secundina wiped her face. "You idiot," she said. "Can you not see? I *am* helpless. A woman like me cannot rescue herself. No woman does. We are dependent upon men because that is how men want it. What am I to do, wait for a federal to come here and seduce me? You make me happier and more hopeful than I have ever known, and then you denounce me for trying to make it permanent. How selfishly cruel. You leave and get to forget me while I have no choice but to stay and think of you forever. How very, very cruel."

He peered down at her. Secundina looked up into his eyes and saw that behind them he wrestled with what she had said, thinking about, she hoped anyway, what he had failed to consider. Then he turned his shirtless back to her, put his hands on his hips, and shook his head.

"It's not that I'm a bad man, just that I'm not meant to be alone."

"What does that mean?"

He trenched his fingers into his hair, plowing them back to his crown. "It's not even that, it's just that I get to thinking about her so badly that I think it will substitute, even for the moment."

"What are you talking about?"

He whirled around, his hands still on his head like they were the only things keeping it together. His eyes had turned suddenly red. "I never planned on laying this on you."

A stone sunk from her throat deep into her belly—a realization, something she too had failed to consider.

"*Querida,* my darling, I have a wife," Garret said, his arms flopping down. "I got a baby too. Well, as far as I know. I haven't seen it yet."

The stone landed, a little cloud of sand particles exploding around it.

"And I'm faithful to them. Well, not, I mean . . ." He gulped and knelt down on the ground before her, taking her good hand in his. "What I mean is I got every intention of going back to them. I told her I would, and I'm an honest man. Laura's setup is not all that different from yours, you see. In fact, if you had been her, I guarantee—"

In the front room the door grunted open in its frame and there was no mistaking it this time. They both heard it. The door shut and footsteps sounded on the floorboards. Garret scrambled into his clothes and dove under the bed.

Secundina conversely felt a coolness wash over her, a reality that, with Garret's revelation, slammed into focus with the sound of the door. Within seconds she was dressed and taking control of herself and Garret with a newfound assuredness. She made up the bed and ushered Garret out from under it.

She left her room and, as she had hoped, found her mother in the kitchen hoisting two heavy sacks of flour and setting them on the counter before scanning the bottom cupboard for a place to put them. She looked up, startled as Secundina entered the kitchen.

"What are you . . . have you been crying?"

Secundina only shrugged. She moved over to help with the flour, feeling her mother's gaze but refusing to meet it. She knew that even if her mother was concerned she would not pursue it. Too much time had passed without asking how her daughter felt to suddenly ask now.

Secundina picked up one of the bags of flour and bent to the open cupboard. The bag slipped from her fingers and hit the floor on its side, landing with a *poomf* and a burst of flour.

"Secundina!"

"Sorry." Secundina grabbed a rag and started cleaning the mess. After a moment her mother joined her. As they knelt there, rounding the spilled flour across the kitchen floor into a mound in the middle, the front door opened and quickly closed. Cecilia paused and looked expectantly to the entrance of the kitchen. The house was silent.

"Who . . ."

Secundina didn't look up, didn't speak. She just kept cleaning, feeling her mother's eyes upon her.

CHAPTER 25

When Costilla shrunk into a cluster of boxes wavering in the sun's reflection off the snow behind him, Garret steered his horse into an arroyo, dismounted, removed the remaining stack of Sibley's proclamations from his saddlebags, and drove them deep into the snow with his boot.

He rode north, the sun intense, the sky cloudless, and the earth so searing and white he saw it even when he closed his eyes. A spell of unusually warm weather had blown in and Garret felt playful. He rolled up his sleeves, coiled the reins around the saddle horn, and with his horse slogging forward along the empty road, tried to remember that old saloon song he had all but forgotten until recently.

> *"Oh Sara Bella Blue was a girl I used'a do*
> *She grew eleven fingers and wore two left shoes*
> *Her breath smelled'a hell, but that was just as well*
> *Cuz Sara Bella Blue belonged to me and no one*
> *   else."*

He sang it robustly, relishing how good it felt to speak English. He grinned, pleased to have recalled it, and when he couldn't remember how the second part started, he repeated the first. He sang it over and over, each time hoping in vain that inertia would carry into the second part.

Shortly before dusk he arrived in San Luis, a Mexican village much like Costilla with slump-roofed adobes and a communal plaza marking the center. A steepled morada loomed before the entrance to the plaza. Passing it, Garret felt eerily suspected as if it a brother of someone he had wronged long ago.

He came to what had drawn him to the town, a wooden two-story building with tall windows looking eastward to the mountains. Above the building's door frame hung a tar-painted sign reading simply, *MESÓN*. Garret stood his horse and felt in his pocket for the pouch of gold pieces Colonel Heffinger had given him. With few opportunities to spend money in Costilla the pouch had hardly diminished and Garret counted eleven pieces. He meant to spend all of them before returning to Mace's Hole.

The interior of the inn was musty and nearly dark except for the dimming sky pouring ghostly from the windows. A small counter stood before a door in the left corner of the lobby, and to the right four more. At the end of the row a spiral staircase led to a catwalk that ran along five more stacked rooms. Immediately to the right of the main entrance squatted two comfy-looking felt chairs and an end table that half circled a potbelly stove.

Garret rapped on the counter with his knuckles, whistling as he did. A thud followed by coughing, throat clearings, and snorts climaxing into one honking spit came from the door behind the counter. A man whose beard was so long and white Garret wondered if he had just awoken him from a decades-old nap stepped out of the darkness. The man had not bothered to put on a shirt and Garret observed a sweeping cotton-white field covering his chest and belly. He was perhaps the hairiest person Garret had ever seen.

The innkeeper struck a match and held it to the lantern stuck to the wall behind him. "You want a room?"

"You got it."

"Got money?"

"Wouldn't be here if I didn't."

"You'd be surprised how many folks try. Not the beaners either, but men like ourselves. How many nights?"

"Not sure yet. Let's start with just one."

"You want upstairs or down?"

"There a difference?"

"One is on top the other."

"I'll take downstairs."

The innkeeper turned back into his room. Garret heard him *hyaaak* and spit again. He returned and slapped a brass key on the counter.

"Yeah it's the Army men that make me give 'em rooms free. They give me these slips of paper that say I'll get paid some other time but I ain't holding my breath. You an Army man?"

"Nope, miner."

"Pssh! You better keep out of sight of the lieutenant then. He'll try and get you. Tried to get me."

"What are you talking about?"

"Lieutenant Randolph. He's here recruiting for Fort Garland. Having a bitch of a time, too. The beaners ain't much keen on fighting. Neither are the white folks for that matter but the lieutenant still tries harder with them. He's your neighbor tonight, should be back anytime so unless you're interested in giving up mining and fighting for the Union I suggest going to bed now."

"I see."

"That all?"

"What is there to do in town on a night like this?"

The whole cotton field rippled as the man laughed. "Son, if you're looking for piano music and whores, San Luis is not your place."

"How about a saloon?"

"Nope, the Penitentes don't allow one. But if you'd like *I* can sell you some booze."

Garret followed the innkeeper into his bedroom, which was humid and stunk of sweat and soiled laundry and was noticeably absent of a spittoon. The man pulled open the top drawer of his dresser to reveal a dozen-some rolling and clinking bottles.

Garret selected a pint of whiskey and a pint of rum, thanked and paid his host, then went to his own bare-walled, cell-like room. He set his pack on the skinny bed and took his bottles out into the lobby where the innkeeper worked up the stove. When the fire caught the innkeeper turned and without so much as a good night retired to his room. Garret sat in one of the chairs in front of the stove, set his two bottles on top of the end table and, alternating swigs between whiskey and rum, waited for the lieutenant.

He saw the man's shadow through the window first, a horseman passing between the light of the stars. He heard the sounds of hooves crunching in the snow around the side of the inn and leading to the lean-to attached to the back of the building where Garret's own horse was stabled.

A minute later the front door barged open, a burst of winter air immediately barnstorming the room, and in walked a young man uniformed crisply in the blue and white of the Union army, complete with kepi hat. He hugged his saddle against his chest with both arms, and it struck Garret how young he was, surely no older than himself. He wore a boy's attempt at a mustache and goatee, the cold-pinkened skin visible below the sparse fuzz. When he saw Garret, he froze.

"Howdy," Garret said. "You mind shutting that door?"

The man's face became suspicious, a little scared even, Garret thought, and for a fleeting moment he couldn't help but suddenly feel the same. The lieutenant shut the door without taking his eyes off Garret. "Who are you?"

"John Harris," Garret said. "Who are you?"

"You Texan?"

"I'm Minnesotan. Why? Do I look Texan?"

"You got a twang."

"I been to El Paso once or twice but never long enough to pick up their sound. Spent a few years as a boy in Arkansas; maybe that's it. Don't worry though, friend." Garret gave a limp, half-drunk salute to the lieutenant. "I'm on your side."

The lieutenant didn't move. He kept the saddle against his chest as if it a shield or maybe a blankie. "What are you doing here?"

"Same thing I've been doing for three years now," Garret said. "Mining. Well, not at the moment anyway. Right now I'm making a trip to Santa Fe."

"You've been a miner here for three years?"

"You bet."

"Where's your claim?"

"To the north. And I'd tell you where exactly except I consider it a good stake and myself a good miner."

Garret saw the lieutenant's guard loosening.

"You say you're taking a trip to Santa Fe?"

"That's right. Going for a little R and R, a civilized place to blow some money, you know."

"Hell, bud, you're going the wrong direction if you're looking for relaxation and civilization."

Garret managed a confused look. "Why do you say that?"

The lieutenant scoffed. "Ain't you heard? There's a war going on down there! Santa Fe just got sacked by the rebels. By Texans!"

"Santa Fe belongs to the Texans?" Garret asked. The warmth of the alcohol was lightening his body. He furrowed his brow. "Was it a bloody fight?"

"I don't know much about that," the lieutenant said, obviously enjoying reporting major bad news as all people do. "I can tell you one thing, they're in for a huge surprise, and after that there won't be no more Texans outside of Texas."

"Pleased to hear it. You want to put down that saddle and help me cap the night?" Garret shook one of the bottles by the neck.

The lieutenant smiled. "All right. But not for too long mind you. I'm heading out early in the morning."

"I understand," Garret said, shoving a few pieces of wood from the pile the innkeeper had left into the stove.

The lieutenant was walking to his room when he stopped right behind Garret's chair. "I'm Lieutenant Tim Randolph."

Garret twisted in the chair and took the man's hand. "Howdy-do Tim."

The stove, stuffed tight, spit and crackled while the two men slouched back and watched it. They swapped the two bottles back and forth. Garret was pleased to notice that despite the lieutenant's forewarning he nonetheless drank stridently. He observed the man's face slouch as the alcohol warmed it, and he thought how this enemy soldier was probably the best company he'd had in quite a while.

". . . You'll never have to worry about eating either because we feed you squarely. Good food too, I'm telling you biscuits and bacon every morning . . ." The lieutenant had wasted no time in starting in on what was obviously a much-rehearsed speech. Garret abided him for a while, at first curious to hear the other side's tactics, but eventually decided there were far more interesting things he could be learning from the man.

"I'll stop you there, Tim. I got no intentions of signing on with the Army. It ain't got nothing to do with you being a Unioner either. Why just the other day I turned down a feller doing the same thing as you except for the other side."

The lieutenant's eyes widened. "You mean a rebel recruiter?"

"Yep. Met him a couple days ago. He made a good case, too.

Feller named Kelly I think."

The lieutenant gaped at Garret for a second then pulled back
on the rum bottle as if to wash down the information. "Another
one from Mace's Hole I'll bet you anything. We caught three of
them last week not twenty miles from here. Recruiting right in
Fort Garland's backyard! How do you like that? Who knows
what else they up to? Maybe looking to burn another mail
wagon."

Garret took a swig, struggling to appear naive. "What's a
mace hole?"

"Mace's Hole," the lieutenant corrected. "It's a big festering
hiding place in the mountains for rebel sheepfuckers. Really,
I'm not just saying that. I heard they actually fuck sheep there.
All these Southerners from the mining camps grouping up to
surprise us at Fort Garland. Been going on this whole time
right behind our back. Thing is there's got to be so many of
them they almost might've done it."

"There been times by myself up in the mountains I would've
taken a sheep. Trade?"

The lieutenant handed Garret the rum. "Yeah, well whatever
they're doing they better enjoy it because Slough's just brought
a thousand troops from Denver. And the first stop's a surprise
visit to Mace's Hole."

"Is the second stop to meet Sibley in Santa Fe?"

The bottle froze before the lieutenant's mouth and his eyes
narrowed. "How do you know about Sibley?"

"Why that Confederate recruiter I told you about. I didn't
listen to him long but enough for him to mention that name."
Garret felt his forehead going hot as his mind squirmed within
his lies like a boy stuck in too many blankets. He felt panic rising in him as he wondered if the lieutenant was clearheaded
enough to ask why Garret would still be headed for Santa Fe if
a Confederate recruiter had just told him an army of Texans

was currently marching that direction.

His lies this evening had been flimsy, partly because of the drinking and partly because Garret told them spontaneously. He didn't know what his plan had been talking about a Confederate recruiter except to perhaps bait the lieutenant, although that still did not explain why he had mentioned his own name. It would not be the first time a person retraced Garret's words and discovered them fraudulent.

To Garret's relief, the lieutenant nodded and took back the bottle. For the remainder of the evening Garret avoided all talk of armies and wars and led the lieutenant through jokes, crude memories of lovers, and even, at the end, a few revelations of one another's family. He thought of how under different circumstances the two might very easily wind up good friends, how regrettable it was they couldn't. When finally the fire burned low and both bottles emptied down to just a few gulps, the lieutenant abruptly stood.

"Well that's it for me, John."

"C'mon now," Garret pleaded. He lifted one of the bottles and swished it around. "Finish what you started at least."

"Sorry, bud. It won't do for me to be sick on a day like tomorrow." The lieutenant wobbled a bit.

"What's so important about tomorrow?"

"I already told you," the lieutenant said, bringing the sight of an invisible rifle to his eyes. "Reb hunting at Mace's Hole."

Garret remained in the lobby and finished the bottles as the fire died and the interior went dark again except for the light of the moon. He tried to think of what he should do next but in his drunkenness found it to be like focusing on a single thing while spinning in a circle. A real soldier would jump on his horse and set a midnight run to alert his compatriots. Then again, a real soldier would probably sneak into Randolph's room first and kill the enemy. Garret knew he could never do that. A part of him—the part that was lazy and cowardly and probably relied upon far too much throughout his life—wanted to just wait and see what happened. And in the end, this is precisely what Garret decided to do. After passing out in the comfy felt chair, he didn't even hear Lieutenant Randolph leave.

When he did awake, it was to a hard slap on the face that sent him toppling over the side of the chair to the floor. Light poured in from the window. He looked up, rubbing his cheek. The innkeeper loomed over him, shirtless and with a ball of gray rags bunched in one fist that he shook in front of Garret's face.

"You pissed in my chair!"

"Wha—" Garret looked down at his crotch and saw a wet stain. He peeked over the arm of the chair and saw another. "Sorry."

"You're scrubbing it or buying it. Your choice." The innkeeper pushed the rags closer to Garret's face.

"All right, all right, I'll scrub it." His head pounded.

The innkeeper dropped the rags into Garret's lap. "And when you're finished get out of here. Check out time is now."

"Hold on there," Garret said, fishing into his pocket until his fingers found the coin pouch. "I'm buying another night."

The innkeeper looked down at Garret skeptically. Garret pulled out two coins from the pouch and held them up.

The innkeeper swiped the coins from Garret's hands. "No more pissing on things."

When Garret had cleaned the chair he walked hunched over to his room, flopped down on the bed, and fell back to sleep.

When he awoke it was dark. He felt about the room until locating his saddlebags and pocket watch. He took the watch into the lobby and held it up to the window. Seven-thirty. Still early. He went outside to the lean-to and fed and watered his horse, then returned to the inn, banged on the innkeeper's door, purchased two more bottles from the dresser drawer, started a fire in the lobby stove, took a seat in the chair he had not pissed in, and ate the meal of tortillas, pigs feet, and lamb the Espinosas had packed for him.

He kept his socked feet propped up on the woodblock below the windows, alternating pulls of tequila and vodka between bites of supper. It was a magnificent inn, he decided, with great big windows through which he could see almost the entire Sangre de Cristo mountain range. If he squinted and looked to the far southern end of the peaks he could even see the switchback gully that was San Francisco Pass. And on a night like this, through windows like these, he could also see what appeared to be a few twinkling torchlights weaving their way up the mountains and toward Mace's Hole.

The next morning he was again awakened by the innkeeper. "What's wrong with my beds? Why you keep sleeping out here?"

The sun shone brightly through the lobby windows, and Garret opened his eyes to see villagers and mule carts passing by.

"Nothing wrong with your beds. Nothing wrong with your chairs either."

"Except one's been pissed on. Do you want another night? If so you've got to pay now."

Garret rubbed his face and stared out the window for a moment. He pulled the money pouch out of his pocket and peered into it, conscious of the innkeeper leaning over his shoulder. He yanked the pouch closed.

"Well?"

"Wish I could but I'm in a hurry." And with that he gathered his gear from his room and rode off.

The warm spell had not yet broken and the road south had become slushy. There were more travelers out today, lone horsemen and the occasional wagon. At one point, Garret spotted an oxcart sunk into the road's sludge, its driver waving at him for assistance. But just like he had done with the horsemen and the wagons, Garret avoided the oxcart by stepping off the path and sweeping wide. After a while, he left the road completely, cutting east into the untrampled snow leading to the mountains and Raton Pass.

Mace's Hole was disbanded. Those rambunctious Georgians whose only mission in this war was to drink and sing and curse the Union, were all dead or imprisoned. Sheltered deep within the mountains and with hundreds of men all sharing Garret's sympathies, the war had always felt far away in Mace's Hole. Now that it was gone Garret understood his illusion and he missed it. He felt as he probably should have felt more often since the night he pledged his oath to the Confederacy, a little drunk and with a throng of glass-raising Southerners patting him on the shoulders. He felt scared. He felt alone in enemy territory with nowhere to hide since, thanks partly to him, the hideout was no more.

He decided to ride to Santa Fe, to Sibley. As much as he hated the idea of falling into the ranks, and likely as a horseless infantryman at that, Garret had three coins, a day's worth of food, a pistol, an army of federal soldiers marching his way, and a slackening talent for lying. Garret needed the safety of his own numbers. More than that, he needed redemption for failing—out of drunkenness, cowardice or laziness—to warn his fellows at Mace's Hole. If the Coloradoans were riding to Santa Fe to surprise Sibley, Garret would ruin their surprise. He would ride in a hero, an accidental spy that might well save the campaign. He might even get to keep his horse.

By the time he came to where the valley floor met the thrust of the mountains, the sun had begun to set. Garret stopped his horse and studied the forested ascent before him. Somewhere through those mountains lay Raton Pass, and once on that road Santa Fe was a straight shot south; an easy day-and-a-half ride. Time was on his side and he had no intentions of riding through the night. Still, he felt nervous alone in the stretching shadows of the mountains. He felt vulnerable. Federals were not his only enemy in this land. He knew of the depredations of the Indians; had even, to a forged extent, seen it played out in Orton's scalping of the wagon driver.

Something moved in the valley, an animal of sorts. It dragged along less than half a mile away, a queer-shaped figure with its neck pointed to the earth while the head brushed at the snow in search of grass. It boasted no antlers which suggested it was a cow elk, albeit a tall, very lanky one. But focusing on the spine, Garret realized what he had at first thought to be an extra shaggy clump of unshed fur was not fur at all, and suddenly he found himself recalling a memory from long ago. A memory from his boyhood.

It was summer and the carnival had come to Little Rock. Garret and six other boys slipped out their bedroom windows while below them the sisters slept. They had had no money so had circled the carnival's perimeter fence, gawking. Outside the petting zoo fence, the boys yanked weeds and fed those creatures whose names they hardly knew. Only later, long after they were caught and punished, were the boys able to match the animals to their titles in a picture book: llama, ostrich, miniature donkey. They had recognized each animal and now, from that experience, Garret did the same.

"That ain't an elk," he said aloud. "That's a camel."

From out on the valley floor the camel lifted its head as if having just heard its title. Garret saw the arch of its long neck like the handle of a teacup. Even from this distance he could make out the thinness of its high legs, the fat round lips and, most telling of all, the giant hump protruding from its back.

The camel gazed in Garret's direction for a moment and resumed its grazing.

"A goddamned camel," he said again, observing that his horse had noticed the same oddity before them. From his waist Garret unholstered his pistol, cocked back the hammer, and aimed at the creature.

His horse rolled one of its eyes up to the pistol hovering above its head and shuddered. It took a step back in learned anticipation. Garret eased off the hammer and stuck the pistol back in its holster. "Now that I think about it, that'd be like shooting my guardian angel."

Garret, deciding the camel to be an omen, dismounted and led his horse a few yards into the trees where he would be hidden yet still in sight of the camel. He cleared a patch in the snow with his boots and laid down his saddle blankets. He made a fire and ate a few hard biscuits. He lay down under his blanket next to the fire and fell asleep wondering if the camel would be there in the morning. The fire burnt down into coals and Garret fell into a sad dream in which a parade of men barged through the trees and scared away his guardian camel.

When Garret opened his eyes, the sun had risen and his horse was scraping its bridle against a tree. He had overslept. He rose and peered into the valley. The camel was gone.

"A giraffe must have come along and gave him a spook," he said to his horse.

After riding most the day up the sharp ascent of the mountain, the trees suddenly opened and the incline flattened. Garret jerked back on the reins, his heart jumping in his chest. The road before him was pulverized, trampled by hundreds of boots and hooves into a winding slosh of snow, mud, and fresh heaps of manure. An army traveling south had just crossed Raton Pass.

But what army? The sheer number of tracks suggested it to be the federals slinking down from Denver. But why at night? Could it be that some of the men had escaped from Mace's Hole? Hope swelled inside him. Had his comrades made a midnight flight down Raton Pass while Garret slept just a few miles below?

Whatever the case, Garret judged the riders to be a safe distance ahead. If they belonged to Slough's Coloradans, at some point they would be veering east to Fort Union to meet the New Mexico troops and prepare for Sibley. If, however, the tracks belonged to the surviving Southerners of Mace's Hole, they could only be going south to Santa Fe and its occupying Confederate army.

Garret, proud of his detective work, nudged his horse down the road to find out who it was he had heard last night in his dreams.

The pass was slick as it wound down the brush-clotted hills. From the top of a few slopes Garret could see for miles along the flats of eastern New Mexico, each view offering no signs of soldiers except for the bedraggled trail they left behind.

A shout rose up behind him, shattering the afternoon silence. "Hold it! Hold it there I said!" A single rider came galloping around a bend in the path above Garret, pointing at him. Garret identified the blue and white of his uniform.

"Just wait there, friend," the man called. For one panicked moment Garret considered whipping his horse and bolting ahead, but suddenly the man was upon him and Garret realized he had considered too long.

"Hey there, friend. Whoa." The soldier eased back his reins and pulled up so close Garret smelled the man's body odor. His horse wheezed and struggled to catch its breath as if it had been galloping for miles. He was a scruffy old man, squab with a gut that poured over the horn and pushed him far back in a saddle that had slid nearly halfway to one side of the horse. His hat sat cockeyed above a face of white whiskers and silver-lined spectacles. He had a lazy eye and immediately Garret figured the man daft.

The man did, however, have a pistol attached to his waist, and noting this Garret decided against taking him lightly. He considered few things more dangerous than a daft man with a gun, especially one that was by federal decree, whether the man knew it or not, Garret's sworn enemy. Garret turned his horse to hide his own pistol-laden hip.

"Watcha doing here, friend?" the man asked.

"Riding."

"Doing what?"

"I said just riding."

"Riding to where? Boy, where you coming from?"

"I'm a miner."

"Speak up, boy." The soldier's eyes narrowed on him. "How come you speaking so soft?"

"I said I'm a miner."

"Where's all your 'quipment? You tell me now where it is you're from."

Garret tried to appear confused but was conscious of his hands trembling. "Iowa."

"Iowa?"

"Yep."

"Like hell." Suddenly the man snatched the pistol from his hip and swung it on Garret. Garret raised his hands. "You're not from no Iowa. You're one of them from the Hole."

With the gun still aimed at Garret the man twisted up the road and yelled, "Hey Benji, Sammy-boy, I got one!"

Garret moved fast. Jumping up in his stirrups he batted the pistol with one hand and, just as the man's face turned, swung with the other. The blow caught the man in the eye and Garret felt the glasses crunch against his knuckles. The force whipped the man backward, and with his arms swinging wildly in little circles he toppled to the ground. He landed with a splat in the slush and for a moment simply lay there on his back, his one eye a sparkling mess of blood and glass. Then, as if he had just been splashed in the face with a bucket of water, the man jolted up to his knees and began to scramble toward the feet of Garret's horse. It took Garret a second to see why: the batted pistol lay directly beneath him.

The man lurched forward, clasped the gun, and rose. Garret drew his pistol, pressed the barrel against the man's forehead, and fired. A burst of red sprayed across Garret's face. The man, his head a gorge of skull and brains, balanced for a moment until collapsing forward. Garret stared at the body and then at his pistol, turning it over in front of his eyes as if it an obscene object just dropped from space.

He holstered the pistol and wiped his face with the inside of his shirt. Blood stained the snow everywhere and seeing it Garret felt himself go lightheaded. He heard a faint galloping and noticed the dead man's horse running back up the trail. His breath caught in his chest. *Benji. Sammy-boy.*

Garret darted his gaze south. At the bottom of the pass the road became a long and treeless straight shot across the plains. Once on it Garret could ride a hundred miles before finding shelter, a place to hide from Benji, Sammy-boy, and whoever else was about to happen upon this bloody mess in the snow.

He spun his horse and spurred it off the trail, disappearing into the junipers leading west and back down into the valley. The horse struggled through the thick, unbroken snow between the trees but Garret did not stop kicking it for hours. Even when Raton Pass and the slain soldier were miles behind, he continued to check over his shoulder expecting to see a galloping pack of red-eyed bluecoats chasing him, and it was during this ride Garret decided he was done with the Army, that he never should have even been part of it.

He needed to get out of the West completely. He needed to go where the Civil War wasn't. But first he needed to hide. He could only assume whether Benji or Sammy-boy or all of Fort Garland were coming for him. He needed someone to hide him—a place where the Union would never think to look for a white rebel assassin.

The sky already dark, Garret turned his horse northwest until he reached the southern road out of Costilla. He didn't know what he would tell them, but if it really came down to it he could always say it was because of her. This time he would be deliberate. This time there would be no spontaneity.

CHAPTER 26

When the knock came (very loud and very late), Vivian and his brother jumped from their beds to find Secundina in the hall and running to the door.

Garret stood on the steps looking harrowed as Secundina jumped on him, her ankles and arms wrapping around his body.

Vivian stood frozen beside José in the hallway. Behind someone barked, "No! No! No!" and Felipe struck past them, seized Garret by the collar, and tugged him into the yard. Secundina released Garret and pounded on Felipe's back just as Lino emerged followed by Cecilia and María. Cecilia pulled at the flailing Secundina and the two women went to the ground. Garret, who was being pushed back by Felipe, spotted Lino and began to beg.

"Lino, help me. Please."

Vivian, his brother behind him, followed Lino out the door to where Felipe and the soldier grappled. "I'm sorry *Señor* Kelly, but we have already done what was asked of us. Your welcome in my home has expired."

"But Lino, *Señor* Lino," Kelly stammered. "Don Carlos has sent me here, and he is coming!"

Lino's eyes grew wide. "Don Carlos is coming here? Wait, Felipe."

Felipe stopped shoving but did not release Kelly's collar. Cecilia pulled Secundina into the house and Vivian heard her scream.

"There has been a disaster. I barely escaped. I was ordered back here to warn you and to wait for Don Carlos."

"Don Carlos wants to meet me?"

"Both of us."

"About what? What is your warning?"

"It is best, I think, that we wait until Don Carlos arrives."

"Tell me now or you are gone."

"Tell him to let go."

Lino stepped forward and put a hand on Felipe's back. "Release him."

"He's a liar," Felipe growled.

Lino dragged a finger widthwise across Felipe's back, stopped at the spine, and pinched at something. Felipe winced, dropped Kelly, and retreated toward Vivian and José, rubbing at the mysterious pain on his back.

Lino moved closer to Garret. "What disaster?"

Garret brushed at his collar and glowered at Felipe. He glanced at Vivian and José. From inside came the sounds of Secundina's continued struggle.

"Given the severity of what is about to transpire, I should tell you in private."

"He is lying, Lino," Felipe said.

Lino crossed his arms and scrutinized Kelly. "All right, come in," he said finally, and retreated inside with Garret at his heels, the soldier's eyes set straight ahead as he filed past Felipe. The two men marched by Secundina and Cecilia, the women frozen in their tangle of limbs and ripped clothing. Vivian saw his sister mouth Garret's name but Garret didn't bat an eye as he disappeared into Lino's study.

They waited in the parlor for a long time, silent except for Cecilia's one attempt to soothe and reconcile with her daughter, an attempt instantly rebuffed. Secundina kept her eyes on the closed door of the study, and Felipe in turn kept his eyes on her. Vivian could tell he wanted to say something. María simply sat on the sofa with her head down, jumping every time there came a bang from Lino's desk or a muffled exclamation of "Every one of them!" Or "But I only . . ." Or, most audible of all, "God. God help me."

When the two finally emerged their faces were white. Lino looked about the room, at everything and nothing, his mind someplace dreadful. Garret wasn't any better. He appeared visibly frazzled, his eyes bloodshot and watery as if he had been crying. Lino, composing himself, stood before the parlor and clasped his hands behind his back. After years of seeing this stance at home and in the morada, the family stilled and prepared to receive their mandate.

"In two days *Tío* Carlos joins us in our home. Possibly indefinitely unless what is to happen in Taos happens in Costilla. Until then, no one is to speak of any of this, not even to the Brothers. No one is to know that *Señor* Kelly has returned and is once again staying with us."

"It is a lie Lino, you *cabron*," Felipe said. "How do you not see that?"

Lino rushed forward, snatched Felipe by his hair and yanked it back. He held Felipe's upturned face under his, his eyes murderous. "I said no one is to say *anything*."

He shoved Felipe's head aside and whirled on Secundina. "You're sleeping in our room." He turned to Kelly. "And you stay in her room. Obviously, you cannot set foot outside this house. In fact, do not come out of that room unless I say it."

Garret nodded and followed Lino, Secundina, Cecilia, and María down the hallway to begin making up the rooms. Vivian remained on the sofa with his brother and cousin.

"I wonder what is happening to Costilla," he said.

"Nothing is happening to Costilla! It is all a fake," Felipe said.

"They both looked scared," José said. "I don't think they were faking that."

"Garret didn't come here because he is scared for Costilla," Felipe said.

"So why did he?" José asked. "Secundina?"

Felipe leaned forward on the sofa and brooded, peering in the direction of the hallway as he chewed the insides of his cheeks.

"Is it her?" Vivian asked.

Felipe shook his head. "No, it is not her. It's just that he is going to tell her that."

"Does it matter?" Vivian asked. "If it's a lie he's still going to leave without her."

"It does matter."

"Why?"

"Because when he goes he will be taking everything she has to give him. Everything she has to give anyone." Abruptly Felipe rose and made his way through the parlor toward his room. Halfway there, however, he stopped. When he turned around Vivian saw something in his face resembling either sadness or embarrassment, he couldn't tell.

"I almost did not say good night," Felipe said, and returned to the boys and hugged them. "Good night brothers. Good night, good night," he said and with that disappeared finally into his room.

Vivian and José looked at each other, then at the floor. Vivian didn't have to ask, he knew that just like him José could not remember Felipe ever hugging them good night.

Vivian and José took turns keeping watch from their room. About every forty minutes one left his post by the cracked bedroom door, roused the other in his bed, and switched roles. But after four such interchanges it became apparent neither slept so much as waited anxiously his turn to keep watch into the hallway.

A lantern burning dimly on the middle of the floor between them, the two sat cross-legged playing three-card monte. It was a game they played often, especially when sent to bed early. Over the years they had accumulated an impressive collection of trinkets under their respective beds in two buckets labeled V and J with which to gamble. Not that the markings mattered much for by the end of each game chances were the contents that had been in bucket J would now be in V and vice versa. It was a perpetual game meant to pass time rather than accumulate winnings, although often enough some pride was won.

On occasion, Felipe joined them and the two emptied a third of their buckets into his lap. They loved it when Felipe played as it tended to bring out a lightheartedness in him that otherwise seemed so reserved or muzzled by all the troubling things about which he never spoke.

Earlier in the night, the boys thought they heard the front door open and creak shut. Both had sprung to their feet and peered through the cracked door but saw nothing. Since then, everything had been silent except the regular *pertunk*ing of one boy's trinket into the other's bucket. They moved through the game silently and systematically, sliding the cards back and forth across the cool floor, every so often glancing at the door and then at each other in shared anticipation. Despite his attempts at hurting his little brother—his attempts to wedge him away from his cousin—Vivian knew he and José wanted the same things, to grow up the same people, to *companero* the same man. And they could too, Vivian thought, if only his selfishness could allow it.

When the front door creaked open, Vivian grabbed the lantern and snuffed the wick. The boys looked at each other and listened. The thick scrape of boots on wood padded toward them down the hallway, slow and soft. A shadow passed the light seeping through the cracked door. Vivian reached out into the darkness, found José's head, brought it close to his and whispered for him to wait. He rose, inched open the bedroom door, and leaned into the shadowy hallway.

The figure stood one door down gripping the knob. He wore a dark sombrero pulled low over his face and an ashen serape. His spurs were silent as if caked with mud, and protruding from one sleeve of the serape glinted the beautiful steel of the dragoon. Felipe, his hand frozen on the doorknob, lifted his face to Vivian and held the barrel of the pistol to his lips. Vivian reached around to the back pocket of his trousers and pulled out the pocketknife he had snatched from his bucket, but Felipe shook his head and Vivian lowered the blade. When Felipe released the doorknob, it rattled and Vivian cringed.

Felipe backed away from the door. In the darkness all Vivian could see was his cousin's silhouette and the steely shine of his spurs and pistol. Felipe's shoulders began to heave up and down with deep breaths. He glanced at Vivian once more and tipped his hat. Then, leaning back on one foot and bringing up the other, he kicked.

The door exploded off the frame. A shot fired and Felipe clasped his shoulder and buckled back. Somewhere Secundina shrieked. Bursts of light shredded the darkness in the hall as five more shots were fired from within the room and spattered the door frame behind which Felipe hunkered, still clutching his shoulder. Vivian felt José run into his back, shoving him forward into the hallway. Felipe ducked in front of them, and Secundina screamed his name bloody behind them. By the sounds of it someone was holding her.

After the sixth shot, Felipe outstretched his own pistol and followed it into the bedroom. From his position Vivian could just make out Garret curled up in a ball in only his underwear on the floor between the bed and the wall. He worked frantically to reload his pistol and plead with Felipe at the same time. He blabbered, offering money as Felipe knelt slowly on the bed and began crawling toward the cowering soldier. At the edge of the bed, Felipe rose up on his knees, slowly aimed the pistol, and fired. The echo filled the house and reverberated under the soles of Vivian's bare feet. The air thickened with the smell of smoke and powder. Garret screamed in agony. Felipe fired again and abruptly Garret fell silent.

Before he knew it, Secundina tore past Vivian into the bedroom and dove for Garret. She hugged him against her chest and wailed. Then, as if suddenly remembering him as he rolled off the bed to his feet, Secundina sprung up and leapt on Felipe. She clung to his shoulders, ripping at his face with the nails of her one good hand.

Behind him Vivian heard the metallic *clack* of a shotgun breech being slammed closed.

"Felipe, *vaya!*" Vivian yelled.

With Secundina still on his back and tearing at his face Felipe whipped his torso and tossed her onto the bed just as Lino came thundering down the hallway. Vivian turned in time to see José lower his head and ram his shoulders straight into his father's knees. Lino yelped and fell forward as Cecilia came running up behind him. Lino stood and stomped José flat just as Felipe careened out of the bedroom and into the parlor.

"Lino stop!" Cecilia shrieked.

But he already had the shotgun aimed. He squeezed the trigger, and Vivian drove the barrel against the wall. It fired and a burst of dried mud and splintered wood filled the hall, and through the ringing of his ears Vivian heard the front door slam. Lino grabbed him by the front of his shirt. "What are you—"

"The stables!" Secundina shouted, and raced toward the front door.

Lino dropped Vivian and waved the shotgun in his face. "You don't leave this house! You either," he barked at José before sprinting after Secundina. Cecilia followed behind him, pleading with him to stop.

For a moment everything was silent. Vivian looked down at José, crumpled on the floor and crying.

He dashed outside and instead of cutting right toward the stables Vivian went left. Somewhere around the house a horse whinnied and Vivian heard the jingle of a bridle. He cut around the corner to see Felipe swinging atop the waiting horse.

"Felipe!"

Felipe spotted Vivian and spun the horse toward him. "Brother, you need to protect your sister. Do not let her do anything bad. Will you do that?"

"Where are you going?"

Felipe grinned, his mouth like that of a jack-o'-lantern. "Can you keep a secret?"

"Yes. Oh yes."

"Good. Me too." And with that Felipe spurred the horse and vanished into the moonlit valley.

★ ★ ★ ★ ★

Part Four:
The Dedication of
María Espinosa

SUMMER 1862–SPRING 1863

★ ★ ★ ★ ★

CHAPTER 27

It was a windy evening in late June. Dust swirled in the streets of Costilla and blasted against Lino's face. The sun hung over the mountains, setting the few clinging patches of snow alight in pale auburn. A few wagon drivers and pedestrians passed him, some of them tipping their hats. Lino pretended not to notice and trudged with hung shoulders, watery eyes, and sand-grinding teeth home to what was left of his family.

He had just left an uncomfortable meeting with the Hermanos de Luz in which several sensitive questions had come up, including where Don Carlos wanted the new community site and when Lino expected Vivian—who, they reminded him, ought to be preparing for induction—to return from his Albuquerque boarding school. Lino answered in the same way he had invited them: by lying. And when he sensed their suspicion rising as every lie piled higher so that it verged on toppling down upon him, Lino lied one more time and said he was wanted at home. He excused himself early, leaving the rest of the Brothers to no doubt turn their discussion on him.

When he opened the door, Cecilia was seated on the couch knitting. A fire spat in the fireplace. His wife, deciphering Lino's mood, got up and retreated to the kitchen where María was polishing glasses. Lino stood in the parlor for a moment, thinking, then followed his wife into the kitchen. He walked past the two women without acknowledgment and made for the cupboards, opening the one directly above the basin—the same cupboard he had opened the night he met Garret Kelly—and felt around until his fingers gripped the whiskey bottle. It had been years since last he got drunk.

He returned to the parlor and took up his rocker next to the fire. He poured himself a glass and stuck the open bottle between his thighs. He tilted his head back and, relaxing his throat, emptied the glass in one gulp. There had been a time, back in Chihuahua, and even more so during his first years in Taos, when Lino considered himself something of an expert drinker. A professional drinker, that being most of what he did. But since becoming Hermano Mayor he had all but admonished the stuff, allowing only one bottle in his home for visitors or the rare cause for celebration.

He savored the drink's burn down his throat and into his stomach. He filled another glass and downed it like the first. Within minutes his head buzzed and his heart lightened. He drank a third glass.

He wasn't celebrating tonight; he was coping. Coping and preparing. Along the blustery walk back from the council meeting Lino had decided two things: what needed to be done would be done tonight, and that to do it he would have to be drunk. He felt the whiskey spreading its assurance, hoisting his burdens, and numbing his fears. Throwing back another glass, he could hear Cecilia and María in the dining room. He wasn't sure where Secundina or José were, and suddenly felt a hard pang of depression as it occurred to him that in this moment he didn't know the whereabouts of any of his children, bastard or no.

Four months had passed since Garret's death. After the gunshots and the clamor in the stables the servants had come rushing out of their quarters and Lino sent Cecilia to usher them back in. He and José wrapped Garret's body in bedsheets, carried him out the house, and slung him over the back of a horse. Carrying two shovels and a lantern they had led the horse to the easternmost corner of the fence line and dug through the snow to the brown crust of dead grass and then four shallow feet into frozen, rocky earth. By the time they were through, dawn approached and a few curious steers had grouped around the corner fence to watch. Lino and José jabbed their shovels below the enshrouded corpse and pried Kelly down into his grave. When the hole was filled, the two tamped the soil and piled a small mound of stones above it. Should anyone ever ask—one of the Navajo servants, a hired vaquero from town— this was the grave marker of Cecilia's favorite mare.

A horse rests under those stones, not the bullet-ridden body of a Confederate recruiter. It was the first story of many more to come: *The gunshots fired that night were aimed at coyotes in the herd, not at the soldier in my residence. Felipe moved out of my home amicably to begin a new life for himself in Santa Fe; he did not kill a man in the night and run away. Secundina is sick with pneumonia; she is not stewing in her room with something damnably worse. Vivian is in Albuquerque receiving a formal education; he did not steal a horse and chase bareback after Felipe that night. In appreciation for your patience during this difficult time of war Don Carlos has agreed to confer upon the people of Costilla one hundred acres dedicated to communal pasture; he is not, in fact, completely unaware of any such arrangement.*

This last promise Lino had made in desperation, and now he struggled to figure out how he was going to amend it without further damaging his credibility and, worse, that of Don Carlos. After the Coloradoans destroyed the Confederate nest at Mace's Hole, they had marched south and defeated Sibley and his force of Texans outside Santa Fe. Sibley retreated to El Paso, and in the wake of his absence there arose reports of abuse, pillage, and rape in the towns his men had so briefly occupied.

And if Lino's place in Costilla—the trust in him—hung by a

thread before, these reports hacked the thread and sent him into free fall. The Mexican memory was a deep one, one that survived generations and surpassed national boundaries, and the Penitentes would not forget his publicly standing behind a Confederate soldier.

One Sunday shortly after the soldier's death, while standing atop the rostrum of the morada, Lino realized that he had lost his audience; that they would never trust him again. It was in that moment, his words catching in his throat and the people turning their heads, when the sensation of falling began. It was as if the realization sprung a trapdoor below him, sending the air rushing upward and his feet flailing for some sort of ground—all while the villagers watched. That is how, without thinking, he had blurted out the decree about the hundred acres. He said he had personally lobbied Don Carlos for it on their behalf, and hearing it, the faces of the audience turned from distrustful to enthusiastic. The announcement was not going to erase their memories and solve Lino's problems, but it would, for a little while at least, relieve them.

Sliding forward in his chair, Lino pushed another log into the fire with his boot. He called out to Cecilia.

"Yes?"

"Where is José?"

"In his room."

"And Secundina is in hers?"

"Yes, Lino."

Lino filled another glass. Of course Secundina was in her room. She had been in there for months. Four months.

"Everything all right?" Cecilia called.

Lino downed the glass. *"Perfecto."*

He lifted the bottle to his face and shook it. About a quarter remained. Lino lifted the glass and was about to pour when he hesitated, decided against it, and tossed the glass onto the couch where it bounced off the backrest and shattered on the floor. Lino made a gun with his hand, squeezed one eye shut, aimed at the broken glass, and fired. He swung the whiskey bottle to his mouth and didn't stop until it was empty.

He felt more confident than ever. His control had slipped a little since the first three glasses but it was the confidence he deemed important.

As that last pull from the bottle settled in and the fire, the room, everything warmed, Lino became suddenly perturbed. How does Cecilia not know? She has to. Does she mean to keep it a secret? Do they all mean to keep me out of it and hope it somehow never comes up?

Well it was about to come up. Right now.

Lino set the empty bottle under his chair. One by one he called out the names of his family.

Cecilia and María arrived first and asked why he was yelling. Lino told them to sit down. Noticing the broken glass and the empty bottle under his chair Cecilia's face grew somber. José was next and Lino gestured his son over to him and gave him an awkward, one-sided hug squeezing the top of the boy's head before releasing him and directing him to the sofa.

Lino threw his head back on the chair and yelled for Secundina. After a moment she appeared, her hair oily and hanging in clumps, her eyes deep and lifeless in their sockets. She was underfed and her spine protruded through her dress and shawls. It was the first Lino had seen her in years without the long black glove.

The night wind wailed outside. Somewhere a sheep bleated.

"Come here," Lino said, motioning her to his side to face the others on the couch. She looked to her mother. Lino reached behind him and pinched her dress and led her around the chair to his side.

"Papá don't," José said.

"Lift up your dress," Lino told her.

She stiffened.

"Lift it up."

Secundina kept her eyes on Cecilia who suddenly began to weep. She stooped over, grasped the length of dress just before her toes, and lifted. Her belly, centered within her otherwise sunken frame, protruded the size of a grapefruit.

Cecilia rushed to her daughter and Lino kicked lazily after her. His head was starting to hurt and his stomach was turning sour. He blamed this on the emotions, all the drama that had suddenly stuffed up the room.

Quick not to lose his confidence, his control, Lino shot up from his chair and pried the two women apart. He shoved Cecilia back to the couch and whirled on Secundina. "Did you think I wouldn't find out?"

She shrugged.

"That is the gringo's baby."

"The gringo is dead."

"But are all his friends? The war is not over. Not all *rebeldes* are dead and buried in the clay."

"Oh God forbid it!" she cried mockingly. "What if they find my gringo baby? *Mi gringo concepto? Mi prole?*"

"They would not find it as funny as you."

"Fine. Good thing then that it's not the gringo's baby."

Suddenly everything seemed to quiet, even the wind. Cecilia's hands went to her mouth. Secundina grinned, a large, hateful grin. The sickness rose inside Lino.

"Who then?" Cecilia asked.

But before she could open her mouth, Lino pounced. A promise, a deal, had been broken, and he couldn't bear to hear it told. He snatched a fistful of the girl's hair and yanked her head back. He glowered into her rolled, defenseless eyes.

José rushed him and Lino mule-kicked the boy and sent him

sliding. He began to drag Secundina toward the door by her hair but his feet tangled with hers and Lino went tumbling. He landed hard on his side, whiskey and bile instantly rushing up in his throat. He kept it down and lifted his face. Everything was in chaos. Feet stomped everywhere and people tugged at Secundina as Lino gripped the hem of her dress. Everyone seemed to be shrieking, even the sheep. All of a sudden the cries of the animals had filled his brain.

He released the girl and lurched to his feet and, the room spinning around him, staggered to the front door, jerked it open, swayed, and stumbled down the step to the ground.

At first, in his daze, he had thought it to be a dense fog hovering within the yard. But focusing his eyes, Lino realized it was not fog he had stumbled into; it was sheep. A whole flock of them. Their dark faces bleated and poked above the churning white sea of wool. The animals milled about in a tight bunch, and when the wind gusted the whole sea of white seemed to ripple.

The shrieks from inside the house continued to ring in his head but all Lino could think about was how all these sheep had escaped their pens, what they were doing in the yard. Then he saw him. About thirty yards ahead Vivian whipped the animals from atop a horse. The boy didn't appear to notice Lino and merely spun in tight circles, stirring the sheep with the whip.

Lino stood and charged the boy. He did his best to plow through the waist-high flock but the ground kept shifting—a heaving, fluffy white pond—and making him sicker. He fell once, then again, this time crushing a squealing lamb beneath him, and when he stood up Vivian no longer spun about. The boy sat watching him.

"Vivian! Help me!"

Behind him something whistled through the air and Lino had

just begun to turn when suddenly his feet yanked out from under him. He slammed face first into the dirt and dragged backward by the ankles. He rolled to his seat in time to see another figure leap on top of him. As fast as he had appeared the assailant clutched both of Lino's wrists and in a blur spun the free length of the lariat around them. Holding the end of the rope around his wrists, he pulled Lino to a sitting position where he then connected the spindled wrists to the lassoed ankles, working with an adroitness Lino had seen before. The roper wrapped the remaining length of the lariat a few times around both feet and ankles and knotted it.

Lino sucked in a big breath of air and was about to shout when a hand clamped over his mouth. From under his sombrero Felipe drew his face into Lino's and put a gloved finger to Lino's lips. "Silence."

The moment Felipe took his hand away Lino roared. He rolled to one side, struggling at his knots, knowing it to be futile. He gave up, closed his mouth, rolled to a sitting position, and through the milling bodies of the sheep strained to watch.

From inside the house there arose a new commotion, and suddenly Felipe burst from the doorway with his arm around Secundina's waist. She did not fight as Felipe led her around the side of the house to where Vivian sat waiting with the reins of the second horse in hand. Felipe released Secundina and guided her foot into the stirrup. He hoisted her into the saddle then swung up behind her, and just as Felipe turned the horse Lino saw Secundina glance over her shoulder at him. She smiled.

Someone came rushing through the door.

"Felipe!" José cried, bolting past his father. "Wait, wait!"

"José don't!" Lino called after him. "Come to me! To me!"

But José only kept running, pleading for his cousin to wait.

Lino watched as Felipe pulled back on the horse and fumbled with something in his belt. He turned in his saddle and Lino caught the glint of a pistol. Felipe drew it at José and fired. Lino howled.

When he opened his eyes however, José was still standing, dust floating about his feet.

"Turn back little brother," Felipe said. "Stay with your mother."

His mother but what about his father? Lino bemoaned silently. His head spun and he flopped back onto his side. He vomited. It burned as it surged up his throat and out his nose before pooling in the dirt around his neckline. Warm tears rolled over the bridge of his nose. When he lifted his head the riders were gone, a softening thunder of hooves fading in the wind. Only José remained, the dust settling around his boots.

"José, son. Hijo, *mi hijo.* Untie me."

But José never moved, staring off to where they had left him behind.

CHAPTER 28

On a late afternoon two months after Secundina's departure, María retired to her room with the sun still up and, feeling resolute and calm, fell deeply asleep.

When she awoke it was dark and the air outside her window smelled of predawn; cool and misty.

Working quietly she set a rucksack on the bed next to her own—the bed where her son had slept across from her for more than a decade—and filled it with all her belongings: three dresses, a second pair of shoes, a few pairs of socks, a scarf, a box of matches, a Bible, a comb, and a small, metal-plated crucifix gifted her by the women of the *auxiliadora*. She had no money. She fell to her knees on the floor and for the very last time in this hated home said her morning prayers.

Lino snored in the back bedroom as she slipped down the hallway. In the kitchen, she opened Cecilia's cupboards and stuffed all the food that would fit into her sack. The food was more than adequate for her journey. But who knew how much was needed at her destination?

María closed the bulging sack, slung it over her shoulder, walked through the parlor, opened the main door as softly and slowly as possible, and stepped out into what she acknowledged to be the next great period of uncertainty in her life.

A deep and warming blue gradually muted the stars above the Sangre de Cristos. Somewhere a mule brayed, followed by another. Lino would be up soon. María headed down the roadway until the hacienda was out of sight and cut west.

The sun rose, warming her back, illuminating the way. The only sounds were of livestock declaring the morning far back in Costilla. Her ankles felt frail each time her feet bent uneven over a rock and already the pack fatigued her shoulders. Nevertheless, María felt optimistic, more so than she had been in years. She felt guilty and vulnerable, yet liberated and purposeful. She removed her rosary from her pocket and recited as she walked, the Hail Marys soon becoming a trotting melody.

It was a warm day in August yet already many of the aspen leaves had begun to change. Walking among them, María pinched the base of a small branch and slid her fingers to its end, scraping up all the leaves until they were a neat bouquet between her thumb and forefinger. She blew the bouquet and let them sprinkle down before her.

Near dusk she approached the Río Grande. The last she had seen the river it had been late in the season and the water low. Now, the river was high, roaring with summer's rain and the last of the snowmelt.

María stopped at the bank, picked up a stick, and tossed it into the river's center. The stick landed amid a section of whitewater that swallowed it and within seconds spit it out fifty yards further down. She turned and followed the water upstream, looking for a place to cross. She knew she was more than halfway to Conejos but that the greatest challenge of her trek—all fifty feet of it—lay directly in front of her. She had hoped to have the river forded by nightfall, but was now having second thoughts. The air had cooled and no matter how far she skirted it, the water remained deep and swift.

After nearly a mile she came to what, at first glance, appeared to be a bend in the river. But as she neared the spot María found it to be the rounding of a large pool created by one massive beaver dam sectioning the river. The dam lined from both sides of a gigantic boulder centered directly in the river like some dead titan. The river's flow brimmed evenly over the complex barrage of sticks and rocks leading up to the boulder.

María examined the potential bridge and then the sky. The sun had set and the light was fading. Although it had not been in her plans, María debated setting camp and worrying about the crossing tomorrow.

She stepped one foot onto the dam. The sticks compressed and submerged under the weight and the current soared over her ankle. Yet the dam felt sturdy, and with one foot already wet and because subconsciously that was enough to make up her mind, María stepped both feet onto the dam and began to cross.

The current hissed past her ankles and suddenly she felt lighter and frailer than ever. She crouched low for balance, her pack seemingly gaining weight. She stuck her heel out and pressed down on the dam, testing it, before her with each step.

When she reached the center of the river María paused. Back on the bank she had failed to notice the two-foot gap between the first part of the dam and the boulder, the small waterfall gushing through it. She looked behind her, knowing even as she did that she could not turn around. Her eyes caught the pale reflection of the moon rippling in the water.

María faced the boulder, swayed, and leapt. The sticks collapsed. Her palms slapped against the side of the boulder as she dropped and clawed for purchase. It was no use. The current ripped her off the rock and into the icy water.

Her head sucked under. The air froze in her lungs and her heart jolted to the sudden cold. She threw her head and gasped, her feet kicking frantically below in search of the bottom, but the water was deep and it swept her downward.

María fought to keep her head and shoulders emerged but the pack, heavy with waterlog, pulled her down. She splashed and craned her neck to keep her face above the surface, trying desperately to suck in a breath of air before submerging again below and swallowing a lung full of water. She started to choke.

Her arm brushed against something and instantly her hands lashed out. Land. María clawed her nails into it. Dragging herself, still choking, onto the shore, she fought to remain conscious. Slipping the pack off her shoulders María forced herself to her knees, pounded one fist against her chest, and vomited the cold water from her mouth and nose. With every gasping breath little stars flashed and paled before her. Her heart pounded against her ribcage.

Working fast, she yanked open her pack and shook out the contents. With trembling fingers she found the box wrapped within a coil of soggy dresses and dumped them to the ground. She felt around until locating a clump of dry weeds which she used to towel the matches. The stars flashed bright and María felt the shock sucking at her consciousness.

She set the matches down and rounded up tinder, scrounging by the moonlight for driftwood and dead willow. When she had a small armful, she ran back to where she had left the matches and began tepeeing the kindling.

María picked up one of the matches between her thumb and forefinger. She looked at it for a moment, said a prayer, struck it. The match fizzled blue, hesitated, then flared to life. María set it to the dead sage at the bottom of the kindling.

When the fire caught she stripped her clothes and huddled naked against it. For the first hour she shivered uncontrollably, uncurling herself only to fetch more firewood. She built the fire larger and larger until she had warmed enough to stand and the flames licked high above her. Nearby coyotes began to yowl and María peered in their direction and saw eyes on the opposite bank of the river, bright and bodiless, flickering with her fire. The sight filled her heart with relief, not that the river separated her from the animals, but that she had landed on the opposite side.

★　★　★　★　★

Throughout the night María fed and watched the fire, drying her dress, falling asleep only in the early hours of the morning and waking with the sun boring down upon her.

Knowing the worst of the journey behind her, she felt anticipation stirring in her stomach as she dressed and resumed her journey. She had waited exactly sixty days to make her way to Felipe. She had reasoned that gave Secundina time to acclimate, to set the terms of her life with Felipe without María's influence. Lino and Cecilia had allowed her to stay under their roof but, plain to her, only as bait. If Felipe returned, Lino would kill him. At least, this was Lino's promise, and María did not doubt it. Of course, Felipe had not come for his mother, and for this María was both thankful and hurt. It was a lonely feeling, an old woman fording a river alone.

And so she believed Felipe waited for her. She had to believe it. She hoped that by now the girl wanted her help, that late in her pregnancy she felt in need of a mother's presence. But what if sixty days had not been long enough? The last thing María wanted was to find that Secundina had run away. Or, worse, that she lay tied up in some corner, a scenario María could not rule out.

She slowed her pace.

It was early afternoon when she spotted the glimmer of the Conejos River. To the north lay a sprawl of low-set buildings. The town had been rebuilt.

María hopped the flowing, willow-choked irrigation ditch her husband and son had dug so long ago. She avoided looking at the collapsed and charred ranch home east of the river, keeping her eyes on the jacal in front of her, its little chimney billowing smoke. Three small corrals honeycombed the home, one containing a pair of milk cows, the second a few sheep, the last empty but presumably meant for the horses. The giant butte with steep sides thicker with brush and pines than María had remembered loomed behind the hut. She felt something pulling at her back and fought against it.

María knocked on the door. Footsteps sounded on the other side and the door jerked open, releasing a rush of warm, sweet-smelling air. Secundina stood there, her hair long and pulled back in a neat ponytail. A rash covered half of her face—a flaking, mud-colored splotch extending from her left temple to her chin. Her expression was impassive, and underneath a large white chemise her belly bulged round and ripe.

María gestured to the girl's face. "That is *máscara del bebé,* the baby mask. I can help with that."

CHAPTER 29

Secundina, following María's order, waited in the doorway of the jacal out of the sun and watched the old woman wander into the sage. María knelt and broke off two stalks of yucca. "They are like sunburn, those rashes," María said. "I had them too." She stood before the doorstep, twisting the stalks in her hands with her eyes down pretending to examine them, waiting to be invited in, afraid that she would not. The rucksack still hung from her shoulders, the bottom of it damp. María's hair was frazzled and gray with only a few streaks of color, and Secundina remembered when it was colored with only a few streaks of gray.

"Come in," Secundina said, stepping aside and shutting the door behind them.

María set her pack on the floor and Secundina followed her gaze about the room. Late-morning sunlight beamed in through the small square portal holed in the wall, the rest of the light coming from the few candles burning atop the altar next to the portrait of the Virgin. Secundina had awakened cold that morning and her fire still burned in the stove. Two thin beds made of hay-stuffed flour sacks lay beside each other on the clay floor. Through the open doorway leading into the bedroom Secundina could see the corner of her own, doubly large bed. Potted cactus and flowers were scattered on the floor, countertops, and ceiling hooks—tokens of affection. Leaning against one wall was a small arsenal of rifles.

"Where is Felipe?" María asked.

"He and Vivian will be back. How did you know where to come?"

"Felipe helped build this home, and I don't think he ever stopped considering it his. It looks like someone must have kept very good care of it since then."

"He says they found a squatter living here, and that a lot of repairs were necessary."

"Still, a good squatter."

Secundina shook her head, not knowing whether María was really naive or just pretending to be. "I don't think he was really a squatter. Come now, heal me."

She led María to the back bedroom. The space was dominated by the bed, an unmade mess of pillows and rose-colored linens. A handsome, hand-carved dresser topped with a jewelry box and more flowers filled one corner while a small rocking chair sat in another. Secundina sat on the edge of the bed, enjoying the shock on María's face.

"Are those satin sheets?" María said.

"Yes."

"Where did you get satin?"

"Felipe had them for me before I arrived. I do not ask for details. It would make sleeping in them impossible."

María stared at her. After a moment she dragged the rocking chair from the corner and sat beside the bed. The two women were silent for a long time as María snapped apart the yucca and spread its cool blood across Secundina's face. Through the oversized bedroom window grasshoppers crackled and a warm breeze wafted along Secundina's neck.

The rash had appeared almost a week earlier, and when it worsened instead of going away, Secundina and Felipe panicked. It had been the first mutual acknowledgment that for all their new independence they were nonetheless unprepared for this baby. Felipe, who had so far been insistent that his mother would come unaided, began to plan yet another assault on Lino's hacienda. Secundina, terrified of a second attack on Lino but even more wary at the thought of María—a potential judge and advocate for Felipe—moving into her new, unjudged existence where she remained the center of his devotions, had argued for a temporary midwife.

But now that María was here Secundina found she was soothed by her presence and, indeed, anxious. Sitting there at the edge of the bed, the satin about her thighs and María's hands working in the tingling yucca oil, Secundina opened her eyes to see María looking at her belly. She sensed the questions coming, the pressing for details Secundina had so blissfully ignored.

"May I?"

Secundina leaned back and let María slip a hand under her dress and feel her stomach. After a minute in which no one moved, Secundina said, "It is a very calm baby," and sat back up. María pulled out her hand and reclined in the chair with one elbow on the armrest, her cheek resting on her fist.

"When will Felipe get back?"

Secundina shrugged.

"You don't know where he went?"

"I don't ask. All I know is that wherever he goes it's always with a lot of guns."

"And when he comes back it is with things like satin?"

"Sometimes, but not always. Sometimes he comes back with nothing at all."

"And Vivian goes too? With the guns?"

"Yes."

María sighed. She gazed through the window, mournful.

"What did you expect, María, to find him tending crops? To be working in a store? Felipe does not work for things. He takes them. You've seen it."

María frowned. "What have I seen?"

"You've seen him take what he wants with a gun."

When María only looked at her, Secundina rolled her eyes and splayed her fingers out under her chin.

"You mean you?" María rocked forward in the chair. "He took *you* with a gun? I don't see any barrel pointed at you. I don't see you locked in this house with your satin sheets. All I remember seeing, Secundina, is you accepting his hand and climbing on his horse."

"He killed Garret."

"You left with him. You are here now."

"I did not want to."

"You did."

And Secundina knew it was true, that she could no longer deny it. Because for all the anguish she could summon at Garret's death, for all the hatred she could, and did, lay upon Felipe, everything was an emotion mustered to preserve her self-pity, her self-hatred. Alive or dead, there had never been a life for her with Garret, just like there had been no life with Omar Chapa or as an unwanted daughter in Lino's hacienda. But, suddenly, there had been life with Felipe, and she had sensed it immediately that night climbing atop his horse, her back against his chest, his arm around her belly.

María must have recognized the admission in her face. "Why then, if you detest him, are you here?"

"Where else would I be? How much longer would I have lasted in Lino's home, pregnant like I am? And when it was born, when the baby came out with its light skin and its brown hair, how long would it have survived? Not a minute. Lino would have lifted my child still wet and crying and snapped its neck. It would live in a hole out in the pasture, next to its father."

María's face softened. The anger left and her eyes moistened with sympathy, and suddenly, despite her resistance to the woman, Secundina ached for that sympathy, the understanding of a mother.

"You want this child then?"

"I . . . I think I need it."

"And what you said to Lino, that was a lie? You are quite sure it belongs to the gringo?"

Secundina nodded.

María leaned forward and took Secundina's hand and Secundina shuddered and began to weep. It was as if the touch, this transferring of compassion, confirmed all the love Secundina had denied herself, and the remorse for ever having allowed it. María put the hand to her lips and then her cheek and Secundina lifted her arm—her bad arm, her gloved arm—over her eyes as if it a symbol for all the true things she had for so long covered in ugliness.

"You've been a selfish girl," María said, her cheek resting on the back of the outstretched hand, "a blind one to think my son never worked for things. He worked for you. And if he is willing to keep working for you and for that child, I think it is time you finally, wholly, let him have you."

Secundina fell into a long, dream-filled sleep that afternoon and when she awoke it was to the sound of horses trotting into the corral, the clink of saddle buckles sliding off their backs, and the *spraw-spraw* of spurs plodding past her bedroom window. She heard them come in, the reunion of mother and son. A pink hue of a midsummer sunset tinted the room as Secundina lay on her side, watching the moving foot shadows below the closed door.

Felipe spoke quietly. Vivian said nothing. Secundina smelled a stew cooking. She heard Felipe ask about her and María tell him she was sleeping. Felipe said he would not disturb her and

María said that no, he should see her. At this there came no reply, only a curious pause in the conversation, which Secundina imagined to be reply enough. Then foot shadows, the jingle of spurs, and the slow, gentle turn of the door handle.

Reactively, Secundina closed her eyes as he stepped in and closed the door. She could feel his presence, his passing shadow over her eyelids, the room seemingly growing warmer. He stood there, still.

In the previous weeks, every time he had come to check on her, asleep or not, Secundina had kept her eyes closed until he left. Sometimes he looked only briefly, poking his head in and immediately out the door, and other times he looked longer. No matter what though, in every instance, brief or long, Secundina knew that when he looked upon her he wished she would say something; that she was all right, that she would like something to drink, that she was cold, anything. She knew every time he wished she would just open her eyes.

And now she did. "Hello."

He smiled. "Hello."

CHAPTER 30

Two days before Christmas, on a night when the wind howled against the little jacal and towels had to be stuffed below the door, Secundina's water broke. She was standing in the middle of the kitchen when it happened. Everyone was there, prepared.

María guided Secundina into the bedroom while Felipe and Vivian heated water on top the stove and poured it into the tub. Secundina watched from the bed as the two bobbed nervously before the kettle as if doing so made it warm faster. She concentrated on the humor in it, trying to distract herself from the pain. They sprinkled a precut potpourri of flower petals into the tub, and when the tub was full they each plopped in a rosary.

Secundina began to scream. María crouched somewhere below her propped-up knees, offering one piece of optimism and advice after another. None registered. All she knew were the bones in her body, the turmoil at her pelvis. She could feel the contractions coming, would instinctively try to repel them until she could not and they clamped and seized her. With each one she squeezed her eyes and saw macabre visions, a cave of flesh being torn apart by a freezing tunnel of light. Bones bending to the extreme like a wishbone at the verge of snap. She screamed until her throat hurt. She thought she saw María pop her head up and grin. Then came another contraction, this one more terrible than any of the others, followed by a great and excruciating churn of her insides. She felt herself go numb and saw a God-sent blackness accumulate over her eyes like ink dripping onto a pane of glass. Secundina grew docile, comfortable. She closed her eyes. She saw relief.

Her eyes shot back open and all of a sudden her cheek stung, and she realized María had just slapped her. Her consciousness began to return and as it did she felt a fury building, not because she had been slapped, but because she had been denied her dark relief.

But then, slowly at first, it occurred to her that the pain was gone.

She heard the shrieking and María calling for the tub. She saw her stand, holding him in her arms, the body squirming, bloody and steaming, and even in her weak, dreamy state Secundina could not mistake the chestnut of his skin, the small little tuft of black atop his head.

She sat up and looked at him in pure marvel. Vivian rushed in with the first tub and set it below the bed. María tested the water with a finger and then gently released the wailing child. She took a knife from a cloth on top the dresser and cut the umbilical, tying its shorter end into a neat nub on the baby's tummy. Felipe stood frozen and scared at the doorway.

María smiled and shook her head in disbelief. She looked at Secundina, then to the doorway. "Come here, Felipe," she said.

Later that night, the room finally beginning to cool and a lone candle burning on the dresser, Secundina lay sleepily on the bed, her hand on the belly of her dozing son.

Across from her, with the tip of his finger clasped in the baby's fist, was Felipe. He rested with his elbow under his ear, stroking the back of the tiny fist with his thumb.

The boy coughed and wriggled, his eyes still shut below the wool hat his grandmother had knitted for him weeks ago, and Felipe leaned his face forward and kissed his forehead. He looked at Secundina and, when her eyes gave the permission, he kissed her, too.

CHAPTER 31

They named the child after his two grandfathers: Domingo Ignasio Espinosa. A week after his birth, the family—Felipe, Secundina, Domingo, María, and Vivian—walked a mile through the snow to the resurrected village of Conejos and its morada.

They were greeted by Hermano Mayor Lionel Gomez—a short, whiskered man with yellow teeth who knew the story of the burnt ranch home to the south and the death of Ignasio Espinosa and for that reason seemed oddly and overly fond of Felipe—as well as the visiting priest from Abiquiú who had come for the occasion. Before a full congregation, the priest married Felipe and Secundina and then immediately baptized their child. Vivian sat in the front pew next to María, brooding.

When they had come to Conejos their life was one of danger, freedom, and fast wealth. It was the life he had never predicted for himself but one he had always wanted. It was a rebirth.

They had started easy, ambushing single riders on desolate roadways. They pillaged saddlebags and pack animals. They took gold, silver, guns, ammunition, jewelry, portable foodstuffs, a giant pair of spurs (which Vivian wanted terribly but said nothing as Felipe attached them to his own boots) and everything else of worth. Then, holding the reins of the victim's horse, they would depart, leaving the poor fellow bound, blindfolded, and horseless.

After a few such assaults, Felipe and Vivian (with six guns between them now instead of just Felipe's treasured dragoon) set out on a midnight mission to a horse ranch outside Ojo Caliente. With night as their cover, they filtered out twenty-two head from the corral and, stopping along the way to alter the brands, rode deep into the early hours of the morning to Santa Fe.

At auction, they kept their hats pulled low and their bandannas high. All around him Vivian recognized traders and sellers from his multiple trips there with Lino but never spotted the man himself. Their eyes looking cool but their nails digging into their palms, the cousins accepted the prices offered, refusing to linger and haggle, and by the end of the afternoon were long gone.

They rode further north than Vivian had ever ventured, swiping eighteen brandless horses from a ranch in La Garita, Colorado, and driving the remuda in one long push over San Francisco Pass into Pueblo where they sold every one.

Their saddlebags bulged with cash. Felipe said little the whole ride back to Conejos and in his silence Vivian knew the burden of his cousin's thoughts. It hurt him that Felipe could not be content; that this dangerous, free and wealthy life with his cousin was not enough. But there was nothing Vivian could do about it. He had known of the discontent all along, known that all Felipe thought of was Secundina and that soon enough they would be returning to Hacienda de Espinosa.

For the remainder of the winter, Vivian did his part to serve the family. He helped with the care of the baby and the keeping of the home while at the same time allowing himself to consciously fall into the background. He did not begrudge Felipe and Secundina's happiness, their newfound love for one another. He did, however, feel diminished by it.

Sometimes Felipe would try and get Vivian to hold Domingo, but always Vivian refused. It was not that he disliked the baby; quite the opposite. He loved the child intensely. Rather, to pick him up, to physically be what kept the infant from the ground, inferred to him an acceptance of some rite he could never disavow. The concept seemed childish even to Vivian, who knew he vowed himself to the baby simply by loving him. Yet, for Domingo's parents to actually watch the embrace would be for them to witness an act he could not deny, a memory he could not retract should he ever leave the home which, more and more, he thought of doing.

For two months following the child's birth the family lived by the law. They kept two cows and purchased food and materials in town with what was left of the Santa Fe and Pueblo horse sales—adventures that now felt like lifetimes ago to Vivian.

On a warm, muddy day in March, he made his decision. Felipe was shoveling manure from the cow pen when he approached him. Vivian stopped at the fence and put his hands in his pockets. "I think I am going to go."

Felipe stopped shoveling but waited to turn around. "Where?"

"I don't know. Maybe south. Where there are people."

"There are people right here." Felipe turned around and set a foot on the shovel.

"Not for me."

Felipe frowned a little, looked down at his feet, and twirled the shovel in the muck. "What is it you don't like about what's here? Domingo?"

Vivian opened his mouth but before he could answer Felipe changed the question.

"What is it you want to *do* Vivian? It is a simple question, for it's obvious you aren't content with farming and ranching, that you are restless. So tell me."

"I don't know."

"You are bored?"

Vivian nodded.

Both were quiet for a minute. Suddenly, Felipe jammed the

shovel deep into the muck, hoisted a sucking glob of mud and manure and, to Vivian's surprise, heaved it. The glob sailed across the pen and splattered against the shoulder of one of the dozing cows. The animal startled with the impact, spun halfway around and threw her head back. The sludge oozed down her flank and leg.

Felipe grinned. "To tell the truth Vivian," he said, his feet making shlopping sounds as he stepped toward his cousin, "and you cannot tell anyone this, but I get bored, too."

Felipe climbed over the fence and scraped the filth from his boots on the bottom rung. "Damn if we are not bored and running low on money. And damnit too if one doesn't remedy the other."

A two-day ride northeast found them high in the mountains at the summit of Sangre de Cristo Pass. It was a steep, switch-backed road veined with rivulets of running snowmelt and strewn with loose rocks that teetered under their horses' hooves, causing the animals to pitch forward and snort with vexation. It was midday and sunny, and Vivian felt giddy.

He rode behind Felipe who slumped in his saddle and held the reins loose in one hand while the other fiddled and scratched at the Spencer repeater balancing across the pommel. They had not encountered a single traveler in their long ascent and Vivian grew increasingly anxious at the sight of his slouched cousin, feeling like someone who had dragged a friend to a disappointing party. He felt responsible for Felipe's apparent boredom, like the whole venture was on the verge of being called off, and as they rode Vivian strained to think of something to talk about that would not seem irrelevant or contrived.

He was rescued when, reaching the summit where the road became straight and level for half a mile before dipping back out of sight for the descent, the ears of his horse flicked forward and a hundred yards ahead two mules approached pulling a wagon.

"Up there, a wagon," Vivian said. Felipe slowed and lifted the brim of his sombrero. Vivian could see the driver seated atop the buckboard, looking their way. He knew they had only a few more seconds before they chose against it or else lowered their brims and raised their bandannas.

"You see that?" Felipe asked.

"The driver?"

"He has one leg."

Vivian squinted. Although he couldn't yet make out the man's face there was no mistaking the odd empty space beside his right thigh, the knotted end of trouser dangling off the front of the seat.

Felipe twisted in the saddle and faced him. "Well?"

Vivian's heart started to race. "I say yes."

Felipe turned around, lowered his brim, and worked the bandanna up over his nose. Vivian did the same and with his thumb popped open his holster.

The driver, less than fifty yards ahead, must have figured it out because suddenly he dove backward into the interior of the wagon. Felipe spurred his horse, his pistol already drawn, and bolted for the wagon with Vivian speeding behind him. The mules froze.

The driver wormed back out gripping a long double-barreled shotgun, but already it was too late. Felipe pulled back his horse directly underneath him and clicked back the hammer of his pistol just as the man turned to look into it.

There was a moment in which no one spoke. Vivian positioned himself beside and slightly behind Felipe with his own gun leveled. The driver was gringo, hatless and half bald with little gray tufts above his ears and a snowy, short-trimmed mustache. He showed no fear peering down on Felipe, only some regret as slowly he dislodged the shotgun and held it above his head.

"Keep your aim, Vivian," Felipe said. "Cock your hammer and remind him there are two of us."

Vivian clicked back the hammer and the man's eyes darted to him. Felipe shoved his own pistol back in its holster and held his palm up to the driver, motioning with his fingers for the shotgun. The driver sighed and handed down the gun.

Felipe swung off his horse and disappeared to the rear of the wagon, leaving Vivian and the driver silently staring at one another. Vivian kept the pistol steady, pushed the bandanna higher up over his nose. He didn't like the way the man stared at him. It was as if he was scrutinizing Vivian, searching his eyes for something recognizable. Even more unsettling was the man's apparent ease at having a cocked pistol aimed at his face and all his cargo about to be pilfered. The man leaned forward atop the buckboard and rested an elbow on his one knee, tapping his fingers patiently against the wood, a smirk on his face.

Vivian listened to Felipe fumbling with the door of the wagon, then the groan as it swung open. The man's smirk stretched into a grin. From behind the wagon, Felipe muttered, *"Puta madre."* The driver began to chuckle.

"What is it?" Vivian asked.

Felipe stormed back to them, the shotgun swinging at his side. He glanced at Vivian only briefly but long enough for Vivian to see the fury in his eyes.

The driver shook his head as if he could not believe the hilarity of it all. He said something, motioning as he did to Felipe and toward the rear of the wagon. Although Vivian could not understand a word the man said he understood the message: If you really want it, take it.

"Felipe, what's in the wagon?"

Felipe glared at the driver, his eyes becoming smaller above the bandanna puffing in and out before his mouth. "How do you think he lost that leg?"

"Huh? I don't know. What's back there?"

"Oy, muchacho," Felipe said, banging one fist against the side of the wagon. The driver, still smiling, looked down at him. "How that?" Felipe pointed to the knotted stump at the man's thigh, and when the driver only tilted his head, Felipe stepped up on his tiptoes and patted his fingers on the stump. *"Donde?"*

The smile left the man's face and it was silent as he gazed down at Felipe and considered his answer. Felipe lifted up both his palms and shrugged.

"Veracruz," the man said.

"Sí, Veracruz." Felipe took a step back. *"Vamos.* Off."

The driver, scared now, appealed to Vivian. Vivian switched the pistol from his tiring arm to the other. When still the man did not move, Felipe raised the shotgun and pressed it against the driver's good leg and Vivian braced for the report. But Felipe only prodded, and finally the man began to push himself up. The driver stood, balancing himself with both hands on the top of the wagon, lowered himself to the edge, spun around so that his one leg dangled, and slid forward until dropping the last few inches. He landed and a book flopped out of his back pocket. It landed on its spine and splayed open. The pages were blank, and stuck between them in the gutter was a pencil. Felipe crouched over, picked up the journal and stuffed it in his back pocket. Now it seemed to Vivian that Felipe was the one smiling.

"I'm going to look," Vivian said, climbing off his horse and leading it toward the rear of the wagon. Whatever torture Felipe had planned Vivian decided he must first witness the reason.

The door hung open, and even before he swept around it Vivian smelled the odor. It was a stench that made his eyes water. Even the horse seemed offended, pulling back on the reins as if it too was wary to see. Vivian tugged the animal forward and froze before the open carriage.

His shadow sent a small cloud of flies buzzing about the dim interior. One of Vivian's initial suspicions had been that the wagon was a mail freight, containing nothing more than valueless letters and a few medial gifts. Peering in however, Vivian saw no sacks bulging with envelopes and neither were there crates stacked one on top the other from end to end. Instead, the interior was utterly empty; hollow except for the single wooden coffin lying loose and askew on top the planked floor.

He spun away, unable to breathe the sunbaked, rotten air wafting out of the door and coughed into his arm. *"Puta madre."*

"Like what you see?" Felipe called from out front.

Vivian retreated further but still was unable to get the smell out of his nose. It coated his throat, something festering and green and furry like moss on a boulder. It seemed more than just rotting flesh. Vivian couldn't imagine what there was to it but somehow whatever was in that coffin reeked worse than any corpse should.

He returned to where Felipe held the shotgun lazily at the driver's waist, the driver balancing with one hand on the wagon. Vivian thought of how the man had smirked as Felipe fumbled at the door and then laughed after it squeaked open. Observing the grim suspense in the man's face now, the downturned eyes like a dog that knew it was about to be beaten, Vivian was suddenly all for whatever Felipe had in mind.

"Hey, *Señor* Veracruz," Felipe said, cracking open the breech of the shotgun to check the shells and then snapping it shut. He motioned the gun down the roadway. *"Diez segundos."*

The driver looked at the road, the long, straightaway stretch before dropping out of view, and back at Felipe. Felipe ground his boot into the mud as if setting his grip and raised the shotgun to the man's face.

"Waaan . . . dooo . . . treee . . ."

The driver set off down the path, hopping wildly with both hands pumping at his sides.

Felipe dropped the shotgun into the dirt, dashed to his horse, and untied his lariat. He jogged after the driver, the lasso swinging above his head, and about ten feet behind him Felipe let the loop fly. It sailed up over the man, loose and wide, and by the time he turned his head the loop was already over his waist and dropping. Felipe jerked back and the lasso zipped tight around the thigh and suddenly the man was in the air, his leg yanked out from under him and his arms flailing.

He landed shoulder first with a muddy *splooch*. Vivian erupted into laughter at the sight of the man's face, his confused expression as he turned around to see Felipe right behind him, the rope swinging through the air.

Felipe, still holding the end of the rope, turned to Vivian, lifted the bottom of his bandanna and grinned. Behind him the driver pulled himself up with half his face dripping with muck. The sight of that combined with Felipe and his jack-o'-lantern smile made Vivian start to choke with all the laughter barnstorming his throat.

The driver freed himself from the loop and took off back down the path. Felipe made a big display of bending over and stretching his legs, shaking his arms out, and cracking his neck. Then he charged. He closed on the man, leapt into the air with both feet out front and rammed his heels into the driver's back. Both men came crashing down, Felipe on his seat and the driver hurtling forward for a few desperate hops before spilling into a face-first slide.

Vivian was wheezing, stuck in that rare moment of hilarity in which no sound comes out and all air is pressed from the lungs even though the lungs keep pressing. He forced himself to suck in a breath and howled it back out. He couldn't help it, even as an alarm began to rise from somewhere within him, telling him to stop, that the scene was growing ugly, that his laughing was what encouraged it.

This time the driver did not rise immediately and so Felipe, after sneaking another look at Vivian, stalked up to the face-planted driver, lifted him by his shoulders to his one foot and, once he was steady, kicked the foot back out from under him. The man crumpled to the earth.

Something was happening; something changing inside Felipe. Vivian could sense it. He saw it in how spastic his cousin suddenly moved as he scrambled back to the fallen driver, clutched at his collar, and hauled him again upright only to shove him back down. He saw it in his hands, the tendons that were strained and the fingers that were splayed and curled inward as if about to claw his victim to death. And despite his uncontrollable laughter, Vivian desperately wanted it all to stop. Something beside a craving for air had begun to balloon inside his chest.

Fear.

If they were to kill this man they should kill him now. Vivian pulled off his bandanna and ran to where Felipe was again picking up the muddy driver. "Felipe stop!"

Felipe, one hand on the man's scruff, whirled on Vivian and instantly Vivian realized his mistake. Felipe glowered at him, the driver still clutched in his hands.

The driver seized on it: balled up a fist and swung. It was a hard hook that caught Felipe firm in the mouth and sent his head snapping back. Vivian froze in his tracks.

Felipe turned his face slowly to face the man and Vivian saw the driver's face retreat from defiance into dread. Felipe wiped his mouth with his forearm, inspected the blood on it, and spat. He pressed the forearm against the man's cheek and wiped it, leaving a bloody smear.

"Get your lasso," Felipe said.

"What are you—"

"Get it."

Vivian turned and jogged back to his horse. He grabbed his lasso and when he turned around Felipe had the driver by his foot and was dragging him back toward the stalled wagon. The man, caked in mud, began to yell and punch at Felipe's grasp around his ankle but Felipe paid him no attention, pausing only to pick up his own rope from the road.

He dragged him past the two mules and dropped him beside the tongue of the wagon, setting a foot on the man to keep him still as he coiled the rope in his hands. "Come here," he said to Vivian. "Help me lift him."

Vivian approached Felipe and then hesitated. The driver stared at him, frowning.

"Idiota," Felipe said, yanking Vivian's bandanna back over his nose.

The driver fought with a renewed fervor. They rolled him to his belly and snaked the two ropes under him, then hoisted the man up to the underside of the wagon tongue where they strained to hold him as they rapidly wrapped the ropes over and over until the driver was snug and each rope double-knotted. He squirmed in his restraints, his face less than a foot from the rocky earth. The man kept quiet but Vivian noticed tears falling into the dirt. The mules craned their necks back and forth and fidgeted in their harnesses.

Felipe stepped aside and reclaimed the shotgun. "Haf good ride, *Señor* Veracruz," and with that he held the barrel of the shotgun above the mule's ears and squeezed both barrels.

The animals hurtled forward, tearing into a run that sent the wagon and the man hanging off its underbelly careening from side to side over the rocky path. He shrieked, the wagon wheels striking a rock and bounding into the air. The wagon landed and the tongue flexed down and Vivian saw the man's face smash into the mud with a toothy *"ack!"*

Vivian and Felipe began to laugh, especially when they saw they had neglected to close the rear door of the wagon, which now swung wildly on its hinges. As the wagon rattled and bounced the coffin bashed into the walls, sliding back and forth. The wheels struck a second rock, the driver howled, and the coffin catapulted out the wagon. It crashed and rolled, splintering apart in a mini explosion of shattered planks and nails, and within the debris Vivian caught a glimpse of the corpse somersaulting end over end before coming to a stop in a limp ball among the wreckage.

Now he was sucking air all over again, at last feeling like it was all right to be laughing. In the distance the mules kept running as they approached the descent down the pass and Vivian saw the rear wheels strike a rock and kick up into the air. Then the wagon dipped down out of sight, the screams of the driver trailing off down the mountain.

Vivian pulled off his bandanna and looked at his cousin. He expected to see a huge, triumphant grin, and was surprised to see that Felipe appeared startled, his eyes squinting down the road.

"What is it?"

Felipe began to run.

Vivian started after him but immediately slowed when he realized where Felipe ran. He watched his cousin sprint up to the wrecked coffin, his feet stopping immediately before the crumpled corpse.

"Felipe, I would not touch that—"

Felipe dropped to his knees and gripped both hands on the corpse's shoulders. He turned it and peered into its face.

"Mother of God."

CHAPTER 32

María was asleep on her cot in the front room when the knocks came. At first she thought it part of her dreams, but when the raps grew louder and more urgent the curtain between dream and reality reeled apart and María gasped. Dull moonlight shown through the drawn sheepskin over the room's one window, but otherwise everything was dark. There came more pounding and María rose, feeling blindly about her until she located the pistol Felipe had left on top the Virgin's shrine. She pressed her face and the pistol close to the door, the cool metal bristling the small hairs of her temple.

"*Quién es?*"

"Lionel Gomez." Lantern light shined through the door panels.

"Just you?"

"Just me."

She unbolted the door and opened it to reveal the small gray figure of Conejos's Hermano Mayor. He held a lantern in one hand and the lead rope to his burro in the other.

"You frightened me."

"I apologize."

"We were asleep."

"We?" Lionel leaned past María's shoulder. "Has Felipe returned?"

María studied him. "How did you know he was gone?"

"So he is back?"

"No."

Lionel sighed and looked over his shoulder into the star-cast sage, for what María did not know. In the distance to the north the few firelights of Conejos twinkled.

"Come in, Lionel. Tie your burro and tell me everything."

She fell back into the home, leaving the door open and inserted a few blocks of kindling into the stove. The days were growing warmer but still the nights lingered near freezing, and with the baby in the house María made a fire every night.

Lionel stepped in, removing his sombrero and shutting the door behind him. María heard Domingo murmur in the bedroom behind her, followed by a rustling of sheets. There came the soft thud of feet hitting the floor. Lionel, hearing it too, looked embarrassedly to María and María assured him with a wave of her hand. She walked over to the bedroom door and said through its crack, "Stay in there Secundina, it is not them." Then she took Lionel's lantern, set it on a shelf beside them, and motioned for him to take a seat on Vivian's empty bed while she took a place across from him on her own. She kept her voice low, conscious of the sleeping baby and his listening mother.

"What is it Lionel? What has happened?"

The old man seemed almost ashamed, his silver hair matted and his hands rotating the brim of his sombrero around and around between his knees. "I do not mean to worry you."

"I'm already worried, and my imagination is making it worse. Tell me."

Lionel sighed again and twisted at his brim, and as he relayed the story not once did he lift his eyes from the hat. "This morning a wagon traveling from Pueblo to Taos was held up on top of Sangre de Cristo Pass. The driver was a horse trader from Santa Fe, a well-known man who had fought for the Americans in the Mexican War. He was driving alone when he got ambushed. He was, I understand, tortured. Another traveler came across his wagon halfway up the pass, the mules at a halt in the middle of the path. The driver had been tied upside down to the wagon tongue, his face having been dragged for more than a mile down the mountain."

María felt her hands begin to shake and clenched them.

"Yes, well, he did not die," Lionel continued. "He came very close, was very mangled, but after they loaded him into his own wagon he made it to Fort Garland and told them what happened. And this, María, is what is bad. The soldiers asked if he knew who did it. He said yes. He said Felipe and Vivian Espinosa."

"How? How does he know?" María demanded, defensive as if Lionel was the accusing driver himself; as if she too did not know deep down that the driver was right. "The boys have no American acquaintances."

"He said he recognized Vivian when he pulled his bandanna down, that he had remembered him as Lino's son from horse sales in Santa Fe. He also said that Vivian called Felipe by name."

María closed her eyes and rubbed them hard with her palms, vague splotches of color exploding in her vision. Something bumped against the closed bedroom door and remained pressed.

"So what happens now? You came thinking they might be here. How did you hear this story?"

"I came hoping they were here so that I could warn them. I was informed of it by two Penitentes from Costilla."

María dropped her palms from her eyes. "Costilla?"

Lionel checked a smile. "I, too, was awakened from my sleep this night. I received a visit from two men by the names of Pedro Guadalupe and Adan Hurtado. You know them?"

"I know of them."

"They ran their horses all day from Costilla just to give the story, and already they are running back so as not to be suspected. They say earlier this evening during an assembly in the morada, an assembly in which every member was present, a gringo marshal accompanied by four federals from Fort Garland surprised Lino and demanded the whereabouts of Felipe and Vivian. At first he claimed Vivian was in school somewhere and Felipe had moved south, but when they told him of the wagon driver and threatened to arrest him too, Lino, with everyone in witness, admitted they had run away. You and Secundina, too. Unfortunately, he also said that he thought you were here, in Conejos."

From inside the bedroom Domingo whimpered in his sleep. The footsteps shuffled away and the cries subdued. María stared at the bedroom door, feeling suddenly nostalgic. It was a dreamy, sorrowful nostalgia in which she felt the loneliness that had hung within the home those two years when it was just her and Felipe; the loneliness that she had felt for the boy who was without brothers and a father. It was a feeling all its own, and it seemed to belong to this home. Stranded mothers and their sons.

María wiped her eyes. Lionel leaned forward on the bed and lifted her hands in his. "You understand, María, that you have many friends, that Felipe has many friends. Was this not shown tonight with the riders from Costilla? Do I not show it now? Do you not know that your husband is remembered? That what he did here, what he died doing, is remembered, and that he is loved for it? Do you not know, María, that your son is loved the very same?"

But María's eyes were not on him. She wasn't thinking about herself, or Ignasio, or even Felipe. She was back in time, enfolded in the feelings of loneliness, uncertainty, and helplessness that seemed ingrained in the mud and wood of the house like a scent from long ago.

★ ★ ★ ★ ★

She spent the remainder of the night in Secundina's bed next to her daughter-in-law and grandson, the hours passing slowly with neither woman sleeping but whispering to each other intermittently in the dark—whispers of strategies, guilts, fears— until finally the gray tints of dawn cracked through the window and María rose, scooped the stirring baby in her arms, and carried him into the front room to allow Secundina some sleep. There the two spent the morning, Domingo in a cocoon of blankets on María's cot, his eyes drifting about the ceiling while María remained statued in front of the window.

By noon Felipe and Vivian had still not returned and neither were there signs of the Army detachment purportedly searching for them. When Domingo, hungry, began to cry, Secundina emerged from the bedroom, her hair disheveled, her eyes sunken. María had been anxious all morning, but somehow the sight of the girl compounded her troubles, the memories of the long night and of all that impended not just over herself but above the young mother and her child. When Secundina picked up Domingo, María told her that she would be outside doing laundry.

The day was brisk and overcast, and carrying the basket of clothes at her hip María felt a few tiny droplets of rain on the back of her neck; the first of the season. The coolness of it, the presage that seemed contained in these maiden droplets, elevated María. They felt refreshing after the stuffy jacal, and although she sensed the rain might become worse, María decided to walk beyond the running irrigation ditch to the river.

She had to search along the bank for a clearing in the willows that had grown dense over the years. Snapping the limbs under her shoes, María set the basket in the dirt and dropped to her knees at the water's edge.

Looking up from the wet dress in her hands she gazed at the

charred spot across the river where once there had been a cabin, the spot where Ignasio had died. She felt a wave of fury toward her son suddenly rush over her, the furious culmination of all the blame she had withheld from him all those years ago, back when she had insisted that he was only a boy and that he had known no better. It was the same fury she had so steadily and painfully accrued for her husband in those years following his return from the war. The years in which she had helplessly watched vindictiveness fill Ignasio until it became all that he was and all that he willed to his son. All that Felipe remembered of him. It hurt María to believe that, but she did.

Gazing across the river at the few black remains of the burnt cabin while anticipating a band of armed soldiers galloping toward her at any moment, María couldn't help but see Felipe as the misguided boy he had never stopped being, the misguided boy who now had a son of his own.

Twigs cracked within the thicket. María shot to her feet. About twenty feet up the river, the tops of the willows were being pushed apart as something, or someone, forced a passageway through. María watched, waiting. The willows became still except for a few limbs fanning backward and bouncing a little as if being sat on. Something metallic clinked on a rock.

María dropped the wet dress into the basket and peeked outside the edge of the thicket. "Felipe?"

The clinking stopped. Everything was silent except for the quickening raindrops spattering against the muddy bank. María forgot her anger. She wanted to run to him. To embrace him.

"Felipe?" This time the fanned limbs sprang back up. Boots sloshed through water and the willows on the opposite side of the river—the side María stood on—pushed apart.

She began to run to him and then stopped. The man burst forth from the thicket, hulking and nearly toppling forward when the last limbs whipped back from off his shoulders. He steadied himself, turned, and María stared into the face of a monster.

At first she thought the face was covered with hundreds of black flies bunched wing to wing in clusters like on a windowpane. But looking closer she realized they were blisters. Tiny chocolate-colored and flaking pustules funneled upward from his bare neck and engulfed his face and ears. They swarmed over his hands, teeming and thick, some so tightly clustered they seemed to be bubbling outward, blister upon blister, and even though María had never seen a victim of the affliction, she knew its symptoms. The man had smallpox.

A heavy beard, brown and filthy with debris, hung to the man's sternum and was capped by a stylish mustache with wavy ends twisted and greased. He wore a ratty beaver pelt hat that had been knocked aslant in the reeds, an oily ponytail wound with rawhide. He was not as immense as María had first thought but instead hunched under a backpack the size of a small horse. The pack bulged about his shoulders and over his head. Tin cans, pots, and utensils, along with what had to be half-a-dozen metal traps hung from chains with their jagged mouths clamped shut like crocodile skulls. Tied to the very top of the sack was a muzzleloader, and holstered to the man's hip a pistol.

At first the man appeared frazzled by his escape from the willows, then surprised at the sight of María. Then, a yellow grin seared across the blistered face, and something foreboding lit within his eyes. Slowly, but not so slow as for María to miss it, the man crouched, poised with his feet spread and his hands ready.

"Dime ont été m'appelez-vous?"

María's heart began to pound. She stared at him.

The man repeated the question then raised his eyebrows. "You speak the Spanish. *Si?*"

"Sí."

"Good. I speak Spanish. At least, *un peu,* a little."

But he must have noticed her repulsion, for the man's eyes crossed to look at his nose.

"Is good," he said, scrubbing his palms against his face. The sound of his calluses brushing the flaking blisters was like sand grinding leather and María observed pale flecks of skin snow down onto his collar. "See, it is good. I am *pas contagieux.* I am no more sick. I am no more get you sick. Healthy, see?" He did a little jig, hopping from one foot to the other, the pots and traps swinging and clanging behind his back.

María turned and began to walk back to the house, forgetting the basket of laundry and keeping her eyes fixed before her. The house was a two-minute walk from the creek, one minute if she ran. She heard the pots and traps jangling after her.

"One moment, please *señora,*" he called, panting as he slowed and began to walk at her side. He smelled coppery, like the dried blood of a skinned carcass.

"Really *señora,* I am good. I am all healthy. I can no more get you sick."

"That is good, I believe you." And she did. She could see the papules were dead, and that the man acted in a way no one in the throes of smallpox could. Most likely the scars would be there the rest of his life. No, what propelled María to the house was the way the man moved, how he carried himself, how he had stumbled out of the thicket and pivoted and the shadow that fell across his face upon seeing her. It was something almost instinctive, predatory. She knew the look, the stance, the crouch like some spider about to pounce. She had seen that shadow over men's faces her whole life; those men in Chihuahua banished from churches and expelled wherever there were children, men whose presences could always be felt, lurking and leering. She had known of such men here in the north, too.

The rain started to fall harder and the air turned colder. The trader kept pace with María, attempting to get in front of her. María quickened her stride with every attempt.

"*Señora,* what is your name? You call for a Philip? Who is Philip?"

"Felipe. He is my son. He is inside with my husband."

The man looked to the jacal ahead of them, to the empty horse corral. From the corner of her eyes María saw the yellow grin spread again between the bulges of black pockmarks.

"This Felipe, he is no help to you? He is, maybe, helping somewhere different?"

"He is with my husband in the house."

"Just the two?"

María did not respond. She was halfway there.

"You are like *mon femme,* my wife. Or like my mother, maybe, because of age. But no important, for they are the same women, always at the house while their men are in different places doing their work. Working *por la famillia, oui*?"

They were almost jogging now and María caught a glimpse of his arm snake out behind her and she felt his calloused hand riding gently along the small of her back. He slid it up and down but María did not run. She bore it, knowing that to run would be to confess herself, to tear away any hesitation that might be holding him back.

"I have food *señora.* Maybe you are hungry? Maybe you and Felipe and your husband are hungry? I have rabbit. Do you like rabbit? Maybe you have things for stew? Maybe Felipe likes stew?"

She was almost there, only a few more feet, a few more seconds. The rain seemed suddenly even colder and María realized it had become sleet. The jacal was a dark blur through the icy sheets, and the blood-smelling man with his hand on her back and the bouncing pack above his shoulders seemed a lumbering hunchback.

She spotted a pitchfork leaning against the corral. She began to reach for it but suddenly the man snatched her dress and yanked her back as if she weighed nothing. He wheeled around on her, his back to the house, and began to unsling his pack.

María screamed, "Felipe help!"

For a moment she thought it had worked. The man froze with a hand on the shoulder strap and the other arm curled around her. He did not even twist around. His ears perked and his eyes darted side to side.

Then the door swung open and María's heart crumpled. There stood Secundina, her eyes wide, the baby clutched against her chest.

The man turned and looked at the girl and smiled. María leaned to the fence post and clasped the pitchfork.

CHAPTER 33

What the coffin revealed sent Vivian and Felipe off the trail to the south and high into the mountains. Felipe spurred his horse until blood seeped from both flanks. They ran their mounts without stopping through alpine forest and jagged spires. When finally night fell and their horses neared collapse, they ducked into a boulder field and spent the night huddled and shivering without a fire.

Vivian did not sleep. He thought back to earlier in the day, after Felipe had run up to the shattered coffin and began grappling at its corpse.

The body belonged to that of a soldier, adorned in slick black brogans, gold-trimmed trousers, belt, and a crisp Richmond gray jacket that boasted two starred medals over the heart. With his forage cap knocked aside the man's long blond hair tangled about a head that was small and bird-like. He was obscenely decomposed. Dark flaps of skin hung off his forehead and over his eyes. His nose was gone, not severed as if with a knife but more like it had been frostbitten and fallen off. Black ridges of cartilage lined the moon-white nasal cavity. A huge chunk of green-black cheek had peeled away and hung at the jaw, revealing a clenched mouth of otherwise normal teeth. Vivian observed similar lesions along the man's hands and parts of his exposed calves.

"He is plagued, Felipe, get away."

But Felipe had ignored him. His hands fumbled at something

below the corpse's side near his hip, and only when Vivian leaned a little closer did he see the object of Felipe's fixation. Sheathed to the man's hip was a saber, appearing much like the swords Vivian had seen on innumerable federals prowling the valley except for the handle, which was composed of a deep black pearl.

Felipe retracted the blade, bowed and golden. He turned the handle to view its other side.

"It is," he breathed. "Dios. It *is.*"

Something had been etched on the sword's blade just below the hilt. At first Vivian thought it was an X carved crudely into the steel. But when Felipe held the sword perfectly upright Vivian realized that the marking was a cross.

Felipe held the sword high above his head. The sun flared off the steel and Vivian squinted. He watched Felipe stare up at it in awe and felt something akin to the jealousy he had felt watching Felipe interact with José.

"We have to go, Felipe. Look at our horses."

He pointed further down the road where both horses had strayed far off the path and were now grazing the still-brown foliage of last autumn. But Felipe only stared at the shimmering blade as if it some miracle.

"Felipe, we need to hurry."

Felipe snapped aware and darted his head from one end of the pass to the other, then back to the sword. "Yes, *vamanos.*"

Hours later, when finally they had stopped to make camp below the slanting boulders, shivering under their coats, stomachs growling, again Felipe held the blade up to the sky and marveled.

"The sword looks very light," Vivian said.

"It is."

"Also very sharp."

"Yes."

"Can I hold it?"

Felipe looked at Vivian, revolving the upturned blade near his face, and after a moment handed it over.

The blade was indeed surprisingly light, and upon sliding his thumb an inch down its edge Vivian brought forth a neat cut of blood.

"Do not get that on the sword," Felipe said.

This seemed stupid to Vivian, and he couldn't help but feel a little hurt by it. Nonetheless, he wiped his thumb on his pants and gave the sword back to Felipe.

"Where do you think it was forged?" Vivian said.

"I don't know. Maybe by the Americans. Maybe by God."

He turned the blade over and over in his hands, careful as he slid his fingers down its edge. He looked at it lovingly, yet also, Vivian thought, somewhat apprehensively; like a mother holding her newborn while at the same time thinking of all the ways her life was about to change.

He must have fallen asleep, for suddenly it was dawn and Felipe was shaking him by the shoulders. Vivian opened his eyes to see his cousin's face in sheer panic.

"It is an omen! A harbinger of something bad! Something terrible. We have to go! We have to hurry!"

Vivian rubbed his eyes, stood, sauntered to the edge of the camp, and unbuttoned his pants. He looked into the sky and observed a ceiling of gray predawn clouds closing toward them from over the San Juans.

"Vivian! What are you doing?"

"I'm pissing."

"That's not what I said to do!"

"Well it's what I'm doing." Vivian shook and spat. "Tell me this omen. Where do we have to go?"

"Home," Felipe said, jumping atop his horse, the saber swinging at his side. "Home and we cannot stop. I feel the devil already on his way."

CHAPTER 34

Secundina was feeding Domingo when she heard María scream. She ran to the door, the baby tight against her, swung it open, and instantly realized her mistake. The creature's mouth was yellow, and when he peered at her through the pouring sleet he grinned. María struggled in his grasp, and with his head turned clasped the pitchfork and raised it.

The man howled as the three dull prongs jammed into his side. He released María and María bolted. The man spun like a dog after its tail, staring in disbelief at the pitchfork dangling out of him. Secundina swung open the door and stepped to the side as María raced toward her. Behind her the man tugged out the pitchfork, flung off his pack, and began to fumble at his waist.

María burst through the door and behind her the man raised the pistol and fired. María sprawled into the room past Secundina, sliding into the stove and sending the boiling kettle of water atop it splashing to the floor beside her. Outside the man lowered the gun and started forward. Secundina shrieked and slammed the door.

María did not move. A dark hole oozed blood out the back of her neck, just below her skull. Secundina bolted the door and scoured the room for a weapon until locating the single-shot pistol atop the shrine and retreating into the back bedroom. She steadied herself on the edge of the bed facing the front door, placed Domingo beside her, and raised the gun.

She heard his footsteps crunch through the grass, then fists pounding against the wood. "Open the door, beautiful. I have rabbits," he called. "We make rabbit stew, *señora.*" He kicked the door and it rattled against its hinges. "Maybe you like rabbit stew and can cook? Maybe *bébé* likes rabbits. Or is *bébé* Philip? Felipe?"

As he continued to kick, the door splintered at the bolt. Secundina rested her dead arm under the sight, squeezed an eye shut, and peered down the barrel.

The door burst open and smashed against the wall. Secundina squeezed the trigger. There came a loud pop and a burst of smoke. The man stumbled backward through the haze. Secundina didn't wait to see him fall. With her ears ringing she snatched the baby and crawled across the bed to the window, ripped away the skin curtain, and slid Domingo out the small rectangle. She held him pinched by the cotton shoulders of his little gown and let go. He dropped a foot and splashed on his bottom in a puddle of sleet-crusted water. Secundina then squeezed out and plunged after him, landing in a half somersault before scooping up Domingo and taking off at a sprint.

The sleet stung her skin and poured down the back of her dress, and the icy puddles and cacti mounds grated her bare feet. Through the sleet she saw nothing except the dark butte towering before her, the butte Felipe had called Ba'ga Ka'ni. He had told her there were hiding places in the butte, dark places tunneling deep into the earth. Brush and pines moated the butte, and once through it was going to be a desperate scramble up loose rock fields and more cacti and abrupt drop-offs.

A shot sounded and Secundina felt the bullet buzz past her head, whiffing her hair. Then another gunshot and this time Secundina lunged forward, lost Domingo, and slid onto her face in the mud. The bullet burned hot in the middle of her back, searing metal lodged tight between her muscles. Still on her stomach she flailed behind her, feeling warm blood amid the freezing sleet.

Somewhere the baby cried and Secundina lifted her chin, her back flaring in agony, and saw him writhing on his back a foot in front of her. She forgot about the slug in her back and tried to drag herself forward but her fingers merely scooped back mud. She heard boots splotching up behind her.

She turned just in time to see him leap and dive on top of her. She felt the air heave out of her lungs, a rib crack. Her whole body seemed to be sinking into the muck. He pinned both of her arms together against her spine with one immense fist. Secundina smelled blood and noticed it smeared along the monster's blistered hand.

The man sat up and scooted back to her hamstrings. She lifted her chin again and concentrated on Domingo thrashing on his back and flailing with his tiny arms to wipe the accumulating sleet from his eyes and nose. She felt the bottom of her dress fling up, his scaly hand snake up between her thighs, fumble at her underwear, and suddenly his fingers were inside. She screamed at the pain, the thrust ripping at her inside walls. He thrust and thrust and then fell back down on her and began to unbuckle his pants.

"Domingo," she whispered. The baby writhed in the sleet just above her.

"*Putain bébé*," he spat, and abruptly his weight lifted. He set a heavy foot down on her spine and reached for the baby. Secundina felt awareness rush back, found her breath, and howled with more pain and horror than she had ever known. His fingers reached for the tiny neck.

Something whistled in the air and landed with a hard *thuck*, and the monster flung both hands behind him. An instant later a shot boomed in the distance, then another buzz, another *thuck* and the man stumbled forward with two holes in his coat. Blood seeped from the holes, the first one high in his spine and the second one lower near his waist. The monster dropped to his knees and lay spasming in the wet ground, his face inches from Domingo's. She saw the monster's mouth open and close, open once more and then stop.

She crawled to her child, the slug in her back like a rod pinning her to the ground and numbing all parts of her body around it. She clawed in the mud, snatched at fistfuls of wet rabbit grass and pulled herself to him. His hand went out to her and she took it, reeling him into her bosom and brushing the freezing sleet off his body. She hugged him against the crook of her neck.

Secundina closed her eyes, pressed her palm against the baby's chest, felt his heartbeat, and concentrated on nothing else: the bullet inside her flesh, the slain monster, the footsteps racing toward her, the voice that shouted her name.

She recognized the voice, and hearing it brought her peace. He was late, woefully late, but not too.

She heard his familiar, purposeful stride as he rushed up to her. She wanted him to see her like this. It would be her final, ultimate shun, something she prayed—as she prepared to die—would forever haunt his dreams.

She felt his feet straddle her. She heard more gunshots, a whole volley of them seemingly miles away. And then he was taking the baby out of her arms.

Secundina's eyes shot open. "*Bastardo!* Give him back!"

But he only held the child in his arms, hunkering his head against some new battle across the valley.

"*Bastardo!*" It came out a whisper. She felt her life draining. She tried feebly to kick at him and missed. "Please. Give him back."

Without looking back, he tucked the child against his chest and began to run.

"*Bastardo,*" Secundina said, and slowly closed her eyes.

CHAPTER 35

The horses grazed in a sunken arroyo while the men perched—binoculars and spyglasses pressed against their faces—on a slight mound amid a cottonwood patch. From their vantage point they reported a woman striding empty-handed toward the jacal alongside an unidentified man, a trapper by his appearance.

"Who is the woman?"

"I can't tell. Here, you look."

The marshal prodded the binoculars into Lino's face. Lino raised the glasses. "That is María. I don't know the trapper."

He handed the binoculars back to the marshal and resumed his seat on an overturned log, his elbows on his knees. He attempted to twirl the pistol in his trembling fingers. He didn't know if he did this to convince the others of his calmness—his readiness and compliance—or if he merely tried to convince himself.

He felt the eyes of the others watching him, all five volunteer soldiers minus Marshal Austen and Lieutenant Hutt on lookout. Lino guessed each one of them to be at least forty. The two gringos were overweight while the three Chicanos appeared malnourished and spiritless. Chicano or not, none of the military men spoke to Lino. They didn't have to; their silence said enough.

Lino peered across the sage, seeing only María and the overburdened trapper. Who was he to her?

He focused back on the pistol, squeezing and loosening the

handle in his fist to get the blood flowing. The sleet had him frozen and the less he moved the quicker his digits grew bloated and stiff.

He didn't have to be here with these old, ragtag, disdainful volunteers. He wasn't here to assist them or Marshal Austen or the other two officers. He was here because he had insisted to Don Carlos on riding with the posse. He was here to mend frayed ends. Cecilia needed Secundina and Vivian home and Lino needed his wife happy. Lino needed Felipe out of his life. Things in Costilla were in upheaval—at home and in the mo-rada, and the only remedy Lino knew was to see Felipe dead in such a way that martyrdom would seem blasphemy.

He was here because he had to be a regulator. The men were going to arrest Felipe. Lino had to see him escape. Or better yet, killed.

"Whoa, whoa, hey, what is this?" Suddenly Austen stepped forward and adjusted his scope.

"Is that a pitchfork?" Hutt asked.

Everyone got to their feet. Lino went to Austen. "What do you see?"

"The woman, she just . . . who is that?"

Lino snatched the binoculars. "Secundina. My daughter."

"She has a baby?" Hutt asked, still watching through the spyglass. "You didn't tell us—oh Jesus!"

A pistol shot blared and echoed across the valley. Austen wrestled back the glasses but Lino had already seen everything: Secundina standing with the baby in her arms in the doorway, María lurching past them.

The men dashed for their horses but Lino took his time. They seemed to forget him as they swung into their saddles and charged out of the grove, Austen in the lead. Lino watched them a moment, climbed atop his own horse, and nudged it into a trot.

A second gunshot bellowed from inside the jacal and standing high in his stirrups Lino saw the trader double over inside the opened doorway. He staggered a moment and appeared about to tumble backward onto the ground, but kept his footing and, after a moment, disappeared inside. A few seconds passed then two more shots blared.

Lino was now a good ten lengths behind the rest of the group as Austen and Hutt jumped off their horses and barged inside the jacal. The soldiers, unthinking and directionless, followed with their rifles aimed in front. Only Lino remained mounted as he slowed his horse and waited. He knew enough from what he had seen and heard to foretell the gruesome scene inside.

But suddenly he caught something out of the corner of his eye, something lumbering behind the jacal and toward the looming bluff. Sleet poured from the brim of his sombrero and through it he saw the trader hobbling toward what looked to be a fallen form on the ground. The inside of the jacal was a ruckus of flipping furniture and crashing dishes, and Lino realized they would find nothing. The man had followed Secundina out the window.

He leaned forward in the saddle and watched the trader flop onto Secundina, the baby writhing above their heads in the sleet. He watched the savagery taking place before him, the forthcoming death of Secundina and her child. He wondered where Felipe was; thought how they would blame him for leaving the girl and her child unprotected. He thought how unforgivable this absence, how it would be known by all.

Lino had one foot out of the stirrup and was about to join the others in the house when from inside a rifle cracked, followed by another. The trader arched, grappled at his spine, and collapsed. Lino kicked back into the stirrups.

"They're out here!" he called lamely, bolting past the house and the two smoking rifle barrels resting on the rear windowsill.

She lay on her side, the child screaming and nestled under her chin, the trader dead on his stomach. Lino dropped off his horse and observed a small hole blasted in the middle of the girl's back and staining her dress a dull crimson.

A pistol fired behind him, then another. Lino ducked, a crazed thought entering his mind that the volunteers were shooting at him. But when he turned two riders barreled toward the jacal, their pistols firing wildly into the group of untied horses milling out front. The horses whinnied and scattered, a few of them stumbling before collapsing onto the ground. Mud and sleet flew behind the racing hooves of the riders' mounts, and Lino recognized the horses to be his own. The riders' sombreros flew behind them by their chin strings and bandannas whipped about their necks. The larger of them, Felipe, had what appeared to be a sword bouncing in its scabbard against his saddle.

The two closed in on the jacal and inside the soldiers fired back. Lino pried the baby from his dying mother only to rear back as suddenly Secundina flared back to life. She cursed him, blood splattering from her lips, but Lino kept his hold on the baby, lifting it by the arm and clutching it against his chest. He hesitated a moment then ran, hearing only faintly the trailing condemnations of Secundina.

He ran at a diagonal, positioning himself with the house between him and the attacking riders. One of the rifles still pointing through the bedroom window searched wildly for a target, and when the dark Chicano eyes behind it spotted him Lino held up the baby.

He sprinted to the window, handed the child to the soldier and pulled himself in after it. He dropped onto the floor of the jacal and was immediately kneed aside by a huddle of soldiers fighting to regain position at the window. Lino saw the volunteer who had taken the baby wrap it in a blanket and then sit next to it on the bed with his hands over the child's ears. The whole interior was thick with gun smoke and a cacophony of rifle shots and yelling—seven men waging war inside two cramped rooms.

Lino crawled to his feet and peered out the bedroom window. Until that moment all shots had been firing from the front room—from the doorway and front window above María's lifeless form—but suddenly one of the riders careened into view and a fusillade of rifle shots ripped above Lino's head. The rider, the sword swinging below him, raced to the still body of Secundina while firing blindly back at the jacal. Lino, his face pressed against the cold clay wall, heard Felipe suddenly howl. He galloped around the fallen Secundina, his fingers clawing at the sides of his head and his face screaming up toward the sky.

He fired again into the walls of the jacal. Why didn't he leave? Lino wondered. Secundina was dead. Then Lino turned his head and saw the answer: the baby squirming on the bed with the soldier still covering its ears.

Lino forced his head higher in between the crammed soldiers out the window. "*El bebé es muerto*! The baby is dead!" He yelled it as loud as he could, so loud it cracked his throat and made him cough. He had only a second to see it register in Felipe, see the knowledge lurch the man inward as if a fishhook had just yanked his heart out through his back.

But that was all Lino saw, for instantly a dozen boots were stomping him to the floor, crushing his chest, and kicking at his head. He felt himself go dizzy, heard the riders yell to one another outside and, just as consciousness prepared to leave him, the sound of their hooves galloping away.

★ ★ ★ ★ ★

Part Five:
The Liberation of
Vivian Espinosa
SPRING 1863

★ ★ ★ ★ ★

CHAPTER 36

A southwesterly wind blasted the San Luis Valley. It whipped through the sage, sweeping with it the deposits of the Río Grande and its tributaries for miles until wind and sand heaved against the unremitting spine of the Sangre de Cristos and shuffled down the range's western base like dirt along a door frame until finally dustpanning into the northern flank of Mount Blanca.

Into this massif pocket the sand collected, the wind carrying for centuries the yellow and black river particles that became mounds that became hills that became mountainous dunes. Ten miles long and seven hundred feet high, the dunes were ever-shifting, ever-growing, and when seen from a distance in the wavering haze they were a lurid vision of gold frozen in its smelter. The Great Sand Dunes.

There was a mysticism associated with the place. A bruja told of wild horses with webbed feet galloping across the sand at night, their prints disappearing behind them in the changing sands. The Tewas sung of the place of genesis, of an underworld called Sipapu. They sang of a black pond within the dunes from which the first humans emerged after climbing a tree reaching out of this nether realm.

A shepherd claimed to have seen the pond. He said that when overlooked, it appeared nothing more than a brackish pool in the sand except that lining its perimeter was a ring of animal carcasses, their heads submerged in the blackness and their bodies beached lifeless. It was a place that after hearing the myths but only having seen the dunes from afar—the frozen smelter—Vivian, even now, foreboded.

Yet that is where they ran, the sky growing dark and the sleet turning to snow. Felipe rode in front, and did not look back. He whipped his gelding with the reins and gouged it with his teacup-sized spurs whenever it sputtered or slowed. The horses had been running all day and Vivian felt his mount fighting against him, pleading to stop and breathe. He followed Felipe even as the dunes loomed above him and a warning tugged at his back.

Splashing across a wide creek, they dismounted and began the ascent of the dunes. Sand cascaded under their feet and Vivian tugged at the reins of his mare, her mouth frothing and her eyes bulging. He pulled harder and silently begged her not to collapse. He begged the horse not to strand him alone in the twilight, the falling snow on the sand.

They summited and before them in the dim gray of the sky Vivian could see no black lake nor webbed-footed horses, only an ocean of sand and snow, stuck waves and untoppled crests. Felipe did not pause, merely swung back atop his horse and, with Vivian close behind him, galloped across the swells.

They raced for miles, their tracks fading behind them in the sweeping wind, and soon the dunes met the flanks of the mountains. They transitioned seamlessly and now fought a new battle up the steep incline, the tumbling rocks and clinging brush, the thick clouds and the moonless night.

Vivian felt the animal's will fading beneath him, the temptation with each step to fold over and rider be damned. "Felipe, my horse is going to die."

Felipe said nothing, only dug his spurs into his own horse's lacerated flanks.

After a few more minutes the mare collapsed onto her side,

trapping Vivian's thigh and dragging him a few feet down the slope.

"Felipe . . ."

Felipe stopped. "Your horse dead?"

"I . . . I think her heart burst."

"Maybe you best stay here then."

"Please don't leave me."

A few lights shown far down in the valley, reflecting in Felipe's eyes and flashing off his huge teeth.

"You want us to stay around now?" Felipe jumped off his horse. "Suddenly you are not so bored and ready to move on?" He walked slowly down to where Vivian lay trapped. He bent over and picked up a dead branch.

Vivian yanked his leg free. "If you can let me ride on the back of you—"

He heard it before he felt it, a whooshing through the air and snow and then a thick *crack* on the side of his shoulder. Vivian yelped and Felipe—nothing more than a shadow with two eyes and gritted teeth—leapt astride of him. The branch whooshed down again and smashed into Vivian's chest. He choked and begged his cousin to stop but the melee came faster and harder and Vivian curled into a tight ball against the back of his dead horse with his hands over his head and cried until Felipe roared, flung the stick down the mountainside into the dunes, stomped back to his horse, mounted, and resumed the hard climb up.

The wind howled through the trees, rattling their limbs and shaking free clumps of snow that dropped on Vivian. He lay curled in a ball, his arms and knees tucked inside his shirt. He kept his back against the cooling mane of his horse and stared dreamily over the winking lights of the valley below. After a while he closed his eyes. He ceased to shiver, to feel the pain of his bruises and abandonment.

Somewhere, perhaps within a dream, something approached. Boots groaned over snow and stones tumbled before them. Vivian lifted his eyelids, which had become crusted with snowflakes, and in the predawn shadows saw a figure descending toward him.

The boots came to a stop directly in front of his face. "Get up brother. I found something."

Vivian let his eyelids close again. "What did you find?"

"Something very old and magical that will protect us. It is not far. *Vamanos.*"

"I don't want to leave. I'm just going to keep sleeping, and maybe later I'll go see your place."

Felipe crouched and slapped Vivian's cheek, yanked Vivian's shirt out from over his knees, and pulled his arms out through the sleeves.

Vivian moaned. "I said let me sleep."

"And I say you go to sleep and you will not wake up. It's freezing brother, you need shelter."

Vivian had realized that hours earlier upon first shutting his eyes and feeling the pain fade away. He had already given death its permission, and he thought how very comfortable and peaceful he had felt only moments ago, and then how suddenly cold and battered and unforgiving he felt now.

"You will die if you stay here."

"It was feeling good."

"If you are ready to die, then at least come with me and we can decide a better way to go about it."

In the darkness, the two scrambled vertically before cutting abruptly north and walking for what seemed miles along the mountainside until the sky alighted over the opposing ridge. Felipe slowed and Vivian spotted Felipe's horse tied to the base of a tree, asleep.

"This is the place?"

A large outcropping of rock jutted above them, flat shale and granite plates bulging from the face of the mountain. Felipe approached the formation and dropped to his hands and knees and suddenly disappeared beneath it. When Vivian crouched low he observed a small opening at the base of the rocks. It appeared smooth and unnatural, as if it had once been cut larger but compacted over the years under the immense weight of the stones above.

"Come in." Felipe's voice reverberated from inside the cave.

Vivian poked his head in and although he could sense his cousin an arm's length away he saw only blackness. "What's in here?"

"Come see."

"Is there room?"

"Yes."

"What if there are bears?"

"*Cabron,* this is not a bear cave. It's a mine. Did you not see the engraving?"

"What engraving?"

"Look right above you."

Vivian pulled his head back out and looked up. Chiseled crudely about six inches above the entrance was a cross, and below that the weatherworn words:

EN NOMBRE DEL PADRE
FRANCISCO TORRES, 1720

"Do you see it?" Felipe asked.

"Yes."

"Come in here."

Vivian traced the pads of his fingers over the engraving. He dropped to his belly and crawled inside.

Shuffling past Felipe, he found a spot on the floor and sat up. He waited a moment for his eyes to adjust but the blackness remained impenetrable and after a moment Vivian began to feel about him. He felt the smooth roof of the cave. It rose almost four feet high. The floor was flat and dusty and seemed to stretch deep into the heart of the mountain. Warm air continued to gust past Vivian, smelling stale and damp. He scooted forward on his seat, feeling ahead of him with his feet.

"Careful," Felipe said.

"Careful of wha—" Suddenly Vivian's feet dropped and dangled out over nothingness. He cried out and flopped on his back, clinging to the surface and squirming in retreat. Behind him Felipe laughed, caught hold of Vivian's collar, and dragged him. Vivian curled up against the entrance. "There's a cliff."

"Yes. But there is something else too. Here, come feel." Felipe grabbed Vivian's wrist and pulled him toward to the drop-off.

"I don't want to," Vivian said, shaking his wrist free.

Felipe snatched his wrist harder, and leaned in close enough for Vivian to feel his hot, sulfur-smelling breath on his skin. "If you want to be a baby, go back to your mother."

Vivian thought of his mother, of his old room in the hacienda, of playing three-card monte in his pajamas with his brother. He thought of these things and was thankful for the darkness concealing his eyes.

Vivian crawled forward as Felipe led him by the wrist. After about ten feet his fingers hooked over the lip of the ledge and another gust of warm air rushed past his face. He shrunk back, inches away from a pit of black, bottomless depth.

"Stop shaking," Felipe said, and guided Vivian's hand across the ledge until his knuckles struck something solid. "Feel it."

Vivian patted his hand along the object. It was smooth and wooden, two carved poles connected by smaller rungs.

"A ladder." Another gust of moist air.

"Brother, do you know what we have found?"

"No. It is not real."

"It is below us."

"It is a story."

"And it is true."

"Let's go, Felipe. Please. We can keep moving. I don't need to rest."

"No. We are protected here. This place is safe."

"This place is evil."

"Don't say that. We were led here. No one can get us as long as we stay. It will not allow them."

"I'm going outside."

"I'm staying."

Vivian crawled back to the mine's entrance and shimmied out into the brightening morning. The ground before the mouth was smooth and flat. Vivian cleared away the thin layer of snow, curled into a ball, stretched his shirt over his knees, and pulled in his arms. With the warm air of the mine wafting against his back, he fell asleep.

When he woke, the sun burned far out to the west and Vivian was sweating. He pulled out of his ball and spotted his cousin sitting shirtless on a rock. The saber lay unsheathed beside him, as did his saddlebags, a rifle, and the wagon driver's stolen journal. Felipe clutched a small pocketknife and appeared to be cutting at some sort of twine laced around his torso. Vivian rose and approached him. The twine was an elaborate vest of braided yucca, the razor-like points curled into hooks that burrowed into the skin over the shoulders and all the way down the spine where it connected to a belt of steel barbwire looped around Felipe's belly.

Vivian stopped short and took in the naked, mutilated back; the old lash marks like latticing brushstrokes, the fresh punctures of yucca and barb seeping a crusted, brackish blood.

He followed the line of yucca down the spine and recalled the way Lino had pinched Felipe's backside and pacified him the night Garret returned.

Felipe glanced over his shoulder. His eyes were moist. "Will you help me?"

Vivian sat down and took the knife and began slicing the *cicillio* and peeling its barbs gingerly from his cousin's spine.

"You are no longer penitent?"

"I am. I just no longer need wires and yucca and pebbles in my boot to remind me of His suffering. My own is enough."

Vivian glanced down at the sword, then the journal beside it. It was the one belonging to the one-legged wagon driver. The book lay open to a detailed illustration of the sword. The depiction showed the handle upright and a sun in the top corner of the page beaming down on the blade and its etched cross, both of which shimmered as if enlightened. Vivian had always admired his cousin's skillful hand, whether it be drawing, writing, or aiming a pistol.

"You are like Don Quixote, carrying around that sword."

Felipe bristled and glowered at Vivian who immediately realized his mistake. "I mean only that you both have swords is all. I didn't mean your battles are imaginary, only that—"

"How many bullets do you have left?"

"Felipe, I didn't mean—"

"How many?"

Vivian unholstered the Colt from his hip and popped the cylinder. He jammed a hand in his right pocket and counted the other bullets with his fingers.

"Nine."

Felipe nodded. "I've got only a couple left in the rifle. We left everything else back at the house, even my dragoon."

"What are you thinking of doing?"

Felipe didn't answer. He stared out over the valley below

them, his eyes glazing over. "Even the dragoon . . ."

Vivian finished removing the last of the *cicillio* and Felipe untwisted the barbwire belt around his belly and let it clang to the ground. He looked at Vivian. "Would you know how to find this place by yourself?"

Vivian grabbed Felipe's arm. "Please don't send me away. I didn't mean to offend you. I really didn't. I'll help you, Felipe, with anything. Please . . ."

Felipe shook his arm free. "I'm not sending you away. Did I say I was? I only asked if you could find this place yourself in case we ever *do* split up. We will need a place to meet."

Vivian searched his cousin's eyes for sincerity, found only heartbreaking impatience. "It was dark last night. I was cold. I didn't really pay attention . . ."

Felipe picked up the journal, removed the pencil from between the pages, and tore out the illustration of the sword. He closed the book, turned the ripped page over, and began to draw. Working fast he filled the width of the page with an outline of the mountains followed by the valley, villages, and sand dunes below. Although hastily drawn, the map was finely detailed, and when Felipe finished sketching the cave and outcrop of rocks Vivian thought he would be able to find the place in relation to the dunes. Felipe marked the cave with a cross and wrote above it, *"La Boca de Sipapu."* Seeing the title, Vivian felt even more ill at ease with the place. He accepted the page, folded it, and slipped it into his pocket.

Felipe climbed to his feet, stretched, and put on his shirt. He picked up the sword and glided it back into its scabbard. He turned around and gazed toward the entrance to the mine, his hands on his hips.

Vivian remained seated and looked at his cousin. "What are we going to do?"

Felipe squinted. "Did you really see what is written up there?

The name in the stone?"

"Yes."

"Because the carving is small, and it was dark last night, and—"

"I said I saw it."

Felipe was quiet a moment and Vivian observed his finger go to the hilt of the sword and scratch it with his fingernail. "It is said that friar, that Francisco Torres, was the first to name not only the San Luis Valley, but also these mountains."

Felipe's gaze floated above the mine to the jagged summits looming above, their snowy peaks radiating crimson against the setting sun. "Sangre de Cristo," he muttered. "Will you really help me?"

Vivian opened his mouth, then closed it. He couldn't tell if the question was for him.

He spent another night huddled before the mine's entrance, and he awoke the following morning to the deep, sternum-shaking rumbles of his empty stomach. It had been more than two days since he had shot and eaten the doe, and as he waited for Felipe to wake up Vivian spent the dawn in vain search for berries among the rock and wind-bent bristlecones.

When Felipe finally emerged from the mine, Vivian helped him saddle the horse and the two rode double at a northeast slant up the mountains until finding a low pass that they followed over to the range's eastern flank.

They dropped in elevation, descending through the trees as the sun filtered spiderweb shadows through the limbs and arched out of sight to the west. The terrain eased into rolling, brush-choked foothills. Soon a thick banging sounded in the distance ahead, resonating among the trees, followed by men's voices. Reaching a slight rise, they dismounted and tethered the horse. With Felipe and his rifle out front, the sword dragging in its sheath by his side, they crawled to the top.

Below them spread a small brown pasture dotted with grease-wood. A log cabin squatted at the center, flaxen and freshly cut and with a small corral set a few feet aside. Three hobbled horses and a mule hopped and grazed like rabbits. About fifty yards away, between the perch and the cabin, three pink, sunburned men constructed a wind pump. Two of them worked together at the top hammering struts into the latticed tower while underneath the third man used a pulley to move up the boards.

Vivian scooted through the brush and flattened on his belly next to Felipe. "Three of them," he whispered.

Felipe squeezed one eye shut and peered down the rifle barrel. He lifted his head. "Wait."

Vivian turned his face back to the pasture. In the corner of his eye he watched his cousin set the rifle flat, twist a stem off a bush at his side, roll it between his fingers, and pick at his giant teeth. Vivian wished Felipe would talk to him, that he would share his plan and thoughts. He wished he could ask questions without feeling bothersome or childish and naive. He wanted Felipe to know he was prepared to do anything he asked if only Felipe would confide in him.

An elbow jabbed into his chest. "Quit that," Felipe said.

"Quit what?"

"Your stomach. Take care of it."

"Do you have any food? How can I take care of it?"

"Eat some grass."

Vivian looked at his cousin, his mouth half open but Felipe only tapped the stem against his front teeth and watched the men. Vivian's stomach popped and grumbled and Felipe frowned. Vivian looked to the ground, snatched a handful of dead grass and wet leaves, and crammed the sticky wad into his mouth and gulped.

After a while Felipe reached into his seat pocket and removed the journal. He opened the book, took up the pencil stuck between the pages and, still lying flat on his belly, legs crossed behind him, began to write. On the other side of the mountains the sun faded.

"Felipe?"

Felipe continued to write.

"Felipe?"

"What?"

"Do you sometimes think about José? How we left him. How he is still there with Lino? Do you think he wishes he was with us?"

Felipe snorted. "When did you start caring about your brother?"

Vivian lowered his face to the ground. He found a pebble and rolled it against his palm and then pressed it into the soil.

"Do you wish he was with us?" Felipe asked.

"I don't know."

Down in the pasture, the sky dimming overhead, the two men atop the tower finally began to climb down.

"Felipe?"

"Yes?"

"Back in Conejos, when they were shooting at us. Did you hear someone yell out the baby is dead?"

"I heard it."

"The voice . . . the man who yelled it. Was that Lino?"

The pencil hesitated in Felipe's hand. He tapped it against the paper, then resumed writing. "Possible."

"If it was, do you think maybe he was lying? What if Domingo is still alive?"

Now the pencil stopped altogether. Felipe kept his head down on the pages and Vivian watched him squeeze the corner of the book until the flesh under his thumbnail turned white.

"Felipe?"

"They killed him. Domingo is dead. All of them are dead."

"But what if he is not? Should we just go see, or even find someone to ask? We could—"

"Shhh!" Felipe snapped the journal shut. "Look."

Below, two of the men were saddling their horses while the other unhobbled the third horse and the mule and led them into the corral next to the cabin. As twilight fell, Vivian and Felipe watched the two men mount their horses and wave to the third before disappearing into the forest south of the pasture. The good-byes seemed brief to Vivian, temporary. He observed the man below, alone now, light a lantern hanging above the cabin's front door and go in. Another light flared inside.

"The lantern," Vivian whispered. "He's waiting for them to come back."

Felipe stuffed the journal back in his pocket and climbed to his feet. "Let's go."

They scrambled down the hill and into the pasture, Felipe with the rifle pumping at his side and Vivian with his pistol drawn and sweaty in his palm. About twenty yards outside the cabin, the horse, having apparently dozed off beside the mule in the corral, spun its head and whinnied. Felipe and Vivian dropped to their knees in the grass.

It was almost completely dark as they faced the front door of the cabin and its overhanging lantern. A man's face appeared in the small window next to the door. The two hunkered lower and became statues as the man pressed his face against the glass and cupped his hands around his eyes. Vivian stopped breathing. He stared into the eyes, blue and warm, above a light gray beard, and after a moment the man turned and left the window. They rose and stalked toward the door.

Shortly before reaching it, Felipe bent over and rested his rifle against the wall. He turned to Vivian who looked at him inquisitively. Felipe pointed at the pistol in his hand and shook his head. Slowly he drew the saber out of its sheath. He put a hand on Vivian's back and guided him until he was flat against the wall beside the door and out of sight of the window. Through the wall Vivian heard the clanking of pots and swishing water. Felipe pressed himself close against the door, coughed, stomped his boots as if just approaching, raised his knuckles, and knocked.

The man called out something in English, something surprised and familiar. The door opened and the words stopped in his throat. Felipe jammed the saber deep into his gut. The man gasped and staggered back. Felipe held the sword tight and followed him in. The man's knees buckled and Felipe caught him with one hand behind the neck and lowered him to the floor.

Vivian stepped in behind him and for a moment he and the dying man locked eyes. The man coughed and a spume of blood speckled across Felipe's face. Felipe grinned and yanked the blade free. He straddled the hacking man, raised the blade until it scraped the cabin's low ceiling, and chopped it down. It whistled metallically through the air and split the man's head from the forehead down the face, the entire skull opening up like a halved watermelon; two neatly stuffed shells of wet brain and glistening cartilage.

Felipe beamed at Vivian, his teeth huge and spattered with little red dots.

They tore out drawers, flung open cabinets, pried apart chests and boxes, upturned the small mattress. They found the man's saddle in the corner, along with two leather panniers and a packsaddle for the mule. They stuffed bedsheets, matches, candles, a brass-handled caping knife and a cleaver, a jar of molasses, a sack of apples, a bundle of carrots, a loaf of bread, and four long cuts of beef jerky into the bags.

Vivian devoured the fifth piece of jerky and crammed two of the apples into his pockets. He found a gleaming silver-and-gold Henry .44 repeater. It looked new, and next to it was an untouched wooden box containing fifty rounds. Vivian slipped his pistol into its holster and grabbed the rifle, determined not to let it go.

"Aye," Felipe said, making Vivian jump. "Now here is something." Vivian turned to see Felipe holding a flat tin box. The lid was open and Felipe looked into it, mesmerized. Vivian went to him and peered over his shoulder. He gasped. Inside the tin piled a small treasure of coins; not the silver Spanish bits Vivian had seen all his life but the golden liberty coins of the Americans. They all but glowed, seeming almost mythological to Vivian who had witnessed them only fleetingly on his horse-trading visits to Santa Fe with Lino or on the even rarer occasions inside Don Carlos's office.

Vivian reached over his cousin's shoulder. Felipe snapped the box shut and Vivian flushed with anger. "It is part mine, too."

"It is all yours if you want, same with that Henry." Felipe stared past the corpse and out the door. "But right now we have to go. Here"—he handed the tin to Vivian—"put it in the bags."

They worked fast, saddling the dead man's horse and securing the heavy panniers over the mule. Vivian swung atop the horse and followed Felipe who led the mule and jogged back up the hill. When they reached the top, Vivian heard voices behind him and looking back saw two swinging lanterns flickering among the trees.

They found Felipe's horse and Felipe worked frantically to untie it.

"Where do we go now?" Vivian said.

"Somewhere where no one has ever heard the name Espinosa."

Felipe climbed into the saddle and spurred the horse forward.

Vivian followed, keeping an eye on the mule and its bouncing pack, listening to the tinkling of the gold coins inside the tin.

They kept to the high country, kept north. They rode in the middle of creeks whenever possible. Veering west away from Cañon City, they uncovered an Indian trail and followed it deeper into the Rockies. They came upon a small cattle ranch and stole a cow.

Leading a pack mule and the cow, they left the Indian trail and slunk down through the trees until finally dropping into a marshy pocket. The spot sunk between the peaks like something had long ago pinched its underside and stretched it down, and water pooled clear and cold in spots after having drained from the snowy peaks.

A thin stream lined with willows and cattails trickled down the middle of the little valley and flowers bloomed yellow and purple and pink—all of them exceptionally bright for the otherwise brown, early spring. A few pine trees cropped up among the marsh while a number of massive boulders scattered at their feet. Felipe pulled back his reins next to one of the boulders, placed a hand on it, and looked up. Vivian followed his gaze to the largest of the mountains looming above them. It was the northwesternmost of them, and its top bowed in such a way there appeared to be two small peaks, one of which was capped not jagged but flat and oval, like a saddle horn.

"See that mountain?" Felipe said.

"It looks like a saddle, how it bows. And the horn."

"It is a saddle mountain. It is *Montura Montana.*"

"I like this place."

Felipe slid off his horse and squatted up and down, stretching his legs. "Then stay a while."

They unsaddled, removed the pack from the mule, and took what they needed from it before stuffing the rest below a boulder and covering it with smaller rocks. Vivian built a fire while Felipe led the cow a little way down the stream and butchered it.

For three days they picked at that cow, roasting every part of it from its snout to its tail and stewing everything after that. When only the skull remained, bloodstained and dappled with black patches of fur, Felipe hoisted it under his arm, strode to where a pine tree lay fallen on the edge of camp, its long dead roots reaching like stiff tentacles into the air, and hung the skull by a root end.

The following night Vivian awoke to the sound of voices. He huddled behind one of the boulders, felt around him, found his pistol, crawled slowly forward, and peeked around the rock. He could hear them. They sounded like they were arguing. They sounded familiar.

Slowly, he stood, pulled back the pistol's hammer, and stalked toward the deep and guttural, black, and brutal voices.

Vivian froze. There, sitting astride the fallen tree before its splayed end of tentacle-like roots, was Felipe. He squeezed a knife in one fist under the hanging cow skull, the blade glinting in the piercing light of the moon. Felipe snarled, seethed, and cursed at the skull and waved the blade threateningly before it as the skull, through eyeless sockets and yellow teeth, cursed Felipe back in his own voice.

At sunset the next day, they saddled the horses, tethered the mule, and rode northward over the swooping flank of Montura Montana. They descended into an immense intermountain basin, a sweeping caramel-colored grassland rippling under a throttling headwind that lifted their sombreros and whipped their serapes open revealing the flashing steel on their hips. The land rose and sunk like trinkets poking beneath a bedspread, and long swaths of soil shone dark red as if lesions in the earth's living tissue. It was a harsh playground of rolling hills, extinct lakes, and spine-like ridges. The dry lake beds shimmered crystalline white: ancient salt deposits of a prehistoric ocean.

Vivian had heard of this place, this high valley rich with game and nomadic hunters. He'd heard of the creeks deep within those ice-tipped summits to the north, the gold they secreted, the prospectors they attracted. It was a vast and secluded hollow explored by the French and Spaniards a century before, and it was to them the place owed its hybrid name: Bayou Salado.

In the dull evening, lights twinkled in faraway cabins and ranch homes, and in the distance to the north, nestled at the ankles of that massive range of mountains, throbbed the coalesced lights of two neighboring hamlets.

"Many gringos here," Felipe said.

They hooked to the east, passing ringlets of stones—old tepee circles that bespoke the comings and goings of the Utes. Vivian's head ached and his lungs felt compressed, and he was reminded of their extreme elevation. Twilight closed as they mounted a long, straight wagon road that cut the basin floor like a seam before jutting abruptly up a steep, red-soiled pass. Lights glowed from what appeared to be a roadhouse at the summit. When they were a half mile below, voices began to sweep down in the wind; loud, drunken voices. Following Felipe, Vivian steered his horse off the road and the two dismounted in a cluster of aspens where all that could be seen were the lantern lights dancing through the leafless branches.

After an hour of cold, silent watch, two figures emerged from the roadhouse. Vivian saw a match strike and a cigarette burn red. The figures tramped down the porch steps and descended into the darkness.

Vivian lost track of the figures and the floating cigarette ember and half expected the men to come suddenly galumphing into the trees before them when suddenly there came the blue flare of another match being struck, this time in a ravine about a hundred yards to their left. They listened.

The men built a campfire, apparently having failed to find vacancy or welcome at the roadhouse. Illuminated by the growing flames, Vivian watched them fling out two bedrolls and sit. A few moments later the smell of roasting beef carried in the air. Vivian began to salivate and braced himself for his stomach to grumble and the elbow that would follow but neither one came. In the darkness he couldn't see Felipe beside him, could only feel his presence; that ever-turning mind prodding the fringes of Vivian's own awareness.

After the fire had shrunk into a pulsating cluster of orange cinders and as Vivian rocked back and forth with his knees against his chest and his teeth clenched shut to quiet his chattering jaw, the elbow came. This time it was soft. The cue.

They crawled the whole way, knives in their fists, each knee sliding inches at a time until Vivian felt the heat from the coals and smelled the cigarettes and beef on the breaths of the snoring men.

He watched Felipe rise up on his knees above the head of one of the men and hold up his knife. Vivian did the same over the other, and in the dying light of the embers the cousins looked at each other and Felipe counted down from three on his fingers.

But something in Vivian—his muscles, his will—froze, and suddenly, with the knife raised above him, he was watching Felipe drive the blade down and bury it into the throat of the sleeping man. Felipe leapt back and the man choked and grasped at the jammed knife, and in the bottom of his vision Vivian had just enough time to see the eyes of his own intended victim burst open and roll about in confusion. The two locked eyes and just as the man started to raise his hands Vivian rammed the blade down. The blade sunk through hard bone into the man's sternum. The man screeched, shoved Vivian to his back, scrambled to his feet and, the handle of the blade protruding from his chest, bolted over the fire and up the dark hill toward the roadhouse.

Vivian felt his face grow hot as he pushed himself to his knees. He could barely see the man's shadow staggering slowly upwards, and before he lost sight completely he unholstered his pistol and aimed.

A hand clasped his arm. "One moment."

As they watched, the man's shoulders stooped, his feet dragged. He looked over his shoulder at them and collapsed.

Felipe laughed. "*Viva los resueltos!* Salute the people that try! Ha!" He took off after the fallen man while Vivian turned to the other who, his hands still fumbling at the knife wedged in his Adam's apple, gradually went limp. Vivian checked his pockets. He pulled out a leather pouch, unlaced the top and brought out a handful of what he at first thought to be gravel. He sifted the rocks through his fingers and dug a nail into one. It was soft. He crouched over and held the rocks closer to the embers.

"Felipe come over here quick!"

After a moment Felipe came sauntering back.

"Gold nuggets, Felipe!" Vivian thrust his palm out. "He had a whole pouch of them!"

Felipe grasped Vivian's hand and plopped a second pouch into it. "So did that one."

Vivian gaped at the pouch.

"And I brought this back for you, too," Felipe said, handing him his knife, sticky and warm.

After that the murders became less clandestine and more callous, and as they tallied by the dozens Vivian grew numb to cruelty and mutilation; his only sensations the thrill of thievery and his darkening suspicion of his maddening companion. They roamed the wide-open grasslands of Bayou Salado, slipping off their horses and crawling on their bellies atop nubby hills or ancient lake bottoms and sniped men like antelope from sometimes a mile distant. They bided in culverts alongside nighttime roadways and ambushed horsemen and wagons. They killed gamblers, miners, ranchers, and men in suits traveling from Denver, and their spoils piled.

Felipe lassoed a man as he exited an outhouse and with the rope tied around his saddle horn dragged him to death. Vivian shot a man leading a pack mule and emptied the pack while Felipe hacked at the man with his saber and then refilled the pack. They kicked open doors and they skulked upon camps. Vivian lost count of everything—the number dead, the days past, the things stolen and transported back to the hideout whenever their saddlebags began to overflow—and it came to be where all he understood was that everything was loathsome, excessive, and stimulating, like some sensory-dulling addiction.

He grew increasingly aware of Felipe's lack of interest in the wealth they accumulated, his enthusiasm seemingly devoted entirely to killing, and it bothered Vivian. Whatever they were—bandits, mercenaries, murderers—he wanted them to be the same, and it pained him they were not. Their values were inconsistent. Their sufferings varied and so too did their motives and mentalities, and this terrified Vivian more than any thought of being caught and hanged or of being somehow reclaimed and punished by Lino. It was terror that had started the night his horse failed, that night above the dunes when it had first occurred to him Felipe would go on without him. And since then the fear had mutated into a vile paranoia in which the two became like strangers, not believing in their partnership, kinship or any one thing mutually, and Vivian knew in his heart that should he ever fall or his horse ever fail him again that Felipe would not wait. He would leave Vivian alone, a boy murderer without a companion or home.

They shot a rancher as he sat atop his horse whipping among a herd of cattle, and Vivian ransacked his cabin while Felipe carved alien designs into the corpse. They roped two cows and led them back toward Montura Montana. Vivian said a silent prayer of thanks. He needed the rest.

They slaughtered one of the cows and let the other graze with the two horses and the mule within the confines of the hideout. Vivian combined the latest plunder with the rest stashed inside the now-bulging panniers and covered them again with rocks. He tended the meat over the fire while Felipe wrote in his journal. The noise of the pencil scratching the paper and Felipe's incomprehensible mumblings irked Vivian. His cousin had grown a thick and soiled beard that bristled up his throat and across his face like some inky moss, and Vivian found he could hardly look at him. After they ate, they went to sleep without a word.

He awoke during the night to the sound of footsteps, the soft bellow of the cow, the unmistakable *srrnk* of the saber being drawn from its sheath. Vivian knew what was coming. He braced himself, and listened to the blade whisk through the air and slice into the thick neck. He heard it chop again, and again, and he heard the head drop to the ground a second before the body.

It had turned suddenly cold and this time Vivian didn't get up but wormed forward with his blanket around him and peeked out toward the fallen tree and its long and furled roots. His breath fumed out before him. It was snowing. He watched Felipe walk toward the tree with the freshly decapitated cow's head steaming in his arms and stake it through the severed neck on a root. Now there were three heads hanging from the tree, the blood of the most recent one dripping onto the tree trunk.

Felipe stuck his hand curiously underneath it as if checking the temperature of a leaky pump, then pulled back his hand, and sat.

He began quietly, calmly even, his finger pointing one by one somewhat accusingly as he addressed them individually. He raised his hands, palms upward, and declared, *"Trinidad."*

And then, beginning low and soft but rising until it rumbled and resounded in the mountains around them, Felipe was screaming. Vivian scrambled frantically back into his den and tightened the blanket over his head and clamped his hands over his ears as what sounded to be a forest of voices—each one of them growling and hateful and rooted in the same lungs—blathered at once. He kept his hands over his ears and his eyes squeezed shut. He started to weep.

He must have fallen asleep, for when he opened his eyes the world was bright and sparkling with four inches of snow. Vivian pulled out the panniers stuffed with loot and packed them atop the mule. When arriving at the hideout yesterday, he had figured to spend a few days here, perhaps even a few weeks since they had stolen two cows. But now both cows were dead and cooking in the sun, and after last night the thought of another night here made Vivian feel sick. He started a fire and waited for Felipe to wake up.

They left around noon with Vivian leading the burdened mule and rode north. Not two miles into the ride they came upon a man picnicking on a bench surrounded with Columbines dipping under the clinging weight of new snow. Behind the bench was a small cabin. The man wore a long, black duster and a matching wide-brimmed hat. They let their horses saunter and Vivian watched the man reach to his side and rest a pistol in his lap. Felipe waved and the man continued eating.

"Howdy," Felipe said.

"Howdy," the man said. *"Buenos tardes."*

"You speak Spanish."

"Sí. I speak German, too." The man gestured at Felipe's hip. *"Das ist ein schönes schwert."*

"What does that mean?"

"I said that is a nice sword you got. Cavalry saber?"

"Yes. Cavalry saber."

"Would not have guessed you to be a cavalry man. You two aren't deserters are you? I won't say anything."

Felipe pointed at the gun resting in the man's lap. "There is no need for a gun with us."

The man stuffed the rest of the sandwich in his mouth and wiped his hands together. He reholstered his pistol. "Got to be careful, what with those rebel guerrillas terrorizing the area. They killed John Addleman yesterday. Not that I figure you know him."

Felipe cocked his head. "What was that word you used?"

"Guerrillas? It's those confederate renegades. Everyone knows it's them but—"

"No, not that. *Aterrorice."*

"Terrorizing?"

"Yes. That is the word. That is right. Terrorize is right."

Felipe flipped open his serape and shot the man twice in the head.

It had begun to snow again; weltering, ice-like flakes. Felipe fastened the buttons of the man's duster under his chin, the matching wide-brimmed hat already atop his head.

Vivian had found little inside the cabin. "Now what?" he asked.

"What do you mean, now what?"

"He said everyone knows what we've been doing."

"Of course they do. We have killed a lot of people. But like he said, they think it's Texans. *Rebeldes.*"

"Still, we need to get out of here."

Felipe finished buttoning the coat. He was black from head to shin. "Where do you want to go, brother?"

Vivian's breath caught in his throat. It had been a long time since Felipe had called him that. Another life. "I don't know."

"Montura Montana? Get out of the cold?"

Vivian envisioned the rotting cow skulls, heard their voices. "Maybe we go someplace else. Somewhere far from here."

Felipe gazed northward toward those two twinkling villages tucked into the mountains. "Those lights. They are from mining camps."

"But maybe we should move someplace further."

"There are miners in those camps, men working by themselves high up on lonely stakes, their pockets no doubt heavy with nuggets and gold dust. Just think how much gold . . ."

Vivian knew what his cousin was doing. "But Felipe, maybe we should—"

"That is where I am going." And with that Felipe turned his back and made for his horse. A ball rolled up in Vivian's throat. He stood there and looked south at the gray sky and the floating snow. He turned around and watched Felipe mount his horse and kick it into a lope. But for a long time Vivian did not move. He held himself still as if demonstrating some independence he knew he did not have.

Chapter 37

The mining camp of Buckskin Joe, located a few miles north of Fairplay at the feet of the Mosquito Mountains, had a rambunctious reputation. In 1860, soon after the mountain man Joe "Buckskin" Higginbottom discovered a nearby lode that would produce a million and a half in gold, the population swelled to a size half that of Denver, and Buckskin Joe was named county seat. They built hotels, banks, groceries, mercantiles, dance halls, and a post office, and talk circulated of naming it the state capital, should statehood someday come.

But three years later, the placers exhausted, and with the mining went the entrepreneurs, the politicians, the families. The camp neared total abandonment, the cabins and stores now hollow boxes leaning in fierce timberline winds, their roofs sagging and caving under the snow. What remained were a few dozen late-coming or else obstinate prospectors and a disproportionate count of four dance hall saloons. Now the only reason one came to Buckskin Joe was to drink, whore, gamble, or fight.

Billy Buck's Dance Hall & Saloon—the first and most popular of the saloons—was open tonight, but not for business. At least, not for business as usual. The men inside—each one a struggling miner secretly appreciating the sudden late-spring snowfall and the call of this grim meeting as welcome excuses for being away from their mutually dry and valueless claims— had pushed together two poker tables. Billy Buck, having contributed a bottle of whiskey as a sign of his support despite his declination to join the group, sat on the edge of his bar dangling his boots. Three bored-looking whores rested their arms on railings in front of their bedroom doors on the terrace. A fire crackled in a corner stove. Already the bottle was empty and between the snugness of the stove and the warmth of the whiskey the men grew emboldened. Only one—the cross-armed, pipe-smoking, eye-patched man at the head—was quiet.

"Tho foo whuf afually therf?"

"C.F. you got so much chew in your mouth none of us can understand you. It looks like you got two horseshoes behind your lips. Take at least the top half out if you gonna talk."

"I afte foo—"

"He asked who was actually there."

"I was. I was there and it was terrible. Poor Sam Sutton. I saw everything, and I wish I hadn't."

"Bull you was there. You stood on Peterson's steps with a bib round your collar and foam on your face. You just watched from those steps and didn't help nothing with Sutton."

"I was halfway through a shave! What was I to do, just run up with half a beard?"

"You can't say you was there."

"Don't mean I didn't see it."

"Fine, Landin, does that mean you was one on the scene?"

"Fellers, I was the one caught the beast by the halter."

"All right, you tell it then."

"It was Thursday in the middle of the day, the middle of Fairplay—"

"Everyone already knows it was Thursday and in Fairplay."

"Nathrop, will you shut up!"

"Yef, thutp upf."

"I was just—"

"Shut up!" they all clamored.

Landin cleared his throat. "It was around noon. I know that

cuz I was thinking about lunch. I had just rode into town and was hitching up, not doing much else or thinking much else, except, like I said, 'bout lunch, when I notice the mule come huffing into the street. And I notice the other folks around too noticing, cuz the thing 'bout this mule was it was a pack mule but no one was leading it. Didn't even have its lead rope. Had everything else though, including its panniers which had slid complete under its belly. You could tell they were full, and also that the animal had been walking for some time. Who knows how far but by the way it huffed I'd say a ways. It just came tramping into town, I guess not knowing where else it should come tramping.

"So what I do is finish hitching up then walk up to the mule and grab hold the halter. Everyone around was watching, coming out of stores and all, and standing there. Well once I catch it, up comes Ted Gibson and old Ann Gibson out of their shop, and oh hell how I wish old Ann hadn't, but you know how she is. She is saying, 'Oh you poor betty, oh you poor betty,' rubbing the mule on the nose. I don't know what 'betty' is supposed to mean except maybe something like baby or darling.

"Anyhow, right away I smell the stink and I could tell so too had the Gibsons cuz their faces are all scrunched up. The stink was bad, like rotten carcass, you know after the sun and the maggots get to it. And so that's what I first think, that inside those upside down panniers is a bunch've spoiled meat, and when I dip my head and look at them I see the cloth is soaked dark and not only that but dripping into the dust. The bags are bulging with things soft and hard. You know, bones protruding.

"I says to Ted, 'Ted, I think we got spoiled meat in those panniers,' and Ted says, 'Sure nuff' and takes out a pocketknife, pinches the collar of his shirt up over his nose, and cuts those panniers right off, not bothering to unbuckle them or nothing. They hit the earth with a splat. Hearing it is how I get my first bad inclination. Cuz even if this mule had gotten away from its master right after the master had shot an elk or something, like had originally crossed my mind, well no hunter would pack his meat so sloppily, just stuffing it all wet and unwrapped into them sacks.

"I says to Ted, 'Ted, something is not right about how that meat's been packed,' and Ted don't reply this time, just bends under the mule and jabs his pocketknife into one've the bags and slits it. It splays open and before my eyes can even connect to my brain old Ann is screaming. Ted steps back so fast he falls over, and there I am just stuck to the spot and staring. I'm stuck because staring right back at me from that slit and in between a whole mess of intestine and limbs is a face. It was Sam Sutton's face, and his whole body'd been hacked and stuffed into those bags."

"Jesus!"

"Oh Jesus!"

"Christ!"

"Jefuf!"

"Lord Almighty!"

"Injuns!"

"So there's the chopped up pieces of a man just heaped in the middle of town, and Miller you're worried 'bout folks seeing you with half a beard?"

"The beard had been real long. You remember it. Besides, that's not—"

"Hold on. Joe did you just say Injuns?"

"It's Injuns that done it. Injuns that been doing all of it, this whole time. If not the Utes, then the Arapaho. I'll bet the Arapaho. You want to bet?"

"I think it's the weather. That is, I mean not the weather that's doing the murdering and chopping and all, but that it's got a part. It shouldn't have been so warm so soon. It's got someone all confused and riled."

"It's not warm now. Look at it still coming down out there."

"Maybe that's a good thing."

"Snowed this morning, too."

"Could be just one crazy feller living up in the trees. A Herman."

"Hermit."

"One of the bluecoats says it's a couple Mexicans."

"Ain't a Mexican. Ain't no Mexicans round here. It'd be a chink before a Mexican."

"When did you talk to a bluecoat Nathrop?"

"Came into McGill's yesterday."

"What's a bluecoat doing round here at all?"

"Don't you know? There's eight of them. Governor Evans summoned them up to patrol Bayou Salado. Major Chivington is leading them."

The man seated at the head of the table suddenly coughed, his pipe spewing from his mouth and clattering to the table in a small puff of ash. There was a lull as the others looked at him, alarmed. The man didn't acknowledge or even meet their gazes, simply brushed the ash to the floor and replaced the now-snuffed pipe between his teeth.

"Did you know what else the governor done? Put up a bounty."

"A bounty?"

"*Rocky Mountain News.* Two thousand and five hundred dollars."

"Two thousand and five?"

"Two thousand and five."

Another lull.

"I think, if throwing things out on this table is what we're doing, then the big one might as well be thrown."

"Don't you do it, Miller."

"What are you talking about?"

"Yef, whuf the bif one?"

"I know what it is."

"Don't, cuz it ain't."

"Might."

"Just say it."

"Don't."

"Rebs. Confederates."

"Goddamnit, Miller! Everything's got to be a politic with you. Anything bad happens, oh well then it's Confederates. It's snowing outside? Confederates. Woke up with a bellyache? Confederates."

"It's a legitimate thought. Lot've people are thinking it, and it might be true. Few reb guerrillas ride into the territory, start terrorizing the people, get things chaotic, and keep even more bluecoats out've the East cuz they got to stay here. Kill the miners and steal their diggins to bring back to the South. No forts for a hundred miles so the Army can't do nothing about it."

"Got a point."

"Got no such thing. Ya'll are ignorant to even think it. The whole idea is contradictory. If anyone is harassing others and meddling in business that ain't their own, it's the bluecoats. Ain't that why there's a war at all? Ain't it?"

"Rebs rode into New Mexico."

"Got a point."

"You're just saying that cuz the captain's sitting here."

"I'm just agreeing. It's an idea we have to consider if we're gonna try and do something."

"Wait. What are we gonna do? What's been decided?"

"I ain't havin a part in no political faction out to harass decent Southerners."

"No one's saying that's what this is. We are just speculating."

"Well I'll have no part!"

"Whoa! Sit down, Joe."

"Yeah, settle it now."

The door of the saloon burst open. A few of the men jumped, their chairs shoving backward in a chorus of groans against the wooden floor planks. An empty whiskey glass tipped, rolled, fell, smashed.

"Heyo, fellers! What's going on here, a sewing circle? My wife's got one of those."

"Cripes that made me jump. Did you jump too? I saw you jump. Why are we all so jumpy?"

"Shut the door, Julius, you're letting in the cold."

"The saloon's closed tonight, Julius. At least till we're done."

"Done with what? I didn't see a closed sign. Damn, C.F., that's a lot of tobacco. You got mule lips."

"You can't drink till we're through."

"You're drinking. And through with what? What is this?"

"It's a meeting."

"About what?"

"The murders."

"The murders? What are you now, a posse?"

No one answered. They looked timidly at the man at the head.

"Well, whatever you are, if you're meeting about murders then I got your next order of business. We got a man and a wife just ride in from the Springs who says they passed a dead man lying in the snow near a cabin on top Fox Hill. Said the man been shot in the head. From how and where they described him it sounds like that man is Charles Binkley."

"Binkley?"

"From the way it sounds."

"God."

"Was he hacked up?"

"They didn't say, only that he'd been shot in the head. Welch was heading that way with the coroner when I left."

"The body's still out there?"

"At least for another hour I'd reckon."

A cloud fell over the table, something sobering and real that caused the men's backs to straighten, noses flare, breaths catch. Once more they looked to the man seated at the head, the man who had so far not spoken a word, and if there was a man to speak next it could be him and only him. They waited.

He rose. "Get your guns and your horses and meet back in five minutes. If you don't have a horse or a gun, get searching."

The man seated at the head was Captain John McCannon. He hadn't seated himself there, had simply entered late and found it waiting. He wasn't really a captain either; not officially, not anymore. He couldn't remember if he had told one of the men this former title of his but supposed he must have. Then again, it was possible they simply heard it secondhand, or even that they gleaned it wordlessly from the stiff, ex-military demeanor he suspected himself to continually intimate; how he would catch himself walking rigidly with little give to his knees and his thumbs hooked behind his back as if inspecting formation. Or how any request he made always carried the undertone of an order, how any question was a demand for information. He suspected these traits in his character, and was working to change them.

But a character, he had so far discovered, was a difficult thing to kill.

Either way, the men left the seat at the head open for him and they called him Captain, and so rather than telling them it was unnecessary and potentially fostering interest for his reasoning, McCannon let it go.

He had come to Buckskin Joe almost a year ago to retire, to

intentionally relocate to a place with a dwindled population and a short future because that was how he felt: reduced and near death. He welcomed the feeling and hoped to die anonymous. Characterless.

He wasn't that old, sixty-two, and in fair health. He didn't feel that way though, and neither did he display it. He let his gray beard grow ever farther down his throat, the bags sink below his eyes, the belly lap over his belt. He liked his neighbors—his fellow drinkers, whorers, and halfhearted miners—and considered them his friends and appreciated them for never testing his past. What concerned miners was the future: where the next lode was going to be found, how much gold will be worth next year, will Jerry Cummings lease out his site, and so on. Still, he would have preferred them to call him simply McCannon.

Compromising his efforts for anonymity more than anything were the murders of late, the indomitable massacre that attracted not only the attention of the governor and the newspapers to his place of retirement but also that of the Army, the very thing that had sent him into exile. He knew of the eight soldiers patrolling the basin, doing little except interrogating strangers and following the odd hoof track. But he had not known Major John Chivington was among these men before Joe Lamb announced it and caused McCannon's heart to lurch and his pipe to fall.

A year ago, McCannon had been Captain John McCannon of the First Colorado Infantry. And after almost two days of seeing his Union volunteers outflanked and sharpshot by Sibley's Texans in the mountains above Santa Fe, McCannon had personally been company in the discovery and subsequent destruction of Sibley's entire supply train. While both forces were busy exchanging fire in the hills, McCannon helped set fire to eighty-some Texan wagons and scattered some two hundred Confederate horses. The act had won the battle and, as Sibley and his now supply-less troops scurried back to Texas, the campaign.

McCannon and his comrades had liberated New Mexico, and they celebrated the night in Santa Fe, reveling in liquor, women, and glory. McCannon treated himself with a cheap, yet beautiful, Mexican *señorita*.

A week later, McCannon's chest and neck flared an angry, bubbly red. He became feverish and thought he was dying. He couldn't piss as his genitals had morphed into some festering bulge of horror. The Army surgeon diagnosed him with syphilis and shot silver nitrate into him, and in a few months McCannon recovered with a few scars, as well as a thin curtain over his left eye, and utter darkness over the other. He was declared blind and the famously moralistic Major Chivington, disgusted with his captain, issued him his discharge papers. The major had not even talked to McCannon about it, simply shuffled the process along while McCannon lay agonizing in the infirmary.

And so he became a miner in depleted mountains, and had been on the verge of a successful twelve months of sequestered gold panning and taciturn salooning when the rampage started and the Army, Major Chivington leading the way, marched back into McCannon's life.

He could avoid them. He had enough dust and nuggets to cash in, stock up, and hole up for weeks inside his cabin—a bottle in his hand, a shotgun in his lap—and wait it out. Let it blow over or else let the murderers come for him, and if they did, that's what the shotgun was for and he'd make a go at it but if that's how he went then that's how he'd go. There had been so many deaths lately even mutilation was becoming an obscurity, and obscurity was what McCannon aimed for.

But he wasn't there yet. Another year in the dying town and maybe so. For now the men still called him Captain and when they invited him to an impromptu meeting at Billy Buck's, they made a seat for him at the head. A character was a hard thing to kill—to let starve and bury—and in McCannon's character lay a contempt for disorder and a fondness for fighting. There was also, he admitted, a touch of pride, an itching appetite for glory that sabotaged his quest for insignificance more than being called Captain or being placed at the head or anything.

And that made life in Buckskin Joe difficult: the pressure, like lying down on a hard floor and having someone heavy step on your chest, of crushing your own spirit. Its contortion was painful, whether by Chivington or perpetually by himself.

A respite—to chase down some thugs and maybe a little lost pride—beckoned McCannon.

Binkley's cabin sat fifteen miles south of Buckskin Joe. McCannon led the men at a steady trot, skirting them around Fairplay, wary of alerting anyone. Pistols jutted from their hips and rifles swung in their scabbards. Each one of them had managed to secure a horse except for Joe Lamb who believed his chocolate-colored burro superior to any horse in any task, whether it be riding, packing, or chasing down killers. They spoke little and the silence intensified the energy coursing through the company as if it one mass organism, ebbing and reforming with every rider that fell behind and then caught up. The energy was pure nerves; an anticipation of blood. The moon radiated off the shimmering white of the fresh snow, and McCannon said a silent thank-you for the brightness. On a sunny day, his vision was like peering through a thick glass of water. At night that water became diluted and dark.

He spotted two dim lights floating in the distance. Lanterns. The men called out and waved. About fifty feet from the cabin, McCannon ordered the men to stop and wait. He dismounted, handed the reins to one of the others, and ordered Chuck Nathrop to follow him.

"What do you need of Nathrop?" Fred Miller asked.

"His eyes."

Trudging through the snow, McCannon soon made out the figures of Sheriff Welch and the coroner, Clifton Cole. They stood with their chins and ears tucked in their collars over the body of Charles Binkley, sprawled facedown beneath a heavy duff of snow.

"What the hell are you two doing here?" Welch demanded. "Who else is back there?"

"Settle down, Welch, we're here to help," Nathrop said.

"Don't tell me to settle, and don't call me Welch. It's Sheriff. What are you all doing out here?"

"Same thing you're doing, Welch, but probably better," Nathrop said. "How long you been here?"

"You saying this is a posse? Ha! I didn't sanction no posse."

"Don't need to. We got what you might call initiative."

"Then you're vigilantes. Is that what you're saying? You saying you want to get arrested? Surely you're not really a part of this, Captain?"

McCannon didn't answer. Instead he crouched over Binkley and leaned so close he could feel the cold off the dead man's skin. He saw no further wounds besides the two in the head. The shots had blown the back of the head into one gaping cavern of brain. McCannon brushed the snow from the man's back.

"Hey, don't do that!" Welch cried.

"Let him," Nathrop said. "We know what we're doing."

"Yeah, you're a real crack detective, Chuck. Man could piss on your feet and you'd wonder why your socks are wet. This better not be a posse!"

The snow atop Binkley was even heavier than McCannon had first perceived, four inches at least, and while brushing it away two things occurred to him.

"Tell me something, Mister Cole, how long you think he's been lying here?"

"Oh you don't need to call me Mister; I ain't vain like the sheriff. I'd say judging by the snow piled about him something like eight hours, ten at the high end."

"It's not vanity," Welch said. "It's proper."

McCannon brushed away the snow around the corpse. He sensed the sheriff taking a step forward and for a moment he thought the man aimed to grab him and pull him back. But the sheriff, like the other two, appeared only curious and McCannon kept brushing, circling the body, and minding his step. He was, after all, not sweeping away all the snow, only the first four inches. He swept until he found what he was looking for.

It had snowed twice that day over Bayou Salado, once around dawn and then again in the afternoon all the way till the present moment. It had been sunny but cold through and through, and the snow of the early morning had become a sun-kissed crust, frozen beneath the heavier and fluffier second falling. Brushing away this top layer, McCannon uncovered a swirl of boot prints fossilized in that original crust.

"Well see that," Cole said.

"What I tell you, Sheriff, crack detective all right," Nathrop said.

All four bent over and began sweeping away the fresh snow in a widening radius around the body. When they got to the hoofprints they paused. There were three sets.

"This one here's a mule," Nathrop said.

"Must be a pack mule," McCannon said, "since we got only two pairs of boots."

"Maybe a third rider never got off the mule," Welch offered.

"Maybe."

"Why you got the rest of your posse waiting way out there

Captain?" Welch asked. "Have them help us."

"They're out there so no more tracks get trampled than what's already been."

"Look here," Nathrop said. "It's the getaway tracks. They head north."

McCannon moved to where Nathrop pointed to a line of hoofprints. The tracks lined straight toward where the other four waited in the distance, toward town.

They would lose those tracks should the trail take to the road which had no doubt been traversed numerous times since then, including just now by the posse. McCannon knew that, just like he knew they would follow them all the same.

As the others watched, McCannon turned his back to the northern tracks, stepped over Binkley's body, and crouched once more. His hands were nearly numb and the icy crust of the snow scraped and burned the tops of his sweeping fingers. Finally he felt them, the hoof-shaped indentations and the bare earth within them. The prints of the killers approaching from the south.

"What are you thinking, Captain?" Nathrop asked.

He stood. "I'm thinking we got some tracking to do."

"You gonna shovel snow all night?" Welch asked. "Shit then I don't care if you are a posse. Shovel away."

"Shouldn't be too bad with six of us," Nathrop said, sounding unconvinced.

"Four," McCannon said. "You and I are following them the other way."

"The tracks coming in? But that's where they came from, not where they'll be."

"Right," McCannon said.

They were walking toward the waiting members of the posse when McCannon remembered the second thing that had struck him immediately after brushing the snow off Binkley's frozen body.

He turned back to where the sheriff and the coroner unfolded a white sheet to wrap the corpse in. "One last question, Clifton."

"What's that?"

"You know what kind of coat Binkley used to wear?"

"Coat? Nah I wouldn't know that. We can go see if it's in his cabin. It's been looted but there might still be a coat left. Why you interested in that?"

"Because that body don't have a coat on it. And today was cold."

The night wore on and the moon sailed across the sky until McCannon lost it somewhere to the west and the night entered that black hour before dawn. Nathrop walked ahead and brooded silently as the two men led their horses by the reins and continued their plod through the snow, every so often bending over and brushing away the top layer to confirm their route. The snow had finally stopped but the men were soaked to the skin, and in his blindness McCannon was all too aware of Nathrop's exaggerated sighs and what he suspected to be forced coughs.

He was also aware of a shadow looming before him, of walking under the auspices of something so massive it seemed to cast a shadow in the dark.

"Looks like the end of the line," Nathrop said.

"Why, what's up there?"

"A mountain, Captain. A great big one. You're not fixing on going mountain climbing tonight, are you?"

"Do the tracks go up it?"

"Yeah, but—"

"Then let's go mountain climbing."

The tracks did not scale the mountain but rimmed its base at a gradual ascent that eventually hooked them almost completely behind the mountain to its southern face before jutting abruptly downward into a secluded pocket bordered by mountains. Mc-Cannon heard a stream trickling somewhere.

He bent over once more in the snow to clean away and recover the tracks. Suddenly it was no longer hoofprints he felt, but boot prints.

"This is where they mounted. Still only two of them. The mule is a pack."

Off to his side Nathrop brushed away more snow. "They're all over the place. What the . . ."

He didn't finish and McCannon heard him jog forward.

"What is it? Where you going?" Deep in this mountain pocket McCannon's world was as dark as ever, and now something occurred to him. What if someone was here? What if they had missed the two that got Binkley only to surprise the other members of the gang in their hideout? What then? How would McCannon, blind as a bat, do anything? What was he doing at all, joining this venture, let alone leading it?

He heard Nathrop walking back to him. "Take a look Captain."

"I can't, Chuck. You're gonna have to describe it."

"Heads," Nathrop said, stopping shortly before him. McCannon perceived Nathrop holding up his hands. "They're cow heads. I have two here and there's another one down yonder that's just a skull. But these two are the whole heads, eyes, tongue, ears, everything. All three were hanging next to each other on the end of this fallen tree. Here, feel."

McCannon felt fur matted with frozen blood.

"Can't be too old if the coyotes ain't got to them," Nathrop said. "The rest of the bones are down there too but they're picked clean."

"You see anything else around here?"

"A campfire ring."

"Show me."

Nathrop tossed aside the heads and marched back toward where he had discovered them. McCannon followed by sound. Nathrop put a hand on his chest.

"Right here, Captain."

"Where?"

"You're standing on it."

McCannon crouched over and sure enough felt a wide ring of stones encircling him. He took a step backward, dropped to his knees, and plunged his hands through the snow and beneath the ash deep into a faintly warm soil.

"Warm?" Nathrop asked.

"Little."

"I don't see anything else. And I'm pretty sure the tracks end here."

McCannon knew that Nathrop was just saying it, wanting to believe it. It didn't matter though. McCannon believed it.

They returned south in the sunrise. By the time they mounted the road leading to Fairplay and back into Buckskin Joe, the snow had turned slushy under the surprise warmth of the morning and it dazzled reflectively so that McCannon's vision, illuminated both top and bottom, peaked.

About half a mile out of Fairplay, gunshots burst within the town like a string of firecrackers. McCannon jabbed his heels into his horse and with Nathrop close behind bolted across the snow.

He smelled the gun smoke before he saw it, the strangely sweet smell of cordite that reeled his memory back to the hills of Glorieta: of two armies volleying shots that thocked into the pines and filled the forest with an eye-watering haze. It rose above what appeared to be a small cabin atop a knoll on the southern edge of town. McCannon had his rifle clutched in one hand, his horse still charging ahead, when suddenly, almost too late, he noticed a mob of people directly under him. He had just enough time to see a young woman who whirled her shocked face to his and then cringed before he yanked back on the reins and stopped the horse inches from the cowering woman.

"Fool! What's the idea?" she stammered, glaring up at Mc-Cannon.

"Sorry. What is all this? What's happening up there?"

"You a soldier?"

For a moment—perhaps on instinct, perhaps on the nostalgia that carried with the gun smoke—McCannon almost said yes.

"No."

"Then put that gun away. This ain't your business. Chivington's got it handled."

McCannon almost dropped the rifle. "Chivington?"

"You blind?" The woman flicked her hand at the ongoing gun battle on top of the knoll. "The major's got him trapped."

McCannon peered atop the knoll. A few thin aspens surrounded the cabin and behind them eight blue-coated soldiers crouched firing at the cabin walls. Even half-blind McCannon could not mistake the towering figure of Major John Chivington. His brick-red mare stood roped to a tree further down the hill. The major barked orders to the men and whoever he had cornered in the house, every so often popping a pistol shot into the door of the cabin.

"Should we help, Captain?" Nathrop asked.

"I thought you said you weren't Army," the woman said, turning around to face him again, her eyebrows furrowed suspiciously. More eyes in the crowd darted up to McCannon.

"I'm not. Who's he got trapped up there?"

"The murderer," a man standing to McCannon's left said,

his eyes fixed on the firefight. "The one's been doing all the slaughter. Chivington must've gotten some early intelligence on him cuz they been yelling back and forth through that door all morning."

"It's just one man, not two?" McCannon said.

"Why don't they just kick in the door?" Nathrop asked.

"Cuz the Nelsons are still in there. He's holding them hostage," the woman said.

"Just one man?" McCannon repeated.

"Just one," the man said. "A Mexican calling himself Vasquez. Come in late last night and someone reported him. The folks inside been yelling that he's a friend of theirs, that he's their guest, except thing is the folks inside are the Nelsons and what would they be doing with a friend named Vasquez? It's obvious he's got them in there with a gun to their heads, telling them what to say."

The windows of the cabin shattered and splinters of wood blasted apart alongside the stacked logs. Suddenly, something poked out of one of the side windows. McCannon squinted and saw it was a bedsheet tied to a broom handle.

"Cease fire!" Chivington yelled. "Cease fire!"

The fusillade dissipated and everything became quiet except for the ringing in McCannon's ears. The cabin door inched open, a hand waving out of it. "No more, no more!" a voice called. "I will come out."

A Mexican man, tall and well-dressed in a dark gray suit and bolo tie, leaned halfway out, his hand still waving.

A rifle exploded from somewhere between the aspens and Vasquez slammed backward against the side of the cabin and slid to the ground. He lay on his side, openmouthed, his hand clutched to the middle of his chest.

"Damnit!" Chivington bellowed. "Who fired? You answer right now! Who fired?"

One of the soldiers, an older-looking fellow with glasses and a white goatee, slowly raised a hand.

"Eggstrom, you fool!" Chivington barked, marching up to where Eggstrom cowered, his hand still raised and trembling.

The crowd watched as Chivington beat the soldier across the head and shoulders with his pistol, emphasizing every blow with each syllable of *"Egg-strom you fool!"*

A couple and their daughter, presumably the Nelsons, surrounded the fallen Vasquez. McCannon couldn't tell for sure but he thought the man looked pretty well dead. The crowd had begun to disperse, muttering in tones less triumphant than disappointed.

On top the knoll, Chivington ceased beating the soldier, holstered his pistol, and turned toward where the crowd had just dissolved. He looked at McCannon.

McCannon whipped his face to the side, raising a hand to cover it. He tugged the reins of his horse and spun it to face Nathrop. Even with his back turned McCannon felt the major's gaze, his suspicion, and knew that one quick glance over the shoulder was all it would take to confirm those suspicions and invite his old enemy down the hill.

Nathrop eyed him curiously. "What do you say, Captain?"

"Come on," McCannon kicked his horse. "For now don't tell anyone what we came upon last night, not even the boys."

The other men had lost the tracks soon after McCannon and Nathrop set off on their reverse route. This, plus the death of Vasquez compelled McCannon to retreat to his cabin and spend the next two days in his chair, a bottle in his hand and a shotgun in his lap. Only occasionally, and only during the brightest time of day, did he venture outside to work his claim. He did it only for appearance, speaking little to his fellow miners except to let them know the posse would ride should the killings recommence. Otherwise McCannon spent the days and the nights alone in his chair, the thunderous voice of Chivington echoing inside his head, guilt ballooning inside his chest.

He knew they should be scouring the mountainsides for new tracks before the snow was completely melted, which would be soon. He knew the other men were thinking the same thing and all they waited for was him. No one really thought, McCannon least of all, that the massacres had ended with the assassination of a single Mexican in a nice suit and a bolo tie.

Chivington was out there. McCannon should be out there.

His cabin, along with his claim, lay alongside one of the lower banks of California Gulch, meaning McCannon lived in shouting distance of the many more claims that ran up the gulch like seaside chalets, as well as Buckskin Joe itself.

On the third morning, McCannon heard the shouts. They carried upward from town along with what sounded like a furious rattle of lumber. McCannon snatched his rifle and ran down the streambed.

In the roadway around Buckskin Joe, four oxen teamed together, pulling a full log cart, seethed and bellowed as a group of men tugged at their harnesses to bring them to a stop. One of the oxen was lame and staggering in its yoke. The cut logs rumbled in the back of the cart and as the team came to an abrupt halt one of them rolled out over the side. Soon after, McCannon spotted a man spilling out behind it.

He landed flat on his stomach and recovered instantly, bursting to his feet, and McCannon recognized the man to be Edward Metcalf, a logger who did some mining on the side and lived in a cabin not far from his own. Blood splotched the front of his shirt and trickled down his sleeves, yet somehow Metcalf seemed not to notice. He jumped and raved. "They shot me! They tried to kill me! I saw them!"

"Who shot you, Eddie? Who'd you see?" McCannon asked.

"Mexicans!" Metcalf looked down at his shirt, his eyes widening in remembrance. "They shot me! They tried to kill me!"

"How come they didn't? Looks like they got you good."

Metcalf patted his chest as if searching for the entry wound. He stopped over his right shirt pocket, felt inside it, and produced a leather pouch. The pouch was blown almost in half and gold nuggets spilled at his feet.

"Oh hell," Metcalf said almost casually, and dropped to the dirt to pick them up.

"How many Mexicans?"

"Two. The shot just came somewhere out of the woods and knocked me straight back into my wagon. It was a lucky thing too, being knocked back, since the team took off running. They must've thought me dead though cuz when I peeked my head up from out those logs I seen them, just standing there in the road. And then they seen me. They chased me probably half a mile, filling the cart full of shots and I think shooting an ox . . . yep, they shot an ox."

"Did they have a pack mule with them?"

"They had no animals. They chased me on foot. One of them had a great black beard and awful teeth. I could see them big things all the way down the road. He had a great long knife too. It hung from his belt all the way to his knees. Like a sword."

"What about the other one?"

"The other'n was younger. I think."

Metcalf continued to talk but McCannon had stopped listening. He was looking for his posse.

CHAPTER 38

Vivian raced behind Felipe, his horse heaving beneath him, the mule all but dragging behind. His teeth chattered despite the sweat running hotly down his back. They had let one get away. They had been seen.

Moments ago, Vivian laid on his stomach, concealed behind an outcrop of brush overlooking the primitive wagon road between Buckskin Joe and, on the other side of the Mosquito Mountains, Leadville. His entire front was soaked with snow and he rested his cheek against the sunbaked steel of the rifle before him. Both horses and the mule stood tethered a short distance back in the trees. Felipe crouched down by his feet and when the oxcart finally came rattling into sight, Vivian felt his cousin tap the sole of his boot and whisper, "Take it."

Vivian waited until the driver, the reins to the four oxen draped lazily over one hand, rode within fifty yards and then pulled the trigger. He saw it blast the man in the chest and fling him feet over head backward into the open log cart. The oxen jumped with the resounding boom, the sudden grunt of their master behind them, and took off in a clumsy trot down the road. Felipe patted Vivian on the calf and laughed. It had been a good shot.

The two stood up from their vantage point to watch the driverless cart parade past them. It swung wildly behind the crazed beasts, sending a single log tumbling out over one of its sides. As it passed, the driver came into view, sprawled out on his side and bouncing with the jostling lumber, the blood speckled across his shirt. Felipe laughed some more and patted Vivian on the shoulder.

Then, just before drifting out of sight behind the back end of the cart, the driver sat up.

Felipe swung his own rifle next to Vivian's ear and fired. The bullet streaked down one of the logs next to the driver, and the man looked up and straight into Vivian's eyes.

They leapt down the embankment and chased after him. The oxen bolted faster with the second shot and gained momentum down the sloping path. Vivian saw the man's head peek up from behind the back wall of the cart and he pulled the Colt from its holster and emptied it. The shots spattered against the rear end of the cart, and the man ducked back down. Vivian kept running, fumbling inside his pocket for more bullets, only faintly aware that Felipe had stopped. The rifle thundered once more behind him and one of the oxen threw its head and bellowed. It stumbled but did not fall, the shot instead sending the other three animals into a deeper frenzy as they pulled at the wagon and their limping comrade until the cart disappeared down the path for good.

Felipe had just looked at him, his eyes cold and his lips pressed tightly beneath his tar-black beard, and in that look Vivian had understood. Saying nothing, the two rushed back to their horses and bolted off so fast that Vivian, the lead rope wrapped around his hand, thought he might yank the mule's face off.

The air was warm, almost muggy with melted snow, and every time Vivian turned around and noted their hoofprints it was like seeing a trail of bread crumbs. Miraculously they came across no one along the long sprint across the open basin and, with twilight approaching, all the way to the base of Montura Montana.

The animals were gasping by the time they reached the hideout, which had become a sinking bog of pooled snowmelt. Vivian slid off his horse and let it trot up to the water, its reins dragging, and drink deep. He looked around for a dry place to sit and chose a boulder overlooking their now-submerged fire pit.

He noticed Felipe still atop his horse, a worried look on his face as he stared at something on the ground. Bulging from the mud as if floated up from shallow graves were the two cow heads. Over by the fallen tree, still dangling by a dead root, hung the third head, the skull. Felipe looked at Vivian, no longer appearing indignant but suddenly scared. "We have to go."

"Where?"

"South. Far away from here. Fast."

"But the horses, how much further can they go? The mule has been carrying that pack for days."

"We will remove the pack and hide it. But not here. They are coming. They have been told about this place."

"How? Who told them?"

But Felipe didn't answer, only looked around him with the same look of terror and paranoia as if the assassins crouched in the mountainsides around them, taking aim.

"Get on your horse. You can free the mule if you care that much about it."

"But it's carrying all our money!"

"Then take it! And don't cry when it dies on the trail."

Felipe steered his horse and nudged it south. He took off at a trot through the middle of the creek, the willow branches scraping his horse's sides. Vivian jumped off the rock and his boots sucked past the ankle into the swampy earth. He trudged to his horse and the mule, his boots slurping beneath him.

They set upon the Indian trail winding steadily southeast and up the forested mountains. The trail became steeper as they went and Vivian was forced to tug harder and harder at the huffing mule, coaxing it along with desperate utters of encouragement.

Soon the riders came to a wide bend that, just before switchbacking still upward, opened to reveal an immense view of the eastern basin, the snowy expanse shimmering a brilliant salmon in the sliver of setting sun. The moon was pushing through, large and full. Immediately below the bend, the mountain ran off at a sharp grade of loose shale. On the opposite side spread a small boulder field surrounded by trees.

Felipe stopped, peered out at the plains below, then at the boulder field. He swung out of his saddle.

"Quick, we need to hide that pack."

Vivian dismounted and together he and Felipe hoisted the two bulging panniers from their braces, the fur of the mule matted and soaked beneath them in perfect outline, and, jumping from rock to rock, careful to leave no tracks, they hefted the bags into the boulder field where they stuffed them into a crevice and covered them with stones. On a flat-topped rock beside the crevice they crossed two dead branches.

When Felipe turned back to the waiting animals, Vivian stayed a moment, looking down at the heap of stones solemnly as if it the freshly filled grave of a loved one. Inside that crevice lay what had to be a thousand dollars in stolen jewelry, knives, pistols, cash, coins, and gold—nuggets and dust plucked fresh from the mountains.

Behind him he heard the glass-like tinkle of cascading shale. He turned around to see the rump of the mule sticking up over the rim of the trail, its rear legs trembling in resistance. Felipe was pulling it down the mountain.

"Don't!" Vivian yelled, and began to run. He bound over the rocks and saw one by one the rear legs relent and step down the steep descent and disappear off the ledge. When he reached the overlook Felipe had the mule's rope pulled taught in one hand, his knife in the other.

"We can just let him go Felipe. We can just—"

Felipe jabbed the blade into the mule's throat and dragged it across. He drew it out but held the rope as the animal let out a weak and gurgling bray, staggered backward a step, then slowly, as if lowering itself to sleep, dropped to one knee, then the other, then flat on its side. Its flank puffed up and down in dying breaths.

"You didn't have to do that," Vivian said. "We could have just sent it along in another direction."

Felipe tugged the lead rope again, dragging the dying animal down the steep mountainside until suddenly letting go and stepping aside as the little avalanche of shale carried it down.

Only when the mule came to a sliding stop halfway down the mountain did Vivian realize that Felipe was laughing. He had been laughing the whole time.

They rode for miles, the moon and the stars casting the aspens around them an alkaline white; long parched bones thrusting upward from the earth. The breeze grew stronger the higher they climbed and colder the later it got. When the mouth of his horse began to froth a chalky paste and the moon threatened to disappear below a distant summit, Vivian asked to stop.

Felipe led them to a short cliff overlooking a small grove choked with cottonwoods. Veining through the trees and glistening in the starlight were the branched rivulets of a spring, and further in the distance Vivian saw a river winding through a shallow canyon. Without warning Felipe dismounted and began to lead his horse down a break in the cliff. Vivian followed.

They built a short chimney of stones and inside it a fire. They ate hardtack and jerky. Vivian rested his head on his saddle and watched Felipe scribble in his journal. The way his face followed his pen—the concentrated scorn—reminded Vivian of a reproachful priest searching for some admonishing passage. Almost every night of their journey he had observed Felipe scratch into those pages.

"Where are we going Felipe?"

Felipe didn't look up. "We keep along this trail."

"But to where? And what about Domingo? What about your son?"

Felipe kept writing. "Not yet. We will go someplace else."

"And keep killing?"

"Yes, and keep killing. And you can take all the treasure you like."

"Is the Virgin still telling you to do this?" Vivian asked mockingly. "What happens when she stops speaking to you?"

Felipe looked up, stuck his pencil into his mouth, and grinned. "Then something else will tell us!"

Vivian searched along the ground, picked up a twig, and threw it into the fire. "That last night at the hacienda? I regret ever having followed you, cousin."

Felipe poked the tip of his pencil between his teeth. "I regret it too, cousin."

"Yet here we have come."

"And thus must still go."

"Killing."

"Looting."

"Mutilating."

"Shooting and missing."

"Screaming at cow skulls."

"Weeping in one's sleep."

"Writing in diaries."

Felipe was trying to maintain his grin but Vivian saw it trembling into a snarl.

"Do you want to know what I am writing about now, cousin?"

"Tell me."

"I am writing about *you*." He said it like he expected it to sting.

"What about me?"

But Felipe's expression had changed again. Suddenly, he appeared hurt, ashamed, and after a long moment of looking at Vivian across the flames, the bottom of his beard shaking with his quivering lip, Felipe snapped the book shut and climbed to his feet.

"I'm going to piss on this fire and go to sleep."

"No. Please don't. I want to sleep next to it."

Felipe, looking somewhere in the darkness beyond Vivian, nodded. He picked up his saddle, carried it away from Vivian and the fire, and plopped it down behind a log and lay down.

Vivian threw a few more sticks into the fire, stuck his arms inside his shirt, and curled tight below his saddle blanket. He watched the fire for what must have been an hour, the shrinking blaze pulsing behind the stacked rocks.

Softly, from his place behind the log, he heard Felipe say, *"Buenos noches, hermano."*

And Vivian whispered good night to his brother, even though it was almost dawn.

CHAPTER 39

Already an hour behind after having to search out and gather the posse, McCannon and his men, minus Jim Landin who had been too drunk on potato vodka to be bothered, galloped down the wagon road leading out of town. As they neared the spot where McCannon planned to swerve off the path and beeline across the ranch lands to that dark hideout, Fred Miller shouted, "Ho boys, we're being followed! There's Death on our heels!"

McCannon craned his neck and in the afternoon sunlight saw what indeed appeared to be Death on his horse. The figure wore a long black trench coat flapping behind him as he raced toward them on a pale nag. He was gaining fast, his black sombrero held tight against the wind with one hand.

McCannon halted and waited for the rider. He slipped his hand inside his coat and rested it on the pistol.

The man pulled up beside the group. "Which one is Captain McCannon?"

"Who's asking?" Joe Lamb asked.

"I'm John McCannon. State your business."

"I been told you're chasing some killers, and so I come up from Denver to join you. Name's Billy Young"

"Denver?" Lamb asked. "What you doing coming all the way from down there? What's your stake in this?"

"My brother. He and his partner got kilt two weeks ago camping below Kenosha House. Man crept up on him in his sleep and stabbed him in the chest."

"That was your brother?" Nathrop asked.

"Jesse Young was his name. His partner was a prospector by the name of Seyga. Same man kilt him, too."

McCannon sized up Young. He was of slight build and seemed jittery, the corner of his right eye twitching as he talked. On the other hand he possessed a long, powerful-looking rifle with a scope, not to mention a fast horse.

"It's not one man we're after but two, one've them supposedly a boy. You prepared for that?"

"Wouldn't have come if I wasn't."

"Then come on. More is merrier."

"Yeah, we were one short anyways, and evens make for luckier numbers," Nathrop said.

"What's with all the black, Young? This your mourning getup or what?" Lamb asked.

Young's eyes fell to his rifle. He rubbed its barrel. "I rode up here to kill someone. Figured this was the way to dress for something like that."

The soggy floor of the basin dappled with melting snow. Shortly after Binkley's cabin they picked up the tracks leading toward a mountain with a summit bowed like a saddle. McCannon stopped at its base. "Look familiar, Chuck?"

"This is it, Captain."

"Then this is where we go on foot. Miller you stay here with the animals and keep a lookout for anyone sneaking around the other end back into the basin. The rest of you keep quiet and step light. Check your chambers, too, cuz if they're where I expect them to be, we'll be pulling triggers before sundown."

But after a slow trudge around the foot of the mountain and a wet army crawl the last fifty yards, the men peered into an empty camp. The tracks continued right past the two cow heads still half sunk in the marsh where Nathrop had dropped them—a carelessness that McCannon silently berated himself for—before hooking upward along a faint Indian trail heading southeast. The trail retreated back into the mountains, two horses and a mule.

McCannon felt the eyes of the other four men as they all stood—horseless, the evening light fading away—and in their silence he sensed neither their disappointment nor their frustration. He felt their embarrassment for him. Even Young, who had ridden all the way from Denver to avenge his dead brother, awkwardly scuffed the tip of his boot in the spongy grass.

"Best get our horses," McCannon said.

By the time the group scrambled around the mountain, met Miller and remounted, climbed back to the empty hideout, and finally set off along the Indian trail, stars twinkled in the moonlit sky. McCannon fell toward the rear, keeping only C.F. behind him lest he lose the hazy outlines of the men and stray entirely. It was an exceptionally bright night, bright enough for a man with decent vision to follow the hoofprints in freezing mud, although not exactly bright enough for someone with McCannon's eyes to see anything more than a vague land of shadows.

"Got something here," Nathrop called from out front.

The column stopped. From the left a sharp breeze struck McCannon's face and he grew aware of an immense cliff beneath him. "What do you have?"

"The mule's gone. Looks like they took a break here cuz I can see boot prints walking around. But when they pick back up the mule ain't with them."

"Where do the mule tracks lead?"

McCannon heard one of the men drop to the ground and begin pacing. Another gust of wind blasted him from the exposed mountainside to the east, and in that moment he suddenly understood what had happened to the mule.

"Well this don't make sense. They go right over the mountain. One of the men, too." The words were followed by the sound of thin rock shards tinkling downward.

"That's where they of disposed it," McCannon said.

"You mean killed it and dragged it down?"

"Probably got to slowing them down too much," Nathrop said.

"Means they ditched the pack, too."

"Or stashed it somewhere. What say we look?"

"No time," McCannon said. "You say the two horses continue on the trail?"

"Yep. Looks like they keep going up into the trees."

"Then that's where we keep going."

They nudged the horses on and McCannon thought of the business before them. The slaughtering of the mule had reinforced in him the fact that they followed not just bodiless impressions in a muddy Indian trail, but two desperate murderers.

He imagined the encounter, pictured his men riding slowly up to the two Mexicans as they slept on the icy ground next to a large fire, peaceful in their self-assuredness. He would ride slowly up to the biggest one, the older one with the great black beard and the wicked mouth. He'd awaken him with the click of the hammer and allow him just enough time to open his eyes and see McCannon on his horse and the business end of a barrel before both man and barrel sent him free-falling into hell's furnace.

Or turning a corner in the trees and spotting the two men up ahead still on their horses. If McCannon was lucky, the light was right, and the two did not turn around in their saddles immediately, the posse might be able to take some shots at their backs. If they were even luckier the shots might land. Otherwise there would be a chase, in which case McCannon hoped the killers rode slow horses. If not, McCannon had no compunction about shooting horses.

Then again, what if the two Mexicans *knew* they were being followed? What if they lay in wait, perhaps up in a tree, their rifles aimed downward at the trail? Then there would be casualties, and McCannon didn't want to think about that. He preferred spotting the two up in the trees early, then picking them off like squirrels.

The more McCannon envisioned these scenarios the more he realized he held no plans for these murderers other than to kill them. There would be no talk of capture, because if McCannon learned anything in the hills above Santa Fe, the battlefield where rifle smoke hovered above the forest and juniper bark exploded above his head, it was that victory is best served bloody.

His skin prickled, his senses heightened. The clopping plod of the horsemen before him seemed louder, the high-altitude breeze felt colder, the smell of earth, frost, and animal turned pungent. Even his vision brightened and cleared, and McCannon soon observed the sun peeking over the summit of the eastern horizon.

He smelled smoke. Faint and unmistakable.

"You all smell that?" Nathrop whispered. The column slowed.

"There! Down there!"

They stood atop a granite cliff overlooking a tapered grove of cottonwoods. At the head of the grove a spring surfaced from under the cliff and branched out into a few dozen thread-like streams interlacing the trees. Further off, a river shimmered in the morning sun. It was the Arkansas, winding down to Cañon City.

"What do you see, Miller?" McCannon asked.

"A horse."

"Two horses," Young said. He peered through his rifle scope. "There's another one in the trees behind the first. Both got their saddles on but I don't see any riders."

"Could be a trap."

"I don't think so."

"What do we do, Captain?"

McCannon considered it. "We need to get down there. Even if it's a ploy, we got no chance at anything from up here. Who sees a quick way down?"

"There's a trail right here that cuts down," Nathrop said. "It's narrow though with a lot've rocks. Steep too. Our horses would make a lot of noise going down it. Further yonder there looks like another path with a better slope. But that would bring us on the opposite end of their camp."

"Our horses stay here," McCannon said. "Three of us are gonna climb down this trail and another two are gonna flank them by heading down that slope opposite. One man's gonna stay here with the horses and keep an eye on everything from up top, ready to yell out in case he sees something that we on the floor don't."

"I'll be that man," Miller said.

"Fine. C.F., you take Young down that other end. We'll give you a ten-minute head start. Once you're down, approach slow and get hunkered in those thickets."

"I don't need to be taken," Young said.

"Nathrop and Lamb, you'll climb with me down the cliff. Once down, we move low and slow. We close them in so that with Miller up top the only direction they'll have to run is east. And if they run that way they hit the Arkansas, and this time of year the Arkansas ain't an easy river to cross."

"So which team shoots?"

"Whichever one gets first sight. But it better be damn sure."

"I want that shot," Young declared, looking around for a challenger. "I think I got those rights."

"Then go. We'll give you ten minutes. But I'm telling you, Young, slow and low, clear and sure. You'll waste your whole ride from Denver being too antsy."

C.F. and Young handed their reins to Miller and began a jog along the top of the cliff to where it sloped down into the tree-congested grove.

"That Young's apt to botch this job," Nathrop said.

After ten minutes, Lamb, followed by McCannon and Nathrop, eased their way into the steep cut of brush and loose stone bisecting the cliff face. They moved at a turtle's pace and just about as low to the ground, keeping a close watch on the horses in the trees.

Dropping into the soft grass of the grove's floor the three men scuttled and ducked behind a nearby willow. The camp sat less than a hundred yards straight ahead.

McCannon whispered for them to fan out, instructing that he take the inside against the cliff, Nathrop the middle, and Lamb the outside. "When one or both of them do finally pop their heads, I ain't gonna have the eyes to take a proper shot so it's gonna have to be one of you. Just make it count."

Nathrop and Lamb nodded. Hunched and with their rifles clutched below their knees, they separated and disappeared into the brush.

McCannon had yet to see the horses. He could still smell the faint wisps of a campfire and, as the sun arched higher, see the many tiny creeks flashing like twined metal. McCannon slogged through the marsh, ducking from willow to tree to willow. No birds sang, no breeze blew. All was silent except for the slow sucking of McCannon's boots. He followed his nose.

There came a snort and McCannon dropped to his knees. The sound was close, straight ahead. Peeking around the thick cottonwood, he spotted the horses. They stood tethered to two trees about fifteen feet apart with just enough slack in the reins to allow them a shallow crop of the grass below. The one nearest McCannon, however, did not eat. It looked at him, its ears flipped forward. It snorted again and this time followed it with a stomp, and suddenly it occurred to McCannon just how close he was.

The other animal lifted its head but instead of eyeing McCannon it craned the other way. Someone was approaching from back in the trees, and now both animals were looking that way. McCannon listened to the steps crunching over the grass and the willows scraping apart. A man emerged. Not a man, a boy. A slim child with a silvery-black, almost translucent, mustache. He wore a baggy gray-and-red serape that opened just enough at the sides to reveal a pistol holstered at his hip. Two barren eyes, as sunken and drained as a depleted mine, peered out from under a soiled tan sombrero.

The boy did not so much as look his direction, merely strode up to the reins of the first horse and began working at the knot around the tree.

Suddenly, McCannon felt a strange urge to save him. He didn't know if it was his limited vision and the resultant heightening of his other faculties, but he sensed something about the boy that deserved saving. It was a kind of remorse, a regret of the things he had done but also knowledge that they warranted his own death in turn, and it was for this knowledge alone McCannon did not want it to happen. It was like killing a man after he begged you to do it. You pull the trigger on a man like that with pity. Shame.

He wanted to suddenly whisper to this boy, tell him to get down, lay flat while we kill your friend, your father, whoever this other man is whom I know nothing of except that he corrupted you. *Lay flat child, and cover your eyes.*

The sky above the grove ripped apart. McCannon felt the boom of the rifle reverberate against the cliff. He saw the boy twirl hard as if a rope coiled half around his shoulders had just yanked and he slammed into the tree trunk and dropped. The shot had come from McCannon's immediate left, from Nathrop.

The horse, untethered now, lurched back and McCannon realized the boy still had the reins wrapped around his hand. He sat upright, one hand jerking high above his head with the rearing horse while just below the armpit a large chunk of side yawned apart, revealing blood and ribs with each thrust of the horse. The boy hung on, his other hand fumbling against his side for a pistol.

Another rifle thundered, this time from further down the line at Lamb's end, and a second cavity blasted open, this time in the boy's chest. The fingers loosened from the reins and the crazed animal disappeared in the thicket. The boy lay on his back, the bottoms of his boots splayed like two kicked-over headstones.

The second horse was going wild at its tether, and McCannon suddenly saw Young appear behind it, his rifle swinging out in front of him, his opened trench coat flying behind him like a cape.

McCannon bolted to his feet and turned toward Nathrop and Lamb and waved his arms. "For God's sake don't shoot!" he bellowed. "It's Billy Young!"

There came a shot and the tree above McCannon's head burst into a showering cloud of bark.

He dropped flat and yanked out his pistol. Young, the end of his barrel smoking, fired again at him. Except it wasn't Young, McCannon realized. The man looked like Young—a long and flowing black coat and matching hat—except for a thick black beard consumed his face. And was that a sword on his hip?

McCannon squeezed three shots at him. The man barely flinched, merely strode to where McCannon now rolled back behind the tree.

Another shot, then another—both of them from McCannon's

left. One of the bullets smashed into a trunk inches from the approaching bushy-faced man and the man hesitated. McCannon seized the moment and fired again. There was a grunt and the man's hand clasped at his shoulder. Another shot from McCannon's left, and now he twirled and raced back into the trees.

McCannon climbed up. Both Nathrop and Lamb ran to him.

"He get you?" Nathrop asked.

"No."

"Where's C.F. and Young?"

"I don't know but hurry. Let's send him their way."

The three took off at a jog, slowing just a little to look down and take in the face of the glassy-eyed boy.

"We might want to walk. Those two are gonna be firing this way any second," Nathrop said.

They slowed, their guns held out in front of them. Behind him McCannon could hear the single, still-tethered horse whinnying, but other than that nothing. After a while, they stopped completely.

A voice called from within the trees ahead, "Captain? Chuck? Lamb?"

"C.F. He's coming at you," Nathrop called back. "Dressed in black and got a beard. Be ready."

They waited. The woods were silent.

Fifty yards ahead, C.F. and Young emerged, walking cautiously with the stocks of their rifles pressed tight against their shoulders. Nathrop waved at them and the two men hesitated. McCannon thought he saw Young's head cock to the side, confused.

They closed the gap. "You didn't see him?" Nathrop asked, somewhat accusingly.

"Bearded man dressed in black? Didn't see him or nobody. Was that who you were shooting at?"

"Him and his *amigo*. Got the *amigo*."

Young stomped a foot. "I was supposed to get first shot!"

"Shut up, Bill," Nathrop said. "It's your fault he got away. You and your stupid undertaker's costume."

"No it's not, it's my fault," McCannon said. "And he ain't got away yet. He's veered eastward out of our snare. Fan out into a line and let's sweep this forest to the river."

Upon reaching the river however—its water high and fast and both banks dry—McCannon realized that once again he had judged wrong.

"Well I ain't heard Miller take a shot. What other way out has he got?" Lamb asked.

No one answered. The silence of restrained frustration devastated McCannon.

When they arrived back at the camp, Miller was there, rifling through the saddlebags of the escaped man's horse. The dead boy gaped at the sky.

"Miller? What the hell you doing down here?" Nathrop asked.

"What do you mean? I heard the firefight, and after half an hour of hearing nothing else I figured you was done. Except where's the other one?"

"Damnit, Miller, that's what I'm saying, why you down here when you're supposed to be looking out up there?"

"You mean he got away? I was looking out the whole time and I tell you I didn't—"

A chunk of tree directly above Miller's head exploded and once more the quiet of the grove ripped apart with the bark of a rifle. Everyone dove for cover. A second shot and the horse whinnied in agony and fell, blood spilling from the hole in its side. McCannon lifted his head and glimpsed the man's figure, dark and vague, high atop the cliff. And just as suddenly as it was there, it was gone.

After a clumsy, sliding scramble to the top of the cliff, the men found only four slaughtered horses, their throats split open and their heads stretched up against the trees to which they remained tied. Young's white mare was gone, as was Lamb's cherished burro.

The tracks led north, back toward where they had started.

They never did find the boy's horse, and in the end Nathrop and Wilson took off on the long walk to Cañon City to give the news of the posse's half success and to acquisition some mounts. The remaining four stoked the campfire back to life, dismantling the stone chimney and enlarging the pit zealously until the flames licked above their heads. They sat around it, passing flasks, recounting the battle.

McCannon said little from his spot beside the fire. After searching the saddlebags of the sniped horse, he had discovered two knives, a Colt .44 wrapped in a white shirt, a shiny Henry repeater tied to the saddle, a canteen, some jerky and hardtack, and over a pound in ammunition. He had also found a second pistol holstered on the boy's hip and a few loose bullets in his pockets. Padding around the body and feeling something crinkle inside the breast pocket, McCannon removed a folded piece of paper. Now, seated by the fire, he unfolded it. It was brittle with old sweat and moist with splotches of fresh blood. He angled it up toward the midday sun.

Illustrations covered both sides. On one, a long, elegantly curved saber filled the page from top to bottom. A sun shone in the corner of the page and beamed down onto a cross that appeared carved on the blade shortly below the hilt. It seemed McCannon and Metcalf had seen correctly; the bearded man carried a sword.

The reverse side of the page depicted a snowcapped mountain range. Lining the foot of the range was a smaller, velvety wave of hills. The scene seemed familiar although McCannon couldn't quite place it. On one peak, directly above the velvety hills and shortly below the summit, the illustrator had penciled another cross as if marking something specific. Above the cross were the words, *La Boca de Sipapu.*

McCannon folded the paper and slipped it into his pocket. Once Nathrop and C.F. returned with horses, he intended to stop at that turn in the trail where the mule had been killed, even though he suspected that whatever valuables the killers might have hidden there were likely being recovered this very moment.

McCannon looked around at the men. They would return to Bayou Salado only half triumphant, with more than a few embarrassing missteps to explain. But, in a tiny camp like Buckskin Joe, a place composed of little more than a few weathered dance halls and a dozen-some mule-headed miners, those unfortunate things always seemed second to the things worth celebrating. And judging from the already lively conversation around the fire, Buckskin Joe would soon have something big to celebrate.

McCannon didn't know what all he would do once he got back, but he figured he'd start by giving the map to Chivington. The major would know what to do with it. And it would feel good to be the one to hand it to him.

For now though, McCannon accepted the flask, and joined the conversation.

CHAPTER 40

The summer passed slow, still, and painfully quiet. The days were long and so too were the nights, for insomnia had struck the Espinosa family. From spring to September each one of them denied sleep like it were a sign of heartlessness or else forfeit, and they remained awake and separate in their rooms keeping watch out windows for signs of the two riders, listening for the sounds of their return. They watched the moon wax and wane over the months, invoking emotions inside their water-comprised brains much like it controlled the ocean's tides. They did this until the days began to shorten and the nights grew even longer and it became cold and now it was autumn and one by one they gave up hope and succumbed to their fatigue and, finally, fell to sleep.

At night, Hacienda de Espinosa divided into light and dark.

The line drew at an angle where the hallway met the parlor, the moonlight cast from the parlor window obstructed for its sidelong position beside the front door. Tonight the moon beamed especially bright, and if the light seemed lighter, the dark seemed darker.

As the moon drifted up and across the parlor window, the shadow yawned wider into the hallway, and soon José was pressing himself against the inner wall into the shrinking dark.

On the sofa before him, concealed within his tent of shadow below the backrest, lay his father. José couldn't see his face, only the oily shock of black hair spilling over the armrest near-est the hallway. The end table had been scooted in front of the sofa, and on its surface as if shoveled from a much larger table was a heap of cigarette butts, drinking glasses turned into ashtrays, soiled kerchiefs, bullets—some upright, others toppled on their sides—a half-empty bottle of tequila standing tall amid the mess as if master of ceremonies, a pistol leaning against the bottle, and a framed collodion portrait of Lino, Cecilia, and José.

José looked at the table and felt nothing.

He didn't know how long he had been standing there at the mouth of the hallway, but he thought he had done most of it half asleep, half in a dream. He felt fully awake now, alert to every pop, crack, and shuffle in this house where everyone slept but him.

The dream had involved a story his mother once told him about a princess who went to bed on twenty featherbeds yet could not sleep because of a tiny pea stuffed under the very bottom cushion.

Or had it been another dream, one that recalled the princess and the pea only as he awoke and found himself standing in the hallway shadows? Dream and memory, what begat which?

José stepped across the line. A clucking sounded from the sofa, the moist pop of a tongue suctioning off the mouth's roof, and José crouched. He heard his father shift, the rubbery moan of the sofa's leather. He waited for the breaths to become steady and rhythmic, then stood and made his way to the window.

The moon, a low and waxing crescent, plunged into frame. José shielded his face and turned away. He waited for his eyes to adjust, staggered by the brightness alighting the kitchen table where one chair stood askew. In front of it on the table was his mother's own leftover state of being. A heap of crumbled bread. If over on the parlor's end table explicated his father's daily regimen, here was his mother's; crumbling pieces of baked bread into scatterings which she then, with acumen, scooped into one neat pile. Sometimes she remembered to throw the pile to the birds. Other times, like tonight, the pile went forgotten.

Sometimes she made him sit on her lap and she held him even though he was too big. And when she finally left, he knew she would try and take him with her.

He turned and pressed his face against the glass. He saw out for miles, the few dim lanterns of Costilla floating on a pale desert like water candles. And he remembered the dream.

A firebug flew across a piercing moon, and far below José had sensed it.

The dream prompted the memory. Like the princess and the pea, in his dream José, through his own extraordinary sensitivity, had become disturbed by a slight changing of light, a tiny brightness within one utterly absorbing. Pressing his temple against the cold glass, he gazed at the shadow of the Sangre de Cristos. They loomed over Costilla. Their slopes, lush with spring vegetation, were ghostly viridescent.

From behind him came a cough and again José dropped to a crouch. Another cough, faint and tiny from back within the hallway, followed by a sleepy whimper. His father shifted and before the chance was lost José slunk across the floor and back into the hallway's darkness.

More little coughs spaced between more whimpers steadily turning into cries. The baby was on the verge of a fit, one that would dash all sleep and silence within the home, and quickly José slipped into the room from which the cries came, closing the door behind him.

Soundlessly he moved to where Domingo lay squirming and coughing on the bed. He knelt, scooped the baby into his arms, and held him against his chest. After a while the baby quieted and fell asleep in his embrace.

A hand, cold and frail, floated from the bed and rested on his elbow.

José leaned in to whisper. "He is back. I see his fire in the mountains."

The hand squeezed. For a long moment it clutched him and José felt his sister's pulse harden through her palm. "Bring him to me."

★ ★ ★ ★ ★

PART SIX:
THE MATURATION OF
JOSÉ ESPINOSA
AUTUMN 1863

★ ★ ★ ★ ★

Fort Garland, Colorado Territory
18 September 1863

To Mr. Ceran St. Vrain:

Ceran, no doubt you already heard of this man Felipe Espinosa, this "ax man" as the newspapers called him before the recent slaying of his companion and consequent disclosure of his identity. Presently thirty-two corpses have been discovered, their conditions mutilated beyond my stomach for description but sufficient to justify the newspapers' moniker.

Espinosa is thought to be in possession of a great amount of pillage and he needs a place to hide. A map was discovered on the body of the accomplice. It appears to lead to a cave in the mountains over which the cartographer has inscribed, "La Boca de Sipapu." On the reverse side is an illustration of a black-handled cavalry saber with a cross etched below the hilt. I have included the map and illustration with this letter.

Governor Evans has ordered me kill this terrorist Espinosa. Between Texan rebels and the Indians my fort is fighting two wars, and this as Lincoln imports our most able men east and leaves me a leftover soldiery of overaged, overweight, underspirited men. I have not the resources to hunt a murderer. I'm afraid I must seek outside help.

I am seeking a mulatto Indian hunter named Tom Tobin. It is said he can track a "grasshopper through sagebrush." It is also said he is a friend of yours. Is this true, Ceran? If so, would you recommend him to such a task?

Awaiting urgently your reply,
Colonel Samuel F. Tappan

Mora, New Mexico Territory
26 September 1863

To Colonel Samuel F. Tappan:
Sam, does Fort Garland already require another shipment of flour? Or is this correspondence of a more serious business?

I have followed the Espinosa case in the newspapers, and I only hope after this violent spring followed by the passing of this silent summer you are not too late. By now that snake has very well slithered back down into Old Mexico.

I have viewed the map and the illustration. I think "Sipapu" is something Puebloan. Unfortunately, I have never known a saber with a cross on it.

Tom Tobin has been my friend almost thirty years. He is the most reliable man I know, as well as the most frightening. Last I saw him he was contracted out to a rancher who was paying him for scalps, and Tobin had six of the nasty things hanging from his mule. I asked him if he didn't think hanging those scalps for all creation to see might attract the ire of a few Indians, and Tobin points to a pair and says that is how he got those two.

I tell people they will know Tobin when they see him for he always rides a dark mule and is always in the company of an immense wolf dog. The animal has dark brown hair and snarls and bites and kills if even you smell wrong. I like to tell people that the same is true of the dog.

If, Sam, you are looking for someone to hunt down the bandit Espinosa, Tobin is your man.

I don't know whether this cave, this "Mouth of Sipapu," exists, but if so Tobin will find it. I will also ask him about Espinosa's "divine sword."

If Tobin has a soft spot it is only for his dog and for a girl named Pascuala living in Arroyo Hondo. Tobin doesn't stay still much, but when he does it's usually with her. It has been some time since last I saw my friend and I figure I owe a visit.

Riding north presently,
Ceran St. Vrain

Arroyo Hondo, New Mexico Territory
8 October 1863

To Colonel Samuel F. Tappan:
Sam, found Tobin. He has agreed to search for Espinosa and will begin in Costilla at the former residence. I have given him the map and illustration and he says he will find the cave as well as any pillage the bandit may have hidden.

You may see him before this letter reaches you, but in case you don't Tobin says the sword depicted on the map belonged to a Sergeant Jesse Talford. Know him? He died last year in Colorado Springs of leprosy, got buried in Taos. Tobin says it is not a cross Talford etched on the blade. He says it is a "T." Thought you would like to know that, Sam, in case you were worried which side God was on. Also, if Tobin finds the sword, he says he is keeping it.

Hoping his mission is quick and successful,
Ceran St. Vrain

CHAPTER 41

The campfire shone below the summit and shortly above the upper hem of timberline so that anyone looking from Costilla could have seen it. José suspected anyone looking from the southern San Luis Valley could have seen it, and the thought was enough to make him glance behind him as his horse approached the jutting slopes. He saw no one, only the few winking lanterns of Costilla and the moonlight glinting off the windows of Hacienda de Espinosa.

He didn't expect to spend another night inside it. Tomorrow he would let his mother take him, for she was like him and had waited only for Secundina and Domingo. Or, rather, they waited for Felipe. They knew Vivian was dead. Tappan, the officer from Fort Garland, had presented the news to the family by unfolding a newspaper declaring the slaying of Vivian Espinosa. But as long as Felipe remained a factor, so did José's sister and nephew.

He had promised Secundina he would not leave until Felipe returned for her, and he wondered if Cecilia had done the same. To abandon his sister and her baby alone with Lino would be next to murder, yet at the same time for them to stay with Lino was suicide, and José feared his mother could hold out little longer.

With the reins looped around his fingers and both hands clamped on the saddle horn, José let the horse thrust heavenward between the pines and thought how soon he could quit being scared. His father was a doomed man, and José refused to be doomed with him. The Penitentes forsook Lino, the Army bullied him, the Navajo servants had slipped away weeks ago, and now it was only a matter of time before *Tío* Carlos reclaimed the flailing hacienda. But before that could happen, José and his mother would escape. They would be free to run once Secundina and Felipe were free to run as well. He had little hope for his damaged sister, her infant child and fugitive husband, but what more could he do but fulfill his promise?

The horse heaved up the steep forest. Approaching timberline, the animal froze. Its ears twisted forward and alert. José ducked low in the saddle and peered through the branches. Fifty yards ahead, firelight danced through the trees. Silhouetted before it were what appeared to be two horses.

José's heart quickened. If Vivian was dead, why two horses? For the first time since glimpsing the fire more than a mile below, it occurred to José that his instinct—his dream—might have been wrong, that perhaps he just had ridden upon strangers. Indians maybe. He considered dismounting and approaching on foot but the idea of being caught sneaking up on a sequestered campsite in the night, including that of his mass-murdering cousin, banished the thought instantly.

Instead he toed his horse forward and began to sing the words to *A La Rueda de San Miguel.*

> *"A la rueda, a la rueda de San Miguel,*
> *Todos traen su caja de miel.*
> *A lo maduro, a lo maduro,*
> *Que se voltee Felipe de burro."*

To the Saint Michael, Saint Michael round,
Everyone brings their box of honey.
When it's ripe, when it's ripe,
Let burro Felipe turn around.

Something rose from behind the flames, something that even illuminated by the fire remained a shadow; a figure wrapped in black from ankles to head. There was no face. José pulled the horse back. The figure held something in each hand, a pistol and what looked to be a book with one finger pressed between the pages. For a long moment the two stared at each other, the only sound the spit-crackling of the fire. Then the black head split apart, and from within that beard opened a grin vile and familiar.

"Brother," Felipe said.

"Tie your horse. Join me." Felipe set the pistol and book in the dirt and dragged a log closer to the fire. José looked around the camp. Besides the two animals—one a snowy white bay, the other not a horse at all but a chocolate-colored burro—he saw nothing except the book, the pistol, and a single rifle tied to the rear of the bay's saddle.

"Where did it all go Felipe? Where is all the treasure you killed so many men for?"

"I never killed anyone for treasure."

"Where is it?"

"There is none. It is gone."

"Mm, I bet. And where have you been hiding all these months? Wherever it was you must not have had a mirror. Or maybe you want to look like that? Maybe this beard is your disguise?"

Felipe forced a weak smile. He tapped a boot on the log's surface and looked at José expectantly.

"No, we must go. Put out your fire and follow me."

"Good! Of course. Where shall we go? I have no food but we can get more. We will get more easy, and I will follow you, brother, however far you choose."

"You are going to follow me to the bottom of this mountain.

That is all."

The light faded from Felipe's eyes and the smile disappeared. It was more than a look of hurt, although what else José couldn't quite tell.

Felipe took a slight step backward. "What is at the bottom of the mountain?"

"Your wife and son."

He took another step back and dropped to his knees. Working suddenly in short, spastic movements, Felipe stuffed the book into his coat pocket. Between the flames José saw him take up the pistol and begin fidgeting with it, squeezing and rubbing the barrel between his grimy palms, his eyes darting everywhere except at José who now realized it was neither hurt nor surprise he saw in his cousin. It was fear.

"They killed Vivian," Felipe blurted. "They murdered your brother simply because he was a Mexican."

"I said Secundina and Domingo are alive."

"He had done nothing, but because he was *Mexicano y Católico* they hunted him, and since I am the same they hunt me, too."

"You aren't listening. I—"

"Came for me, brother. You came to join me." Felipe suddenly rose and ambled over to the horse. "We will ride wherever you wish José, do whatever you want. If you are hungry I will get you food. If you need other things I will get that too. I know places where there are gold chunks the size of your fist, and beefs fat with green grass, and . . ."

José had stopped listening. He watched Felipe pretend to fumble with a loose saddle strap; the brother who had left him and the stranger who returned. And in that moment he understood.

"You knew."

The hands paused on the strap. Felipe fell silent.

"You knew and yet this fire is not for them."

"The fire is for you, brother. And you came."

"I'm here for Secundina. And we are not brothers."

"But we were."

"No, you are a distant cousin. That is all you have ever been. Even long ago, before you shot your gun at my feet and deserted me and got my real brother killed, that is all you were, *un relacion lejanas.*"

"That's not true, José. I remember what we used to call each other, you and me and Vivian. We would call each other—"

"Enough! I'll take you to your family Felipe, but after tonight we don't see each other ever again."

In the firelight, moisture glistened in Felipe's eyes. He looked about and gestured to the burro. "I brought that for you."

"Give it to my sister." José turned his horse and nudged it back down the mountain, not stopping or looking back.

He was halfway down before he heard Felipe's horse and burro behind him, the loose stones tumbling under the clop of their hooves.

Half a mile south of Hacienda de Espinosa and shortly below the scaling forests of the Sangre de Cristos, the road to Taos branched southeast to San Francisco Pass. It was at the edge of the forest overlooking this junction that José had promised to lead Felipe. Secundina said to have him there by first light. Spying the road and the valley beyond from their place in the trees José watched the eastern sky warm a metallic gray.

The air was still, the woods silent except for a lone crow perched on a limb directly overhead cawing in reproach. José peeked at Felipe. His face craned up at the bird, his mouth gaped in dumb wonderment. His duster was open revealing the pistol on his hip, and behind him the rifle hung laced beneath the saddle's cantle. Felipe twisted the reins anxiously in one hand while the other held the lead rope to the packless burro.

Felipe's eyes dropped from the crow and to José who jerked his head forward and stiffened.

A rooster called far off in Costilla. From their viewpoint, José could see the town and the hacienda below it. But as the sky grew ever lighter over the valley, he saw no woman emerging from that hacienda, a child bundled against her chest. José saw no one at all.

He envisioned his father catching her as she attempted to slip out the door and immediately banished the thought. There would be no hope for Secundina after something like that, and José would not allow even the image. Despite his feelings for Felipe, José loved his sister. He loved his nephew, too, and because he loved them he could not help but weep for them as they wept for the husband and father who had worked so hard and for so long to get their love. And it was because of this that even though he would never say it to him, José believed Felipe deserved them back.

"José?"

He turned in his saddle and what he saw nearly made him jump. Felipe's face was contorted into a painful grimace and tears streamed around his running nostrils, draining into his beard.

"Don't make me do this."

There came a shout from the valley and José jumped. It was a man's voice, followed by the creaking rumble of wagon wheels. Another shout, a *whooah*, and the wagon rolled into sight between the branches. It traveled south from Costilla and slowed as it approached the junction.

José glanced behind him, his mind still reeling from his cousin's plea and now the surprise of the wagon. Felipe's face was soaked with tears and snot but his eyes had widened as if staring into the dark end of a long muzzle. They stared past José at the wagon, and swiveling back around José saw the reason for Felipe's daze. Secundina sat high atop the buckboard.

"Vamos!" José said, and dug both heels into the horse's ribs.

He burst out of the trees, his horse galloping through the sage. He kept his head low against the dewy dawn air, his eyes fixed on the wagon less than a hundred yards away. He made out the skinny frame and long black hair of his sister and, on the far edge of the buckboard, the driver whose identity José could only guess. Among the Penitentes Felipe had many supporters, and Lino many enemies, and by the looks of it one must have spotted Secundina and Domingo sneaking onto the road.

Secundina leaned forward and turned to José who yanked back the reins. The driver looked at him and the wagon came to a halt. For a moment, frozen across their short distance, the two parties simply stared at one another. José looked for the frail arm, the sharp cheekbones, the dark eyes of his sister but saw no such things. Instead the woman atop the wagon was full and beautiful with two healthy arms folded below a large chest, blushed cheeks, and warm green eyes. There sat no baby in her lap, and the man beside her was no Penitente. The man beside her was a gringo.

The two continued looking at him confused but unconcerned, and for a second José felt his face flush hot with embarrassment.

Then he heard the hooves galloping louder behind him and turned just in time to see Felipe racing past him.

"Felipe!" But Felipe did not respond, merely spurred the white bay harder and tugged at the rope leading to the snorting burro in tow. The woman and the driver frowned. José charged forward.

Felipe drew up directly in front of the stalled wagon and its two horses and José saw him begin to speak. He whipped at his horse and caught up.

". . . but Santa Fe is much too far of a ride. Much, much too far if all we are looking for is *un prostíbulo*," Felipe was saying, one finger making little cavalier loops in the air. "Surely there must be something closer."

"We need to go, cousin. Right now," José said, offering an apologetic look to the couple. The woman was forcing a polite but uncomfortable smile while her fingers twisted in her lap. The gringo, an older man in a pinstripe suit, appeared irritated but at the same time perplexed, and José could see he did not speak Spanish.

"Why brother? We are in no hurry. This is *Señora* Delores and her husband, Philbrook. They are telling us the nearest place to whore."

José glanced at the couple who were obviously saying no such thing. Delores leaned to her husband, raised a hand, and whispered in his ear.

Felipe's face darkened. "Are you whispering about me, *puta*?"

She gasped, looking as if just punched in the stomach. Beside her the gringo's face flushed, clearly understanding the insult.

"Okay, Paco," the man said, cracking his knuckles before swinging both legs over the driver's box and dropping to the ground. He strode toward where Felipe remained atop his horse, clenching and unclenching his fists.

Felipe turned his head to José and winked.

"Felipe—"

With a showy deliberateness, Felipe opened one side of his coat and reached inside. The man stopped and somewhere, as if at the other end of a long tunnel, José heard the woman scream. The pistol leveled before the man's belly, held for a moment, boomed.

A hole blasted open in the man's shirt. His mouth dropped open and he stared down at the wound, his eyes flaring wide just as a dollop of blood, jellyish with fat and flesh, spewed out in a thick trickle. The man looked up at Felipe, dropped to his knees, and fell onto his back with both hands cradled over his heaving stomach and his lips opening and closing like a fish out of water.

One of the wagon horses reared back and began to thrash. The woman screamed louder and when Felipe, his hideous mouth stretched grinning, raised the gun at her she cowered into a ball. The pistol fired; once, twice, three times, and José buried his eyes in his shoulder. When he opened his eyes Felipe's pistol was aimed and smoking and Delores Sanchez remained tight in her ball, her knees tucked against her chest on top the buckboard. Three bullet holes had blasted through the wagon's front, one to the woman's left, another to her right, and the last directly above her head.

The two horses reared and fought forward in their harnasses. Felipe lowered the pistol and moved off the road to let the wagon and its shrieking occupant glide past. José backed aside and watched in a daze as the wagon jostled down the road like the end of some ruinous parade.

Felipe raised the pistol above his head and fired into the air. "Tell them I'm still riding *puta*! Say Felipe rides with José!"

CHAPTER 42

Secundina heard the pistol shots, five faraway pops that tensed her spinal muscles and stung the scar in her back like a dirty finger pressing on a peeled blister.

Lino appeared to hear it, too, or at least register it in his dreams as he choked on a snore and flipped from his side to his back on the sofa, the whip-crack-like pops fading away outside. Secundina halted shortly outside the hallway, Domingo blessedly asleep in her arm and weighing achingly against her cracked rib. After a moment Lino's snoring resumed and Secundina continued toward the door. Something was wrong. She had to hurry.

She was three steps from the exit when he croaked, "You are up early."

She whirled. He lay on his back, his head on the armrest, hands crossed over his chest. His eyes were crusty and bloodshot, his face peppered with the beginnings of a beard, and his oily black hair spread over the armrest like a splayed mop end. He eyed her with one corner of his mouth curled upward, appearing amused not at catching her in the act of something suspicious but rather as if aware of how he must look and proud of it. It was the smug complacency of a man who's hit bottom and no longer fears falling.

"Domingo kept me up," she said.

Lino dug a finger into one ear, pulled it out, looked at it, then wiped it on one of the bunched rags atop the table. Secundina glanced at the table—the soiled rags, the cigarettes, the empty glasses, the gun, the whiskey, the portrait—and when he noticed her do it, he smiled wider. She thought of the time José had shown her his booger collection, his delight in her disgust.

"Starting to regret that baby?"

"No."

"Thinking of taking him outside and holding his little head in the creek?"

Secundina turned back to the door.

"Stop. Come here."

"I need fresh air."

"I said come here."

Secundina hesitated, torn. Something had gone terribly wrong outside. Something was wrong here, inside. She heard no more gunshots but time had become suddenly much shorter. They were waiting for her, wondering where she was.

Secundina wheeled around and approached him.

"Sit down," he said, gesturing to the rocking chair to his left.

She circled around him and sat.

Lino sat up and coughed hard into a raised sleeve, his eyes seeming to burst redder with every wet hack. He gazed at her sitting expressionless with the baby cradled against her belly, reached for the half-empty bottle of tequila, and hoisted it, causing the propped pistol to fall clattering. He took a swig, crossed one leg over the other, and set the bottle down between them.

"I was having a very good dream before you woke me. My cousin Ignasio was in it, which normally would have annoyed me since he occupies my thoughts too much when I am awake. But I was happy in this dream because he was upset, crying. He was groveling and asking my forgiveness. At first I gave him a stern look that said I didn't know if I could while inside I rejoiced. But then Felipe was there, or rather he was already

392

there and I only noticed him then, like the way in dreams people just suddenly *are*. And I realize Ignasio is not apologizing for all the things I thought he was. He is apologizing for Felipe, for ever having forced his son on me.

"So I make my face even graver like I am acknowledging the terribleness of what he did. I am enjoying the groveling more and more you see, because it was what Ignasio still owed me when he died. Then I see that Felipe is crying, too, and I become excited because I think he also is going to beg my forgiveness. And that is when I finally comprehend it. Ignasio is not apologizing to me. He is not asking for *my* forgiveness. He is asking for his son's."

Lino tossed back the tequila bottle. Through the window behind him the sun spread down the mountains like a portcullis about to close.

He dragged the back of his hand across his lips. "I was not disappointed though, not in the dream anyway. I guess I am now, thinking about it. But in the dream I was just amused. I said to Ignasio, 'Why are you apologizing to him? You are dead because of him. Why are you asking for his forgiveness when everything bad that has happened is *his* fault?' But he cannot hear me. It is like he cannot even see me, like I am watching from a hiding place even though I'm standing right there. But Felipe can hear me. Felipe knows I am there, because after I say what I do he nods. And nodding and crying he says, 'I understand.'

"And then you woke me." Lino gulped the tequila with his eyes aimed down the bottle at Secundina. Through the hallway behind her she heard two faint thumps as her mother stepped out of bed. In a few minutes she would be dressed and joining them, and then things would get even more troublesome. In a few minutes both parents would be wondering why José had yet to emerge from his room.

"You hate me, Secundina, because you think I am why things are like this. You blame me for Felipe and Vivian as if I wrote their fates. Your mother blames me for never fathering them. The Penitentes praise Felipe as a Robin Hood and so decide me a villain for ever trying to bring him home. Yet Don Carlos finds me embarrassing because I did not. Well let them blame me. Why should I care?

"Keep on hating me, *chica,* even though you are wrong to think their choices were not their own. Like a breeze the influence of others might sway a person one way or another, but in the end the decision to walk with that breeze, against it, or to just sit down and bear it belongs to him with the feet on which to walk and the ass on which to sit. I am not their father, and I never needed to be. Felipe is no Robin Hood who fights for the poor. He fights for himself and I cannot bring him home if he does not want it. He is his own man because everyone is a child of God. And so who was Ignasio to ask his son's forgiveness?"

Still cradling Domingo in her lap, Secundina traced her fingers under the bottom of his chubby arm to the soft flesh of his tricep and pinched. At first, deep in sleep, he did not respond, but when she pinched again harder his mouth shot open ushering out a hoarse rush of air that turned into a shriek. His arms flailed and he began to writhe in the folds of Secundina's dress.

Lino grimaced. "God, the thing is crying again. That baby is damaged, Secundina, he screams more than any baby should."

"He is a baby. Babies cry."

"Not that loud. Now he's going to wake Cecilia and your brother."

Domingo was in full fit now, shrieking so that it reverberated in the empty drinking glasses on the end table. Lino put his hands to his ears.

"He needs air," she said.

"Go." Lino waved her away. "Think about what I said about the creek. I would never tell."

Secundina whisked past him and out the door.

The sun had slid down the face of the Sangre de Cristos and was about to spill across the valley. The air was brisk and warming rapidly. Secundina strode around the side of the hacienda, rubbing Domingo's arm. She snuck one last look behind her and began to run.

The pain knotted in her back and her cracked rib flexed agonizingly with the baby bouncing against it. Yet the pain was peripheral, something noticed but unacknowledged like the soldiers that had held her down and dug out the bullet lodged in her left deltoid with a torched Bowie knife while in her dream state all she could think about was Felipe, where he was and could she please just see him? Could she for the moment just squeeze his hand?

Up ahead a figure crouched on the ground below his horse. He had his back to her and seemed to be inspecting something draped in the road.

She sprinted, crashing through sage and yucca that clawed at her legs through the thin hem of her dress. Domingo wailed louder and without knowing it Secundina chanted between breaths: "You are all right. They are all right. We are all right . . ."

The man turned to her and Secundina hesitated. He was a gringo, a traveler judging by the bags on the back of his horse. Then she looked at the thing on the ground and stopped. Another stranger, dead with what looked to be a bullet wound seeping from his stomach below his folded, blood-encrusted hands.

The man rose and said something to Secundina in English. She wouldn't have understood it anyway. Her ears were ringing and all other receptors used for understanding had gone numb.

There was no sense in what lay dead on the ground or in the utter emptiness of the valley. Secundina sat, legs stretched out before her, Domingo writhing in her lap.

Something drew her attention south, and in her swimming vision she saw yet another strange rider approaching. He was dark, an Indian perhaps, and seated atop a mule while a tremendous wolf paced along his side. Secundina laid back and rested her head among the sage, and closing her eyes she wondered how much of it was a dream.

CHAPTER 43

"If they catch you, they will kill you," Felipe said, turning his horse and spurring it back into the mountains, the burro trotting along behind him. The screams of Delores Sanchez faded with the rumblings of the wagon as her husband lay bleeding in the roadway. José stared down at him and told himself that he should help.

He told himself to run home this instant, that there was no time, that he better do something. You cannot just stand here. You better do something. You better run home and find your mother and tell her it was not your fault, that Felipe did it and you tried to stop him except he tricked you and if that Tappan man from Fort Garland comes again, Mamá, you must hide me or else they will kill me. He told himself to press his wet face into her dress and tell her not to let them kill him, that it was not his fault.

He looked for his sister and saw only a rider in the distance, some gringo coming his way. At the edge of the forest in which only moments ago they had been hiding, Felipe disappeared back among the branches. Suddenly José was alone.

A hundred yards away the man stopped and eyed José, unsure. Glancing toward the hacienda and seeing no one, José kicked his horse and bolted after Felipe, following him deep into the mountains.

★ ★ ★ ★ ★

How far they rode and for how long José did not know. Miles and hours. Never did Felipe look over his shoulder to check that José was still with him. He did not have to, and knowing this José hated him even more. Yet he found he could say nothing of it, that he was mute to burying Felipe with condemnations or renouncement. If Felipe would say something—to turn in his saddle even once to *see* his cousin—then perhaps José would not feel so vulnerable and dependent, and maybe then he would have had the courage. But because Felipe ignored him José could only follow, hating his cousin for pulling him further and further away.

They crossed the Sangre de Cristos, plowing through clinging swaths of melting snow and hooking northward along the range's eastern flank. They entered a shallow canyon shortly above tree line and José heard something scrape atop the canyon wall. Suddenly there seemed to be sounds everywhere. José became aware of every squirrel tittering in the forest, every trickle of snowmelt, every tiny stone grinding beneath the horses' hooves.

They left the canyon and fell into the trees. The forest grew denser and the summits to their left sharpened and climbed. It was all new to José, as far north as he had ever been, and the realization startled him, as if the passing into this unfamiliar place meant that nothing would ever be familiar again. And José supposed this was true, for nothing right now seemed so strange and so far from home than the very person he followed.

They came to the funneling headwaters of a creek winding down a sharp gully thicketed with scrub oak and aspen. Felipe dropped into the ravine, curving their path again eastward and down into the lowlands. Their animals had been trotting since sunup and as the western sky reddened their legs trembled at the joints, their tongues chalky with dehydration. Only the burro, without rider or pack, appeared healthy. They entered a tall cluster of trees looking out to where the stream plateaued out into the plains.

Felipe pulled to a stop. "I am tired," he said, swinging down from the saddle and leading his horse and the burro to drink. José dropped to the grass. At his feet were the few rotting remains of a deer carcass: a gnawed skull and spinal column and two peeling front legs with the hooves still attached. José picked up one of the legs.

Felipe had his back to him. "Better give your horse some wat—"

José swung. The air whistled between the cloven hoof and the leg smashed into the side of Felipe's jaw. It sounded like a wood-block and Felipe's head whipped to the side. He crumpled, landing on his side and then looking up wild-eyed at José.

He opened his mouth and blood and tooth gushed out like stones tumbling in a flood. "I had to save the woman!"

For a split second José thought he was talking about Secundina. But Felipe had not saved Secundina, had in fact done the very opposite, and José realized he was talking about the Sanchez woman. He swung the club back and hammered the hoof into Felipe's ribs with all his fury. Felipe howled, his hands sliding from his bloody face to his side. José raised one foot and stomped the face, grinding his heel into the nose.

Felipe hacked. Blood splattered from his mouth and nose and across his face. He tried to speak, choking on the blood, bone splinters and teeth. "It was because of them. It's their fault I had to—"

"It's because of you!" José knelt on top of his cousin and snatched him by the hair. "It is your fault Felipe. It is *all* your fault."

José climbed back up and hoisted the leg above his head again. He hesitated. Felipe's eyes had rolled into the back of his head and he started to convulse. José lowered the leg and, for the second time that day, stared at a dying man and struggled to decide what to do. It had not been his intention to kill Felipe. He had had no predetermined objectives for this assault, only unrestrained rage. Although sobered some, José could not let go of that rage, and he held no compunction about letting his cousin die.

Then he remembered what it would mean if Felipe died: José would be by himself. His terror at being left to fend for himself had goaded him throughout the day's long ride, and to suddenly be alone in these unfamiliar woods on this wrong side of the mountain under this darkening sky as they—whoever *they* were—hunted him, was to José the equivalent of death. Of being shipwrecked in deep and dark waters. Because in the end, no matter how they forced his maturity—his brother's death, María's death, his father's deterioration, his mother's anxiety, the promises his sister exacted and the atrocities his cousin committed—José was still only thirteen. He was a boy, and he still got scared.

José dropped the club, bent behind Felipe, and hoisted him to a sitting position. The blood that had pooled in his mouth spilled into his beard and down his chest. José hit him on the back until Felipe gasped, coughed, and started to breathe. José rose and stood over his cousin as Felipe rocked back and forth, his hands clutching his knees, coughing. He buried his face in the top of his knees and mumbled something.

"What?"

"I said I know!" Felipe blurted, and suddenly he was weeping. "You are right."

"Why did you come back?"

Felipe sobbed between his knees. "Because I was afraid by myself."

"By yourself? Secundina wanted to go with you. She would have . . ."

But suddenly José understood. It struck him with the impact of something long and tragically evident.

Felipe dragged a sleeve across his eyes, leaving a stripe between the blood and grime. He looked up at José beseechingly. "I came back for you."

José felt the hate rush back inside him, no longer so wrathful but rather pitying and remorseful, the object of it crushed but unrepentant. "Damn you cousin."

"We were brothers."

"Damn you."

Felipe grimaced, fresh tears squeezing from his eyelids. He began to rock again, clutched two handfuls of beard, and as José watched in horror ripped the gristly clumps from the skin.

"Jesus, Felipe."

There came a sudden crashing in the trees above them. Branches snapped and willows rustled and up the slope José observed the aspens bend sideward and snap back.

Almost perfunctorily—his face looking neither scared nor surprised, just tired—Felipe pulled the pistol from his hip and held it out before him, his elbows balanced on his knees. He sniffled. The two horses and the mule craned their heads up from the creek and turned toward the noise, ears pointed and alert. José, his heart pounding anew, considered running but quickly decided against it. He crouched behind his cousin.

From within the racket there arose a song. The tune filled the ravine and tunneled down it as if carried by the stream, a joyful melody in a strange tongue. Within the verses was what sounded to be laughing, wet wheezing chuckles that muddled in the singer's mouth like he was sucking on something. Felipe lowered the pistol, set it at his side.

The willows burst apart and there, perched before them in

the fading light atop a dark mule, loomed a nightwalker. He was a skeleton, his face as pale and creviced as the moon. A few wispy strands of hair as snowy as the tail of Felipe's white bay hung from the top of his skull. He wore buckskin leggings and a breechcloth below a soiled long-sleeve shirt. Clavicles protruded above the shirt collar. A leathery scar sunk over one hollow eye socket, and hanging from his shoulders was a small backpack.

"Hello, Blanco," Felipe said.

"Espinosas! See what I have, a mule!"

"You look past death, old chief. You look terrible."

Blanco laughed, the same wheezing chuckle and José realized he was toothless. His lips pulled in like wilted cantaloupe.

"Then I have found proper company. Rise up now Coyote Mouth. What have you to eat?"

They built a fire. The woods grew dark. The burro Felipe had towed all day was slaughtered and filleted.

"What if someone sees this fire?" José asked. "Or smells it?"

The chief drew his steak in from where it sizzled at the end of a sharpened willow branch above the flames. He dropped the slab onto a flat stone on his lap and began to grind it into a mush with a second stone.

"No one will sense this fire," Blanco said.

"How are you sure?"

"Because everyone is too far away."

"Who is everyone?"

The chief shrugged, gestured a hand around him as if to suggest the world. *"Everyone."*

"But they are looking for us."

"Only one of them was, a man with a dog, and now he is not."

Felipe scribbled furiously in his diary. The pencil stopped now and he looked up. "He lost our trail?"

"No. He is dead. I do not know about the dog."

Felipe tapped the end of the pencil against his lips. "Thank you."

Blanco hoisted a pinched glob of meat. *"Salud."*

Felipe returned to his writing and Blanco tilted his head back and dropped the meat into his mouth. José reeled his own steak from the fire, examined it, and bit off a piece. He kept his mouth open, breathing in and out in an attempt to cool the bite. The meat was astonishingly tough and gamey, the strip being mostly muscle, yet the bite awoke in José a ravenousness that had so far this day been stifled by fear. He tore off another piece and gazed at his companions.

Blanco, once chief of the Moache Utes, destroyer of colonies and paladin for the land as it was. Felipe, son of Old Mexico, troubled crusader against the world as he saw it. They were two generations and two cultures lost to the same new nation. Someday they might be mythic for their campaigns, their violence, but for now they were only holders-on: two starving fish floating around a shrinking pond, parched driftwood stuck in the dried, cracked banks. Two scarred faces eating burro in a ravine.

"Tell us a story Felipe," Blanco said.

Felipe kept his face on the pages. "I have no stories."

"You must have some stories. What else could you be writing?"

"These are not stories to share. Not with you."

Felipe continued scribbling and Blanco tsked before shoving another handful of mashed burro between his gums.

"You then José. Tell me the story of how you came to join the great bandit Coyote Mouth."

"I don't want to."

"Chinga Espinosas."

"I have no stories," José said. Felipe kept writing.

Blanco frowned, his one eyebrow seeming to suck into the empty socket. They finished eating in silence. When he was done, Blanco removed a cigarette from the breast pocket of his shirt and held the tip in the coals.

"I knew a man once," he said, placing the cigarette between his lips and puffing it to life in large billows of smoke that wafted up his face, "with a great hatred for me and my people. The man had a family, and one day he came to me seeking a deal. He said, 'I am leaving soon and do not know when I shall return. I am leaving behind my wife and youngest son, and in exchange for their safety I offer you this,' and he produced a pouch of gold coins. 'It is everything I have but I promise you double should I come back.'

"It was a small pouch containing only few coins, and I have never had much use for gold as it is too soft for a tool or weapon yet too hard for anything else. More and more the others have come to value it but only because the Americanos do, and so now I think it not only valueless but dangerous. But that was not why I refused the man and countered his proposition. This meeting happened during an important time in this land's history. It happened during the confluence of the Nuuci, the Mexicano, and the Americano, when all parties were enemies and held within each was the belief that only one could survive.

"I told the man to keep his gold, that I would protect his wife and son. When he asked what I wanted I told him nothing except that he tell his family the truth behind their safety, how I provide it as a symbol of our alliance and friendship.

"But the man refused this and insisted I take the gold. When I asked him why, he said it was because we were savages, and that it would be blasphemy for him to teach his family otherwise. I asked him, 'Does this mean if you return we are to resume our rivalry?' and he said, 'Yes.' And so even though I had no use for it, I kept his gold and told the man very well, that when next I see him he must seek me out and deliver the rest of his promise. And after that, we could once again be enemies.

"The man leaves with two of his sons, and he is gone a very long time. During this time, I am true to the agreement, and when I raid the village closest the home where his wife and son live I order my braves to spare them. Soon after this though, an unexpected thing happens, something wholly accident. A few boys of the tribe, one of them my nephew, befriend the man's youngest son. It should not have been so surprising, for who else did this boy have but his mother? If during this truce the boys could not be enemies, what could they be but friends? And so I allow it, and I do nothing with the gold but keep it hidden, and because for the time being we are friends I even send gifts to the mother and her boy, meat and such.

"When finally the man returns, it is without two of his sons, and he is sad and hateful. He does not seek me out again. He knows I have gone against his wishes and so am not entitled to a second pouch of gold. At this time I get the first pouch from where I had hidden it and distribute it to my daughters.

"The boys of the tribe never played with the man's son again. When I asked why, they said they had gone to the boy and he threw rocks at them and told them never to talk to him again. And so I thought about that final component of the promise I made with the man, that should he come back we must return to being enemies, and I realize I had embarrassed him with my gifts to his family, and that by allowing the boys to be friends I had defied how he wished his son to be reared, undermined the boy's impression of us. I realize I must atone for this and fulfill the man's wishes, and thus that I must kill him.

"I came to his house one night. I had my knife and I was going to slit his throat in bed so his wife and son would know, so they could see the savageness the father prescribed. But when I look in the window the man is not there. I see him instead seated far off in the sage, alone under the stars and in the cold. He is watching his neighbor across the creek. The neighbor has a fire, and from where I am hidden I can see that fire reflected in the man's eyes. I can see he has found another enemy, someone to hate even more than me and my people, and I decide there is no longer a need for me to fulfill the last of our promise. And I was correct in my decision, for before he died that man succeeded in bestowing his lessons upon his son."

Blanco flicked the last of the cigarette into the fire. "But now I wish I had kept the gold. Now I have nothing." He rose, crouched over the body of the burro and began cutting away the hind quarters, stuffing the strips into his pack.

Felipe had stopped writing sometime during the story. He blinked now, snapping out of a daze. José looked up at the chief. "Are you leaving us, Blanco?"

"Yes. Eventually they will come for you, and I cannot sit around for that." The chief turned to them and waved a hand. "*Adios* José. *Pooneekay vatsoom ahdtuih,* Felipe." And with that, Blanco vanished down the ravine.

Felipe sat staring for a long moment, his face deep in thought. Suddenly he jumped to his feet, his journal in one hand, and jogged to his horse. He untied the rifle from his saddle.

"What are you doing?"

"Making a deal," Felipe said, and ran off in the direction of the chief, the rifle pumping at his side.

CHAPTER 44

The girl lay on the ground with her eyes closed, the baby writhing on her stomach. The man knelt over her and pressed the back of his hand to her forehead and tried fruitlessly to coax her awake. In the roadway lay a corpse, folded hands frozen over a wound in his abdomen and a line of blood streaked down his cheek from his mouth. The wolf dog approached the body and sniffed.

"Who done it?" Tobin said.

"Some kid, a bcancr. Ran off when he saw me," the man said, reeling his hand in from the girl's forehead as her eyes flipped open.

"Where?"

The man pointed into the mountains. The girl sat up and babbled something in Spanish.

Tobin examined the hoofprints in the road. "Sure only one?"

The man was trying to listen to them both at the same time. "That's all I saw. Hey what do you think she—"

But Tobin had already spun his mule and lashed it. With the wolf dog sprinting at his side he charged through the sage and into the forest, the shrieks of the girl and her child chasing at his back.

He had his Hawken muzzleloader, Bowie knife, buckskin outfit, the wolf dog, the mule, a canteen, a thong necklace attached to his custom percussion cap wheel, and a leather bag containing a powder horn, powder caps, linen patches, nipple pick, nipple wrench, elk jerky, hardtack, an empty burlap sack, and Felipe Espinosa's double-sided map and illustration.

He had purchased the Hawken in 1844 at J&S Hawken Gunshop, in Saint Louis, Missouri. It was fifty-five inches long and weighed twelve pounds with a thirty-nine-inch, octagon-shaped .54-caliber barrel and double-set triggers. With the invention of his percussion cap wheel—a gear-like instrument with small projections around the edge on which fitted the caps—Tobin had honed the time it took him to load and fire to a deadly eighteen seconds (about three more if he was in the saddle, five more if at a gallop). He'd killed a buffalo from farther than three hundred feet, a Ute from two hundred some. Fourteen short notches scratched along one side of the barrel.

The Bowie knife was a sixteen-inch, two-pound cleaver with brass inlay along the broad side for shock absorption. Tobin had wrapped the pronghorn handle with leather for grip. He got the blade in 1847 following the siege of Taos Pueblo. At the time of the Revolt, Tobin had been working for Simeon Turley making Taos Lightning, and when the rebels surrounded the distillery and set it ablaze, Tobin had dug a hole through the wall and escaped into the night. In the days that followed, he and the American retaliation hunted and herded the insurgents until all that remained were a couple hundred Mexican and Indian rebels fortified inside the pueblo's ancient adobe church. The Army let loose the batteries, spattering the church with howitzers, grapeshot, and cannonballs. Tobin hacked at the heavy front door with an ax until he breached a hole through which he then began systematically lighting cannon shells and tossing them inside. When the battle had ended, Tobin walked about the carnage and noticed the giant blade sheathed to a legless corpse. Since then he had carved three notches into the butt of its horned grip.

His outfit—the colorfully woven buckskin coat, vest, and

pants—was Arapaho and a belated gift from Governor Evans. Ten years earlier Tobin had been recommended to then–Secretary of War Jefferson Davis to lead an expedition of Indian agents traveling from Washington DC to Los Angeles. Tobin guided the caravan along the Old Spanish Trail, and the trip was mostly unremarkable except for the obscene number of mules lost to the parched and broiling Mojave, as well as the bizarre experiment these losses ultimately prompted.

In his report to Secretary Davis, one member of the expedition, Edward Beale, suggested the United States consider importing an animal better suited to navigate the hellish deserts of the western frontier, something that could go days without water and walk more than fifty miles without rest while carrying more than five hundred pounds. He suggested the United States import camels, and Congress agreed. Seventy-five of the creatures were shipped from Egypt and dispersed throughout the southwest.

Four years later Civil War erupted, Secretary Davis became President Davis, and the Camel Corps experiment was forgotten—the Army selling the animals to private buyers or simply releasing them to roam. Tobin had heard about this long after the fact from Governor Evans during his presentation of the buckskin outfit in partial payment for the wages Tobin never fully received for guiding the expedition. Tobin was happy enough to get it, there being only two such outfits in existence—the other one belonging to his friend Kit Carson, although Tobin didn't know what Kit had done to earn it.

As for the wolf dog, one week during the height of the Mexican War, the Army handed Tobin a stack of documents and sent him on an eight-hundred-and-thirty-two-mile delivery from Santa Fe to Fort Leavenworth. He had with him only his Hawken, his horse, a blanket, a lariat, and two spoonfuls of salt. He set off alone, racing across the vast, shelterless Indian country of the prairie. Daring no fire, he subsisted on raw buffalo and antelope when available, and he slept three hours a day. He went through five horses, two of which he commandeered from American travelers while the other three he stole from Indian herds in the night—each time stalking up and roping a fresh mount and leading it half a mile away before changing saddles. The third time he did this however the other horses spooked and the Kiowas awoke. There were four of them and before they even had the chance to gather their weapons Tobin had the Bowie out and was upon them. He lopped the heads off two just as they were getting to their knees and he had the belly of the third slashed open a second after he rose. The fourth began to run and Tobin blasted him in the spine with the Hawken.

When Tobin sat down to cut the three notches into his knife and one into the barrel, he heard a whimpering. Sometime during the violence the pup had slunk out of the camp and was seated in the grass watching him, unsure. Tobin whistled and the pup approached, and in the starlight he made out the wolfish snout, the bristly tail, the blackish-gray coat, the front shoulders already thick with muscle. He looked into the wolf dog's two brilliant irises, one of them a milky blue and the other a deep Mars red. He held out his hand. She sniffed, licking the fingers before suddenly chomping down on them. Tobin snatched the pup and stuffed her into the front of his coat and the two rode the rest of the way to Fort Leavenworth—the wolf dog's small head poking below his collar—then all the way back to Taos. He never named her, and she had been with him ever since.

Now he climbed up through the trees, his mule following the wolf dog as she sniffed the ground in search of the trail. Tobin was glad Tappan had given him the map; might not have even agreed to do the job if he had not. Felipe Espinosa had a bounty but Tobin didn't expect to see it. It wasn't because he wouldn't be successful. Compared to other assignments this one was easy. Felipe was desperate and just a few miles up the mountain, and Tobin would have him shot, lopped, and notched before the day was over. Rather, after almost thirty years of doing business with them Tobin had come to learn that the main form of currency issued by the Frontier Army was the verbal promise. Thus, the map felt something like collateral. He meant to keep whatever might be stashed away in that cave, particularly the sword.

The wolf dog stopped, sniffed along the pine needles, looked up at Tobin and panted. Tobin swung off the mule and looked. There were three sets of prints, two horses and a burro—the same he had observed around the corpse in the road. They trailed deeper into the forest and straight up the mountain.

Who did the other prints belong to? Pack animals? Tobin doubted it. The man back at the road said he saw a kid.

He snapped his fingers and the wolf dog's eyes went to his. He pointed to the prints and nodded. She bolted up the trail, nose to the ground, tail wagging.

He followed her above timberline and all the way to the bald summit, the Hawken balanced across the pommel. They stood atop the tapered southern slope of the Sangre de Cristos. To the north the range swelled and jutted upward in a rising staircase of snow-lined peaks. To the west was the brown autumn grandeur of the San Luis Valley, the San Juans shimmering in the distance, and to the east endless prairie.

In a broad swath of snow Tobin spotted three sets of hooves trudging single file over the ridge to the eastern side. After that, though, even the wolf dog lost it, and once more Tobin had to dismount and scour the soilless rock face for loosened stones, trampled spiderwebs, or hoof chips before finding where the trail hooked abruptly northeast, hugging the mountain's eastern flank while descending steadily into the trees.

The wolf dog scampered out front, pausing only to inspect the occasional pile of cooling manure before springing forward under the mule's snout. Her shoulders were rippling sinew and her tail long and bristly. Yet beneath all that, Tobin knew she hurt. She was old and if her heart was not tired her body was. It betrayed her in her sleep, when the shoulders trembled in such arthritic pain the tail cowered. She was a wolf dog who had crossed the Mojave, an Indian-killer with claim to three notches on the Hawken's barrel. He loved her and she loved him, and he knew the day he left her at home would be the day her old heart finally stopped.

They dove into timberline and the limbs shadowed the sky. To his left the mountain became sheer. Ahead a crag jutted from the side face like a thumb and Tobin followed the wolf dog inside the crag as the mountain became sheerer and the path fell into a shallow canyon.

The wolf dog could be reliable sometimes up to seventy yards with consideration to wind, humidity, elevation, precipitation, foliage, and target. This canyon was too short and its walls too narrow for anyone to be in it with them and for her not to know. Within the hour Tobin knew the trail would end and suddenly before him would be one, two, or possibly three men. Tobin wasn't used to hunting Mexicans. Neither was he new to it, just not as refined in it as he was hunting Indians. Indians were craftier than Mexicans, but Mexicans were brasher and carried better weapons. There was a dignity in fighting Indians that there wasn't in Mexicans. Indians killed with less by thinking more, and that's exactly how he himself liked to do it.

He didn't hear it: saw only the ground around him become dark with a rapidly shrinking shadow; felt the bristles on his neck that told him this would hurt, alone and too late. Suddenly the sky came crashing down. The first of it landed on her, he saw that much. Then blackness as the tumbling rocks buried him.

Something had happened. How long ago? What?

He lay on his face and when he gasped he sucked dirt. Something heavy pressed on his back, holding him down.

He heard a yelping and opened his eyes and lifted his head. At his side the wolf dog lay pinned, her hindquarters buried in loose stones while her front legs pawed forward in a desperate attempt to escape. Tobin tried to reach to her but realized his arm lay pinned under his chest and the stones on his back. Suddenly the wolf dog's whining turned to snarls, then a terrible barking. Tobin followed her gaze and in his swimming vision a pair of moccasins walked up and stopped before his face. He thought he heard a knife pulled from a sheath, the soft ring of steel on leather. The wolf dog lashed forward, still pinned, her snapping jaws clipping just inches from the feet. Suddenly Tobin's hair was being yanked.

He felt the cold edge of the blade on his forehead. The hand tugged harder and then there was the sawing and wet peeling of his scalp ripping away.

Tobin's head dropped into the dust and swinging before his drooping eyes was his own curly-black scalp. The wolf dog whined and snarled. Beyond the moccasins, the mule galloped down the canyon. The moccasins swiveled and seemed to hesitate. Then, after a moment, they began to chase the animal.

Tobin felt thankful to be left to think. He needed to figure out what was happening. The animal barked. Something bad . . . something terrible had . . .

★ ★ ★ ★ ★

He could feel her. A paw scratched at his forearm, the hard pads and stone-shaven nails. Tobin forced his lids open. She lay there, sprawled on her side and whimpering with her two front legs scratching at him. Her hindquarters remained pinned and one of the rear legs appeared crushed. There were stones everywhere as if spurted from some blowhole in the mountain.

Tobin tried to breathe deep but something pressed down on his lungs. He propped up an elbow and rolled and the stones toppled off his back. The effort sent the blood rushing to his head and suddenly it was like standing up into a hot iron. Fresh blood fell warmly down his forehead into his eyes. Tobin sat up and gingerly touched the wound and felt sticky, hard skull.

He crawled over to the wolf dog and pushed away the rocks. She climbed up and immediately sat back down, licking madly at the fractured leg.

The blood continued to seep past Tobin's eyes. Every few seconds he felt a wave crash over his consciousness and threaten to suck him back under. Sitting cross-legged, he flung off his coat and vest and then his undershirt. He shook out the shirt, aware that he had not washed or even removed it in at least a week, and draped it over the top of his scalped head, tying the sleeves behind him like the corners of a bandanna. His scalp screamed in agony under the salty, sweat-stained bandage.

He got to one knee and the wolf dog rose with him. She looked at him and whined, her hind leg hoisted halfway to her belly. The sun had sunk to the other side of the mountains and the clouds above flared a fading pink. He had been unconscious a long time. Tobin looked up at the short cliff wall from where the rock pile had been pushed. He hadn't paid attention. He should be dead.

Like a vague dream from many nights ago, Tobin remembered the moccasins, their approach and then their departure as they chased his fleeing mule. He looked around him and supposed he should be thankful that in going after the mule his assailant had left him with everything but his scalp. The Hawken lay unharmed at his side along with his bag.

Tobin drank from the canteen and poured some in his cupped hand for the wolf dog. The rest he splashed atop his head. He strained to remember where he was, what he should do next. He had never heard of any man ever surviving a scalping. He needed to get to a doctor, or else a good seamstress who could sew up the scalp with a patch of leather.

Leaning on the Hawken, Tobin climbed to his feet. He swayed. The wolf dog limped a few paces down the canyon with her muzzle to the ground. She slowed and looked back at him. Tobin looked into her eyes and understood. He agreed. And in the fading light, he walked behind her.

The mule tracks followed the tracks of Espinosa, and it was more than a mile before the moccasin prints caught up to the dragging reins. He saw where they mounted and continued along the trail.

Darkness fell, and Tobin put all his trust in the wolf dog. There were no tracks for him to see, only moonlit flashes upon the steely coat of his guide. Shaved lead glimpsing a white light. He entered a waking dream and walked for hours.

They slid through a bank of loose soil into a dense ravine and a jolting stream of cold creek water rushed over his ankles. The gully wound eastward down the mountain and Tobin splashed sure-footed down it in a shimmering corridor of willows. His feet grew numb to the icy water. He held the Hawken with both hands before him and in the black predawn hours descended the narrow stream like some clandestine tightrope walker.

The wolf dog stopped and lifted her snout to the sky. Tobin smelled it too, the thin smoke of a dying fire. It wafted downstream from the northern bank. Tobin squeezed through the brush and out of the stream.

There, thirty yards ahead, surrounded by aspen and willow, he saw them. A few red coals smoldered at the center of the camp, and in shivering, fetus-like balls around it curled two figures. A pair of logs had been dragged in front of the fire, and tied within the trees on the opposite side of the camp he made out two horses, one of them the color of sun-bleached bone. He could locate neither the burro nor his mule but it was still dark and Tobin couldn't be sure of everything awaiting him in the shadows.

He lowered onto his stomach and waited, the wolf dog dropping at his side. They disappeared within the tall grass of the ravine and as the dew formed along the blades and the wet stains in the shirt atop his head coagulated Tobin felt no cold nor pain but only patience, and in her fixedness he knew the wolf dog felt the same and like him felt serenity in the moment, felt the comfort in their shared purpose, the mutual solace in knowing not how the thing would be done and only that it would.

The sun crested over the eastern plains and flooded the gully. Enclosed by trees and shrubs, the camp seemed almost spherical as it swirled with the last eddies of smoke so that it was like looking at light funneling through a brilliant orange marble.

One of the figures got up from behind the log and sat a moment, rubbing his eyes and scratching his oily beard before climbing to his feet and stretching his arms wide, the smoky rays pouring past his silhouette. Low and guttural, the wolf dog growled, and like an epiphany Tobin knew his plan. He set the trigger of the Hawken with a dull click, then brushed his fingers up the spine of the tensing beast, feeling her bristle.

He whispered to her: "*Vaya.*"

She streaked across the grass. The arms fell and the bearded face turned as she leaped. Tobin had time to see the shock in his eyes as the wolf dog flew through the air and clamped her fangs into his throat. She tackled him backward into the smoking embers, his feet flying above his head, and suddenly the two were a swarm of ash, snarls, and bloody screams.

The second figure bolted up and Tobin followed him with the end of the Hawken. He gave the boy a second to stare down at the scene in wide-eyed terror. Then Tobin leveled the sight and tapped the trigger. The Hawken bucked and thundered. A plume of fire exploded from its mouth and the .53-caliber slug slammed into the boy's chest and smashed him against a tree. He slid down, blood smearing the pale aspen bark.

Tobin dropped the gun, climbed to his feet, and marched toward the snarling tangle of limbs, fur, and teeth. He took his time, reaching across his waist and drawing the giant Bowie from its sheath. He squeezed the leather-bound antler of its handle.

The wolf dog ripped at Espinosa's throat, opening up the bloody circuits and windpipe. She seemed impervious to the embers at her feet and Tobin smelled the scorching flesh of the man's back.

He put two fingers between his lips and whistled. The wolf dog leapt aside and began to bark into Espinosa's ear. Tobin bent down, snatched the bearded man by the hair and dragged him to one of the logs.

The man gurgled something. Tobin bent the head over the log. The wolf dog barked and snarled.

"What you say?"

Espinosa coughed and blood spurted onto Tobin's face from the opened throat. *"Bruto,"* he wheezed. *"Bruto. Bru—"*

Tobin chopped the blade down, and the last breath of Felipe Espinosa never made it to his lips.

CHAPTER 45

The portrait of Lino, Cecilia, and José was taken two years earlier in Santa Fe just months before the arrival of the Confederate seducer Garret Kelly; back when everything was well and as it should. It was the first and only photograph any of them had ever taken, the only camera they had ever seen. It had stood on a wooden tripod in a restored stable-turned-studio. A fading yellow curtain hung as a backdrop and stepping before the lens of the great collodion box they had all felt nervous, as if the lens was an eye that perceived not only their forms but their thoughts.

The photographer dragged a pair of chairs in front and instructed Lino and Cecilia to sit and José to stand at his father's side. They waited like this as the photographer loaded the plates and made his adjustments, not one of them daring to speak, move or hardly breathe. The machine before them was foreign and intimidating and it felt like being in its house uninvited. The photographer told Lino to smooth his cowlick, Cecilia to pull her dress lower over one ankle, and José to stand up straighter, and they became even more self-aware. He told Lino to place both hands on his thighs, for Cecilia to set one of hers on top of his, and for José to rest one atop his father's shoulders. Each one hesitated at this command of affection and the moment was painful. But eventually they did as instructed, and the photographer disappeared under the camera's little black curtain.

Lino felt alone with his family, and all pain, awkwardness, and uncertainty left him. He knew only the soft pads of his wife's palm over his hand—her fingers laced into his—and on the other side his son's small hand on his shoulder, the bottom of his forearm pressing lightly against Lino's shoulder blade. Suddenly Lino felt something akin to the first warming effects of a whiskey shot, only better. It was happiness, and not the kind he was used to that was too often derived from pride and so tainted like a sugary juice squeezed from a bitter fruit. This was happiness coming from love. Here was his wife and son with their hands on him like he was their shared source of care and security, which was always how he had wanted it. The picture took almost a minute to take, and it was the happiest Lino had ever been. It was what real love felt like, even if it was staged.

He was drunk after finishing the rest of the tequila, and with Secundina and the baby sitting dazed and mute at the kitchen table and the gringo who had delivered them gone and Cecilia on her knees wailing into the front of Secundina's dress, Lino stared dumbly at the portrait. José had left him. To do that the boy might as well have pronounced his father dead. Cecilia was going to leave him. He was dead to her, too.

She began to shriek at him to do something, to go out and reclaim their boy, and Lino snapped into awareness. He strode into his office, removed everything from his pockets, slipped the cold barrel of his .44 Colt into his waistline. On his way out, he paused again at the portrait and for a moment considered taking it with him. He left it where it was.

He walked slowly along the little foot trail between the hacienda and the stable. To the north Costilla was silent like gossipers interrupted by the presence of their topic. A few diminished islands of cattle and sheep floated in the pastures.

The servants' quarters stood deserted. Here was Hacienda de Espinosa, and taking it in Lino remembered the time he had tried to kill himself.

He had done it all wrong then, impulsively and with the wrong equipment. If he had done it right he would have made a proper noose and not a lariat, tied a stronger knot, jumped from a higher height, and, most importantly, done it alone.

That was why he would go to the desert. The desert was the suicide's accomplice. The desert was where you could sit and see nothing for miles and be assuaged in your emptiness. The desert held nothing of familiarity, nothing that might argue on life's behalf like a precious family portrait resting on a nearby table. There was no one around to try and stop you, someone that might sense your purpose or later attempt to resuscitate you. The desert was a city of undertakers, and when you are dead the coyotes come out of their homes and scatter your bones for the sun to blanch in its vast oven.

Lino finished saddling the horse and climbed on top. The barrel of the Colt pressed into his thigh and he thought how the gun, too, was something comfortingly reliable, an easy pull of the trigger and then instant blackness. No consciousness. Nothing. He nudged the horse south. He gripped the reins tightly in his hand, and he thought what a gift God gave man to control his own fate.

CHAPTER 46

Upon searching the camp, Tobin found only the remains of a half-eaten burro, the clothes on the Espinosas' backs, and the saddles on their horses. In the inner pocket of Felipe's long, black duster he found a green silk kerchief with a rabbit embroidered in one corner. He found no pistol or rifle or golden saber.

Tobin unwrapped the blood encrusted shirt from his head. He wet the kerchief in the stream and tied it into a bandanna over his scalp. The wolf dog sniffed at something at the edge of the camp. Tobin went to her and saw the prints of his mule— the slight skiff in the dirt where someone in moccasins had jumped into the stirrups.

In the end, Tobin never needed the map to find the cave. He merely followed the trail on top the white bay, the limping wolf dog out front with her nose in the tracks of his stolen mule.

He rode late into the afternoon and high atop the mountains, the sun baking his scalp inside the kerchief until he began to feel his pulse through his skull like fists inside the walls of a burning house. The burlap sack hanging from his saddle horn had begun to stink. A thousand feet below him the sand dunes shimmered in roiling golden waves. Beyond that the lakes, streams, and rivers of the valley reflected silvery in the autumn sun. Set among these shining bodies were the clustered dots of Costilla, San Luis, Fort Garland, La Garita, Conejos, San Rafael, and the other settlements of the valley. Far to the west the San Juans hunkered under a sweeping shadow of an approaching storm cloud.

There arose a great outcropping of stone, the earth around it trampled and littered with what appeared to be half a year's worth of manure. The surrounding trees had been stripped of most of their lower branches and Tobin observed a large fire pit thick with ash. Pieces of animal skeleton lay scattered. Tobin tied the horse. The wolf dog was already ahead of him, sniffing around the mine's entrance and glancing back impatiently.

Tobin noted the moccasin prints in the dirt intermingling with an array of older boot prints, and followed them to the entrance. Etched in the stone above it he noted two inscriptions:

EN NOMBRE DEL PADRE
FRANCISCO TORRES, 1720

And below that:

Y EL HIJO
FELIPE ESPINOSA, 1863

The cave's mouth had shrunk over time—a healing wound in the mountainside—and Tobin crouched to peer inside. He glimpsed only blackness, and, as he had feared hours ago along the trail, a wide sweeping of dust where items had recently been dragged out of the darkness.

Knowing he was too late, Tobin dropped to his belly anyway and crawled inside. The wolf dog whined at the soles of his feet and when he told her to stay the word reverberated within the rock walls. It was a good ten degrees warmer inside the mine and the air felt damp. Tobin found he could stand with his head ducked under the low ceiling. He felt around with his feet, the floor flat and pebbly, before kicking something solid. He toed around for the object again and suddenly the floor dropped away under his foot. His weight had been leaning forward as his foot padded along and when it plunged below the ledge Tobin threw his body backward and sprawled, landing on his side with both legs dangling over the invisible shelf. He pulled them back and once again kicked at something solid. He felt for it and his hand clasped a smooth wooden pole. Two poles, he realized, a ladder—an extremely long one judging by its firmness against the precipice.

He stuck his head over the ledge and spit. A moist, warm air blew up over his face and there answered no sound. He plucked one of the brass percussion caps from his necklace wheel and dropped it. It whistled for a second through the stale updraft and then was silent.

There, his head dangling over fathomless depths and into infinite blackness, Tobin recalled the legend of this place, how Padre Francisco Torres, a missionary accompanying a detachment of conquistadors, had established this gold mine by enslaving a hundred Pueblo Indians. It was from this mine high within the mountains the padre had one day stood overlooking the grandeur of the valley below him and named it San Luis after his hometown in Seville. And as Torres watched in awe and the soldiers stood guard, the Puebloans meanwhile dug deeper and deeper. They dug all the way through the mountain into the earth and beyond its molten core. They dug all the way into the underworld: into Sipapu, the birthplace and end place of all the People, and there they summoned all their ancestors and all their children-to-be, and one after the other this netherworld army climbed the ladder and out of the mine.

They swarmed the Spaniards, hacked through their armors with weapons ancient and forthcoming, and drove them off the mountain onto the sand dunes below. They killed all except

Torres, who while fleeing across the sand came upon a sudden black lake within the crests. The padre plunged into the water, swam into the middle, and turned to see that all his pursuers had stopped and lined the lake's shore in somber silence, watching. Behind them the sun set a bloody red upon the snowy peaks, and as the first of the hands reached within the water and clasped the padre's flailing legs, Torres had only time to exclaim, "Sangre de Cristo . . . Sangre de Cristo," before the hands—hundreds of them—pulled him under.

A sudden rush of warm air rushed over Tobin's face and frantically he scrambled backward out of the cave. The whole mine seemed to grow hot as he squirmed out from under the low opening and into the sun. He sat up and leaned against the outer wall for a moment, panting. The wolf dog looked at him confused.

Upon first noticing them Tobin had thought about adding his own name beside the other two inscriptions above the cave. Now he decided against it. He decided the legacy of the dead to be long enough, and instead rose, patted the wolf dog's head, and returned to the horse.

He climbed into the saddle, and with the two heads bulging from within the burlap sap, Tobin left to go see about his own.

CHAPTER 47

The boy had grown over the summer. His arms filled out chubby within the sleeves of his gown and his legs stretched below the hem. The little tuft of hair on his head spread and seemed to steep darker, and already a few transparent wisps sprouted from the corners above his lip. He was a normally calm and contemplative child, which delighted his mother who took the disposition for good presage. His body was warm and often she would slip a hand under his back just to feel the heat between him and the sheets.

He slept less than other babies and would stay awake for hours beside her on the bed, his limbs swimming in the air, his fists squeezing and releasing. She would lay propped on her elbow and watch him perceive those things beyond her. His eyes were hazel, adult and knowing, and sometimes they became fixed on forms she could not see. She had seen cats do the same thing. The boy's eyes followed the shapes as they moved across the ceiling or into the room and toward them and she wondered if what he saw were ghosts.

She believed he was attuned to his father, that as long as both lived there existed some shared realm between the two consciousnesses, like the elliptical created by two intersecting spheres.

She believed the love between her and the boy belonged also to the father, and that the boy wished to have him back and for the three of them to be reunited in the same home in the same bed. She believed he wished it if only because he learned to by sleeping with his ear on her heart and listening to her dreams.

And so it was that early morning while propped on her side and watching Domingo pedal his limbs and stare fixedly at the ceiling that Secundina observed the limbs slow and stop, the pupils in both eyes enlarge, the mouth fall open with a little pop of the lips. He gasped, the elliptical burst, and Secundina understood.

Felipe had died.

Around noon there came a knock on the door. Secundina answered it with Domingo under her arm. It was a gringo, a young man, tall and handsome.

He tipped his hat to her. "*Buenos dias.* Is Lino in?"

Secundina shook her head.

"Do you know when he will return?"

"No."

"Hm. Would you mind if I waited inside for him? My name is Lucien Maxwell. I'm Don Carlos's son-in-law."

Secundina stepped aside. Maxwell entered and looked around. Secundina took a seat on the sofa with Domingo on her lap and after a moment Maxwell lowered himself on the chair across from her. He set his hat on one knee and tapped his fingers on its brim.

"What is your name?"

"Secundina."

"You Lino's girl?"

"No. I am Cecilia's."

"Oh. Who is Cecilia?"

"Lino's wife."

"I see. Where is she?"

"She joined some of the Penitentes this morning in a search party."

"A search party? For who?"

"My brother."

"Who is your brother?"

"Which one?"

"The one they are searching for."

"José."

"What happened to him?"

"I wish I knew."

"What about your second brother? Where is he?"

"Dead."

"Oh."

Secundina looked at him. Maxwell gestured his hat toward Domingo. "Does he belong to you?"

"Yes."

"Who is the father, if you don't mind?"

"I do."

He was quiet a moment. He nodded slightly and tapped his hat. "I think I know."

"Then why did you ask?"

The air inside the hacienda became thick and hot. Outside grasshoppers crackled and a cow bellowed in the distance.

"Do you know why I am here?"

"I think so."

"Tell me."

"You are here to dismiss Lino and order us off the property because Don Carlos is too cowardly to do it himself."

Maxwell blushed and Secundina could see it was not because he disagreed.

"Don Carlos and Lino have had a long partnership. It is unfortunate what happened in the end with Lino and, um, the baby's father, but not as consequential as you might think in the Don's decision. He is old now with too many acres. A fellow by the name of Gilpin has made an offer for this land, including the hacienda, and the Don is going to accept it. But he wanted Lino to know first, and is even letting him keep the cattle."

"Lino knew. If I knew, so did he."

"I still think it best if I tell him in person."

"You might be too late."

Maxwell's fingers stopped tapping. "What does that mean? Where is he?"

"Lino left yesterday. And I don't think anyone will ever see him again."

"You mean he ran off? Somewhere for good?"

"Somewhere for good."

Maxwell stared at her. His eyes widened as he comprehended. "Jesus."

"I think he was afraid the Penitentes or Don Carlos would feel obliged to offer some final kindness, like those cows you mentioned. He didn't want that."

"But he left you."

The words struck her with such impact the breath pressed from her chest. It was as if hearing it said out loud had suddenly made it real.

"We are getting used to that," she said, squeezing Domingo.

"Jesus."

His eyes were mournful, this sympathetic young gringo whom she had only just met, and for the first time since learning of it this morning, Secundina began to weep for the father her son would never know.

"What happened here?"

She pressed her face into the back of the boy's neck. "I wish we knew."

It was dark now and it started to snow. Her mother had still not returned. Secundina built a fire and set Domingo before it on the sofa. She sat with him and watched the flakes fall down the chimney and hiss on the burning logs.

Outside there came the clop of hooves. Leather creaked and a bridle chain clinked faintly as the hooves came to a stop outside the door. Secundina listened to the footsteps approach the house and plop down something heavy that rattled the wall. Domingo listened too, quiet and motionless.

She left him there, went to the kitchen, and found a knife. She was about to the door when it banged four times in front of her face. She slid loose the bolt and inched the door open.

At first she was not sure what she saw. She had an image of a wizard she had once seen illustrated in a children's book, a man with thin and flowing wan hair and ancient features. A crisp breeze funneled past them, and Secundina detected traces of animal fur and blood. He was toothless and missing an eye, and stuck through his belt hung a brilliant golden saber.

She saw his eye go to the small kitchen knife in her hand and he smiled. A mule stood idly behind him, its reins loose in the snow. Despite the bridle it wore a packsaddle. A rifle hung cockeyed behind the rear brace.

"Eh?" he said. He looked down and lifted a knee and Secundina opened the door wider to see him tap one moccasined foot against the pair of tan panniers slumped against the exterior wall. The packs were immense and bulging and one by one the chief swung them past her into the room.

"What is in them?" she asked.

But suddenly the old chief was no longer interested in her or the packs. He stared over her shoulder, and Secundina followed his gaze to where Domingo's tiny foot bounced over the side of the sofa. He grinned, a great pink chasm of gums. He held an upturned palm and gestured with it toward the baby, and Secundina stepped aside and let him past.

He strode through the room and stopped to hover over Domingo. Secundina stood behind the sofa and looked down next to him.

He squeezed the child's big toe between his leathery fingers. Domingo sucked on his knuckles and regarded him with intent round eyes. The two looked at each other for a long moment. The chief smiled and moved to the fireplace, crouched down, and reached one finger into the ashes. When he rose, the finger was dark with soot and as Secundina watched he traced the finger down Domingo's forehead to the bridge of his nose, uttering something in his language. The chief smiled down upon his work, nodded at Secundina, and walked back toward the door.

She followed him and when he had stepped outside he turned to her, reached to the back of his waist, and produced a book. It was leather bound, worn and creased as if it had spent its life stuffed inside a pocket. The outer leaves of the pages were soiled and a few hung loose between the others like foiled escapees. It was a journal. He placed it in her hands.

She watched him walk back into the falling snow, unharness the packsaddle from the mule and let it fall to the ground. He swung atop the animal bareback, and with the reins in his hands the old chief galloped away into the pale night, the sword beaming at his side.

Secundina closed the door. She returned to the fire and sat beside Domingo. The boy crossed his eyes and stared in wonderment at the dark ash streaked down his nose. Secundina opened the book.

The Diary of Felipe Espinosa

Dedicated to my wife and son:
Domingo, may the only thing you and I share be our love
for your mother.
Secundina, if I am in heaven, I am waiting for you.

ACKNOWLEDGMENTS

Although a work of fiction, the historical events, characters, and settings at the center of this story demanded research that would not have been possible without the helpful people at the Denver Public Library, History Colorado, the New Mexico Office of the State Historian, and the Fort Garland Museum.

Additionally, the research and writing of this novel extended over my time as a student at the University of Northern Colorado, the University of Denver, and Western New Mexico University, and I wish to thank the librarians, history and writing professors who guided me throughout.

My gratitude goes out to one of Colorado's preeminent historians, Virginia McConnell Simmons, whose books *The San Luis Valley: Land of the Six-Armed Cross*, *The Ute Indians of Utah, Colorado, and New Mexico*, and *Bayou Salado: The Story of South Park* I referenced almost daily. Same goes to Andrew Perkins and his thorough book, *Tom Tobin: Frontiersman*.

Phil Parkinson, Sherri Brooks, and Marilyn Weishaar were three of my earliest readers, and I will forever be grateful for their eyes and input.

I owe an enormous amount of thanks to the welcoming, encouraging, colorful members of the Western Writers of America: a family of authors whose genre is the American spirit.

I am fortunate to have worked with two saints of the publishing industry, the editing wizard, Hazel Rumney, and the marketing ninja, Tiffany Schofield. Thank you both for all you do.

Acknowledgments

Thank you, Chip MacGregor and Holly Lorincz at the Mac-Gregor Literary Agency for all your expertise, enthusiasm, and innovation.

I had a constant companion during the writing of this novel. Tobey, thank you for keeping my feet warm below the desk and for taking me outside to throw the ball every time it started to get too frustrating.

My mother has supported me in everything I have ever pursued, including this novel. To say I could not have done it without her is an understatement. Thank you for being my hero.

And, finally, to my wife, Catharine. You kept this book together. You kept me together. And while I know I'm not always the best at expressing my gratitude and affection out loud, the great part about the printed word is that it's forever. So, Catharine, thank you, and I love you.

ABOUT THE AUTHOR

Adam James Jones received a BA from the University of Northern Colorado and an MA from Western New Mexico University. His short stories and essays have appeared in numerous publications, including *Southwestern American Literature, Weber,* and *Darker Times* (UK). In 2012 he was awarded the Homestead Foundation Fellowship from the Western Writers of America. He lives in New Mexico with his wife, the actress Catharine Pilafas. This is his first novel.

For more information, visit www.adamjamesjones.com.